MW01612872

## About the Author

Dr. Rudofossi is a professional who actively traverses both fields of policing and police psychology. As an active professor, teaching police psychology courses at John Jay College of Criminal Justice, and as a retired police det. sergeant [NYPD], he has written a novel pulled together from more than a superficial glimpse into the field of policing, intelligence gathering, criminal profiling and operations such as hostage negotiations, detective investigations, counter-terrorism and drug interdiction. Adding to the original and novel work of the author is the experience of knowing deeply and of actively expressing the darker side of the unconscious and existential struggles of police and suspects.

This novel is a work of fiction that is illuminated with hope even in the most tragic of moments in the human condition. The author is an experienced and well published non-fiction real deal cop doc, and although no real person is characterized the fictionalized characters and the crimes are as complex as the psychological imagination underscoring the world of police and policing from a psychological perspective.

Dedicated to Cop Doc Allan Brenner, Captain USMC and SFPD Captain Police Psychologist; Professor Dr. Charles Brenner, Professor Richard R. Ellis and Harry Julius Rubenstein First Class Firefighter hero, poet and violinist, and Firefighter Ari Greunzweig, along with all the NYPD Fallen Heroes: Including my pal Det 1st Grade Paul Heidelberger; Detective 1st Grade Chris Hoban; S/A DEA Kiki Camerena; Det. Lt Joe Petrosino, and Det 1st Grade Liu and Det. 1st Grade Ramos, all who gifted the world as heroes in their own unique way. None of us can walk a mile in their shoes – not now and not ever -- may they rest soulfully until resurrected when they will live once again!

Dr. Daniel Rudofossi

# THE NEW YORK COP
# DOC JOURNALS

AUSTIN MACAULEY
PUBLISHERS LTD.

A CIP catalogue record for this title is available from the British Library.

ISBN 9781786128737 (Paperback)
ISBN 9781786128744 (Hardback)
ISBN 9781786128751 (E-Book)

www.austinmacauley.com

First Published (2016)
Austin Macauley Publishers Ltd.
25 Canada Square
Canary Wharf
London
E14 5LQ

# Acknowledgments

First and foremost, the essence of what makes us humane beings is the infinite within: The Almighty.

The greatest blessing of all is my wife Dongyu who is truly my best friend; Love of my life; soulmate; and inspiration for aspiring to actually complete and put this book to print in her own brilliant and loving style.

Dr. Prof. Stu Young who provoked me to write this book as a mentor. Captain Dan Mahoney, bestselling author, for his suggestions and heroism: Eddie Money, his bro, for the effulgence of a two tickets to paradise. Dr. Kitaeff as a peer support who gifted me with his comments, all helpful and ingenious. Lt. Prof Latorre who is a brilliant hero, for his many conquests and for lighting the candle in the darkness to myriads. Emmanuel Martin, an artist, who inspires with lit candles the homeless lost souls. Dr. Shayes for keeping us all well and healthy!

To family: my wife as my soulmate for life. Mom and Dad with love, Baba Xu Feng and Mima Wang Min, our kids, Jon and Emily, and sisters, Mara, Viki, and Leslie. Dr. Conroy, a cop docs' cop doc and Dr. King an odontologist sleuth and healer. President FOP Cops 4 Cops, Det Sgt., Jim O Neil,

# Prologue

The cold brisk air held the crisp Oak leaves in a chill, as the gentle pressure built to a lulling whisper and fluctuating winds shifted and collided through the flutes in each branch. Whistling echoes riddled the old Oak tree with the ravages and aches of age. Its regal leaves crackled as fragments shattered in gusts of expiration, others, hardly noticeable, fell off in gentle exhalation. Silent wisdom bore witness to two centuries splashed with the palette of artistry, decadence, opulence, genius undone, and scores of crimes against the hidden poor. Epiphanies of the heart and soul rose to a pitch under the Oak canopy. The massive Oak's advice to the daft, weary, and preoccupied, hurled acorns in cadence, sounding – alarm. Unheard, the Oak persisted as twenty generations experienced shade and shadow under the looming gentle giant, hovering over the crossroads of urban life. Noble scars sketched in its very flesh the evidence of stage carriage screech marks colliding as narcotics, horses and humans played squash, intoxicated by hubris and mayhem a century past. Sleuths and alienists of yesteryear met under the hub where screech marks left their indelible ambiance to foreshadow a crime scene analysis; a century later, in 1984, a Jaguar sports car, commandeered by street crime officer Anti-Crime Unit., slammed two perps in a failed carjacking into the arms of the Oaks Justice on their road to perdition. Records leafing through yesteryear swirled into the waves of postmodern enclaves squeezed into the Heights of Brooklyn, the county of the King. Street cop and Oak Tree bonded in survival.

Markings carved out, visible and unseen, screens in the creases of skin and muscle, bark and sap, drawn taut in the angular cuts in the Oak's bark as it ages. Marks succumbing to ineffable destiny, where the fates seal life in the furies of spring — sprung — as sordid love affairs of courtesans and men of gentility vanquish in mayfly minutes. The aegis of Cassandra reverberated in hardened wood as colliding pathos of frigid portends of winters solstice ushered out the warm soothing air of fall, linking the discontent of many hearts sensitive to varied changes in the wind. Among those disaffected by winters, early nights and gloomy veil was Allan Cannon. Allan stopped and remembered the Oak Tree marking as he headed toward his car.

No new jaguar for personal use, but an old second-hand Cadillac, a cheaper and practical workhorse. Allan was on a high knowing the exquisite hardship of the Columbia University Doctoral Dissertation Oral Review and Medical School had recently achieved cornerstones. His life at 45 had turned the point of middle age. The Oak barely noticed him as the lingering effect of rum and coke leaked out its last depressing impression. Allan telescoped back to the day he commandeered that Jaguar and received a Command Discipline – a penalty for being too street savvy and too high maintenance in his choice of car. On tap, Allan hardly paid attention to the dark figure in the corner of his eye, as he was reminiscing about his unit boss and delegate who bought him a jaguar bar to wear with honour: Instead of a purple heart, he got an R.I.P, no good deed goes unpunished in the NYPD.

As the shorter, stockier guy moved into the shadow of the adjacent Maple tree, Allan sensed something awry. His heart began that flutter of recognising malevolence, while looking as dumb and harmless as a croc lying passive in the Mara River. The visible perp was eyeing him as large, but easy, prey as he pointed his index finger like a stylus at the sky and touched his brow to target Allan. Allan knew well the nonverbal interchange meant that Perp One, with the knife, would be the backup confederate for the hidden Perp Two. Allan's snapshot assessment was on the pin of the needle of life — his own — as his heart and sweat began to run involuntarily. Allan knew they planned a double over on him to sandwich him with slice, shoot and dice, leaving him for dead. The opportunistic Perp Two figured if the easy picking suit resisted, he'd push the knife against his cheeks hard and fast and Perp One could shoot him if any further difficulty arose.

Perp One and Two noticed the six foot plus business guy's Tag Heuer wristwatch and Goldman Sacs handbag attaché, figuring he had a few hundred in cash and three credit cards. The turnaround would be an easy hit, small risk and big pay. Allan contemplating his own intuitive nature, felt his street cop survival mode of identity flash a shift as potential prey became predator.

A mountain lion taken for a doe in the head lights emerged. Allan Cannon's street smarts kicked in as he could feel the beating of the perp's malicious heart pounding with visions of anticipated easy money and pawn shop schemes, blinding them to the strength and size of their alleged prey.

Allan heard the pop of the switch blade violently open as he felt the steel metal grimace his handsome face. He saw the unfolding scenario, where he'd take down the muggers amidst the Maple, and around the Oak tree as he visualised the inevitable holes in his chest, and slicing opening his neck wide, if he did not act with lightning speed. Shadows mirroring unholy dances escalated as Allan felt and heard the unmistakable rack and load of what he narrowed down to be a 9mm semi-automatic stuck in his back, right where he predicted it would be. Allan glimpsed the silhouette of the lanky long-haired dude grinning as Perp Two screeched in a hoarse, repulsive voice,

"Mother-fucking punk Wall Street suit, give me your wallet or I'll waste your miserable fucking life."

Allan's fear compressed his awareness into a telescope of momentary panic enveloping him. Allan thought he'd forgotten what instinct had taught him in seven years on the streets of Brooklyn North on the midnights to eight. He was wrong: For the perps, he was dead wrong!

The darker cast of Allan's shadow was now set into automatic mode as Perp One clumsily tripped forward and his blade again cut across Allan's face, although aimed for his neck, it nicked him on the side where it caught a token of its intended mark. Allan heard the shorter, heavy set Perp One emerge again from the darkness as the swift slice of the razor cut a narrow tear and blood oozed as his pain felt sharp. A red dark-flow of blood triggered Allan's street crime cop senses. Seemingly, out of nowhere, Allan bent as a reed in a storm as he turned around somersaulting, pulling his seven round clip Colt 45 automatic fully drawn to a full blown counter-attack mode and fired four rounds into the guy with the knife, and three into the guy who was holding the 9mm.

Allan looked on incredulously as he realized each of seven rounds shattered the silence as they all hit their marks. Allan's private sensibility would now be public scrutiny as the blasts of each shot's volley raised the hue and cry of infernal perdition as his calling card.

Allan was flush with pain and revulsion as the sting of his slashed face and warm blood gushing down his cheeks was felt under the buzz of adrenalin coursing in his veins. The slow motion effect of surrealism was emerging as Cop Doc Allan Cannon looked at the perps pathetically laying in their own schemes gone awry. The riveting twitches of arteries emptying out blood through holes in Perps One's chest as his head dropped and his body convulsing in rhythmic shakes rattling on the cement block he crumbled onto, as his last breaths laboured to draw one last gasp of air. Perp Two with the semi-automatic now looked absurdly comical as his heavy jaw was ripped open where his empty threats now rung with the reverberations of impotence in echoes of deafening silence after two shots split his jaw wide open in gaping horror as his shattered teeth bleed dark red. No words exited from the shallow breathing aspirations of Perp One's life as he was expiring and perp two was torturously hanging on to life.

Radio Motor Patrol Cars (RMPs) began aggressively jumping up on the curb as Allan was standing in shock. Uniform officers commanded him to stay put and not move or be shot. Allan was ready to identify himself and was told to slowly surrender his weapon as the uniformed officers drew a cordon around him. Suddenly, Detective Tommy Ryan barked out in a deep gruff bellow, "He's ours – he is Doctor Sgt Cannon" as he stuck his square jaw out of one side of the unmarked RMP with a red bulb on top, while on the other side of the RMP, a Roman-jawed dark and ruddy complexioned head peered out as he swung the recorder side open. He said,

"That is street crime, Sgt Cannon. Boss, we're here for you. Give him room folks."

Detectives Tommy Ryan and Antonio Pacificio were on their way back from Brooklyn Central booking at the 84 pct when they heard the deafening thunder of the 45 caliber full metal jacket rounds buffered as they cross-marked their targets. They thought it was a hit done by drug dealers with heavy fire power. The legendary Captain Commander of Detectives, Maloney, was on his way as en-route they notified him via city wide radio. Det's Ryan and Pacificio were tending to the crime scene for moments which appeared like an eternity to Allan when they ordered some rookie cops to secure the inner perimeter as they took Sgt. Cannon into the shadows of the Oak Tree.

The crime scene lay across from 31 Grace Court. Allan explained to Dets Ryan and Pacificio, he was visiting a writer friend at 31 Grace Court. 31 Grace Court at Brooklyn's Heights prestigious enclaves – uncomfortable bedside mates with Redhook, and looming Bed Stuyvesant, which earned the coveted title as being the all-American homicide alley. Allan's life at forty-five was filled with gifts, many wished for, and few had by most. Along with the boon from many blessings he had, was the bane of many dark moments as he was finishing his M.D., Ph.D. Allan had been slightly inebriated from a few rum and cokes on the rocks as he cheered his beloved dad, a military man lost a number of years ago, prematurely, to trauma unsung as he had picked up the refinished firearm he carried. Allan's Dad was survived by his mother, an architect of edifices, whose indefatigable soul, mind and soma drifted since his death in and out of storms of seasonal drifts where the sunrise and sunset of life's many coloured portals left grieving unmourned.

As Allan was debriefing and groomed, he had no time to think, but was stunned at the devastation his .45, which was strapped on to avoid being lost, was going to be safely stored to honor his Dad's military service. The extra fully loaded clip was not Allan's service revolver or off-duty and he only fired it as sport, but it turned out to be a lifesaver.

Allan was no stranger to the mean streets and had worked Murder Row Capitol next to the Poets Row of Brooklyn Heights where his dreams to be a doc were tilled in one too many shallow graves he witnessed as the hushing lullabies of children were never sung as death drew the hood down prematurely. He knew from having parents who taught him tough love, that children born to parents who proffered gold spoons left their fruit to spoil, while kids born to parents who had gold fillings would work hard to make the rush real. The rush and tide of hope cried out to him when despair leading for most cops spelled the bane of the job as broads/guy's, booze, and bets drowned their dime to the dollar love affairs with traumatic losses gone south.

Allan stood recalcitrant as a Jack Russell terrier, refusing routine and capitulation to the prosaic pall of the beats allure and choir practice. He found the grace of

17

G-d as his rebirth toward life in a rational pursuit from the heart – healing lost souls.

The ambiance of the crime scene would not dissipate as the winds blew and the whistling could be heard in a haunting way. An equilibrium of sorts settled as the police car's rear view mirror captured the shadows of trade winds, where capital gains lost in a crap game called life and settled its sundry scores.

Brooklyn was itself protégé to the Height's winding roads that sunk into the layers of its sediment: cement, blue-rock, blood, and aspirations of art witnessed the Brooklyn Bridge suspended as a link between those who have, and those have not. Like the county of Kings, and Queens, the Isle of Manhattan lay in the intercourse of triangulated boroughs.

Allan, complex and enigmatic was left dangling in the space of ill at ease waiting as the old Oak tree bore witness to the indulgences that humans partake in, when on their harried paths of scheming not day dreaming – thud goes their lives, un-hooded and benighted in valueless blight. Allan returned as the crime scene was framed in yellow and black tape laying the moribund trail of two ambitious street perps dusted by the doc, who never buried the cop inside his rear inner-sight vista. A crap game of sorts mirrored the shadows from the neon lights bathing 31 Grace Court as police turret lights blinded the view from the Brooklyn Bridge holding court between the boroughs. The Oak Tree, on cue, shed a whirling flush of yellowing leaves in his dark black reflection of grace and the Maple Tree in hers shadowed him as a canopy of teary eyed realization struck Det Sgt Cop Doc Allan. He was really alive! Markings of trauma hidden in this massive Oak tree left imprints of crime scenes on the trunk of its half-life of

150 years. As Allan described to Tommy his transfer from the Bureau to the Medical Division as a celebration, he shared with him the day was ominous when he was asked to join the ranks of 'police surgeon'. The dream and bane was the bittersweet success he achieved; as the Chief Surgeon celebrated his star, Dr. Allan Cannon, he left a banquet and dropped dead of a heart attack that night.

Cop Doc Allan, as he was being called, had never been a conformist. From the onset as a street cop, he could move from the world of law enforcement to academia without fanfare. Allan was a cop's cop on the street, and now a cop's copdoc in the clinic. The Oak tree bore witness once again to the inimitable cop doc and two denizens of the concrete jungle as one more mark brandishing death with the flip side of redemption. Markings of tempests past left their symbolic tokens as new initials carved into the unerring bark after the mortals passed in the whisper of settling branches laying hearts bare. New initials had R.I.P. for two new perps to join the legions of clowns and hyenas' laid low in the forest above the asphalt cornerstones of sardonic glee and folly. Crimes of the heart etched on long branches, armed with unrequited perfidy held court in the frozen space of time as the heroes of yesteryear became the new unsung heroes to today. The Oak noticed the Cop-Doc and rued the day as a reporter from the Post said, "Hey 31 Grace Court was the address where Arthur Miller wrote his classic, A View from the Bridge."

As time inexorably moves forward, it remains stuck like amber drops from maple tree wounds, freezing the ever fragile leaves alive and in love with life for an eternal pith of moments undone in frozen death. Antonio left after a preliminary investigation and Tommy left his card as the trauma unit Dr. Allan developed and one of his peer support officers drove him along with Captain Maloney to a place of solace to unwind and to deal with the aftermath. The year was 1987 as Christine greeted Allan Cannon in the special wing of the ER Room reserved for celebrities and cops in shock. Captain Maloney set up the situation that was a respite from the media and its scavenging vultures as the curtain was drawn.

The Police Commissioner and the CEO of NYU Medical gave Dr. Allan Cannon hypnotic sedatives and other medications. A leading esoteric hypnotist was called in to fade the memories through a radical neuro-cognitive technique. Allan was susceptible to this method and whether placebo or not, it worked. The cop docs trauma of doing the double justifiable homicide past into ethereal screen memories he vaguely would remember. The D.A. Assistant of Homicide Prosecution sensitively closed this case as justifiable. Miraculously, Allan would be returned to duty with a full load soon. The perps were unknown, from the former Soviet Union and would not be missed by their government. They were filed away, along with the secrets of that very night.

# Chapter 1

## Sipping from the Chalice of Homicide Alley

The chalice from Tommy's communion slid off the Night Table. The half-filled crystal goblet of Merlot cracked his deep sleep as fractionated crystal took the shape of three mirror images. Images shifted as Tommy pierced a glance into the semi-coagulated red wine with a crimson hue bathing its dye in incandescent light.

Focus on the double image of two triangles in bold inter-twined relief, one down and one up, intersected. Courses of angles, seemingly oppositional, conspiring to eternal life and refined beyond death's pall. A pall that carries the geometry of love as abstract art. The circuitous routes made to escape from death's cover itself.

Grabbing the yellowing sheet called a bed cover, once pure white as Tommy's innocent ideals, now soiled in his sweat. The sheet veiled his skin like an elastic Saran wrap. His numb leg broke into a pin cushion of tingling pain. He couldn't recall what he was dreaming of. He mumbled to his lover, "It sure wasn't good."

Begrudgingly awakening to the wintry cold, he looked at his engorged stomach. Tommy felt the aches of ageing to mid-life as his speech flowed into a low undertone gurgle, "Dreams of being an actor far and away. Hollywood is for the birds. Is this what Boris Karloff felt like after playing the Mummy? Hell being a detective in Brooklyn North isn't that bad after all."

Tommy turned and eyed his lover Christine. Silent in repose – hiding ravenous delight at first. He listened to her low tone murmur of snores, orchestrating her exhaustion in a finale of a deep breath and sigh – as she paused, sucked in air, then silence – Relief.

He thought in a deep reflective moment: My sweet lover, how deftly sleeping: She lay. Christine could artfully make an art of what would be grotesque for most others. She hardly moved. She was softly breathing. Moments of abrupt shakes, sighing and heaving wrested from her breasts; the tremors from working relentlessly: in Cadence's of City life. Pausing, he bounced his hate over his need to leave her and go back and forth between his place and hers – fear of losing his sense of self. If I could only get up the courage to really make the leap.

'Leap' resonates as much more than a word: Leap – what a word to express the subtle and yet so poignant – less than grounding in a storm.

'It' hit Tommy like an electric jolt. Tears brutishly started to well up out of the corners of his green eyes. Drawing him in as his eyes became glazed as the vision of the attractive social worker found raped and beaten. The orange hue glistened with a haze when he was in the 'identity-mode' of pursing investigator.

The image of the Raggedy Doll in dried blood mocking him as part of the crime scene surrounded by human faeces tore at his olfactory ducts with revulsion. Indeed, Tommy's initiation to Brooklyn North Detective Squad: Midnight Watch was a 'whore of sorts'.

Midnight-watch and tours of duty in the NYPD: He remembered the dark humour of other senior detectives creating an impenetrable wall between him and his own sea of feelings; His sea of passions and blasting emotions.

Desperate, oh so desperate to be released in anger, fear, disgust and loss: Silent and hidden emotions that hover overhead as a silent catacomb, entombing his passion for life. A ceiling like a storm cloud of guilt unearned, and yet owned.

Tommy tried as he did, and would, but could not block revulsion – interspersed with morbid attraction. Yes, the twin magnetic poles of the whore of investigation desire, and animadversion.

Tommy remembered his first homicide investigation and whispered, "I am Detective Tommy Ryan."

The push and pull of being a city detective among the finest sleuths of NYPD. Tommy saw his first victim's pretty black painted toes. Toes beckoning mourning never to be had. The curtain on the cold and sterile Kings County morgue refrigerator dropped.

Initiation rites are a bitch — a cold case — his first homicide. In the harried squad room, there was one case after another, a typical insane day of case loads in Brooklyn North. Like speed loaders in the year 1994, which left a third grade rookie detective like Tommy washing memories away. His tears un-spilled in each barrel of beer and sexy images shifting focus.

Images he could remember of one chick that danced away and swirled around into another. Sexy lustful dervishes in which he indulged his senses as if he took score.

Taking score of his escape from trauma and losses telescoping down memory lane like a gullet waiting to receive a crushing 45 caliber slug like a tasty salty anchovy: Anticipation yielded to escape. Still, the air narrowing and Tommy could only gasp in sweet-bitter desperation.

Tommy, the rookie detective, learned he could escape as his lips gulped down Lager from the frothy cup as he kissed the next lady's sweet lips with his alkaline breath. Alkaline infused with musky smells and his sweat. An aphrodisiac for women with fire in their souls. He remembered a beautiful Irish bartender he made out with. Red hair and light blue eyes, three hours with a deep breath in between. He couldn't remember her name, although he remembered the dimple in her cheek and the deep azure glint in her bluish eyes. Pages of losses unraveled in sordid memories washed away. Losses filled in tomes he could write about, but never did.

Aggression and sex on each poker card of a crumpled deck of a Seattle cruiser lost in the Puget Sound. A nightmare in illusion or perhaps the delusion one can escape the nightmare by daydreaming away one's grief and love unrequited.

Illusions also of lost love whisked away in Tacoma, like the Serial Killer he nabbed for dusting a NYC officer. He played cards with a grifter chick in the mocking game called, War, with her seductive insipid adolescent like Stewardess Blonde hair. The type who married men for her sport. He, nonetheless, also succumbed and owned his year-long decent for their secret romp as they banged away in her lair called the Red Lion Inn.

It was there in the red walls where she trampled his heart in the real war waged in her seductive parlour. She played games people play such as her conscienceless card tricks of strumpet and crumpet eaten in the morning veranda, overlooking Washington State's rain and fog. A gift for his visit as she returned to her community as a born again Saint in league with the Devil himself. Leather clad dominatrix outfits suited for her next male victim: Grifter in wait. Tommy was not amused anymore: Rue that year of East to West Coast.

Tommy tried to rid himself of negative thoughts and the intruding images. The more he resisted, the more he sensed his conscious control slipping away. The focus of his eyes became hazier as the blue borders in his carpet became coursing arteries in the highway of his carpet stains. Time never heals all wounds – 'It' festers and awaits – awakening when the mind can no longer hide it. 'It' slinks into the recesses of the brain, where unconscious caverns hold shadows never too see the light, but draining its very source within while blinding one to the light with-out.

Debauchery and Mayhem markings made remnants of late nights with Christine. Spotted passion, abstract and creative as cubic art dotted with intense connection of male merging into female. Suddenly, the split crystal re-captured Tommy's attention: New décors of serial fractions of red pools of blood lay where Merlot wine dripped over crystal – shattered. Sanitizing the spills of Merlot only made 'It' more potent in effigy.

Tommy began to shake his head like a pit bull. Trying to shake the haunting images: No mistakes.

As routine as his eccentricities – his bright star shone more intensely as he tried to dim the intensity within. Perhaps, quelling storms without that permeated within. That is what made his intuitive sense so keen and in step with his smarts on the mean streets he meticulously preened of sadistic perp's and twisted rabid mutts. Mutts are the ones even the everyday Joe Q. Perp hates.

Tommy felt frustration turning into anger as the image returned. 'It' came back! His anger folding into rage at a beautiful lady dying in terrorism on a domestic front. He solved Teshana's murder in Bedford Stuyvesant Marcy Projects, as Housing Bureau – NYPD Detective.

A woman killing a younger one in jealous poverty of purity in her mind's own font of pride. Pride endlessly tormenting her jealous mind as the bounce of a glance bosomed into competition.

The lust of being the fairest lady of all in the hooded man's glance. Tommy peered in his mind's eye as the doll like stature of her ebony body opened and left partially stitched up, appeared hauntingly statuesque.

He hawked a glance at the holes where the wounds made their mortal penetration. The sewn stitches bow-tied in meticulous precision, as the beauty of her corpse danced for justice undone.

The coagulated droplets orchestrating a hue somewhere between Royal Purple and Carmine Red were awesome in their ugly majesty. Like the beauty of a rose petal frayed with age and dry to the touch, he imagined. Anything to avoid thinking of 'It'. Bells in the church rang as the time on the Bergen Street strip of churches that ministered to the mendicants and knaves with heart and souls not yet vacated.

He viewed himself as if he was walking through the Marcy housing project on Dr. Martin Luther King Boulevard, which stunk of stale piss. The 13$^{th}$ stair in the stair well under the roof landing where she lay dying. A young woman in the cusp of life's promise left on the stairs ladder. The ladder of rage unwilling to surrender life – forcefully surrendering her soul's ebony to primrose as the angel, named 'Death', smirked.

Dying, as her soft and delicate hand trembling upward in a pleading motion yielded suddenly. Almost motionless, she lay in her stark beauty as an Ebony Heiress with deaths glee mocking the sacred shroud that draped her face. A requiem unspoken in words: The pith of Tommy's anguish screaming without a whisper heard. His angst unheard in his first experience of surreal departure of soul from function. Setting in as frozen 16mm still frames in slow motion as consciousness slipped away – gloved in the dark arterial blood of death.

The stench of fear embedded in acerbic uric acid, the last piss in the wind prior to her bid adieu. Adieu as thick blood seeped onto his soft leather black Rockport's buffed to a Corfsam shine to counter the poverty and ignorance he faced in the project hallways and roof-landings littered with crack pipes of dreams unanswered. Teshana's beautiful face fatefully reserved for the morgue Auditorium, with the curtain on her unique dreams drawn.

Auditoriums are places of recreation and anonymity. Tommy had an association to his premed days and a recovered image of a cold pink fetal pig in his biology lab in the Brooklyn College Auditorium. He stared at Christine's backside with her bikini Victoria's Secret underwear wedged half in her left butt, her coccyx prominently bulging and the split covering her right side which he would softly kiss and nibble.

Tommy's trance was breaking, he drifted and mumbled out loud in what seemed like a holler and yet an almost inaudible murmur. His whisper was unheard. Tommy laid his head on Christine's backside as her goose bumps articulated her responsiveness in sweet exuberance. Christine's silent, artful ingenuity that was playfully teasing Tommy was blown with sudden encompassing blitzkrieg passion. She listened to Tommy start to do the NYPD rant every real cop could do as quick as a drop of a dime, "I should've stayed pre-med. Instead, what did I do? I friggin' get a Dunkin Donut coffee; a steal donut sprinkled with roach and mice droppings hidden in dark chocolate and a lousy TeAmo dollar cigar every shift from the 24-hour gourmet Bodega."

Tommy felt numb as his painful mirage of past images displayed in his mind's eye bled like a long stream of disappointments he articulated as if someone else were reading them. Tommy shuddered at the pain in his gut and the pounding in his head.

Pounding as the drum of masochism: As if to torture himself more, he said in a louder pitch meant to be heard as if to see if Christine would respond in a temper, or with temperance, "Imagine an office on Lexington and Park Avenue as a Ph.D. or M.D. taking a stroll, sipping an espresso for a buzz at Starbucks and 59th Street, lighting up with a real Macanudo ablaze in the gusts of the East River winds."

Christine heard his mumblings and interjected like a harsh whip with a light feather tip. She loved to peak his male ego with a tease and provocation as a lioness. She loved to have him dominate, and in turn dominate him. It was a game they played as passion teased her mate with a measure of reason.

Christine playfully biting her lion – drew blood – as she licked his drops of chagrin before it could coagulate into insipid stale ruminations. She let go with sardonic wit as she swallowed his blood and sweat as sweet sour drops, "You ought to be a writer, Tommy: That's the ticket old boy: How about a detective novelist? On second thought, hum ... Tommy, imagine the East River winds intermingled with the MTA and Taxi fumes. You need those mean gusts of noxious air massaging your lungs at the apex of a twisted human made monstrosity, this fine city of ours. Yeah, Tommy, Mr. M.D. Ph.D., what about all the malpractice suits, the HMO's, PPO's, Lover boy?" Pausing in a soft hiccup, Christine backed up a little. Realizing Tommy was hurt and in a passive aggressive response she mastered living with the King of Drama – she being the Queen, supreme gently whispered, "Believe me, honey, it's like. Oh man you can't win for losing in this big city; it strangles your Adam Apple and strips you of your fig leaves."

[Tommy frowned with a grin of frustration – he could be so gullible to his woman's barbs – even if done in playful swipes. He was so sensitive for her approval and she knew it. Although he dared not admit it, ever. Even more petrified of being abandoned, he pretended he could not care less if left.]

Christine, sensing his sensitivity, said directly, "Under all my teases, honey, it would be nice for me to see the fig's fruitful response to me, lover boy. Babe, I love you as you are. You are an NYPD Detective – yummy honey, you are my Shield."

29

Christine turned around and pinched Tommy's nipple. She kissed it as she stared at how easy it became hard. Christine felt her own nipple turn erect at the thought of what she had done. She loved his passion and her own since they became lovers: Educating his savage within to dominate and be dominated by her own needs, "Go back to sleep, baby, I'll clean up the mess in the morning."

Tommy looked at her, "What mess, babe?"

Christine felt Tommy's taste in her mouth and his smell as she leaned close to him. She emerged after taking him inside her mouth, which ushered the words she followed up with in-deed. No mess after all. She kissed him as he wrapped his body close to her, cupped her breast and teasingly tickled her nipple – returning the pinch with a sweet grin – he was her own as she knew his secrets and indulged her senses within his: slowly both fell asleep.

Suddenly, Christine's soft skin broke his inner world of silence, he slid his body next to hers – real close. So close he could feel her rib cage vibrating next to his feeling, a mix between horniness and agitation, she pushed back into him. Nothing turned her on more than his boyish charm with a manly and masculine touch; power, not force, was her aphrodisiac. Tommy was called the scrapper and he was a knock out as a street cop, but gentle with his girl. None of whom he could commit too and propose the M word as he called it – Marriage. The winds of being content with the angst of commitment winding down the road of sleep lulled his mind to a hush. Christine's thin fingers, a lithe size five brushed his chins nubs. Her fingers instinctively cupped his cleft chin as he dozed off. Tommy's weary head lay on Christine's supple breasts as he slipped into a dream-like maelstrom of memories.

# Chapter 2

## Haunting Memories – Unspoken

Memories of trauma and loss unspoken haunted Tommy. Christine's breasts, with a nice drooping, lay somewhere between sagging and uppity-snuggled warmly round his face. Her breasts cushioned his loss, as he slowly pacified his angst. He thought how preferable her softness was to the pressed jacket he would roll into a makeshift pillow that felt like a church pewter at Central Booking in the all-nighters' at the 84th precinct.

It was there as a Rookie in Brooklyn North, where he learnt to drift into his own little world. He sort of half slept, while his eyes remained open: Like a lone sheepdog, he could escape the fear, the anger and the rush of running to a heavy job on the radio.

Tommy's attention shifted as he grinned in a mischievous way when he thought back to those days of blue blood, pink panties and green pastures. Endless watering holes with the boys after tour. The endless pink panties he would ravish in lavish attention of fiery passion, drowned in a pyre of a bottle of rum with a pinch of rocks and coke after each stand for survival in the hood.

Lonely days flowed into on-duty nights of shots fired and corpses accumulating in the hefty like zip lock bags for the morgue disposal. His squad supervisor ribbed him that the charred coffee he drank could be Ivied; as much as the beer after 6pm that he swigged after a night of getting wasted. The flash of a thought in Tommy's mind echoed a vision in silence,

"Illusion and watering holes of choir practice like church sessions that become rote – child and adult versions of fantasy and escape – reality washing away in one addiction after another."

Tommy and Christine had commiserated in the echoes of loss: Christine, too, had her silent untold pages of grief – left moldy in her sealed shut closet.

Christine lay silent, thinking of her woes as an ER RN. Once a cocktail waitress, Christine turned to altruism after a stint in being an FDNY, EMT, which was an incredibly hot uniform for Tommy. They would endlessly role play – credit given to the imagination of the public safety male-female dynamic – unleashed. Who says FDNY and NYPD are competitors? Each offers the other what each yearns for and cannot achieve alone.

Christine mused about her feelings toward Tommy. She was no less a man's woman. She had many romps with many men before settling down with Tommy: She could open any Heineken bottle with a strong swallow and twist of her tongue. The foam would explode with timed precision as she took in each drop as Tommy watched with anticipation and glee hidden in a boyish grin. She swallowed a lot of bitter sweet losses in her days, but was ready for Tommy's lager alone.

The days of blue knighthood eclipsed as Tommy hugged Christine firmly, as he felt her warm breath buffer him from the cold world outside.

The Seventh Seal of bachelorhood was checked-mated with the seventh heaven and ready to be parcelled out!

Christine's moisture was strongly scented. Her imprint was unique as he sensed her in his primitive nostrils, arousing him to piqued erect attention.

She gave Tommy refuge in her soft feminine hold. He in his reciprocity delivered a sense of security from the cold world outside her one-bedroom apartment in Carroll Gardens. Tommy and Christine were far from the skells of the street, the junkies, the dealers, and the skin head racists, the pretentious liberals, and the radical nation of Islamists, and the rotating doors of Criminal Court. Tommy was free from those cursed lectures of high flouting brass at roll call, that told him how and when to do his job.

He heard the echoes of the street Reverend preaching doom and gloom reverberate with equal disdain. That preacher man like an old fixture tarnished in time but still shedding some dim light. This eccentric preacher man was a fixture of a gas lamp displaced in the hood. Tommy could not help kind of liking the Reverend in a way of amusement. The preacher man would come on TV all the time protesting this injustice and that one. Like a familiar Tom Cat hooting on his mansion fence, fat and pat, while the other cats meowed in tandem.

The fat cat reverend laying his vertical eyes on run-down dilapidated cat houses with his free eye for a tromp, while preaching redemption songs. Redemption was as far away from Bob Marley's genius and soul as Moses from Pharaoh. A tromp when the sun goes down and preaching stops in the stills of nights trap of temptation. At the end of his romps, good old 'Reverend-Irreverent' as Tommy snuggly named him in his silent wisdom stopped screeching. Tommy liked his tenacity and realised all in all that the Reverend Irreverent, like himself, was addicted to the trauma drama. He was a player, who took his fix like a junkie peering from his window of cynicism and hypocrisy when night descended in Brooklyn.

Not a care for the rest of the purring begging Tom cats he preached hate and division too as he cozily connected with the authorities he so glibly derided.

Tommy too had no patience for the bull-shit passed off as Junior's Cheese cake in the usual media politics. Tommy, in that way, liked the Reverend's cacophony as harmless nonsense, but in an absurd way, at least a protest of the inanity of murder in the Hood.

Tommy's mind sauntered into sleep's seductive pull as he picked up a memory of the civilian complaint he just received yesterday from a drug dealer and pimp daddy. His mind was squeezed into the gruff bellow of his Squad supervisor as his double chin triples as he swallows nuts meant to be chewed.

Tommy is surrounded by the ambiance of steel blue grey paint peeling away in the Squad room as the dusty smell of old couches, ready for the sandman, or Christie's antique road show lay in squalor. The Squad Room: A room of stench and smoke for the finest sleuths: Paradox and illusion is a whore, waiting to be understood.

For Tommy, there was a desperation and fantasy born of constantly being partners with life and death. The hope one would not become the statistic of a hero loomed in the back of one's mind as a cop and a cop's lover.

The image of the father figures fixed all around the squad room: Super Chief Maccione of the Detective Bureau plastered like an ancient Roman and Romanesque Caesars next to the Union Bosses. Both bosses ironically met under the same streets of the winding Tammany Hall underground of yesteryear to strike deals for who was going where, when and how?!

Boss tweed of Tammany Hall was left penniless by the Canal Street Manhattan Bridge, hooking Williamsburg to Lower Manhattan, in an effigy of smoking mirrors and echoes. Echoes leading to the past, unchecked, flip forward into the future.

# Chapter 3

## The Future of an Illusion – Echoes

Tommy awoke with a rough shake of his head. He quickly gained clarity as he envisioned reality with gusto.

"Hum…" Tommy whispered to himself while speaking toward Christine's direction,

"You know, honey bunny, I'm too damn fixed to this job. Christ, I better get married to you one day or lose you: I better not let you go."

Christine, a nurse at Methodist Hospital, pretended she fell asleep again, but heard every word. She grinned to herself; she always listened to his mumbling so typical of his restlessness and the wall he put up whenever she tried to get intimate, not only sexual, with Tommy. She was so tired of the shifts in the ER room as a Nurse Manager where she, like Tommy, got to know her patients. Patients who were like phantoms in the night of their anguish – one door redemption – the other window death: The angel of light and death wrestling in the subtle whistles of winds colliding.

Soil dancing in shadows of slugs that break wind with a grudge and edge – never silent and never comfortable with destiny's dance. Christine shifted from the aggressive musings to the raw sexuality of her needs: Full renewal.

Christine remembered the prior night's decent and the passionate promises and closeness coming teasingly to the precipice of intimacy she desired so deeply inside. She grinned as she felt a twitch in her thighs. Christine almost resented the way her pelvis reacted by just a hug, a brush of Tommy's muscles pumping hard in his gentle, but deep-pitched, voice.

She felt secure and snug in his strong embrace and really liked that macho cop stuff. Christine dare not admit her passion was so piqued for Tommy's macho behavior to encourage him to go overboard. She felt like letting go and telling him what she desired – regretting political correctness placed her Detective in the box of trappings hardly masculine on public display.

She yearned for his gentle foreplay, but ached for his unbridled power and penetration playfully teasing her. All fantasies are played out with tendencies to displace on the opposite sex the desires of one's own darkest dare. She lay in fantasy of him ravishing her with controlled power and dominance in courtly love.

Christine playfully fingered his curly black hair and deep eye lashes nestled in dark and deep furrowed brows, like the deep she used to play in as a kid in Wyndham, N.Y. She nibbled the muscles in his huge arms, kicking up roughhewn hills in the dark hearth of her rural past.

Christine swooned in her thoughts and images of playful games with Tommy. She paused and slowly moved over closer and let her right hand slide, as if accidental, onto his chest. She allowed herself to dwell in this brief fantasy game that entered a visual scenario in her closed eyes. Thoughts slipped into visions — passion fuelling her flow.

Lowering her left hand, feeling the chemical changes inside and that sense of erotic thirst for the opposite sex, Christine was highly piqued for his response. In a surprising feeling of delight, Tommy realized her covert desire and slowly started to tickle her and placed his right hand over hers. They let go and explored how very excited they both were: Christine and Tommy both giggling playfully as they felt her moisture flowing.

Silently, they looked into each other's assenting and accepting eyes. How soft and reactive she was to his caresses. His tickling her thighs and breasts felt like soft vibrations teasing her with his masculine fingers. She felt the ache for him opening her flow as her panties were saturated with desire. Christine slowly put her left hand in his and led him to feel how enamored she was with him… He pulled off her panties and very seductively looking into her eyes, placed them in his mouth while feeling the most incredible surge of primal desire to his core. She did not wait for him and she pushed them from his mouth and her eyes piercing into his said,

"Tommy, I want you too … real hard!"

Christine's mouth engaged his as she pulled his tongue in her mouth and twisted her tongue under his. [Shuffling was heard] Suddenly, a weird sound by the window distracted her attention. Christine bit Tommy's upper lip as she tasted some drops of his blood in her month as he pulled out with an "ouch." She felt a shudder like going from a hot steamy shower into frigid icy air, the change in feeling was violent.

"What the hell is that, Tommy, did you hear that?" Christine looked up instinctively and in shock thought she saw a dark figure. She said frantically in a high pitch, "Oh shit, Honey, look, did you see that?"

Christine grabbed his arm real tight — it felt like a bear's paw. Tommy pulled his head out from under the cover, ignoring his few drops of blood.

"Hey, what the hell can that be?

"Yeah, I heard it, I think I saw something babe, you?"

Tommy muttering and shaking his head like a Grizzly Bear as a shiver went through Tommy. The shiver quivering to his barreled chest, racing across his shoulder, to his chin to his naked butt, and back through his face like an electric jolt.

Christine couldn't move, she smelled his sweat. Turned on by fear and excitement, and before she could respond to him, Tommy's powerful right triceps brushed her face; he grabbed something by the side of the bed, while his left hand slid over her mouth, "shush" he muttered as he leaped over her.

She could feel her own heart pounding, her breathing expanding, and the stillness in the air cut like a razor as the hard wood of his ancient snub nose .38 revolver passed over her head. He instinctively aimed point blank at the window as the frame beckoned back a blank stare. Tommy jumping over her with his powerful elbow, rushing toward the window bruising himself and inflicting a sharp pain for a moment, hardly noticed his bruise. Christine noticed, thinking my poor Irish boy, always getting nicked and bruised.

Tommy now encompassed his natural stance, poised as a Grizzly Bear throwing his 230 pound 6'2" Irish body with a vengeance against the wall. Mouth opening wide, canines showing and panting heavily with anticipation. Tommy switched into his street cop identity mode. Fiercely passionate, a surge of adrenalin rushing with primal energy, swelling his veins every time he looked into Christine's eyes, ready to love Christine again.

It was different now. Chills went through the back of Tommy's head. Tommy felt it tap his shoulders like a friend who was warning him of danger. Real danger ushered in a thought and the word oddly emerged as a black on white sign colored red as 'Foe' landed into his consciousness.

Tommy lifted the aluminum slats parting the old and grayish dusty, once glossy white blinds. Adrenalin coursing through his dilating pupils that surged like sand sharks, lurking in the murky dunes of pitch black underwater caverns.

He looked. He shifted his head behind the shutters and said, "Nothing, no one in sight," as he sighed a deep breath of relief. A halfhearted swallow could be heard as he was trying to convince himself whole heartedly. Everything is ok.

Tommy looked out of the window, and down the Brownstones of Brooklyn Heights, lining up as old cornerstones fading into shade of catacombs, reminding him of some airy grave yard. He caught a glance and double backed as his six sense heightened. Tommy could swear he could read letters out of the cobblestones: The cobblestones' cadence hummed in silent whispers. Whispers trying to tell him some secret un-discernible scribbles at the crossroads where the underground railroad of African Americans escaped human bondage centuries past.

Then she emerged again. His nightmare, where he could affect no help; the haunting lady of African origin at the crossroads of Bedford Avenue and the Cut. The cut was another old name for, Dead End. She was across from Brooklyn College. It was not Brooklyn College but an old shanty area.

Lucy, as she called herself, was peddled for the few bucks she begged for after she lost her ability to barter her body. She was a modern slave for some cult of strong arm atheists preaching hatred of other nations in their own fiefdom as the Nation of Brothers in the hood of Legion's Halls.

The legions warned about in old and new testaments. The beggar lady he brought to Kings County Hospital who could not be rescued and he could not solve her murder. It was she who was the haunting image of a slave woman freed in the underground railroad of yesteryear.

A hall upside down mimicking liberation as enslavement marches on in addictively amusing oneself as the wealthy brothers for the 'people' trade laundry money loitered with common folk's blood, sweat, and tears.

A woman G-d himself created in his own image and breath from Adam's rib as she lay like some cheap discarded animated piece of trash: Trash in the Dead End Zone, where kids play games of street hockey with a discarded can of old Beer crushed into a new object of play. Imagined transitions in objects without a soul made soulful as the magic of faith. A puck in a discarded can of beer. Imagine that, Tommy reflected as sleep was enveloping him.

Tommy tried to wake and make notes in his log, that he hid in his firearm safe. A Moser fireproof safe cut in the floor of his back room. He could not wake as the cut of the LIRR cargo train drew him back into childhood as he was draping some ropes to play Tarzan and Jane with little Suzie next door. Escaping from the claws of the city streets, he always pitched his own fantasy world as all city kids do.

Tommy connected to the kids of his beat in their irascible color and wild expression. He identified deep inside as a kid of his own Irish, Black and Jewish Ghetto he survived as a child and teen. Rough times.

Nothing made sense to Tommy that night, something inexplicable was about to happen – Déjà vu! Tommy absorbed those uncomfortable feelings without saying a word, out loud! He scribbled down what he could remember of his dream like state. He wrote those words and some others and folded into an envelope he licked and closed. Folded into the cut in Christine's bed and slid it in. He suddenly got diverted and distracted.

His cop sense you know he thought as he could not figure out why he was bothered. A frigid chill returned creeping up his arms and a tightness in his chin and cheeks tugged at him. The hair on his forearms felt the tingle of a mild flash of sweat as nerve cells fired away at their sadistic leisure. Cops hate the uncontrollable aspect in themselves perhaps more than the chaos each is taught and learns to fight against in others.

Tommy sat back in a supine position in his worn armchair. Finally, unsure what to do, while attempting to stifle his fear, he turned to his inner-sight.

Tommy looked to Christine, somewhat pathetic: His face reflecting a little boy who drew cadence to the nuns in our Lady Help of Christian Catholic School.

"Honey, you know that skell by the window – it was probably nothing, right honey?"

Tommy answered the rhetorical question as if he did not want to hear Christine's answer,

"Yeah," he went on, clearing his throat, "just a rough week for both of us, yup … too much hot and heavy love making."

Tommy looked up to Christine as if he was an altar boy with a smirk and a grin – continuing,

"I bet an afterimage after all the excitement, a stray fear that popped into our mind, in your terms, a shared delusion or something like that, huh?" He reflected again in his vehement mind's eye, silently and then barely audible,

"Christine, oh, yeah. I can just imagine that; call the job and chicken out. Over what, a feeling huh?!? What will the other guys think? Worst, the bosses will come and then the stiff shirted intelligence squad members in their cufflink's. Worse, the medical division alcohol counselors will interrogate me. Bull. You've been hitting the bottle, huh? Perhaps worse, a little fantasy you got going there, huh? Let's have the department shrink take a better look at what's going on with you."

Christine broke Tommy's silent monologue with vehemence as her bluish grey eyes pierced his green eyes vision. Seeking reassurance, she said,

"Some vagrant? Likely, Tommy, he's some homeless 'skell' as you put it my horny hairy beary."

Christine's thick Italian Brooklyn accent brokered humor, which Tommy adored at times, hid from. Silently assenting when she was upset as he would lay still, fearing her moody outbursts, they would pass.

Her expression now intimated genuine anxiety, looking perplexed, shivering with goose bumps betraying her fear.

Tommy just sighed,

"You know you're right, probably a harmless bum!"

Tommy was silent. He held Christine hard and long.

Christine sensed he was shaken up, and yet he was seasoned. Christine, like most cop girlfriends, never sensed Tommy was really scared. Nick named 'Bull-Warrior' for his bull terrier type tenacity. Tommy was invulnerable in Christine's eyes.

Christine remained silent. She felt the tight hold and warmth Tommy was expressing in silence. Christine let her thoughts slow down like a locomotive out of red ember heated coal. She looked at him and just lay on his chest. Tommy peered out of his semi-open eyes pretending to be calm. That deep relief of letting the steam just fly out like an overheated kettle, and then peace after that shrilling noise, cools to a simmer. She whispered to Tommy,

"Beat's all! But that is the aftermath of being a street cop and an ER nurse, babe."

Tommy, hardly able to stay awake, whispered,

"Yeah, babe."

Sleep slowly gripped them. A tingling buzzing in his ear, a gnawing instinct pushed the fringes of his consciousness to stay awake. Tommy thought to himself, but let go in a low voice,

"Maybe I should call Antonio at least…"

Tommy interrupted his natural flow of ideas and he thought better in the noise of his silence, still he went on as if in a soliloquy;

"Why bother my partner, he's probably busy. Anyhow, if anyone was there it was probably some loser skell that was trying to get a hand out and soused out of his mind. Poor bastard! If I go out and catch him, he'll rotate right out of the slammer. Quick in and quick out – who needs the crap from the department for an off-duty BS collar?!?"

Christine heard his mumble and was lost in her own world of making sense of her own ER Traumas. Thoughts slowly collapsed into images and into the ether of dream clouds.

Clouds descending as an image of the triangle's unbeknownst to each other but intuitively sensed and visualized in synchrony shadowed the contours of the dark walls, hiding secrets yet untold.

A triangle in which both willingly and silently resisted and assented. Trauma and denial wed in sexualized aggression — the derivatives of war untoward — hauntingly illusive and cutting in 'It's' reality of blood and orchids, trees and fertile hearth.

Man and woman so different and so fittingly ecstatic when fused as one. The moment of truth when she expresses, "Oh G-d!" Christine erupts as she looks in his eyes and realizes, as he does in that same moment, they are one and the same. He becomes what she is missing. The tree that marks the space of his roots insertion into the barren earth — filling space with meaning and yield.

Tommy yields once again and surrenders to being swallowed in Christine. Her fertile hearth, without which he would lay like a dried log not a vibrant tree. Christine lifted her head and before she fell off the edge she said to Tommy, "Only a fool could take life's journey as literal and its many lessons as concrete, Baby. Life is a mystery and surreal as the reality we try to make of it. Thank you for being in 'It' with me. I love you!"

Christine and Tommy slowly relaxed in an embrace quixotic and to an outside observer, perhaps symbiotic. Night was chillingly present in their dark abode.

Morpheus enveloped their union as an interloper as sleep deepened in their own melee of fear and passion.

# Chapter 4

## Shudders of Ek-Stasis

Fifteen minutes passed when Orpheus was pushed aside as Tommy awoke suddenly gasping for air. Tommy felt as if the angel of death grabbed him as Morpheus let go of his hold on the lovers. He grabbed for Christine to reassure him. Christine looked with a dazed look and in shock as he cloyingly asked for her reassurance that he was really alive when awakening.

Christine nestled him in her breasts as she reassured him that he was in-deed okay. He gradually awoke as all battle weary officers do after falling asleep on the domestic front on the streets of NY's warzone in Brooklyn North, it is the solemn year of 1991 going through his cycles of rest and trauma dreams. His dad was a tough scrapper and union leader, who fought in the Infantry and suffered from the same toss and tumble night sweats, as he called them, during Second World War, when he was attached to the fighting 69th Brigade. His shrink gave them a name he preferred not using as it signalled fear and weakness, 'Night Terrors.'

Tommy was shaken, but felt a resonance with being alive and well. Night terrors he knew were aching to sabotage his peace of mind when he once again noted he awoke in sheer horror. He did not remember fully crying out to Christine and saying,

"Am I dead? Oh my G-d! I died. [He rolled his eyes up into his sockets and cried with tears coloring his abject terror in a glazed over howl as he yelped out] "I am dead. Help! I cannot breathe oh dear lord have mercy. Jesus is that you? Christine, am I alive?"

Christine tried to share with Tommy the terror of awakening to the fear that he had died and been resurrected in about 15 minutes. Her consistent love in being there with him gave him the sense of security and warmth he needed. For Tommy, it was a dream, a surreal twilight zone experience as he awoke celebrating being alive. The immense fear of being dead clashed in a celebration of breathing, in realizing he was indeed alive. How morbid, Tommy mused. Christine was worried about Tommy, but as she knew that her own terrors dealing with being an ER Nurse resonated deeply within her, it did with him.

The feeling as if the murder he investigated as routine and part of the job swept over his senses and invaded his unconscious mind. Tommy shook off the sleep he felt as if an entire nighttime had been swept away in the under-current of fear lay barren and exhausted as a banana peeled.

Tommy's awakening from sleep pulled and pushed like a dynamic within him. Christine felt an urge that cascaded like a stream of warmth in her navel down. Above that sexual boundary, it was mental with Tommy, as images he resonated with increased his desire and the physical responses that followed his attention. Christine's moisture released female pheromones and he absorbed them in his masculine nostrils.

Tommy's fierce desire to embrace Christine below her navel coalesced with his spiritual desire to gently probe the complimentary sex. Tommy naturally began to make love to Christine, ever aware of her need over years for him to be ever aware of her desires for him to, caress her and kiss her deeply all over. She followed his movements and his rhythms. Matching each the other's hunger for what the other lacked as she lowered her head to embrace him.

In an offering of solace in primitive and ecstatic rites in polar and parallel directions, they united. United and unfettered in an ancient passage in which surrender is complete and where the twain meet in honest release.

Tommy entered Christine with swift and strong undulations. As a true Spartan, he parted his Athenian mate as she moaned and almost quivered in release. She grabbed his back as if it was a buoy in a surly sea of her passion. She felt his raw power, and he her persuasive softness. He anchored her swaying waves as he firmly gripped her around her side and squeezed her as kisses enraptured him into her. She deeply swallowed his wanting eyes. Locked in a wisdom and connection the politically correct feminists and male chauvinists could not break, natural as Adam and Eve.

The embrace intersected in an intercourse of eyes, tight fits, and souls as Christine dominated in the moment of release – shifting her orbits and hips – reverberations in her rhythmic quivering with his. She and he rose together as Tommy exhaled. The fact he had reached the Rubicon, paused and civilly leaped with her.

His genteel way with all the trappings of a gentleman belied his passion. He felt the moment when coming into her domain without caution was destined to beckon release. Christine in turn was shaken by the image of a Knight with a six pack bulging and taut chivalrously sweeping down and embracing her as she lay open. The timeless portals where saints and demons are borne on the wings of desires lust, as the passion of love implodes. Unexpectedly matching Tommy, she erupted in their peak decent from graceful ex-stasis.

Falling with a rush she felt heat on her egg sown in her fertile hearth with enlarged entry; Surrendering in unison. Tommy visualized succumbing to her as a willing victor, vanquished in the joist as Christine's saliva parted with her guttural expressive,

"Knight, oh my knight: How muscular! Yes, dominate me, harder inside!

Penetrate my sheath – plunge into me." Her saliva dripped in his outer lips attached to hers as she licked his tongue that wrapped on hers. She felt her watering mouth as much as she tried to stop her flow as he swallowed her taste in his kisses. She surrendered to faith in the Creator, despite her doubts. The faithful always have their temptations at the cusp of epiphany and unity in the image of their Creator. At the moment of shuddering release in vibrations from pink to red, Christine felt Tommy's stream as if she heard him breathe in her trachea the word, 'REDEMPTION'. The outcome of passion settled in the reddened petals and olive hues of hard branches of compassion spent in pale sighs – singing a song in outcries of passion penetrated with reason that their time had come.

The Criterion film of the Seventh Seal lay on the side of her night table open to sight.

Tommy lay with his sleeping giant gloved in the love he felt for Christine. A love that was more than he could really know, or admit to himself, without feeling his sense of self slipping away into her buoy. He lay his head on her stomach and heard the beats of her pulse as it excited him to think how close to her uterus he was. Men are not beasts and need be aroused by love as much as lust. He was in love with the idea his lust turned into love that penetrated her as a Knight bewitched and took a leap never taken before.

The usual once around was not enough and the unique smell of Christine pervaded his primitive brain as they lay in the bed wrapping his thighs over hers like a pretzel. The heat of the sour and sweet; hard and soft texture of a pretzel – piqued in synchrony as she let go. Both minds visualizing the color of yellow and white merging in the shadows of dark and red passion grew as Christine's lips pleaded for his strong arms and entry into a portal as a seashore ever present and ever lost in reality.

Intertwined in bold relief of the hard and soft play of heat and friction embracing. Male and female scents perfumed and pervaded their nostrils in a way either alone could not. Her power and his mingled in harmony where hard thuds lay in soft echoes that mirrored the depth of energy conserved. Power united, delivered when knowledge that one may survive all the injuries with the genius of the other double, hidden in opposites. Male strokes female and she, he – each the other with what one yearns to be and possess and the other has. Penis envy is really vaginal envy, only one becomes the other in the space of the experience of desiring each the other interlocking course that is sexual on one dimension and purely existential on the other. A good fuck is always and certainly a mind-fuck without the drama, only the trained wisdom to surrender to the truth of desire and the acceptance of reality as dream and wish fulfilled.

An equality buried in the acceptance of the inequality of love when warring competitions stop and inner-sight lets go of conquest to victory of becoming human. Think of it, thought Christine to herself in silence, but as all fantasies she spoke it ever so silent and demure in pretense. Tommy heard, and was totally turned on. Christine needed to turn off but was heavily in heat with her dissociative switch on. Lust was love as she yearned to be her man, as metaphor becomes reality in secret fantasy as orgasm passes by in silent whispers.

Tommy wanted to merge inside of her. In the same desire to be her, that is to experience letting go as if he was her for the moment of reverse potential. Cells do it when they are activated on a subconscious neuronal level of sodium potassium and so do man and woman. It keeps the ritual hot and messy, as it does exciting and mental, as do all mind fucks played only in the sacredness of man and woman. Each fitting the other halves as a whole gestalt.

Christine almost ready to let go as she raised herself and wanted to shower after they climaxed in an ancient heightened rush. She stood time on his small head, where death and rebirth of ecstasy is held beyond ego. The overlay of the harsh realities of their daily numbness and work life threatened the portals with its usual storminess of dramatic goodbyes. Like a long rest after a feast by the king of the jungle Tommy paused, and reflectively while holding his lover tight, felt her kisses.

He knew it would come again as pheromones lit up. Kisses she placed on his muscles percolated their dripping cadence. Christine's bluish Lagoon eyes mirrored his green eyes in a radiant color. Tommy read her feelings with an intuitive script in a way incredulous to him as much as it was a mystical experience. Tommy lowered his head and gently kissed her navel, looking up shyly. Suddenly, as if punched into reality, sweat glistened on his forehead and on his lips pinched by an angel, "I'm tired of playing around. I know I love you deeply. I want you as my wife!"

"Simple as that: Well? Christine, what about it?" Christine had tears in her eyes as her light skin was laden with dark rouge of rueful passion subdued for so long, now enveloping her countenance. Her phases she went through. Her mood swings sometimes with anger and threatening violence toward him. Tommy tolerating her watching male workout DVD's, playgirls with men's photos left in the bathroom hamper under her undies. Her feeling ugly after she relieved herself when she texted or complained of being too fat, or ugly. Sometimes, she would text him during the day and accuse him of not ever proving his love and being all pretense and sweet words, but no proposal.

Christine's tears and sweat fell softly on him. Like dew watering the cactus he drew sustenance in caverns beneath the surface of her earthly being. He touched the wet droplets with his finger tips and tasted the sweet acrimony of her tears as she breathed heavily and nodded, with a broken, "Yes."

"I love you too, even though you are not perfect either. I cannot find anyone as near perfect for me as you, darling." Her saliva was bitter sweet in his hot lips. Even her saliva had her and his taste commingled. She looked with piercing and pleading eyes, her voice became fierce and threatening, "Don't fuck with me!" His eyes met with hers with burning passion, hope and pain: "That's all I can think of doing, not fucking with you, but only you! Every imaginable way, forever and ever, you little sexy fascista."

Tommy shocked her and pulled out the diamond ring that would be a shield and amulet for their love. Placing the ring upon her finger without brushing their teeth and showering before she could speak. He kissed Christine deeply and longingly as their tastes commingling with genius, such as the original taste of male and female coalesced in love. She took pause in resonating on the thought which turned her senses on and off almost at the same time.

Such was the rebellious nature of Tommy, he was unbound. He knew her psyche well and wanted to push the extension of herself in to him and him into her. He was wiser than he let on to her.

In her Puritan exterior, she said,

"Oh, honey, stop playing with our boundaries too far." Tommy said with defiant love,

"Nothing is dirty in love and war. Now that we will be married we can do and be who we are in our messy world, with Spartan strength of love and loyalty."

His eyes pierced her armor and she acquiesced in passive resistance to her own longing of his wild passion which like a Mustang must never surrender his center. Stretched her flowing responses like a stream that could never be fully plugged. Frustration was counterpoised to release in tension: Cables pulsed in her swollen canals needy of being filled with space unraveled. She was not as piqued for his fantasies, but she loved Tommy and his passion.

Christine in ingenious moments of ecstasy and multiple quakes shuddering in redemption ushered in exquisite insight as she spoke to Tommy and told him,

"Time only assumes its protean shape in the expansion of space ready to splice the delicate membrane of human resistance — that is the tragedy of man and woman — we are the same: Longing and disgrace in messy outcomes — it is genius unfurled! It is the origins before the schism of power politics and the loss of innocence. The enemy of the circle of Oedipus repeats in the bedrooms as draws are re-opened in the passion of Antigone's dirty secret." Tommy turned and in excited enthusiasm of a half drunk sailor said, "Wow! Darling, you really are a freaking genius, honey, you really are. That has always turned me on about you when you get these rushes of moods and come up with these insights that press me to the wall."

Tommy understood in part, but was absorbing the power of her insight. He loved her brilliance and in part was upset by her teasing play that turned him on and got him obsessing as well about her dark side.

Tommy calmed himself, knowing regardless of her shifting provocations, she was loyal to him. Christine, being an incredibly committed lover, was never boring. Christine turned on by Tommy responding with excitement about her mind as well whispered as she released with achy resolve as her saliva rippled out as his active thrust turned to passivity as he surrendered to her willingly. They recapitulated to instincts, and feminine ingenuity vectored in the war of orchids gone mad. He was ready to let her take control as she moved on top of him.

Love without one word littering the meditative trance of merger falling off into the precipice of slumber without even being aware of the altered state. They fell asleep before his second climax … Tommy rose again and deeply as intensity engaged her mouth with his, it was as if he could not get enough of her emotionally and he said with honesty and resolve,

"I am finally at peace, I do love you, Christine!" Pausing in reflective excitement, he said,

"I mean I love you in all your colors and dark side as well! I trust you as my wife to be!"

She pulled at his condom and then immediately put the sheath back on. She instinctively retracted into an assertive resistance. The shell that acts so bold on the exterior, but so cold within, grabbing his hand to hold it in place.

Tommy with equal exclaim and unheard brilliance used his uncensored voice, "Fine, Christine. Okay, place that balloon on the obelisk. The balloon that places the ballast of life in the most precarious horizons. The horizon where hot air clashes with eternal returns, that forebodes one world and clashes in the collision of borders of love dancing into tarantellas of hate. Hate and love in up and down motions sketching the lines between heaven and hell." Tommy continued, "Do you really love me and will you surrender to our love. Your instinct was right, screw it. Let go! I mean the condom." Christine said firmly,

"Have you lost it? What about getting me pregnant?" Tommy calmed with baited anticipation already feverish with desire to orgasm with her without bars and doors.

He said with boyish charm, "So what, we're forever my fascista. You are in your 30's, I am in my late 40's. If not now, when? I never want to lose the opportunity and let you get away. I have gambled and lost – not this time and not with you!" Christine with tears in her eyes and extremely aroused and exhausted said, "Tommy, why now? We can continue being lovers and best friends."

Tommy said I never told anyone this, but the last words out of that dying social workers lips I keep hearing is, "I never even got married, help me, don't let me die, please officer…" Christine responded with sensitive and loving eyes to Tommy's pleading answer he so desperately sought. She wisely paused and whispered,

"Honey, neither one of us will ever have to say that. I love you forever too, I can't believe you really finally asked me after all these years. There can never be another replacement for you. I would be lost without you." Tommy said, "Yeah, me too, I was just terrified of getting hurt again like in the past, but I can't bear the thought of another man sweeping you off your feet."

Christine's feeling of love, warmth and security was heightened by Tommy's masculine celebration of her femininity. The *shudder of ecstasy* caused her thighs to tremble in the most ancient of embraces: *Spontaneous synchrony cohered as his eruption cascaded into her emerging waves bellowing out a sonorous disruption to lust as love emerged triumphant.*

It is hard to let go of elusive fantasy that borders on the frame of requited love after being un-requited for so many years, such was Tommy's experience: Christine started to ache as she felt Tommy's finger open her lips as she murmured words unspoken. She let go in venal directions not mercurial such is the nature of woman in distinct contrast with man's folly in pretending naivety. Man's genius lies in the shadow of woman's dark brilliance, so does all light give birth in the darkest of caverns. Dawn foreshadows dreamers in the nesting of peaceful premonitions. The center is eclipsed as it falls from gravities pull. All dreams born in lust are preludes to nightmares. All of civilization comes from the love born of passion to merge man with woman as one heart and soul. The illusion of life's immortality made so by the substance of dreams persistence. Such is the substance of requited love. Pause in the refrain of rebounding into the trapeze of triangles crisscrossed. A unique love of sorts — borne on the wings of lust. Alas the nature of the human condition, and its consequent tragedy in comic relief.

No matter how much pretense and show — it is the error — the comic tragedy of this experience we call life. Dreams are not the sublime aspect of life it is the substance of what portends the beginning and end. A fusion of origin with ends in mind from the very onset of the first kiss to the finale: Conscious fades, their eyelids shut.

# Chapter 5

## Dawn to Dusk – the Seventh Sense of Persistence – Detective Intuition

Antonio thought he heard the phone ring. He saw one ring from Tommy's beeper. Not the department issued one, but his private one. Only one missed ring in cyberspace, a missed call. One link in the chain of communication, a long pause in a drip of a drop from the faucet of life where salvation gasps her last reach of air.

Unrequited love of a father for a son flashed in Antonio's mind. A mind which had deep and haunting reviews of each step made. Yes, he knew about his ability to focus with a hypersensitivity and intuition that could jump like a nerve pumped with electric shock jolting reality. He mused the Almighty looked at his children he made with Justice tempered by mercy for his many sins as a Catholic. Antonio, as a suffering Saint in his own eyes, shed a tear, a bleeding heart, then a heaving in his chest. A blurry haze moved off as he conjectured in the twilight of his strong Catholic guilt. Antonio's shroud around the secret war he struggled with. Antonio the historian without portfolio, read voraciously.

Beginning with Antonio's teenage sojourn to Italy, when in the hinterland of some slope in Rome he visited Bologna, he felt his calling to be a Franciscan Priest. Antonio's cousin Nando, with sadistic irony, introduced him to his first girl right after he professed his becoming a 'Father.'

An Asian beauty, who asked him if he wanted a date; his cousin smiled and offered her some cash. He said great, a movie or dinner? Next, she said, close your eyes and stay still as he felt her peel his clothes off and devour his innocence. He opened his eyes in shock and then intense pleasure as he watched her rise and fall on him, absorbing all he offered her in the corridor of his unzipped pants and his messy outcome.

At that moment, a struggle was born that to this moment has not ended. Women were placed on pedestals as the Madonna as was his ex-wife, and then there was the loving and slutty type who was all he ever wanted sexually. The opposite sex in love denied in the face of war piqued, and relentless in his adoration of black on white, or white on black. The entire world was in a ceaseless struggle that never stopped as gravities pull in endless iterations. Drama King was Antonio's police nick-name.

Antonio mused as his newest lover, sprung into his mind as she captivated his attention or better said held his whole being in captive imagination. Her smell, her purple panties with Victoria Secret sketched as her moisture resonated in his nostrils. He would put his nose to her panties she left teasingly behind for him. She was fully aware of the debauched desire they shared for she would synchronize her fantasy with his; her playful scolding when she was away on a medical conference and asking him if he was behaving; her lips kissed and her beautiful body was thrust out like a witch's tit as he stopped himself suddenly calling his lust out-loud, "Infernal!"

The heat was infernal in his heart as he struggled toward the mount of purity. Such was his conflict up and down in his Sisyphus routine. Night in and day out rites of passage stuck in his mind's eye for four and a half decades of his life.

Antonio realized he had awoken from another dream of wish lacking fulfillment. A gnawing at his stomach like a nightmare giving birth. A birth of the double that Antonio hid: Like his Playboys in his draws of secret desires suppressed into the tombs of repression. His existential convulsions of an awakening of feelings of being in love and fearful eternal damnation with his desire to marry his girlfriend, Mary, the physician, professor and neurologist and incredible lover. He admitted his desire and his want to marry her, in spite of the impossible differences – he was Brooklyn Italian and she, Hong Kong, China Town.

She wanted to keep him as her lover boy cop detective. Maria loved his masculine touch and power as she sadistically teased him and he succumbed in masochistic satiation. Satiation not as passive but in aggressive resistance expressed in their sexual connection. Maria was secretly, and in her style, defiant of all stereotypes in her outward Political Correctness.

She was rebelling against her heritage as a Chinese intellectual raised in a melting pot society. Maria wanted Antonio to conquer her completely. She would let her mind free in her orgasm saying he was her Emperor and she his concubine. She wanted his strength to conquer her fears, but he was so enraptured in his own guilt complex – they both danced in blind darkness as to why they survived every struggle and adversity but could not marry. They were so alike it was truly almost comical, but in its very real suffering, humanly perverse in its tragic pith within the existential moment of trial and choices.

The imagery was incredibly surreal for Antonio, and yet in a weird way, as tangible as an Entenmanns's Crumb Cake falling apart as it yielded to his jaws, clenching the sweet sugary fix as his saliva devoured his lusty appreciation of such aesthetic delights, as eating. He grinned to himself as he felt pride in his Roman heritage. The soliloquy continued for Antonio, who still yearned of becoming a Priest in the Catholic Church after such debauchery. Debauchery that even St. Augustine would blush at. His favorite tome was Nikos Kazantzakis, the last temptation of Christ. The passion and the sweet desire of woman, power, pride and vengeance that resonates with alacrity like lightning flashes blinding the power of his soul. Crucifixion seemed the just layer of content for the short flashes of insight and supplication when he would push away the very love he so desired from Mary. Like a May fly, so were his insights and so were the waves that pulled him out to sea. Manic nights draw bows of endless returns as the shore laps the sandy beaches where heroes don't return – Lord Byron disappearing one stormy night still could be heard off an ancient Grecian Isle echoing romantic poems to his Mary. Prometheus unbound – the detective poet warrior, Antonio – hid under broken clichés lapping the shore of his discontent and unrequited love.

Antonio grabbed the crispy New York Post crackling, smelling of acerbic hard black ink, scrawling pen notes over the gray pages poured out like NYC cynicism. Concrete reality etched on another tragic day in the city. Just another shitty day as Antonio opened up to the sexy girls in advertisements he loved to look at with boyish fascination.

Following with clockwork rhythm was Antonio's self-condemnation: Harsh self-accusations of being immoral and weak to such temptations as looking at the models iterating like crucifixions. Antonio writhed in grief that emerged in heaving and chocking reality in between these poles of Saint and Sinner in his own secret struggle.

Antonio had fallen asleep as he had read Nikos Kazantzakis' modern sequel to Homers Odyssey as Poets and Poetry clashed syntax, semantics and the rules of grammar around his desire and profligate stoicism.

An autobiographical struggle of good and evil, material and spiritual, the sacred and profane: Priest or Street Crime Cop Gigolo, as he saw it. Antonio breathed a sigh of relief as he held Nikos's book close to him; while St Francis Nikos's other book was in sight. St Francis, like St. Augustine, gave up his lustful desires for the light of faith in his religious ascendancy. Like a scope on a 9 millimeter Glock, his blanket of books was his object of security as a transition between this world of crass materialism and his real self-yearning for spiritual succor.

Books that held potions of distilled elixirs transformed from others struggles helped Antonio with the comfort of relief in not being alone in the vagaries of his own life. As Antonio grabbed for the on-switch for hot coffee, which was left over from yesterday's Mr. Coffee machine's brew. Antonio remembered the dream he had forgotten as he looked in the black coffee in this stained mug.

Antonio was in a dark tunnel on the IRT number 3 on its way to Flatbush Avenue. The train he was on was colliding with the canal it was twisting against. 'IT' swayed back and forth in rhythmic movements of a face paced rush. The train ushered in screeching stops and thrusts in the darkness as the lights yielded a full stop and the conductor came on the air saying, "we are out of control folks it looks like we are going to crash." Out of control, next stop Flatbush. The Train was like a banshee expanding without an exit and without stop. The torturing exit between the tightening canal underground finally twisted until it turned into a long king size bed. No crash now as Antonio was laying on it and his estranged son was silent and grasping on tight to the sides – as if they both were suspended in space. It was as if Antonio magically transformed into a harsh surrealism of Dali's painting as a clock stopped in the precision of physical time, dangling into human time. Time flashed its illusion into the image of the Jesus of Salvador Dali in mirrors colluding with reality as Antonio saw his son hanging on for dear life as the crosswinds of past reverted back from the future. The persistence of time was a mirage of surrealism, the tapestry of trauma dangling as an erection left placid as much as Dali's brothers birth and death – unrequited Oedipus.

Antonio sensed the electric voltage enveloping his mind as he was drenched in sweat. Sobbing as he realized the surreal dream had transferred from the traumatic loss of not being able to save his son. His son left gripping the bed for life, and yet falling into the maelstrom of deaths final swirl of experience as living – closed.

Antonio awoke and cried, tumbled onto the floor. His black and white pillow case was colored with sweat and spittle. Antonio had gotten used to these nightmares, which always followed with a convulsive like aura.

The death of his son, Tony Jr. was a long time ago and he had moved on. So it seemed. Antonio tucked away all painful memories as routine as the hundreds of traumas experienced in his shift; Shifting from one night into the day of each new horizon.

The midnight shift signalled his time of work when other normal people slept. Antonio awakened himself and left his ongoing soliloquy for a different night of day.

Antonio loved the streets. The release of another tour triggered his resources to march forward as a good street soldier cop for another day. Alcohol Anonymous had its place and so did he, 'one day at a time.' The buzz in his beeper vibrated it was 2200 hours, or 10pm normal people's time; 2 hours after dusk.

Antonio lay in restless agitation, as he was wont to do, staring up at Stucco ceiling painted in light blue azure as if always a snug sunset as he envisioned it in his mind's eye. It kept away the hideous one eyed monster that spoke to others in his dreams that said I know who you are Antonio. Antonio remembered this recurring nightmare as if he was an ancient soul in transmigration to the present; A messenger within a message.

But he was a sinner and attributed it to being a sinner, not a saint. Hiding as a man who had a secret sought after, but hiding his true nature, Antonio hid his worse fears to be displayed in gray nightmares. Antonio pondered on the fact that his Priest, Minister and Rabbi all loved him, even the Sufi's hiding in the hood had got to know him and loved him. He could not figure out, 'why?' The one who did not like him was the Islamic brotherhood and Imam who wanted him thrust into hell in the hood area. Antonio caught him in a set up. Antonio uncovered the hungry leopards secret Lair in Bed Stuyvesant.

All the while, Antonio's mind was mulling over his ideas fixed as stains in his worries "Why was Tommy so late? Didn't he know they had a tour of duty in two hours?" Tommy would come early to 'chew the fat' as they would say before each tour began, with regularity. Tommy did not call, and nowhere to be heard tonight. Antonio called him on the phone. No answer. Antonio then tried his department phone.

Apparently, Tommy was not at home, or was he avoiding him? He wouldn't answer the phone. Was Tommy shutting out the outside world as cops sometimes do when the shit rebounds off the fan of life's intense moments. But Antonio was his partner in police work: Sacred brothers.

It was getting close to the 12 x 8 tour, he thought, "Where's my gumba? Tommy where the hell are you?" Maybe he was soused like the times when he broke up with one of many women he thought he loved in one of his ninety-day wonder relationships. Life was one bitch, he hardly paused to get her real name. Did it really matter? He had a penchant for the feisty, twisted, and the tortured. Maybe an illusion of his own childhood sweethearts Antigone's box, ever open and greedy to snap shut her treasure, the remnants of flesh devoid of spirit!

# Chapter 6

## Slip sliding away – Dawn into Dusk

Antonio's thoughts drifted again. The facts stood, Tommy kicked the binge drinking through NYPD's Psychological Services and was even seeing some Psy.D. Dr on the side. Tommy appeared to be really in love with Christine, not just a fleeting infatuation. In fact, Tommy was with Christine in the longest relationship he ever had. A real and sincere relationship finally developed. Antonio reflected to himself out loud as he was wont to do when anxious,

"Maybe he had an accident and was in the Hospital somewhere?

No! Can't be; if Tommy was hurt then the Department, would have immediately notified me, especially since he's my partner. Bad news travels like a large looming police turret light. Good stuff is slow as molasses and twice as thick, when it is finally delivered it is sticky and like silly putty captures the reality and the images of illusions in its gummy surface. Then again, hum, maybe he was in an off-duty shootout. But if he was hurt, I would have seen it blasted on the news. This is just not like Tommy. What the hell is going on? What if the bosses see we did not sign in first? They would freak out. We are both going to get a rip of at least five days pay, or worse."

Antonio thought he could cover for a while, since they were very deep undercover and put in a lot of overtime. He thought still and then just thought of a charge of Official Misconduct, etc. It only takes one drug dealer who is out for blood to tag an ace detective. Perhaps it is his ultra-jealous and zealous ex-wife spying on Christine, and him living in 'sin'. Or maybe, worse, a mistress that provoked Christine's Ire, maybe blood thirst on her tongue for her future husband's infidelity, imagined or not; maybe that crazy or when his freaky ex-wife was after him with a vengeance.

The 'what if's rattled off like a rust bound freight train, clanging at each link in the chain that commandeered his course with the threat of derailment shouting her cadence out loud. The bedroom shivered with stale air cold to the breath. Antonio's bedroom echoed the vaulted portrait of his inner life, the Island within the island called Manhattan.

The idiosyncratic hyper-intuitive detective par excellence in his neurotic web he wove for the femme fatales he invited in and compulsively re-enacted his childhood unfulfilled wishes. Believing in his thirst for getting it right, this one would be the one he could really rescue. Each one more of a drama queen than her predecessor type. Antonio chose, and all his brothers knew, but just kept silent about it. The stark reality was being ensnared each time in the web he laid for his lovers. Reflections into his past were as hard to uncover as the womb like contradiction of fury and tranquility his life had become.

Yet, boldly outlined like an artistic impression in contrast to the separate compartment of his mind was an extreme orderly devotion and control. A Playboy was half hidden in the front of his cabinet, earmarked to the graphic pictorial of empty release when he was in the mood to be alone. Old sport editorials were strewn around, a few loose commendations in the closet gathering dust, with a week old Haagen-Dazs ice cream container coloured in inviting, resplendent green mould.

On the right side, above his bedroom, a speckless King James Bible lay with gold overlay shining through the dull withered tome of ages gone by with original calfskin from the 19th Century. A crucifix nailed tight above his head as Rosary beads dangled off the night table, keeping away demons and ex-lovers. Antonio's off-duty Model 64 .38 caliber loaded handgun lay with the wood butt naked and in sight. In sight, right under the pyjamas he left on top of it. The sons of Italy label was proudly displayed on his desk. His courage vaulted as he shook off his procrastination.

Deciding on definite action, Antonio drew his old and trusty .38 Smith and Wesson out of his cobra holster and punched it out. He delicately opened up the cylinder, checking to make sure the rounds were in. He counted all six bullets. Finally, he gently blew the lint that was ever present and sealed shut the cylinder with a flip of his wrist. The cylinder clicked with immediacy and authority. Antonio looked at his hidden service revolver Model 64 S & W. He paused and suddenly pulled out an unauthorized .380 caliber pistol with a clip for backup, surprising himself with his snug feeling of being ready to use all his arsenal, just in case. He had picked up the pistol from a perp he tossed, as he flipped him into an informant. He was ready for action as he slid into his bedraggled Guess Jeans, old but ever worthy.

Before going, he sat for a moment, while heating up his rancid and old cup of coffee with film on the surface as the microwave blasted the 54 seconds necessary. As the numbers slowly counted down, he glanced in slow motion as frozen frames in his eyes recaptured Tommy bailing him out of harm's way and taking a shot for him. Tommy had denied doing it intentionally. Antonio knew better. The feeling that something might be awry-entered Antonio's mind over and over again. In equal and opposite direction, Antonio rationalized that Tommy was fine.

Antonio remembered the wild ties he soldered with his partner. The scenario of a shooting popped up an unsolicited open canal that telescopes in reverse momentum: These moments surfaced with hyper-intensity. Antonio remembered being a subject in an internal affairs investigation. He felt the probe was as acceptable as incest in Ancient Rome with one's sister while father is reviewing the consequences of indulgence gone sour and wayward bound. He had a perverse loyalty to the department and being a detective. Most would have gone south after he did his job right and some perp drug dealer's allegation almost got him bagged for a legitimate shooting. The thought fixed in his mind like a mosquito he crushed that was drawn to his arm. The Mosquito sucked away at the bulbous vein filling up on his blood, as he watched as if in a daze and trance. It hit him that she was a vampire, as he took his fingers and closed in on his Kamikaze attacker. Letting go in a dispassionate curiosity of cop and perp: Pop!

Antonio thought hard, "What could have happened to Tommy that stopped him from picking up the phone. One thought drifted into another like dominos in a kid's game. The momentum of one Domino falling into another as energy built into a sudden crash. The need to escape into action coupled with fear raced through Antonio's blood.

His breathing was short and deep. He felt immobilized. How could he face the prospect that his best friend in this whole world was in trouble, serious trouble? Antonio fought the gut feeling with a rational comeback, "Calm down. Why jump to conclusions? It's probably just Tommy playing and acting out his usual pranks?"

The Seventh sense, that cop sense of intuitively knowing the unknown and in an unusual way that is almost always on the money. Trying to talk himself into a calm had the effect of making it much worse. He was in a panic. It worked as well as placing margarine on a red hot frying pan!

Antonio spoke to himself aloud to hear his own words, "We had a sacred bond, when we were kids, I know Tommy forever, we joked when he was taught what a Brooklyn Sicilian brother was, along with that class clown, Allan Cannon, the other wonder kid from Brooklyn's 29th Street boys. Allan, a half Italian Jew and Catholic was worse off than being fully Irish, Jewish, or Italian Catholic – in some ways, a lot better. He reflected, as Antonio was apt to do in his curiosity as distractions for whatever reason that LaGuardia fellow, the legendary Mayor of NYC who even Maria have rivaled Giuliani that Antonio took pride in as being Italian American as well as half Jewish American. He thought back to the time, when as kids, they would hide in the railroad dead end of Avenue I and look at girly magazines. They would gather with Kevin Misnadeupu, who like Allan Cannon as the Jewish kid, was the token Black American kid.

Martineu Voltaire the French kid who was all too cool was the director in Mayhem and mischief as well as the defender of Allan and Kevin in his own ingenious way. They would all prick their fingers and put it together and vow loyalty to the end of time. Each boy meant their vow at the time. Antonio remembered the vows at the pivotal time of crisis with soothing cooling down in the midst of Mayhem plaguing his own conflicted mind.

What an assembly of asses, Antonio reflected. He thought, we would all tease and ride one another in jest, but we really were as close as can be. That big jovial laughter that would break out like a braying ass was Tommy's awful imitation of an Irish brogue. They would call us the Flatbush 29th Street Dead End Boys. Antonio remembered how he ragged on Tommy for a lot of stuff, all in jest. Antonio really liked the guys like they were his own brothers, including Allan, Kevin and Martineu. He meant it when he called each of his childhood chums, "bro." He wanted so much to see at least Tommy happy. The only one he kept in touch with. It was weird having that memory so distant and yet so comfortingly present in his time of woe. To think of Tommy and Christine being happy replenished Antonio's soul. Believing it was possible for another brother to make it to the marriage canopy after being a street cop and detective left Antonio teary eyed. Antonio desired the freedom of marriage for himself. He hardly admitted, but a wishful prayer for Tommy and Christine was dimmed in his own awareness of a sense of his own failures in marriage and love. Coveting was sin looming large in Antonio's mind.

The next visual image flooded Antonio's mind with abject fear. Fear that Tommy and Christine were in deep trouble. He thought he felt a knife thrust in his side. Like his nightmares, his daymares as he called it, provoked a worse unwelcome image without relief of sleep. Antonio visualized a hazy surreal future crime scene where he was participant and subject. Antonio shuddered at the thought of such a hateful mis-deed. He learned to argue with himself. He convinced himself it was just a bad thought, not reality.

It burned Antonio as he inexplicably looked at his watch and it was 1111 pm or 2311 hours in police time. Where the hell was Tommy? Antonio decided he would go in to the detective squad and leave Tommy to deal with the boss later. Antonio reasoned, Tommy could talk himself out of an Irish brawl on St. Patty's day without a scratch. I am not responsible for him when he decides to just not be responsible. Antonio's self-monologue from the recesses of his mind ended as he started up the 90's Ford Bronco and choose to go to Tommy's. He got ready to peel away. Compulsively, he lifted up the key to his ignition as a strange unwanted feeling brought a chill over him.

A strange feeling inexplicably ushered in, as if dusk had ushered in dawn. But *what dawned on his Darkness – was not light.*

# Chapter 7

## Police Seventh Sense: Never ignore the whispers almost unheard

The hue of grey was dank and dark as Antonio bent his muscular body as he descended into his Ford Bronco with stealth. The pillow on his seat and his 80's police leather bomber buffered him from the shocks of the road. He was ready for any weather condition, and sleeping anywhere including his truck if need be. Antonio floored the metal so hard he almost hit a Johnny Pump as he swerved out of his driveway. He immediately mused it must have placed itself there, out of nowhere, right in his face.

That was Antonio's reactivity when he was stressed: Self controlling, and as jolting as fingering an electric socket. He grabbed his own face, held it as if it belonged to some other Joe, and slapped it. Antonio did this to wake himself every day. He loved to imitate the commercial he saw and imitated with his dad. As a young fellow who forgets to shave, and on his way to work remembers the little nubs emerging as an army ready to strike anew at every dawn to dusk: Reminders of the hardships of being a man, a cop, a dad who lost his son, a father who never was.

That strange feeling that gnawed at Antonio re-emerged. It hit him harshly as he felt a warm sadness as Miles Davis Jazz melted into Blue's with the beatniks of 1958. His rookie days enveloped him in the classic sense even though it was early 1991. Tears welled up with the volume of his new tape he bought in the Village by NYU where he received his B.A. in literature.

Rookie days of sweet naivety when he swayed to the left fence in life, politics were all about social justice and being free and bohemian in pathos. Pathos re-directed as he matured into the conflicted man he had evolved into. Sexual heat and retreat besot his psyche at the time he became a cop and swore and oath leaving behind the love of the wild, restless days. He turned in his idealism and sophomoric days for a pension and a shield against pain – so he thought. He knew better now. A price for everything: His grandmother said, "Why buy the cow if you could milk her sweet baby boy?"

Antonio's wet tears slipped out as emotions overwhelmed him in a deluge of searing pain. The woman he loved last was lost like Paradise. She, the ideal idyllic dreamer, lover, and best friend splashed in a puddle of embryonic fluid. Embryonic fluid that bleed in his suffering his own choices of women, both domineering and controlling in their jealousy who attached like a placenta to his rib cage.

The genuine woman he wanted in his heart he could not marry as much as he loved her. Enlightenment in a match as in a mate checked – in. Like Antonio, not too left, nor too right. Not stuck up and un-prudish, but not a surly curious nymph. The days of a nymph in her orbit, ready to open her petals like talons to stroke her man who stopped to swoon in revel – would wind up peeled and revealed in flesh and bones. The Devil is a woman too who dines on her man's soul. Dinning within the hammock of primrose oil rubbed in the loins of entrancing hypnotic suggestions. Thrusts of bare daggers that go in sealed sheaths in the knight's night.

Italian tradition shook his loins. Conflict was the landscape painted in the fibre of his soul as to what he wanted to do, but defied as a rebel; a rebel leaping to the edge of a horizon. Peeking out and envisioning a new hill on the horizon, a new way of seeing life: So scary as the anxiety of leaving go of old patterns in the stones hedged on the road ushered him back home again to comfortable conveniences. Hedged in stones cemented in concrete ideals as Egyptian Hebrew slaves of the past, who could not leave the masochism interlaced with poison for the ambiguity of freedoms angst.

So pain re-birthed and aborted in every new relationship as perdition raised its ugly banner in the legions of daymares past.

His blue eyes shielded him from the pain as the dark bushy eyebrows hawked over his thick eyelashes. Blinks magnetically drawing in women who ravaged his masculine Mediterranean features.

As with all wise fools Antonio was hardly aware of his striking features as ladies of all fashions and spaces playfully paused. Ladies of the night, the day, of fashion and of feminists unrepentant drawn to play with their lips. Brushing hard maple sap tasting in rituals as they pierced Antonio's veneer and desired to taste his intrinsic soul in the wistful winds of New York City Boutiques.

Orpheus was fixed in the Menageries of each lovers' mind. The singing Peacock stripped of his flying wings. Still denuded of his flight he intuitively knew as the magnetism of Olga who loved him as much as she breathed. She tried to free him from the flight of risky lust with marriage. At the moment of plunging in sacred heart's sealed with genuine love – he withdrew – love interrupted.

Until recently, already in his 40's, Antonio suddenly realized he was attractive. He reflected in the mirror of his vanity as his Romanesque cheekbones clenched his handsome smile with Spartan mirth.

Mirth as in the Praise of Folly which Erasmus the Literati captured side by side with St. Thomas Moore's Utopia: Death in comic relief – a relief in a play on words in which perfect ideals invariably end in deadly serious tragic repercussions.

Erasmus H.S was stately in its haunting shadows built on Utopian dreams laying the ground for underworld schemes. Antonio paused as every tour on his way to the midnight watch with stealth he caroused the side streets to evade discovery on his way to Tommy.

Utopia of St Thomas Moore, a martyr of the soul, as Antonio fancied himself, died for his faith as he had his head handed to him as Barbarians do – the embroidery of a silver platter as a royal dish of head laced with arsenic. Protocol of polite, yet high savage society – the hidden shadows of corruption and white collar crime. Aha, wise poets who make us laugh in their silent tears behind the veil of smiles and mirth. Erasmus, his Mom's H.S., the one she spoke of in the good old days of East New York.

Never to be good for him in the lost days of yore as illusive as the past portends of the future to come.

Antonio felt the surge of his state of mind shifting without control as his moods emerged with merciless and sudden lightening speeds as if a fire sparked his martial side. He overcame the bluish hues in his mind as they turned red. Spartan equanimity of his investigative ingenuity mode placed its Athenian side as his consummate diplomat in dealing with the greasy defense attorneys, or slick pimp daddies and human slave traders. Secretly an actor in need of an acting career, he yearned, for he used hyper-intuitive ingenuity to move in his world of loss encased in the amber of trauma. Frustrated with the tortured memories of dealing with death at every door he knocked on as the Midnight watch witnessed 1000 of actors forgotten by history dying by murderers as much as King Leonitis of Sparta died by the hand of Xerxes of Persia.

Antonio, a centurion without portfolio, felt like stars lining the unsung heroes in the armies of shadows in Paris, Israel, and Langley in Washington DC.

Antonio's imagination was ingenious as he would wrestle with perps in defense of his partners in street crime. Earning his Gold Shield, Antonio mustered courage with placing himself as a Lion along with Leonitis in the midst of fighting the hired Jackals of Xerxes – a Street Cop Diplomat Warrior. Of course, he never mentioned this metaphor to anyone as he kept the fact his mother was Greek in origins.

Secrets are the zestiest morsels hidden from anyone, even the one who holds them as his domain. It may be that secrets are meant to be shared when they become the hold on reality – when trauma smashes through with pain of losses unimaginable in the silos of gathered hits on one humane being – even a toughened Italian-Greek American Street Detective. Antonio could never understand whom he could let go with and share his world with?

His priest may think him possessed when he confessed. When he shared it with Olga, she asked if he would mind having 'Leonitis' pumped up in her bedroom. He just retreated into metaphoric expression and left the harshness buried in poetic license kept hidden in his own self-talk which began to sound like a rant.

Antonio realized he was working himself up all over again as his 'what if's haunted him relentlessly. It was non-sense, he had no evidence anything was wrong. He did look at the evidence that Tommy may have hit the bottle again and was getting laid somewhere without Christine knowing. That gnawing seventh cop sense, or as people call it sixth sense tugged away at him like an unwanted image of a lost love. He finally gave in after a struggle and choose to listen to his seventh sense – that is, his police sense. Antonio convinced himself it was not all that bad to cover for his partner. Yeah, he contemplated, while it may cost him a rip by the boss with three chins so what? They were both going to be late regardless it was now 2333 hours.

Antonio was convinced he would find Tommy, he always could and they would be laughing about it later. Anyhow, Tommy was the better able to talk them both out of a rip by the bosses. Antonio moved down. Flushing Ave, passing the Chinese slaughter house where birds of all feathers were slayed together. The ride through Flushing down to the Marcy satellite of the NYPD Housing bureau got him into a turnaround as the

81

admixture of anger bordering on rage. Thoughts cascading made him shift mid-stream. Antonio jumped as he imaged Tommy hitting the bottle again, or getting laid while he was covering for his lateness, or just being a wisenheimer. Just imagine, at my expense and some shoofly catching him, and me covering for him.

Antonio flashed his hidden dirty secret he left unconfessed and un-redeemed when Tommy drunk and unconscious lay on the living room couch. Christine, in a moment of delirium, jumped and he betrayed Tommy's trust and succumbed to lust with her. He blotted out his one-night affair with Christine. Fear eluded the borders of terror and sunk in with sudden intensity. Antonio spoke with the angel he felt watched over them by grace of the Almighty,

"What if he was hurt, I mean, hurt bad?"

No one answered, but the echoing of vivid and real images of cops shot, stabbed, mauled, and hit by trains. One scene more fantastic than the other slowly and violently entered the unwitting eyes of Antonio. Mercilessly, images of Tommy and Christine emerged as monochrome frames of black and white stills. Still as dawn faded into the black contours of chiaroscuro as lights dim shadow devolved into the double minor flaps of time.

Vaguely remembered images of old-time best buddies Kevin Misnadeupu, the incredible gifted Jazz musician and actor who Antonio would play act with as drama unfolded. Competition for the one girl, Suzie Guggenheim as Allan Cannon would philosophize and draw analogies of what all men shared in common the pursuit of the ideal woman.

Susan would make out with one boy, and then the other and no one was even bothered as Martineu Voltaire had oddly observed and figured out a way to capture this all as frames of Polaroid shots. Shots sequencing portals that silenced the group in a moment of pause as genius unfurled in seeing their secrets come true as metaphor becomes reality.

Martineu delighted in shocking his friends with sage advice way beyond his years. Silently cold air crept under Antonio's shirt as shivers spurning small goose bumps on his powerful chest, struck his legs as they were tweaked for running and his face held taut. Why had he remembered his version of 'our gang', no longer there for him, or with him?

Versions abandoned to the wind. Perhaps someone troubled his own house and inherited the wind, but he could not believe who and why he did. Antonio paused in the mirror and felt pain in the illusions of the past haunting him this very evening.

Still, this night, Antonio yearned to know what happened to them. He sought the fraternity, but never had the courage to seek them out.

How weird Antonio felt as if everything he yearned for was overlapped with a voice that negated him, his wishes most deeply sought and his achievements silenced.

Echoing the mirrors entrancing look, he pushed the border of his cortex and pledged to find out one day, where did these harsh and critical voices emerge from?

Voices receded like an undertow as Antonio felt his little hairs on the back of his neck rise slowly and with sharp awareness. Antonio felt a queasy sensation as if a vice grabbed the back of his head. His vision was glossed over with specks that were ethereal, yet visual, and ever present.

Sweat trickled off his face into his mouth as his own taste in his mouth was bitter. Bitter for a moment as sweet memories of being with Olga last week, when she kissed his sweaty body after he worked out. She had a thirst for salt that she said could only be supplied by him as she plunged her tongue deep into his Roman mouth. His forehead was anointed in drenched heat, sizzling the wet release of fear made visceral as soon as it evaporated.

Antonio took her ploys as a pity party for him – how could he be that lovable? Non-sense, just illusion he left behind as another man made her pregnant, never to be his again. His heart was racing and pounding palpitations as he visualized being a trembling Lion with an unbreakable Armadillo in his clenched jaws.

Antonio rolled up Sackett Street in Park Slope doing about 66.6 mph as he passed a place where older Italian folklore had it that Mafiosi had Lions in their basements to carry out the ancient duty of death with the honor of being eaten by the King of the Beasts. He felt relief as he spotted Tommy's old convertible Mercedes Benz on the street.

So typical of Antonio, he was distracted as he glanced up at a fleeting shadow and observed a female with long hair, pitch black with a glossy shine that was dark and inviting. The Chinese woman he spotted as being from Beijing: He knew this fact with felicity as he had an animate taste for women of yellow color. After all, he was Roman inside, but fancied himself as Marcus Aurelius more than Nero and Caligula who he viewed as animals in human guise.

Antonio, from hours of taxing debate with his splits in identity, shone his exquisite talent to debate heatedly with others. In passionate heat, he merging over desire and sexual tension in relief always sought the reverberations like sonar in the echoes of his female ideal. The Mediterranean male — Asiatic female dance that intellectual fascists tried to censor in their desire repressed in their need to burn at the cross those they could not aspire to emulate. The racists, who assumed Chinese was weak and meek, could only salve their jealousy by projecting their own weakness by deconstructing others that competed with their own.

As if reading his minds, little perversities synchronicity bounced in her lithe fingers as she brushed her hair back in a flirt. Wei Cheng, his lover of two months, he had almost forgot about, tapped her lips with a corner of her index finger. Ms. Cheng slipped her lithe finger in her mouth, and sucked on it. She then seductively placed it in Antonio's large lips.

An amateur violinist and bonafide pianist scratching the taut lines in a harpsichord screeched a tease in his chest as it pounded in distraction. White and swarthy men with strong chests, and hair that protruded in a teasing fashion, unwittingly like sweat pheromones for a woman who was starved in her own culture for her desire unleashed. Wei Cheng, a hard lover he forgot.

She turned and gave him the one look over. It was a long and mutual furtive glance followed by a ruby parlor like hue that rubs off of fleeting ships in the lunar night. He could not help notice, as he got close to her nape, the lightness of her black hairs and her opium perfume drifting into his nasal passage fired his primitive brain creating a stimulating feeling in his whole body. It clashed with his feeling of anxiety and he felt a moment of repose as he relished the angst of the unknown.

The mysterious lady smiled somewhat and gave him the impression of acting demure. Her intense interest was given up by her prolonged and deep glance sparkling from her eyes as fringes with lace in the dusky moonlight repeating her other gestures spoken in silence – interrupted once again!

He knew Wei Cheng was the rebound after Olga and before Mary. He promised her a rose garden, but gave her the buds of thorny dried rose-bush tea in place of hot and alive caresses. Antonio forgot her name, but realized she was the pianist he loved in a flash fire of passion and senses left unfulfilled.

# Chapter 8

## Submission to Domination – Paradoxical Intentions

The parlor of a cathouse in Eden, west of Canal Street as it was called, where men of ill repute habited woman for lack of love and a full house of lust on each card faded away. Unsure and insecure, deep inside the machismo wall, submerged Antonio's desire for the real as the surreal emerged.

Antonio was jolted like an electric shock. Out of nowhere, another smell erupted like an unwanted image of death on a January night. The air was permeated with memories of a crime scene in the harbor of South Street Sea port bay. Adjacent to China town was the oldest section with the richest neighbors and dirtiest hidden laundry list in Wall Street.

Littered cheap beer cans reflecting dim light while rats sauntered busily, taking popped morsels off a murdered DOA swollen with water and tumescence as it was placed in the body bag. Rats scurried along as if washing the decks of human waste with their ravenous ragged teeth. Cats, less brave and taken prey by a flock of rodents hid in street alleys, so as not to be washed away in the mass migrations into indiscriminate parleys and street battles.

Antonio autistically stared in space as his memory filled with one visual image telescoped to embracing a life in a picture of the victim, a smiling sexy member of the female Tongs.

Antonio was awoken from staring into space and his fixation as the demure lady moved into his space and he noticed she was beautiful in complexion and her lips were darkened around the edges. She was elegant and not typical in her movements. She was not Wei Cheng, she was Lisa Wei Feng, J. D., the hot D.A., Bureau Chief.

Antonio's impulse and instinct compelled his call to her attention to the fact it was late and unsafe to be out this late at night. He apologized for calling her lover, mistakenly. She elegantly surrendered her number to him and said,

"I am going to meet with a friend. A quick bite. I will be heading home afterwards. If you behave, we will see what can ensue. I don't pursue men, they pursue Wei, but you are a handsome kind of look alike of George Clooney. Interesting street cop boy, I am liberal you know, unlike you. You are a cop, are you not? I know a Republican from East cup cake Long Island, or perhaps Bensonhurst originally? Don't answer, I know sweetie. You dig my scene. If you play your cards right, you could be lap sitting, on me." [Antonio backed up a few inches, sweat now was beading down his head as he stared at her bemused and irritated, but excited sexually].

"I am only playing with you; do you know who I am?"

Before Antonio could even catch his breath and thoughts and re-direct his speech she said,

"I am an attorney with the DA's office. I am a Columbia undergraduate and NYU Law. My Dad was a General. A man, a real one like you, hum, maybe, kind of like you, at least as far as your reputation goes. I know who you are. Here's my card, boyfriend." A spark was felt as both eyes met for one more long glance. His hand slowly enveloped hers as sweat beaded its blossoming rise and fall from the temples of his handsome face. They exchanged numbers and cards with secret mutual illusions, after niceties.

Antonio said, "Come here Ms. Lisa Wei Feng, Bureau Chief, please." He moved forward as his breath touched her mouth, as the cold air puffed up in a cloud so small it was almost imperceptible. She moved forward and darted her tongue in his mouth. French kissing deeply and passionately for what seemed an eternity ended abruptly. With planned precision, she withdrew with trained precision and said, "I do not want you kissing anyone else!"

In a slight of hand with a troubled but deep almost haunting passionate glance as if they were lovers from some other time, she stared deeply into his eyes. "Here is my card. Don't get in trouble." Lisa Wei looked in his eyes and gently whispered in a very feminine way, "You're a great kisser, Antonio. When you become my lover – which you will, you can trust me! I will do anything for my lover. Anything my man desires. I don't bite, unless I like you. I am me." The card dropped as if it was animated in suspension fluid as it fell in his palms opened. It read black raised on white,

Lisa Wei Feng, J.D. Chief of District Attorney, City of NY Homicide Division 100 Centre Street Room 715. "You remember me now, lover boy, you promise me your loyalty and love and marriage; dump that shit doctor. Drop her. We are meant to be. You need me."

Stunned at her play, Antonio regrouped and headed for Tommy's place. He mused that Tommy would get a kick out of this. Antonio could hardly wait to share his story with him. This may be a great night after all. All the angst leaked out of Antonio. It was as usual like a pin pricking his ego had been released with the possibility of the real one – this one would be the right one. Left bewitched and bemused – no resistance as he scurried along to get ready for the tour. He was now anticipating listening to the excuses Tommy had. He reflected, hum I got tangled so easy with Christine. He understood the same with Tommy. His mood shifting in to an elevated and positive light as the darkness of the street was illuminated with the Halogen on the Street Post from the 19th century left like a stark reminder of omens to come.

Lisa Wei slid away in frustration as he deeply kissed her mouth and tasted her tongue with his. He did not even remember when they had been college lovers back at NYU. She was self-conscious of her neoplasty to correct her very Chinese nose. He loved that feature, but she hated it. She imagined all men loved and watered over the Vogue models. She wanted to change her facial structure like the Caucasian woman. Little did she believe Antonio when he had licked the inside of her nose and said it was sweet nectar. She wanted to believe him, but felt so self-conscious all the time. Lisa Wei would wake and when he would kiss her passionately in the morning, she would get up and slam the door shut and tell him, "I am ugly – you only want me to get laid." She would say to Antonio, "My breath smells and I need to wash my panties in your sink. It is so messy and dirty can't you clean it better." It was if she would train Antonio in getting him to say and do the inevitable in their neatly matched personalities. She intuitively and unconsciously provoked the response she wanted sexually. He would kiss her passionately and kiss her all over without any release. He would not let go until she was heightened in her furies, expressed in moaning orgasm, doubled in his follow up penetration. His Roman ego would not let go in effeminate fear but in Spartan masculine response piqued to rescue her from her own insecurities. Antonio was a gentleman in the core of his being.

Opposites in reality are essentially the exquisite compliment of one another: Without each other they are two lost ships: Engaged in passionate balance, they are dynamic and oscillating creativity in flailing motion of a doomed stream liner.

All he did seemed the opposite – it was if he got turned on by her very turn-offs. Her temper was like his mother, fiery and ethereal as she got what she wanted she calmed and opened up in literal and metaphorical dimensions. She was so extreme in refusing to acknowledge she really loved him. Wei Cheng was so pissed as to how Antonio could forget she was his first lady that was Chinese. He, in reality, loved her and suffered from her loss a lot more than he would imagine, or even understand consciously.

Wei Cheng felt his passion, which remained sacred inside her heart. His leaving and going on to the detail and training scarred her existence. Existentially crushing her more than she acknowledged was the feeling when he left her empty and alone.

She wanted him to propose and stay with her, Wei Cheng pianist acted in the opposite style to procure payment for imagined and real betrayal.

Wei Cheng played the Columbia University man-game as she was taught by her female Columbia classmates. She pushed him to the brink so he would come and supplicate himself before her. She hated passive men and loved to be dominated sexually – loving his rough, slip shod style. But deep inside she loved him to surrender to her completely. Like Antonio, she had been totally unaware of her own unconscious desire. She imagined the cute way he looked at her body which articulated percolating goose-bumps as she began to drink Starbucks bold coffee with her man. Antonio would place drops on her and lick them off and they would share coffee and drink it from each other mouths. Her inner thighs betrayed her wants as she licked his hairy chest. For Wei Cheng, she never was with a strange male who was hairy in a way like a gorilla; Antonio, her hairy man. Antonio did not seem to appreciate when she called him her hairy monkey, gorilla, which meant her lover boy. She loved the warm heat and developed muscles aligning his body. He broke in sweat and in swells of male passion. She would lean onto him as her senses were piqued in smelling his glands and tasting him as he was excited in her embrace. Wei Cheng, pianist, gave up musician dreams for Law & Order. She awoke to realize she was now much older in her late 30's, a new name Lisa Wei Feng no longer innocent although she could not let go when they would meet and stay for hours in Barnes and Nobles. Antonio studying his philosophy; Fredrich Nietzsche's 'Use and

Abuse of History', Soren Kierkegaard's 'Fear and Trembling' and, Arthur Koestler's 'Scum of the Earth' for starters. He was not only super bright and she knew it, but he was neurotic as hell, but a good soul and would make a great husband. She knew she overplayed her cards. She let him go and retreated into the comfort of her culture. They were younger. Twenty years is a whole career in public service cop or ADA. A lot had passed, but not her most secret fantasy of him marrying her. Antonio's incredible passion and creativity had an almost adorable neurotic quality. She giggled when she remembered he would kiss her toes and under her foot as she slapped him and he took it so well. She could almost orgasm with his masculine fortitude and power. He was an artist in bed as much as he was in his secret sketches and poems. She accused herself of marrying a Chinese businessman, who while a good provider, was a player. He left her for a Secretary in his firm. He claimed she had a rough temper and a loud mouth. It was hell for Wei Cheng. She had married within her race and culture, because it was easier. She has loved her white devil and she let him go for pacifying the needs of others as if the Creator would want his creations to be unhappy. Her ex would pay for her expenses and send money for her needs but she was wont for his passion and love which became an illusion. Her vibrator lulled her too sleep, but not peaceful serenades she dreamed of.

She cursed her ex and his evil bastard ways in the silence of her purgatory as she fantasized about her Italian lover who was gone.

Antonio had drifted apart and had let go in their young adulthood pursuing empty dreams without real closure. Culture had been the artificial door that sealed the play in possibilities shut, not personality! She knew as day was day, and night was night, and time was the bitch that kept stealing her dreams for personal desire away like a wicked step sister!

Her desire was melded as much as the fit of Antonio's erection in her soft mound which she imagined had his flag of truce and unity in messy and sweet impurity posted to ward off no others allowed inside. Messy was what she loved as genuinely righteous now with much wisdom under her draw bridge. She was, after all, no long the pianist artist Wei Cheng. She was now a new lady of distinction, Lisa Wei Feng, J.D. prosecuting attorney.

# Chapter 9

## District Attorney and the District of Love: Passion and Seizures

As the District Attorney Chief, ADA Unit Head of Homicide Lisa Wei Feng, J.D. her man, Det., Antonio of the Brooklyn North Det Division was subordinate. She would be the boss at work, and in her home. She had made contact and would break it to Antonio in time that she was his past lover. Antonio was hot into Lisa. She knew she had him snagged in what appeared to be serendipity but was tracked as a lioness on a male bull from his hoofs to his horned head, Lisa delighted in the lust for everything male within and without him.

Deep inside, she mused she was a bitch and loved to play him. But she also felt in the stirrings of her sweetest music she loved him and simply wanted him as her man. She would have him nuzzle up to her as a repentant boy with tears as he shook in anticipated delight. She finally had begun to reclaim redemption she felt lost but now knew there was a power larger than he and she. Hum, perhaps.

Wei gazed beyond the horizon of time and visualized her past emerge in the living space of her dance classes as a little girl. A place she would never be again as the bully girls had pushed her around and touched her roughly and pulled on her dress, humiliating her as a spoiled rich kid, whose dad was a general, but not in the face of girls who were jealous and mean hearted.

She quickly shifted into longing for Antonio's protective arms and chest she loved to touch, kiss, lay on and play with his hair. Playing out in her minds expanse in a slow repeat scene she was getting married. In a splendid white gown with yellow trim and black lace and Purple stockings, she was ready to take him and possess him as her own.

Antonio in a stunning look almost angelic in his ruddy complexion was ready to take the leap. His best man, Tommy, was handsome in her mind but not as much as Antonio. Antonio was decked in a dapper pin stripe suit with a black and white tie. He was well shaved, except for an overcast handsome shadow of about eight hours.

Wei had not forgotten who Antonio was at the core. She wanted him and also had given up on the racial issue and knew what she wanted for all times was Antonio. She imagined with aching resolve to pursue him as she knew serendipity was a myth, grace was not.

She had nowhere to really go, so she headed for the IRT train uptown and local as she checked in her bag and her .25 Berretta kept her lithe fingers company.

She would not waste her passion on an illusion when her man would play her song soon. Lust – maybe, but love would prevail. Oh, how sweet to be a powerful and feminine genius. She luxuriated in her healthy narcissism. She stopped and resonated as the image of her placing red lipstick, playing kitty for her Lion sizzled in her minds eyes as she lay a lair for her man and their marriage. Milton said paradise was lost – but Lisa would regain Paradise as re-visioned in her-story.

# Chapter 10

## Last Temptations: Rattle the Doors of Inception

Antonio reveled in his revelry of being picked up by a beautiful ADA Chief of Homicide, Lisa Wei Feng. He had no hang-ups about the playful possibilities of having this new attractive and sexy woman in his life. She was on the far side of education for his comfort. She made more than him, unless he took all his overtime in cash. Perhaps she would be the one. Although Lisa had rank on him, he would protect her and be her partner in love and crime. Unaware of his ruddy complexion turning blush as anxiety ingeniously compelled his response of sensing and smelling his lover's desire.

Antonio committed to following Lisa's feminine ardor with pith in every moment as he imagined her naked trail. He imagined the many ways he would follow her as her tease could only come from a woman well versed in masculine arousal, the male mind and psyche.

In simultaneous mystique, as if in synchrony, Antonio felt a vibration and ring that echoed a message that chimed in with his pre-programmed 'Waiting in Vain' by Bob Marley and the Wailers. It read,

"Wow, yummy kisser boyfriend, more to come – no pun, darling, your girl, Lisa."

Antonio in knee jerk reaction stopped his impulse to immediately respond in bold sexual texts. Instead, he exercised restraint reflectively, and etched poetic:

"Brilliant countenance, sweet and moist lips, the pride of the Lion, my Lioness Roarrrr …" Lisa Wei Feng, texted,

"Call me darling when you get in …"

Lisa visualized him kissing her all over with his facial nubs shadowing his handsome face. Her playgirl collection was meticulous and each male model on top was covered in sanitized plastic wrap with cardboard. It looked as if she collected them as trophies of her independent brash style hiding her real shyness and desire for the ideal man. She acted with brash bravado, as if these male models were comic displays of toy boys she could pick and choose from. Like the cyberspace male sites she visited, she felt turned on by males in very unconventional and perverse positions. Driven in compulsions, she released wild fantasies with men till relief stopped her aches. Her need for control of her obsessions of possessing men and fantasised sex with them, left her feeling dirty and ended in purging with vomit all over herself as she washed herself clean. Shoving her two fingers down her throat as the wretching vomit splashed out in the latrine waiting to bury her shame and desire: Open and shut cases of obsession and compulsion in mens' draws as in her legal cases shut tight. She stirred in her whirling thoughts as her little straw sucked in the transfusing drops of vertical non-dairy creamy drip in venous abandon into her mouth. She let each drop dribble down her coffee cup as her lick spittle melded with the pure black coffee. She played with the stirrer as she swallowed the mix.

Lisa felt confident as the leader of her own destiny. She was certain she knew men in her own mind. She read them, and up to now, knew how to seduce men and keep her man intrigued – but could not hold any for long enough to marry her. She stayed away from the guides like, Why Men Love Bitches. She liked being her own person, outside of culture and societal demands as a unique lady. She knew she wanted to take control of Antonio without caring to analyze what that meant to others. She hated bitchy feminists and their fascism in radical splinters rupturing the freedom gained in play between man and woman as female chauvinism spiked in inverted nightmares.

Strong and gentle as she reminisced about Antonio's embrace and his breath buffering her from the cold air ushering in. Lisa felt his arms, hard and muscular, as she ached with desire just imagining him holding her strongly. She dreamt of Antonio touching her body and artistically sculpturing her every nerve: touching, smelling, and entering her psyche with strength and perspiration drenching their bodies.

She wanted to smell him, taste him and go down on him. She imagined how nice it would be. A lion, he said, fueling her pheromones as she envisioned in her mind's eye the new film, the Last Lions she viewed by herself. She would be the woman who could see a movie by herself as her answer to Sinatra's don't tell me how to wear my hat. As the male lion in raw power licked and entered the lioness with power. She felt heat all over and played with her coffee cup as she held the curved banana in her car seat and touched it, taking it in her mouth and feeling the girth and texture with her tongue. Incredible sensations of hard maple oozing sap as she placed honey on her banana. The banana, she would have all for herself. She chomped down on the banana and stopped herself with a threatening vision.

She was not wont to share her man with any of the predatory chicks in her office. They were younger and flirtatious 'babes', all over the ADA and Central Booking Office. She felt angst like a sharp barb as her eye muscles twitched uncontrollably, yet hardly noticeable, in her pocketbook mirror. The idea of Antonio sneaking kisses with some bimbo bothered her. Lisa had been in therapy and knew her possessive jealousy cost her many a relationship with men that had fallen in love with her. She distanced herself from her own tendencies in her own mind. She let that possession of rumination go and said 22 times aloud, "Let Go: Let G-d in trust." The calming effect of escape from anxiety in dreams of other places and people helped.

Lisa was a devout Catholic. She remembered the Priest Father Francis Limine. Lisa's crush nurtured her carnal desire for the taboo father. She bathed her relief for him in the confession booth. Ever handsome, honest and with integrity to the end Father Francis never crossed his own carnal temptation – in-deed. She pitched with ingenuity as she gave him Nikos Kazantzakis's, Francis and the Last Temptation of Christ. She argued that St Francis, and even St. Augustine, confessed carnal thoughts and desires. If Father Limine only let go once, they could repent together. If he chose to leave the flock, she could afford to care for both of them as an Attorney. Didn't he ever watch the Thorn Birds? He reminded her he may have felt she was the most beautiful young lady but he was her spiritual father. He loved her 'agape', but love erotica was forbidden. Erotic for Lisa was never cheap porno – the process of making love was erotica's sheath and sword springing roots in fertile ground.

Limine as man could not act on any urges Lisa had, as tears were served with impassioned appeal for his response, Father Francis slipped one time where his passionate lips sealed the cross section with Lisa's pursed lips. Lisa covertly knew Antonio's hidden secret; he too was called to be 'Father', but his wandering ways and eyes left him fatherless. She barren without child, he a detective in which tragedy dulled his transfer of being her seminal King.

# Chapter 11

## Triangles Entombed...

While love agape enlarged with empathic resonance, hints of romantic love, Father Francis Limone never indulged Lisa. But yet, on the last night of his conscious awareness, a miracle happened. Lisa was crying at his bedside in the Hospital as the Monsignor read him his last rites. He had tears in his eyes and so did Lisa. Francis confessed in whispers that he loved her, and always had. But he could not sacrifice his vows for mortal love. Lisa intuitively lowered her mouth and kissed his lips. A kiss that would have to last for an eternity. One night slipped into for-ever and forlorn in the unrequited dreams of a 22 year old Columbia University Sophomore as Father Francis Limone at 32 was dying of a beating he suffered after a severe mugging.

He refused to surrender the identity of the killers to police who had interviewed him earlier. Antonio held Lisa in the longest kiss of perhaps both of their lives. She felt his breath exhale its last breath in her deep throat as his saliva and male sensuality slipped into permanent sleep. Father Francis slept deeply, never awakening.

Lisa awoke from her bitter-melon taste, sour in haunting the corridors of her memory as if she was weeping over her Sainted lover. Anger swelled in unrequited love stealing the requiem of forced diligence as dues paid in the process of roles fixed in dead seriousness. Lisa mused over Antonio, who resembled Father Francis as she stifled her achy desire and felt the burning tears of loss in her eyes. She felt emptiness.

At that very moment, empty chains of reasoning shook Antonio's resolve as he looked around for Tommy's Corvette, or Christine's Fox Volkswagen. The twinkle in his eye reflecting his thoughts that he still had it. He felt flattered that a younger attractive Asian woman had such sweet desire, even if it was a game she was playing. Antonio suspected – it was a game of check mate he would win Lisa true and blue. A rush of good feelings broke into a sweat as easy as his passion ran, his dispassion snuck in worry. The twinkle was dimmed in a transient sty in his lower eyelid. Catholic guilt transfixed his focus.

An image of a crucifix emerged with Antonio laid out on it like a sword between his chest armor right where he imagined his heart lay bleating. Bleating like a lion caught in the mob of laughing hyenas with gnashing fangs in the night. He sheathed that sword and embraced optimism – a light in the cavern of his twisted fervor alit.

Short-lived euphoria and Antonio spurted out, "Oh shit," barely audible like a hiccup unwanted, grotesque and involuntary, he felt frozen for a moment as electric impulses electrified his face and charged down his shoulders. The hair on his forearms started to rise, as he noticed something on a corvette which held smudge. It was Tommy's car. Antonio rushed over, stood up straight and slumped down as he pulled the red framed background and black lettering on yellowing white as two days' worth of tickets, shoved in the grid between the dash board read. No Parking Zone. Shock and revulsion moved in as Antonio eyed Tommy's car ticketed, something wasn't right, why wouldn't he throw his department plaque out and move the car on Saturday during the Day, and Sunday night. He was banged with about 3 summonses called Uniform Appearance Tickets.

It was not like Tommy. Tommy was no rookie and would never forget. Tommy was way too meticulous to pay the city a penny that was not due, and known to be owed. A dinosaur, as cops with time on the job were called, did not make rookie mistakes. He would have called into the Police Benevolent Association and made a complaint about another officer leaving a ticket. Even a brownie as ticket and parking enforcement officers were called in the good old days before PC.

Antonio's neck felt like someone was grabbing him in a vice grip, queasy uneasiness rippled through his racy thoughts like a python crushing a rabbit: Bombarding Antonio like a Kamikaze were racing ideas. His head hurt with the pounding reverberations in his chest. Nausea overcome him as sensibilities were shot to hell. He just couldn't get a grip.

He stumbled, as clarity of thoughts were bungled as anxiety, angst and agitation all took a piece of his mind. The spare key was somewhere in his wallet. He had to dig in the overstuffed compartments Tommy had given him. The key was not there. He remembered the times he walked a tightrope when he was in a jam. Tommy bailed him out every time.

He tried to get a hold on his sensations, which were wild. All he knew was Tommy was in trouble. Antonio slapped himself in the face as he went into his police search and rescue identity Mode. He ordered his thoughts with amazing lucidity in the heat of the moment. All real street cops and detectives learn to master this ability to function under the worse pressure by adaptive dissociation: He had to keep his head when he interned through the daily brawls in street crime fighting which made guerilla warfare seems like a benign shuffle.

Antonio remembered his peer support training, telling himself, "Think clearly, and take sound action." Antonio was ready to kick the door down, but remembered Tommy's spare key was under the carpet in the front driver's seat of his Bronco. Antonio rushed in to the front door of the Brown Stone with Two Old Cement Lions on either side, piercing with eyes of green granite. He hopped up the stairs like a banshee to the second floor and slowly moved toward the 3$^{rd}$ floor. Slowly and silently, he gripped the door knob leading to the third floor corridor as he opened the door. It creaked as he was punching out his .38 and entering into the familiar and secure apartment ecology he had as a haven in his most gloomy days. He was on the third floor.

Antonio banged on the doors of Tommy's neighbors, tinning his way in as the young Irish guy kind of heavy and with a dark hood under his large jacket yelped out as he was caught moving quickly down the hall, "Hey man, I did nothing officer – it was not my weed, I promise."

Antonio breathing heavily said, "Listen, kid, where is your apartment? I am not going to collar you. I am not interested in your bullshit; this is serious let me in!"

The kid said, "Okay, officer, it is 3 hum, 3 B. Promise not to lock me up I have some weed on the table. Please don't lock me up I am in college."

Antonio with stern force and in a way that signals someone is scared sputtered out, "Listen kid, just open the door and let me in quickly. Give me your landline. I think a cop is in trouble, your neighbor in apartment 3D. When you hear the cops come tell them where I am."

The Irish kid gave him his landline phone and Antonio dialed, while pointing in the direction of Tommy's apartment he spoke in a heavy and deep voice as he spit out to the squad Boss, "Lt Kevin Life Spillane. No boss. I am not covering for Tommy. Listen, boss, I'm going in right now – better get here soon to back me up, soon. I mean now. Something is wrong, boss, I feel it - [pause] no I haven't been drinking."

He put the phone down. He told the neighbor kid to wait outside, right out front of the building, and if there was a shot fired to duck down behind the post boxes that jutted out and warn the officers responding. "Remember 3D. Don't forget it in a panic."

Antonio paused and reflected in that split second flash before taking a leap forward, I should call Lisa Wei Feng, but something in him, held Antonio back. He did not know, or understand what was stopping him from calling her for assistance. It was ego, fear, or lack of trust. He wanted too, almost pressed his cell with her name on it. He hesitated to make that call. He pressed the text and stopped it midstream. It was saved on his beeper with the Address 172 Sackett Street, Apt 3D 10-13. Antonio forgot to get the kids name and number he wasn't thinking routine but action. He would get it later.

As he entered the Apartment, without waiting for back up as protocol demanded, Antonio barked out in an undertone that sounded like a whimpering plea half wishful and half morose in his terrifying anticipation, "Tommy, Christine, hello? Come on, lovebirds, where are you?" "Oh Mother of Jesus, Maria, please where is my gumba?" Out loud like a prayer that echoes in silence, "Come on, and speak up!"

Antonio was scanning the living room in the railroad apartment that was sprawled out like a crucifix. A lacquered simulated wood teak coffee table was a depository of a pack of half smoked Pall Mall cigarettes, a week old TV Guide and a paper sheet with OTB horses, a coffee from Dunkin donuts and a half eaten discolored apple. He looked in and around the couch with videos including that horror crap Tommy loved and always denied he liked. When Antonio asked Tommy he always said, "You know it's my kid brother's, not mine, he likes that horror crap."

Antonio scanned the familiar map in his mind of Tommy's apartment, nothing was out of place everything looked in place – quite normal. Still, that feeling of discomfort etched its tingling across his arms folded in as if to ward off shock, yet all was safe and all was quite normal.

Antonio felt freaked out that kind of sense of foreboding – the sixth sense cop intuition. The chills seeped in like an army of tiny ants that move across the borders of one's wall almost imperceptible, but silent in the hidden malevolence marching in cadence. His lips were cold, he was scared and angry. He looked up in into the kitchen cabinet and nothing was out of order – he opened up the shelves and not an item out of place. He looked in puzzlement and found a red Victoria secret underwear in a baggie behind the canned Palm hearts. He lifted them up and looked. They were stained with a brownish twinge hue that felt dried. He brought it up to his nose to smell if it was secretion, or blood from a period. He smelled the odor and it was pungent of female sexuality, oddly, it excited him in a way he turned off immediately, and placed back in the bag. He left it on the kitchen sink shelf.

The bathroom area intersected into the bedroom as railroad apartments were from an era bygone: Chilly, yet windowless, where Antonio felt the cold rush through his bones – a cold brush of wind in airless space as cobwebs spun bring shivers to the most Spartan of men.

The heat was on and you could hear it hissing like a recoiling viper in the Serpentine foreground as the door was shut tightly closed.

Barely breathing as a trained homicide detective he did not want to get in his own way. If someone was in there, he wanted stealth, he knew he broke it. He realised he should not have taken out the underwear, it was evidence, but evidence – of what? Of whom? He wondered, "Why am I making something out of nothing?" He pounced into the door, but it opened violently on the impetus of his rush. He pulled the shower curtain back and felt like a little boy scared of whom and what would be behind the veil he opened with his strong fingers. Terror permeated a trained and tough as you get Homicide detective of the NYPD.

Nothing there! Emptiness and a dry shower tub combo – the old type with the pipe high and angled over the bath – as if it could have been a crouched hang man waiting for a new fool to slip through its noose. A ring of soap scum and short hair from a man, and a few long strands of blond hair. Antonio felt an odd sense of relief. A reprieve he was imagining things as Mama used to say, "Such a boy, such an imagination." Poppa would say, "Build those muscles, Antonio, my boy, you need them to be a ditch digger. No shame in working those muscles as long as you are an honest boy. A job for an Italian American like your Papa is no shame."

Like ghosts he heard his Poppa in the records of tapes stored in his mind. Records that hold treasures that open our minds to the associations that make sense when we least expect it. Antonio knew too intuitively how to listen to his self talk. His associations he learned were like bells in the church of his mind when facing something to come – good or evil – they rang with chimes.

Antonio paused and reflected that Son of a bitch Tommy was out with Christine. They had a ball and wanted me to cover. I can't believe I worked myself up. That freaky wild man put her undies in a plastic lunch bag to preserve her smell to savor when she was gone and remember her until she returned. Now, I have her in my nostrils too. It is my vivid imagination, Mama was right. Antonio felt a longing for his poor Mama, and he loved her and missed her deeply then.

He moved forward to the last room and said, 'not for nothing, one more final room.' It was the guest room he would stay over in. They never slept in there. It was the guest room.

He haphazardly opened up the guest room door as the hoary frosted cold air hit him, as did the unmistakable smell of blood. The odor hit his nostrils and his sense was numbed with death. He looked away. He looked back and stared at the layout on the sofa bed.

There lay Tommy and Christine, woven as if they were sprawled as a cross twisted onto one another with pools of crimson and carmine red blood in darkening hues. Tommy's eyes were wide open as he looked toward Christine's eyes lost in reddened bloody sockets where her baby blues should be. The Satan White Egyptian broad cloth was saturated with sardonic irony of purity bathed in profane sacrifice – the healing duo – detective and nurse torn apart in their love angled as a cross inverted.

Death is an honest dance, where one finds their soulmate as the one who truly dances their last dance with one another. Antonio resonated on this utter absurdity – yet inconceivable truth – in utter horror and stolid silence. His thoughts were entombed as he could not speak or move. He looked and thought as if in a trance unbroken and linked to an eternity in a flash of revelation crossed into oblivion.

Antonio bowed and keeled over like a whale harpooned, as blood and desperately sucked in air constricted in a blowhole through a torn pipe of slaughter. Antonio could not catch his breath as he heaved up stuff from his bowels he never knew anyone possessed, never mind himself. The stench and wretching suffocated his air flow.

Antonio's muscles let him down as he moved toward the wall grasping for traction to hold onto. There was none, no traction – just blood scribbled with characters he could not see through the haze of his eyes. His eyes were riddled with pain as if sulfur welled down his eyelids and trickled over his face.

He wailed and cried out in hideously magnificent shrills as if a whirlwind emerged in chaotic harmony,

"No, my G-d – not my brother Tommy and Christine, like my own sister!" Antonio felt the world turning and spinning around as he could not get his bearing. He felt lost and rapidly losing basic orientation. He felt as if his soul was departing as a figure appeared in the side of his eyes moving forward toward him. He was unsure if he was awake or fainting. He remembered and grabbed for his beeper and a portable landline as and it fell. He could not remember the basics but flipping it open he pressed a name he could not read, and fell as he felt a banging sensation. He tightened his huge right triceps to mobilize his right side up as he leaned into the wall crawling upward. Reeling with dizziness and vertigo as loss of conscious awareness was enveloping him as the fog intensified. Fear of dying riddled his body as he did not know if he could have salvation for his mortal sins.

Antonio was all alone – his sense of self was torn from his grasp. He stopped in his blindness and prayed in a fetal like position, "Please, Lord almighty help me, this is not happening, I am in a nightmare." Everything was spinning in an empty world devoid of life.

Consciousness was running away as he desperately sought her, clinging to her as if too life, the virgin maiden in his minds eyes. The virgin he fantasized about as a boy and had not seen since he saw his father dressed in his wake. His dad looked like the clay doll. The DOA we all succumb too at the end of our life. The clay casing lost all of its animations that our bodies possess and victor over as the soul cries at its departure and is redeemed to its heavenly source from earthly abodes. Try as all mortals do to delude ourselves life here is eternal; the journey is immortal. His Papa's soul departed as the image fading as consciousness was slipping away stung Antonio. He felt his Dad maligned for being a natural social democrat during the Duce's Nero like rise and fall in impotence, as all fascists are destined to decline in their end. His Papa was neither socialist, nor fascist. Too clever for either pigeon hole, he was a hawk and loyal as one to his mate and family.

Strong and potent as he wished to be, Antonio was haunted and to his Papa he turned for security, but only saw shadows in the gray lining of the pocket Tommy had upturned. His other father emerged as Antonio gurgled fighting to say, "Our Father who art in heaven, hallowed be thy name, in heaven as on earth." Antonio lost his muscle's voluntary motion in his Jaw. His Romanesque Jaw was sealed with the heaviness of being, as his eyes lids becoming droopy as heavy film noir lids shaded his red eye flight in Tommy's guest room; A graveyard for all three, Tommy, Christine and Antonio. Hazy was consciousness slipping now in hallucinatory fragments as sleepy seduction was wooing him over to midnights allure. Perhaps even deaths cold enchanting wasteland would be the last rites of Stravinsky's Spring of life sprung as wishes left unfulfilled swallowed him in her ethereal abyss. As all consciousness awareness and memory was eclipsing he imagined feeling the warmth of strong but feminine hands strangling his throat."

He pulled free in a weakened state as he felt a needle pain in the back of his neck. Grabbing for his mobile phone in a flashing lucid moment he dialed, and yelping, "Lisa, help…"

He saw a figure overshadowing him. He imagined as he was unable to answer in shadows. He imaged Lisa Wei Feng, "Antonio, darling, I love you dear, sleep baby boy, sleep."

He felt the pressure on his neck pull him down. Dead Silence as the sound turned deep purple haze. Princes CD Purple Rain was the last image on the floor in-sight as the mess occluded in pitch purple haze swallowing the world of Antonio's light.

# Chapter 12

## Silent Purgatory: Picture Stills – Shade to Monochrome

Lisa arrived first on scene, trailing in 172 Sackett Street, Apt 3D with her 25 automatic that lay snug in her garter belt now squeezing hard in her hand. Snug like stolid metal, without any connection of what she was going to actually do with it. She had shot at the range. Her life with Law enforcement and military task forces had little connection to the stormy streets pitter patter of hard grey melancholic rain of shells sprayed. Sprayed and splayed with the messy splashes of blood, guts, and brains as a crime was in the process of unpeeling. Stretching out the moods of despair she angled her way in as she pulled out her DA Office ID. Her sweet little, ever illusive, girly deadly pistol: A quarter size, 25 Caliber Berretta.

She hesitated to rush in where only US Rangers and Street cops dare tread uninvited. Something intuitive pressed hard and kneaded her tight back shoulder blades, she felt and knew some bad stuff lay in the path she wanted to walk. She felt confused, dizzy and could not remember how she got there. Her pistol looked wet with a dark tinge of red and hair, she placed it in her outer suit pocket surreptitiously.

Unlike Antonio, Lisa had the advantage of forewarning. Stench from the room door lay open like rotten eggs and vomit exposed to the cold air blasting her soft skin as she moved forward ever cautiously. Antonio had left in his wake a trail of dank and putrid stench as the odor hit Lisa on entry with a visceral response. Odor was experienced as vicarious sensations that sheared into her senses. Senses after seeing photos taken including the slaughter of one million souls in Sudan by Muslim extremists. The warlord Hadid who maneuvered to Mogadishu with the terror king Osama Ben Laden and Al-Qaeda taking credit for what was a co-viral contagion, not a coordinated one in 1994.

Lisa Wei Feng was moving through her sense of scents framed in frozen framed Chiaroscuro as lime flavored Brazilian Rum sour and sweet evoked progression to her affair with a US Marine. A wholesome, clean cut, guy named Frank Shaffer from Suffolk County Long Island. He was back from the 93 counter-insurgency in Somalia and Mogadishu.

She met him on the LIRR going to visit her friend who lived in East Islip. He looked like he was ready for action and yet held a gentle and demure smile that semi-grinned and exposed a heavy heart she could resonate with. She heard the battles, which sounded like Brooklyn North street crime police operations on the midnight to eights. The very streets Antonio had skirmishes with in the torn out streets in East NY when potshots hit with a twang in the middle of the night's dawn.

Frank would reminisce each time after sexual encounters he performed on Lisa Wei with the deft skill of a field operator. A field operator where he let the rope of intimacy tautly released with perfectly measured distance onto Lisa Wei. She, in turn, remembered the tension as extreme excitement piqued and relieved in her red flush that evidenced her break with illusion into the moment of shared reality.

Before she could lead the waters of balance after such intimacy, Frank broke the peace with stories of Warlords who starved the civilians in Mogadishu under the rain of terrorist's fast and hard fire. Mohammad Adid's reign like all terror criminals, was done-up – by the U.S. Rangers and the follow up USMC troops! Lisa loved the courage and stamina of her boyfriend in recon. She learned to associate even more pleasure with warlike ferocity as the tempo and signals of intimacy as it was shrouded in mystery. Perhaps, in part, a choice to apply for an ADA position. Frank was a motivation for her next move.

She knew from street crime to the detective squad in Brooklyn North, Antonio's tracking skills were like a hunter seeking out the drug lords who made deals with the devils in the hood. The darker predators of terrorists, hues who laundered women like rags torn and sold to adorn their short lived treasures. Flash back to that excruciating loss striking as a quantum moment in the heart of her psyche was a fast forwarding memory of Frank saying,

"Those fuc_in' smells in Somalia and Sudan hit me first and never exited my brain. Real human beings looking like a rack of lambs aligned in the streets. A brain stem screeched to a halt on the cobblestones in ancient cities. Humans flayed, where the Almighty could see repeats of shells littering and realigning with the blood echoing back to ancient warlords using cudgels no different than the new techs and soviet machine guns, except they were pagan instruments and rituals then and now disguised with excuses of holiness to lay murder raps on the innocent."

He described how he could not shake war memories, smells were imprinted with nausea and hate that provoked feelings and emotions of revulsion and exquisite tasteful attraction to destroying the genocide collectors. Imprinted forever were the dead smells, as he put it, that were cordoned off in the zombie zones he called 'Dawn of the dead.' In spite of Trazadone, and Ambien – Frank could not sleep well. Not even after sex.

He stirred Lisa's imagination as well with anticipation as she loved his macho side as she reveled in his war stories; war stories which were vented without insight as to its real impact, loss needing, expression and re-direction. Which each war story told, nightmares resurrected into casts of crystal portends that coordinated his early demise, spoken and unheard in a final finale of accidental death. Lisa's loss of Frank nestled another trauma left hidden in her zeal to punish and satiate anger left unspoken.

Franks wry humor was dark and dank as he set a barb as metaphor laid transparent in her mind's eye, he barked out his thoughts, "Even a dead mouse in a trap stirs me in the night, babe." Frank Shaffer liked Lisa Wei when she did not shower for a day or two as it made her so much more feminine in her smell, which seemed to eradicate the stench of deaths smell. She felt excited by his desire and in silent assent for him, tolerated her strong smell he delighted in for her sacrifice for Shaffer. Both felt sacrificial rather than sweet repose in dancing.

War was the game they played and breaks in peace as the design they prophesized in self-fulfilling strategy. Oh, the games men and woman play are such puzzles she mused in self-indulgence as she fast forwarded in memories space as only seconds were elapsing in physical time as inches were being conquered in 172 Sackett Street, Apt 3D.

Lisa Wei knew Frank was tamable. She had him in training. She lived by ascetic submission for the pleasure of dominance. Shaffer had complimented her needs with discipline of taking in her pungent and acerbic smells with cravings she could only puzzle in and adore. In a shadow of Franks upbringing as in every masochist, lay the hidden sadist, the Marque de Sade peering for a ruse. Rousing to collect grievances for offenses imagined that in-deed were instigated. This was misunderstood in the folie a deux of both conspirators as much as the fit of sexual intercourse and inter-dependency's natural flow were felt, acted and done with tactical efficiency.

Lisa Wei, in this chaotic moment, glimpsed the truth. The truth as illusory as a string of illusions, like legislating morality or correcting culture that just does not work in reality. Try as some will – nature prevails as the Almighty sees – fit. Their play was sexual excitement to tensions coil.

Tragic was the pop of extension pulled to its breaking point. Lisa Wei Feng awoke to the ring of danger with the news and the ceaseless calls that Shaffer hit a Dividing line on the Grand Concourse. His Honda sedan flipped and his unseat belted head hit so hard against the windshield he never gained conscious awareness. Layered in the tragic momentum of crushing losses complex and complicated for Lisa's life. The fact that after a spat, Shaffer told Lisa she lacked heart and could not understand him. She was incensed and knew that was untrue. She held back from saying what she knew of his suffering and why she was so hard on him at times was love, not hate. Instead, she kept to scripted roles and yelled back at him, "You are crazy, you selfish, self-centered man. Leave through that door and do not come back. You can get hit by a car and I will not even look to throw you a towel but pass over you. You are a prick, one big mean one."

She got furious and had forgotten her words and never meant what she spewed when she saw red in her eyes. They lit up like two dragoons fluttering on the angular lunar iridescence breaking the shadows in midnight's breach. Fury that glowed in the night's queue on the boulevard of illusions.

Illusions breaches titled 'Grandeur' – the other entitlement froze time; Two minutes of drenching memories of Frank submerged suddenly as Lisa's awareness awoke in the present. The corridors on the railroad walls fading to grey as she stopped and leaned onto the fine art print in red frame of Chagall's dreamy Jacob's Ladder laid lightly nailed into the wall. The motif in red relief highlighting the Angel of Death hovering above with Sword in hand as the man lay in his woman's protective embrace.

Lisa Wei Feng was not narcissistic, although many alluded to that character. She was wounded earlier by an overbearing mother who did not let her be loved for being herself. A father who doted on her and never taught her reality except as a princess who remained passive to Mom's control. Dad loved her and it was in older males she sought comfort like Southern Whiskey. The wounded quarter seeking her mirror side and finding in Frank they were half-initiated to the awakening of the

Cock's morning crow in the pecking order of competition.

She never realized in the moment that Shaffer's nightmares of waking and trying to escape as if he was going to leap frog right out of the window in stark fear was not weakness. It was the most complex of losses closing in on his world of security pulled from under his waist belt. He wanted Lisa Wei to wrap her arms around him and snuggle him in his moments of losses. He yearned for her to provoke warmth and comfort that lay at the bottom of the tide of waves never shoring up her love and passion. Guilt, she realized, in lost souls in need of a beacon of a life tower. Instead, soul's unanchored and buoyed in illusive neon lights of a tempestuous sea of life's hazards. Lisa was low on emotional empathy at the time and showed him an austere cold breast. She gave Frank Shaffer heat and sweat as sexual as a canine female in bitchy posture – her false self. 'It' did not nurture him with what he needed most as the inner tension of love. Regrets tormented her soul.

Lisa Wei Feng felt Frank Shaffer was a wounded man, nothing a kick in his butt could not cure. She knew it would work, her friend Susan who was an ardent anti-feminist had told her tough love and he will eat out the cup of your palms. Trust me. Lisa had not only known this to be true, she firmly believed the tougher her boundary the more tough grounding of soul into her man would emerge.

The frames of her own measured beguiling were real enough with her musical craft as a pianist. She disciplined herself as much as she sought disciplining her man with effect.

She ushered in her own serenades in such high strung dramatic plays – a fantastic treatment: Her favorite, George Gershwin, mustered calls of piano rolls in the lower east side swank clubs at Rivington and Forsyth Streets. Rivington shouldered in the blades of Chinatown, where her first generation Beijing mother actively sought release of her frustrated life in her narcissistic extension in the perfect child; The microcosm of the American Dream girl.

Like all dream girls, idols formed as Cinderella's and Peter Pan's that feel the heat of oppression in crystal slippers and burning emasculating brushes. Judgment lay in mother's dominating selfish shadow living her daughter's life. Lisa Wei's substance was dwarfed by her mother's ethereal life as the selfless mother who tyrannized her life with her own selfish legend. Cloned in genetic relief as cultural engineering not biochemical in bankrupt foreclosures. Forestalling reality forever, her mother left the imprint of the wounds of a martyred dowager never living her own life and cruelly foreclosing and controlling her daughter's as her own escape. A narcissistic pleasure of suffocating love without growth, was the legacy her Martyr mother left behind.

Lisa Wei wanted Frank unconsciously to sense her pain in scripts that repeated old roles played on the screen of Chiaroscuro as the next black and white Poster near the guest bedroom in uncanny focus illuminated her experience. She still could not hear sound as the street ambiance hid any breathing if any were to be heard.

Is it not ironic that Lisa Wei Feng drank in little sweet aperitif's, where she sucked on the scavengers of the world, the shrimp cocktails? Swallowing the tail of cocks, or a cock's tale – drunk in the auspicious dark genius of the idea as world under Schiller's Liquor Bar on Gershwin's Piano Roll on Rivington Street. It was there she found the cross currents of her past and present. She mused in her unconscious about the romantic Friedrich Schiller, who posited that Art is the daughter of freedom.

She made her decision to first become a pianist which she labored under her mother's dreams. It was her returning haven to drink her pain away to become an intern ADA, she had known deep inside one day she would be the DA of Manhattan.

The gifted child, all too perfect, as she was taught – so she aspired to teach Frank Shaffer. Guilt and denial is a wicked gap in the hearts ordinary pathos when it falls in the holes left un-full-filled, as the Ventrium leading to the Vena Cava. Shaffer had a rough slipshod exterior while his heart had a warm melt down for her love – she in turn in tragic irony gave mercury rising in polar directions, instead of hot fudge in pink icing, along the lace of her garter belt at the end of dusk. She did not realize at the time how powerful traumatic losses could actually sink in overtime if left unspoken and un-mourned. She could not face his wake and funeral she did not attend.

Her own fear of death seemingly did not match her zeal as a prosecutor consciously. But Lisa Wei's genius carried her well. She grew, as all human beings do, at NYU Law School. Guilt led to self-help books, but she never set foot in a shrink's office except for a brief breakdown in college. That would mean, no matter what the system, EAP, or Psych Services promised she promised she did not trust the system – she knew it too well. She couldn't risk being labeled 'psycho' and lose her promotions. Too great a price to pay for peace of mind. War inside was better than outside, she learned that as a kid and crystallized it with her lover Frank.

Ironically, in spite of her Ivy league education and her 'liberal-attitude' she was not quite so liberal with her soldier lover boy issues. But, that was back in 93' and she had changed and matured quite a bit in substance.

In her attorney mind, she liked 'either-or', 'fear and trembling' as her hyper-focus remembered into the telescope of the past to hold onto the wisdom of Soren A. Kierkegaard. Soren's wisdom. The sage appeal was that the individual in absorbing wisdom from G-d in silence, at times can grieve and appeal in thunderous bellows louder than words spoken. She learned to suffer in silence – intuitively G-d would hear her.

Her existential angst was tolerated better as she was wont to change her heart in a drop of a dime in her 20's, which shifted in her 30's and 40's into a conserving anxiety she tolerated. In a way, like Antonio, she had a duality. Her double of impulsive release in the comfort of convenience as her hyper-focus of structure in form expanded. She had, in compromise with her loss of her US Marine, sniffed, smelled, and developed a keen ability in that sensorium of flesh and blood. By incorporating an aspect he emphasized, she never fully lost the object that tied him idyllically to her scent of a man. That memory emerged as if it was yesterday, even though some long years had passed the visceral record fixed in the stain of smells in her mind.

Smell he had rubbed like stale putrid onions into her mind after he disappeared from her emerged again in explosive intensity. Three minutes had gone by and she abruptly awoke to the present.

She smelled dead bodies and flesh, the putrid decay in the back room of the railroad apartment on a 90-degree angular hit from the guest room. The narrow scope of vision yielded shocking waves of death ingested in her nostrils and vision as she passed into the Maelstrom and spotted Antonio down. Darkness descended suddenly, without warning. Lisa Wei began hyperventilating as the biting cold clatter of teeth gnashing uncontrollably distracted her for a split second. She almost passed out in her weakness of heart as she was in shock. Shock striking mortalities fine line with death un-initiated.

Lisa entered the room and made out Antonio was in the cross bow of being taken down. She was beyond being incredulous as tragic irony twisted its unraveling plot with intent. Her boyfriend she sought out after all these years of hope promised her a garden of roses, now just thorns in demise. Hope resurrected in a crime scene, where a $2^{nd}$ grade detective renewed hope anew laying in a pool of his own piss. Blood of his partner and his girl lay fused in relief. Blood laced her arms and layered her cheeks as she looked at her hands, warm blood was rapidly cooling.

It made a Coen brothers flick look like a serious melodrama. Where was the line to be punched – it was full of holes. She was aching from passion, now filled with the disquietude of paradox as illusion, perhaps delusion surfeiting her date with Antonio. It was beyond belief. She moved forward as Lt. Kevin Savage emerged on the scene with,

"What the fuck! Get down here, now! Forthwith our boy is out. Get the bus here forthwith and the duty chief yesterday. We have the Riding DA hyperventilating. We are unsure how long Ms. Feng has been laying here in shock. Rush that ambulance, make it two – forthwith!"

Tongue in cheek took on a new dimension for Lisa. She could not protest as she was breathing shallowly as Lt Kevin Savage looked on. Lisa scanning the surreal still frames, black and white 16mm repeat. Tears flowed down as she caught Antonio's image slumped in pitiful malaise. No sensibility could be mustered for Lisa, as she walked by in a daze, which the police investigators attributed to shock. Ms. Feng, due to her position as District Attorney, was left unchecked. No search for weapons or contraband on her person was ever affected by investigators. The only intrusive actions taken were Detectives asking Ms. Lisa Wei Feng if she was ok, and how they could assist her. After all, no one questions the authority and power of the aegis of the people of the State of NY. She was untouchable. She was beyond the law like an executive seal, she was beyond the law of the land as she represented the law. Lisa Wei Fang fell into a stupor by some hazardous airborne chemical.

Antonio struggled to awake as a light that was painfully bright was pulling him toward awareness. Irritation, coupled with soreness, hit him as he looked down and felt the dull pain of tubes irrigating his body with clear fluids. Some fluid looked like amber drops as monitors plugged to a cruel computer screen as ESU carried him and Lisa out. In a hushed buzz, anyone that was anybody in the Department emerged to ferret through the crime scene.

Antonio saw members of his squad around, Chief McKinney from Internal Affairs bureau with beady eyes and a quadruple chin, as one layer of adipose fat cascaded into the others eyeing him. Layers of fatty tissue that could not find a ridge to hang onto like fat jelly rolls. He was the Commissioner's top hound in Command. McKinney, who wreaks havoc on officers under scrutiny and shatter's any cop's soul. He could not recognize the duty Captain, although he picked out two shoe flies from the Police Commissioner's Special Squad.

His Detective Benevolent Association Delegate Mo was there and she looked at him with affection as a puppy. She whispered, as one would to a child,

"Do not say anything – not yet, Tony, she wiped his head and kissed it gently." Lisa Wei as distraught as she was being treated for shock, mustered strength to get up and said, "This is official, don't harass Det. Antonio. Give Detective Antonio space. Act professionally. He does not need a cheerleader or cheap thrills."

Mo grimaced at her with cat-like ferocity and smiled, "He is on the DEA Board as a precinct detective delegate and I am citywide delegate. If you want the DEA President here, that could be arranged." Montana was called Mo as a street cop who worked her way up on the streets of Harlem as a detective. She was a bi-racial straight shooter and was heavily into Italian American cops, the more macho, the hotter for her. It was no secret she had the hots for Antonio: as many women on the job did – he was the only one who did not ever really know how much so. He loved her, but like a sister, not lover. He was not Egyptian, he would joke. He tried whispering to her, he could not express the words in his mind. A disconnect horrified him. Antonio was thinking in a dizzy way, but could not speak. He wanted to say, but could not get the words out:

"Is this a nightmare?"

"Am I fuc_in' dreaming or what? Slap me, please, Mo – wake me up."

"Am I fuc_in' constrained to the bed? What the hell is going on here?"

No word was uttered.

Mo looked helpless but stood by his side, supportive and looking sick to her stomach. She feigned being okay but her dark complexion paled white as if she was ready to check out. Mo was no easy victim; she was stand up and loyal to the man in her life. She was no lightweight, but quite heavy and knew how to play kitten or mountain lioness. Mo had no problem standing on lone watch over Antonio. He was at a loss and she knew it and sensed it.

The Lioness was ready to pounce, perhaps on the DA Chief who was treated with kid gloves. But there was no use, she realized something had happened between Antonio and Lisa Wei. No one to pounce on. So it seemed at this point. Her brother in blue, which permeated any lines of race, religion and culture was in hot water. She stood guard at his side. The Medics and EMT's began their work of rescue. The declarations of death usually would be left to the Forensic Odentologist Dr. K. D. with many years of experience, a true cop doc was there side by side with the Forensic Examiner ME for NY City.

Whispering in the corner, which looked more like Grand Central was the hospital room of Bellevue. The Gargoyles guarding the façade from a century past as demons hailing the possession of their own Perimeter with Concertina wire. An observer could see inlaid within each small window the weaving of thin iron. This layout was down to keep the patients in, and the outsiders – out. It was less than a day and Chief

McKinney started to bellow as he eyed Antonio curiously and yet in a subtle way threw a predatory gaze.

Inspector Kwan, whose presence was strikingly different, was acting Commanding Officer of Brooklyn North Homicide Division, NYPD. He was tall and slim and with his Oxford button down white shirt, starched, and with a power tie of red and blue stripes flamboyantly speaking power and ambition, he whispered to the Chief,

"Antonio is one of our best. He is wild, yes. Maybe a street cowboy, granted, but he is not a killer."

Antonio's daze and stupor yielded to a semi — attention as some of what was being spoken, was heard. He just listened, moving his head to the left and right as when a dog is perplexed.

At that moment, a man walked in. He was characterized by a beautiful NY Times journalist, Anna, two years his senior, as being a little geeky, attractive, and being incredibly intelligent. She was some sleuth herself, later in realizing he was a genius and she up for the intrigue as much as his sexy style — they became lovers. In spite of her irascible ways as others saw her; he immediately realized her beauty, her edge and her sexuality which she was very playful with him behind closed doors. Anna magnetically attracted him to her and her to him in solid knots. For him, Anna's eternal intrinsic worth in comparison to the Jane Does of the world was inestimable. He would later marry her. It was not an easy odyssey, but nothing is in the world of writers and police. That was Cop Doc Allan Cannon, M.D., Ph.D., Dr. Sci entrusted with finding out the mental health of Detective Antonio. A Cop Doc was defined as a police officer/detective sergeant and a clinical psychologist. His assimilated rank by virtue of being a doc in the NYPD was an Inspector.

Allan could not give a shit less about the power differential. He was confident in his training and education which was as intense as he was. What he cared about was, what he could do to help an officer down. Like the cleats in one's heel on a slippery mound he gained traction in the most difficult of internal cases and everyone knew it. Administrator or Director were titles he got, but his genius lay as a poet warrior doc at heart. Cop Doc Allan Canon had not yet read the reports delivered by hand to his home in the City of NY; Nor, the Internal Affairs Private Personnel Index on Antonio: Allan broke the rules of the job, to keep his integrity as an idiosyncratic psychologist and a cop, Dr. Alan, refused to read the very preliminary 61 complaint reports and follow up 5 reports on the investigation of the double homicide. The arch way of his single mindedness was to first gain a rapport through the icicles of that frozen stare way beyond him. That numb and stark look of being dumb-founded at the shattering of what life itself means.

Antonio looked at Dr. Cannon as he thought to himself, who is this guy packing a 38 bulging in his trousers as visible as his suit. No Glock, but .38 S & W. was right in the open while the big bosses parted the way to let him through. He was in his late-40's with a ruddy complexion and handsomely etched features coalesced into an amalgam of what was a strange mix of French Jewish features in his face. Like Antonio, he had a Roman Jaw, and a cleft in his chin. He was built athletically and had a powerful chest and very developed arms. His eyebrows hung on his forehead like snowy owls' wings, with a perpetually deep and inquisitive look.

Dr. Cannon had his cup of instant Starbucks coffee bold he put down on the night table near Antonio.

"Hi, Antonio I am Dr Allan Cannon, just call me Doc Allan. I am a cop, like you, but I am also a doc. I am here to find out what happened to you. I am here to help you and want to understand you. Is that okay?"

Antonio seemingly nodded. It was not clear to Allan that he really understood his line of questioning, but he hoped he did. Allan was far from standing by exact protocol in an area he was pioneering in his treatment of repetitive trauma and loss. He continued in an empathic expression.

"So, Officer Antonio, I will ask some questions which you can hopefully answer, has anyone told you why you are restrained like this, and with IV tubes?"

Antonio was lying in a semi-supine position looking like a beached Sperm Whale, bleating in his imprisoned and panic stricken exhaustion of confinement. Antonio looked so pitiful in a world lost and forgotten in his reclined hypnotic state of extreme trauma. Laying there, he was still in the throes of the crime scene and the pain of seeing ones mirror image fixed in an eternal position of ultimate vulnerability. Antonio now twisted his head toward Dr. Cannon in an effort to respond to the question he heard again.

Nothing audible came out, just a crumbling of words littered in the space of times moment of communion like a chalice fractionated in a triad of a cross or star inverted. Antonio tried, but as panic stepped in, an autistic perspective emerged. The extreme intensity of the crimes enveloped Antonio's rational self and all that was left was his emotional purged self – burnt out.

Cop Doc Allan looked into Antonio's eyes and felt his soul resonate: Dr. Allan Cannon experienced Antonio's terror without one word uttered. It was experienced in what shrinks call counter-transference. It was clearly almost like being in hell: It felt as if purgatory ushered in as frozen picture stills. Still frames of trauma frozen in the space of time as pictures of the crime scene were blown to page size in view of Antonio and Dr Allan.

Hell for Jews was for 11 months, for Catholics it could be an eternity. At least for Det. Antonio and Cop Doc Allan, it was likely purgatory had been awaiting the placement of still frames inviting them to come out of the cold into the heat of the murder case. Lisa Wei Feng, ADA, Chief of the DA Homicide Division was outside the door on official business, unofficially. She was treated and released with Ambien at night and Zoloft during the day. Despair laid bare the room of the Bellevue Asylum in spite of the nice décor all gilded in soft sheaths of what lay under the covers: Deep cover.

Purgatory could not be wrestled with – it resonated in Antonio's air drums as silence bellowed her deafening reverberations of fear and withdrawal.

# Chapter 13

## Projections transferred in Cop to Cop Doc Encounters

Cop Doc Allan Cannon came into the waiting room of the Psych Ward Lock Down. He had his Starbucks black Coffee straight up with no milk, cream, sugar or frills – period. Dr Allan Cannon was feeling as if he was ghosted up the corridor leading to the Hospital as he walked upstairs eschewing the elevators to get a workout whenever he could. Not into fanfare, Allan liked the earthy feeling of his roughhewn Rockport gumshoes flatfooted in its black worn lackluster, where sweat made designer fashion look like courier sandals.

In the glint of his eyes, Allan was being tagged by a wannabe hopeful, who just failed the Captains test for the third time. Lieutenant Dimdum Sum of Field Internals Affair Unit (F.I.A.U), who waged war behind his desk of tag a cop. His target was cops who ate an extra ice cream scoop in the Italian Bakery. Lt Dimdum Sum was the son of a big Whig and never did the real time as a street cop. In reality, he never pounded the beat as did Cop Doc Cannon and Antonio. He said in a hardly baited breath, waiting to see Antonio crucified by Cop Doc Allan as a dejected psycho-cop, "Hey Sgt., I am sorry if I shocked you. It was unintentional. I mean [with heavy accentuation] Cop Doc Allan [pausing] I suppose you are going to put the major rejects, malingerers, and shifty shaky cops who are minorities like your own tribe and the neighboring ones in Bed Stuyvesant on the couch for a relaxing spell. I know you shrinks would love to give them Long Island tea and broads to rub them day and night on the city payroll, huh!?! Maybe you'll assign them painting jobs for recreation, I suppose? But no dice to roll in Antonio's case as you know shit will fall from the sky and hit your face if you allow him to get off. I know you will hang his Italian Ass if you are smart."

Cop Doc Allan did not bother answering. Allan was too polished to answer instigators crafting a pit to fall into and envelope him in. With relish, as a laughing hyena, Lt. Dimdum Sum brayed and laughingly spit out the next line even more malicious than the first, and now more personal.

"In fact, Cop Doc Allan, rank as you put it in your writing is very important. Well, check this out, I am not into nice pinko Jew Boys. I am a real Lt. I think you should know as a Sergeant there is deference you owe me by city charter and protocol. Even snooty college kids who get into Ivy League schools need education sometimes in the school of hard knocks, or they can get knocked off their high horses and bridges. Just telling you, if you get my drift." Dr. Cannon looked down, and with intent, bent forward, indicating measured submission and did not utter a word and turned his eyes away from Lt. Dimdum Sum's gaze. Lt. Dimdum Sum went on with his glowing rant in front of unidentified plain clothes officers and heavy set folks in the waiting room. He lowered the pitch of his rant as he noticed some may have been eavesdropping. "I know and have my eye of the ancestors on your ass Sgt Allan Cannon and you do not impress me. When you waste city time after your cops suffer from a 'critical incident and you let them steal from the government instead of doing their job: I suppose Sgt, Doc Allan Cannon?" With biting sarcastic irony Dr Cannon was in typical form, sizing up his antagonist, who he knew plagued good officers as a racist and anti-Semite. Lt. Dimdum Sum snugly awaited nabbing cops, mostly innocent ones, on any rap he could. There were many effective and decent IAB detectives, but this was not one of them. Cop Doc Allan Cannon, being Jewish American, waited in analytic calm. Lt. Dimdum Sum lay in his own waste like a snug Scarab Beatle in the rue morgue looking to scavenge another tragedy with opportunity to use his pincers. He had his little memo pad he titled 'after-midnight delight' a journal of seeing officers he ambushed and devoured in their worst moments. Lt. Dimdum Sum knew he had gained a victory as Sgt. Allan Cannon went beyond his realm of sensual delight in submission, rather than what Lt. Dimdum Sum anticipated with glee. Gleeful to a good cause to rip out a complaint and spew gossip in sardonic pleasure, as all sadists do, by underscoring Sgt Allen Cannon's insubordination.

Cop Doc Allen stayed silent as he knew what was to come, and in strategic layout, saw the tactical hits as hypothesized. He was disrupted before going into the room to do his assessment of Antonio. He was annoyed by such disruptions as this anti-social assault. But he knew from the side of his eyes and his intuitive style some folks in the corner who also were quiet, listening, and one in particular. Cop Doc Allen Cannon put his ear forward, tilted his head to the right and allowed the Lieutenant to stare him down. The Lt. went on in alleged humor,

"I am not bothered when a rogue cop eats his gun, I am also not bothered when the inferior sicko's do it. A good shooting done and finished is a good job when it is final."

Lt Dimdum Sum was hunting for any reason to shut down the "sissy pinko program" as he saw fit to call the assistance program chartered by the mayor's Office, The Union Leaders and blessed by the Police Commissioner to run by a Cop Doc. Cop Doc Allan turned and now lifted up his head and with a dead eyed stare looked deeply into Lt. Dimdum Sum's eyes. He paused, reflected as he supped his coffee with a smattering of his lips to accentuate the noise as he faced off, and in a voice of calm equanimity said, "Lt. Dimdum Sum I think you need an education about rank and duties. I am going to suggest a solution to ask Chief Julius Markowitz and Inspector Castor O' Shea in the corner over there."

Lt. Dimdum Sum was stunned and with shock on his face writhed in undulation of fear. Fear leaking out like someone who just peed in their pants, gushing out;

"Hey, Doc, I am only kidding. I meant no harm. I was only ribbing you. As you know, it is not really what I meant, you know that? Who can't take a joke?"

Cop Doc Allan turned now looking away and straight at the two men: One with an Eagle on his shoulder, and the other with four stars moved forward toward Lt. Dimdum Sum. Cop Doc Cannon pauses and in a whisper said to Lt. Dimdum Sum,

"Tragic is the moment you lose your heart and soul to hate and ignorance. Man has his plan and G-d has his design. You want to play a Scarab Beatle and eat flesh, and drink blood of your peers. If you have a head for sadism, be prepared you may be eaten by a mongoose that relishes the crunching of flesh eating, and soul sucking snakes. I suppose you did not recognize Chief Julius Markowitz and Inspector Castor O'Shea, shall I introduce you to them Lt. Dimdum Sum?"

In his dulled powers of observation and self-sabotage that blinded him to seeing the four-star Chief of Personnel Julius Markowitz and Inspector O'Shea. The two brass warriors walked up to the now shaken Lt and said,

"Listen, Lt. Dimdum Sums, I am not Doc Allan Cannon, who has an assimilated rank per the Police Commissioner as Deputy Inspector, which is two ranks your superior. Dr. Allan Cannon can suspend you right now. I, or the Inspector, can see you next in the Trial Room in the department with a list of charges related to official misconduct and stalking behavior related to Cop Doc Allan. I like tearing down little men with Napoleonic complexes in my beloved Department. I bet you did not know, or care who I am as Chief of Personnel, but now I know you. Today you made me cringe, realizing the rumors I heard about you were true, I have files on every member who is a problem child and you are one of my favorite rug mice now. [Turning to Doc Allan Cannon he asked him],

"Doc Allan, do you need your shoes polished by this mouse in the house? We can arrange that after I may demote him: Perhaps he can be demoted to house mouse supervisor for the rest of his career. But, if you prefer to charge him with insubordination, defamation of character, EEOC complaints and suspension just let me know now?"

Lt. Dimdum Sum's face turned red with plum stark fear. Like all bigots caught in their own traps of malaise trying to target others with their own incompetence and hate he became teary eyed.

Cop Doc Allan went over to Chief Julius Markowitz and they spoke in a hush in the corner for 15 minutes. Chief Markowitz then walked over to the almost shaking Lt. Dimdum Sum awaiting the worst and he said,

"You are fortunate. If it was up to me, I would squash you for the shit bug you are! You could not measure up to the Cop Doc and you better thank him for the fact he is letting you ride. He felt you were acting out of your own insecurity and fears of being real in our world of real cops. Real street cops do not need to play with brutality and bullying. I respect the good Doc or I would propel the shit out of your beer belly pot luck. Let me ever hear you belittle any officer like you did and you will not know what hell on this job can be. I have my Jewish eyes on you. Remember that when you go to your next Klan meeting. If I ever find out — you will not have to worry about your Shitlers list. Covering you and me shadowing your every move, is something you can be assured of." Lt. Dimdum Sum awkwardly and with shame as a little terrier that bit a Mastiff's heel, backed away with nothing to offer but his dim lit stupor, which yielded to speaking some of his confession,

"Inspector Cop Doc Allan Cannon, I am sorry for being so out of hand. Gee, thank you for saving my neck. I know I did myself in the back of the neck!"

Dr Cannon looked and said with quiet calm,

"Lt. Dimdum Sum, think before you talk. Remember now that your conscience has caught up with your egotism. Surpass fear and realize change is possible. Listen to that voice in your heart. Life is a gift and while you can – change in mistakes you've laid out as your path. Don't thank me, thank G-d. Maybe you can rebound in the space of humble expectations and change in your private confession and re-direction if you realize not every Jew has horns and every man of color has ardor to do you in."

Lt Dimdum Sum was stunned more at the intervention and as he slid out like a slug in muddy mess. The slimy trail left behind as he tracked backward to the hospital door was left slimy. Lt. Dimdum Sum almost tripped over himself on the way out, as the door slammed closed bolted away. He bolted into the darkness of anonymity.

The cold dank streets of the city swallowed him up.

Dr. Cannon let go and let G-d with all his travails. He genuinely heralded the opportunity for Lt. Dimdum Sum to learn a lesson in humility and fair play unearned.

Allan Cannon took a breather and reflected on what had happened. He was either loved or hated. That love – hate fault line was the dividing rites of being a Cop Doc in a major department – or a lackey Doc for hire.

The Chief and Inspector met him as they spoke in whispers in the corner as hands were shaken. Dr. Cannon in his typical manner of eccentricities left without a trace into the room where Antonio lay still in his seated position.

Dr. Cannon immediately sensed and felt the aura of pain and suffering and a tearing in his gut as he felt the portals of silence embrace his core.

Antonio looked as if he was faceless: a persona non grata; a shadow of what Doc Cannon had gathered about this hard-nosed and keen detective. An officer with a hyper-intuitive sense of doing the keenest investigations with heart, soul and humanity. Earning the respect of his peers in the best sleuths of the world, NYPD Detective Bureau. Allan knew this was not going to be easy, he felt like fleeing himself and that caught him unawares.

Why did he feel like fleeing on entry as a tenured Cop Doc with a likable detective? He immediately noted in his well-trained pick up of coordinates of emotion, feelings and sensory awareness what the counter-transference helped him navigate in countless patient's angst, anxiety, depression, suicidal risk, perturbability, fear, panic, and lethality. That was the pickup of everything a patient threw at him with hovering and now almost uncanny attention. Cop Doc Allan read the patients feelings as if they were a screen projection.

He was at the door of Antonio's state of mind. Seemingly lost in mindless chaos as he was ordering the symbolic sensorium into a sensibility in his clinical senses first. Cop Doc Allan took the fragments of loose associations and senses and put them in rhythms. Rhythms sensibly scored in penned words, and recorded notes.

Dr. Cannon scribbled down with frenetic energy handwritten notes unreadable to all others, save, Dr. Cannon. He was after all a Detective and Sergeant, he learned always to write on the fly sheet on his flip side of the memo book on patrol to make his notes readable and interpretable to himself and no one else. It allowed him to be his own interpreter and no one else allowed entry – a bit of street cop wisdom asking no one's permission and not for sale, or compromise.

'Keep Them Guessing' was posted on his Police Surgeon outer-leather Shield holder … Dr. Allan meant that for cops and docs to see, and think about. He loved provoking thoughts in his students and in his peers. In the tradition of the warning that Erich Fromm, wrote in the forgotten language he doggedly and with a scrapper attitude fought for the power not force in the dimensions of words.

Semantics underlying concepts at their core, hidden in between the litter of cheap words at the cost of genuine expression in the raw nudity of meaning stripped bare.

What the scratch in the clinicians notes portrayed was different to the official analysis. The official bureaucratic version was one he needed to etch out his existence as the Chief Psychologist. He etched out with the feeling of puke in esophageal regurgitation, male Caucasian Italian American detective showing 'remarkable symptoms of dissociation, de-compensation and regressed primary cognitive thought patterns.

Dissociation was an important expression for the altered states of consciousness that Antonio exhibited. Remarkable, meaning that the intensity and severity of the symptoms that were atypical. De-compensation, meaning he could not compensate for the normal expression of the status quo of life on the mean streets – the cruel cold indifference encountered in the bureaucratic shuffles after dealing with life and death with amazing regularity until the psyche becomes desensitized to the Devil in the details of being a detective.

Dr. Cannon picked up the emotional constriction of Antonio as he was able to absorb the veil of death and violence discarded like the waste of fast foods put in a garbage disposal. A steady staple of losses in death experiences that were treated like the tossing of burgers blamed and embalmed the officers as if each was a clone of the other. It reminded Allan of waiting for egg salad or tuna sandwiches at Day School. The kids who waited patiently and decently were beaten by bullies for compensation in concessions at the cafeteria. Allan felt Antonio was one of those kids and he was as well. A training ground for being a kick butt cop and the denial of 'It': Denial becomes the victims who survive the bully's mantra. Bullying by whom? Bullying by an indifferent system that eats up cops and innocents living in the hood: The hood Antonio had worked in for a number of his formidable young adult-hood years?

Dr. Allan Cannon asked himself as he writhed in witnessing to often and too well the uncensored hell that is ferocity breed in unnatural concrete jungles surrounded by Eco-ethological niches of Lost Souls and who is behind it all? Who is the social engineer, a hidden Dr. Moreau, or Josef Mengele the physician and cultural anthropologist advising the powers that be? Who is behind the fury in the intestines of the beast?

Dr. Cannon's drift into the space of questions that plagued him as a cop and doc did not leave room for pause. Necessity provoked answers to questions needing answering by the Cop Doc. Humility, resonated as he knew he only had – tentative hypotheses – at best. Human nature and the unnatural cataclysms of zealots, radicals, and well- and ill-meaning utopian thinkers causing more hellish trauma on earth than the salt of the earth ever has, but what could he do but heal one victim of the system after another.

Dissociation and Trauma responses were still underscored in primitive forms within his profession as psychologist/psychiatrist as one of eleven anxiety disorders. Dr. Cannon was blasting away at the indifference of his profession with inept and compromised labels.

Labels targeting a bottom line which held no buoyancy in a complex world where humane beings could not be fixated on dimensional or logarithmic scales.

His private notes scratched out, illegibly, DX [Diagnosis, 'Police Complex Trauma Syndrome' – Experimental traumatic neurosis – H1, first and foremost hypothesis]. TX [Treatment modality].

The term H1 meant his first hypothesis-1. A hypothesis being a trajectory in the way of prediction as to a relationship: A relationship operationally defined and measurable — between the diagnosis and the assessed factors involved as effects on the patient's prognosis.

Dr. Allan Cannon allowed his existential frame of reference to explore his emotions and feelings as he was taught by the great psychoanalyst, Charles Brenner, M.D. He asked himself, were the factors involved in trauma exogenous as happens when a raisin is left to burn in the sun too long. The poem, a 'Dream Deferred' as Langston Hughes the poet rued, and Lorraine Hansberry drew out in the drama of the heights reached in the struggles of hoods in Chicago as in hoods in Brooklyn Bed-Stuyvesant?

Was Antonio suffering from bleaching his ecological niche, where ethological survival pushed the pull to identify who, when, where, and how the faceless murderers did their ugly deeds by overly identifying with each one? In-deeds needing confession in a system of justice in want of repentance. *Who rescues the detectives analyzing death in the grail that speaks in hauntings of victims trails destined for the rue morgue?*

The police, firefighters and EMT folks who are scorched with too much shine – shrivel like Raisins in the sun. A native son burning under the sun of intense tragedy without a real hood to shield the intensity with comfort? Could it be a TBI [traumatic brain injury] such as being hit with a blunt object in the neck or head area that was affecting Antonio's limbic system, or was it more diffuse as in his ethological, or existential executive functions of the brain?

Factors endogenous and exogenous as a major and severe loss infused with too much drinking and wistful nights to wash out the pain where sex with the wrong woman and STD follows, perhaps.

Perhaps the factors were organic as in the growth of a tumour in the brains limbic system and with the tell-tale hypoxia of pressure on the brain stem, Medulla oblongata, and Pons: Was confusion in behaviour and regression to a state of catatonia induced organically as in a neurological disorder? Gershwin's temporal lobe epilepsy signalled when George heard and sensed in olfactory hallucinations smelling burning rubber years before its emergence. Perhaps Antonio's semi-conscious speaking of burning rubber smells signalled a tumour.

Hearing and seeing things is not always madness but created when a part of the brain as the temporal lobe is affected with a hyper-sensitivity that runs like a double pirouette into hyper-intuitive insight. An American in Paris was analyzed as being played at least a 100 times by technological analysis, as requested by Allan. It was also recently heard in his portable Emerson CD player as the internal affairs report of the behavioral layout of Antonio's room was re-visited in the free-flowing conscious awareness of Allan's mind. He found it of profound interest that this detective was as idiosyncratic as he was, and as creative in his reasoning ability with other homicide cases as he had begun reviewing his files.

Memories, for Cop Doc Allan, synergized with alacrity, veridicality and acuity in novel forms when stringing together relative facts with quantum jumps in the gaps in psychological autopsies. He remembered his conversation with his famed director friend, an idiosyncratic intuitive rarity, Emmanuel Pomartini, MFA. In their weekly meetings, his notes on Vaslav Nijinsky, the male genius ballet dancer and director, who choreographed his way to madness – was a retreat from reality's rejecting dagger.

Meaning, society is sometimes not ready for the infusion of certain tunes that awaken the absurd notions of conformity to a mad system dehumanized and legislating a new bold world of political correctness: Looney is a convenient label to discard folks with visions beyond the fads.

Perhaps that is what happened with Nijinsky, and perhaps with Antonio? Cop Doc Allan scribbled again illegibly, to himself on cue.

On cue and break behind every comic expression lay a tragic punctuation – marked with traumatic impact. Allan was not yet satisfied with this hypothesis as he developed it further.

Hum, he reflected that perhaps the labored breathing and sub-clinical asthmatic wheeze causing this retarding feature of personality and blank expression was due to ontological insecurity in a divided mind and soul as in Schizos-Phrenos. That term was defined by the Scottish analyst, R.D. Laing, who felt a broken soul in at least some cases of schizophrenia laying behind the layers of madness.

A retreat from reality was a defense against societal madness that made sense. Sensible when in measured unraveling of double-bind messages of saying I love you and overly smothering parent's narcissism tyrannizing the normal development of children in overly suffocating indulgence without boundaries and intrusion.

Dr. Cannon's trauma expertise laid out Ontological Insecurity as critical in understanding such symptoms.

Insecurity comes from a fear of inner-expression, rather than fear of outside censure. Desires from within maybe unleashed as if one has acted badly.

It remained haunting the child that never had the time to grow into emotional adulthood. Physical adulthood is requisite with the maturity of function. Function, at times all the way up to the genius level, can be stymied on an emotional level when the adult is still grounded in the chicks nests with an overly intrusive mother. Adaptation in functioning is a compartment separate from flying in interdependent vulnerability with a real mate as in marriage – when leaving one's invulnerable shelter – is a true liberation feared more than death itself by the subject of a double bind by a narcissist mother who cannot let the adult daughter/son fly as they wish too. A shelter long gone and empty for it never had, nor will have the love so needing nurturing as to promote an existential sense of self and finding inter-dependence with one's soul-mate. Some call it soul-murder and perhaps Dr. Allan Cannon felt it was.

Fear to exist and become – where losses shadow illusion – in place of reality. Onto-logical comes from the word 'to know', as in Hippocrates guide to physicians of the mind to 'know thy-self'.

If one does not dare to know one-self and dis-owns knowledge of self as in self-less musings, that patient is less than his/her self. Allan knew this maybe the case in Antonio being left as Sisyphus in search of his myth to live by. What was hidden under Antonio's birth? What marked the trauma of original losses of ideals of nurturing never to be had in its sordid and perverse substitute.

Losses need mourning! Mourning resonated deeply with Dr. Allan. He came back to Lt. Kevin Life Savage who was part of their weekly meeting of artistic poets for expression without oppression from within and without the Police Bureaucracy. The moral compass of circles infinite nautilus in the rap sessions during work hours cleverly unraveled in his twenties and early thirties.

Detective Lieutenant Kevin Life connected to Antonio, which was also a mystery to be unraveled. That is the synchrony of events. History's way of repeating one existence into the other, with seeming serendipity as an excuse for avoiding G-d, does not throw dice. Only humans deny the voice of conscience and G-d, more comfortable in their own delusions in creating false gods with small g's: Hubris and arms against a sea of troubles in the games played where avoidance only defers payment from the source of all Creation, the Creator.

The inimitable charm of Lt. Kevin, who put Man-child in the Promised Land to shame and sham. His exquisite vision as a musician iconoclast shattered the myth of who he should be with sublime insight. Dr Allan remembered talking with him about Bob Marley and the Last Man on Earth as 'Legend' in which the fifth column sabotaged all that is valuable in fighting for religious freedom by pressing atheism as the only press worth printing. The vision of Lt. Kevin, who off-duty, was known as 'Life' – engineered a second calling as a DJ who broke new ground. Life broke into tears un-spilt. Dr. Allan, analyzing Antonio by comparison, asked with poignant alacrity as a soliloquy, 'Is it a wonder a homicide detective can reach the record of a stylus needle holding the pulse on inhumanity in a humane soul until it reaches its breaking point? Perhaps, Schizos-Phrenos is a temporary causality of war's insanity, mused Dr Allan.

Dr. Allan Cannon scribbled another note to himself, that Antonio was ushered into his twilight state of existence under the rubric of escape into madness? Temporary solutions to permanent catch 22's. Allan was as in everything not standing down from his wisdom.

Allan insisted with the pioneer Cop Doc Rudofossi to recall what police, firefighters and EMT's experience as 'critical-incidents' into Police and Public Safety Complex Trauma Syndromes. Reductionism and minimization cut the heart of life. Eating the excess fat of what surplus funds get you when you micro-manage health care is simplification of what is complex trauma into acute stress. Incidental like coincidental made it sound as if a cop slipped off a curb and yelped out "ouch", similar to a 7 year old, who in routine predictability, is called a 'cry baby'.

Disrespecting loss was for the birds. Dr. Allan would not toss out the Eagle, who thought he was a chick, without allowing the Eagle to know he had wings for flight. Nijinsky, Kafka and Koestler were a triad of tragedies un-scored as just too much. Allan scratched out in his clinical notes, 'grief work needed – loss un-mourned' – artistic expression as conduit as he allowed his creativity to articulate and refine his clinical sensibility.

Dr. Allan threw out his fear when he placed losses in perspective and boldly wrote on official notes that Detective Antonio suffered from Police and Public Safety Complex Trauma Syndrome: He did not know exactly how it developed, but he knew this tentative diagnosis warranted attention.

Dr. Cannon knew in his gut what others would think in derision. As ever, those in little left corners, as in right corners of politics, would label any novel way of thinking, 'hubris'. Dr. Allan Cannon knew he had the grip on complex trauma syndromes as much larger than simple labels made for mis-managed care and intellectual fascism. He knew the madness by peers who con-formed to the system in prescribed one fits all technique-custom fit for grants. Labels conforming for the sake of a few more dollars – just did not cut it. Even if all the corners of fat were gelded together in a large banquet of gluttony, he deferred even a tiny bite of fat for himself: Integrity!

Integrity of leaving colleagues who knew better in – 'snug convenience to wallow in mediocrity – was a fine and just 'Desert' as verb, adjective and noun.

Like Freud, he would go far in his own voice and not be controlled by a language archaic and brutal to the humanity of his officer-patients.

For, Dr Allan practicing with the integrity of the classic founders of therapy of which he was trained by personally was more than stepping stones. His police supervisors were a connection to a meaningful aura of responsibility. When he was pressed in a media showdown with shrink peers who never saw a shot, but insisted they were experts in police and trauma psychology – he glibly pulled away. He offered an analogy and said, calling Complex Trauma – 'Incidents' was like comparing Moses surviving the Nile River in a basin filled with Nile Crocodiles and Egyptian Archers to an Upper East Side kid in the community pool losing his Smurf doll as equal and the same to one another. That is Political Correctness, wiping the slate clean and anaesthetized – everything and everyone is equal and the same: Delusional – madness!

Complex is complex trauma syndromes and is not, if anything, a simple critical incident. These altered states were shifts in the awareness and the ability to think clearly as a detective as well as a humane being in general communication: Allan was wont to do that and did not mince his words as litter to play tunes in the marching band of kinder-garden technocracy.

As he placed his coffee down, Dr Allan Cannon's inner vision laid out his knowing the cause of Antonio's state of mind. It was going to be excruciating to pull open a wall shut tight. The aesthetic delight of the cop doc as an artisan working from chosen words laid out a strategy. The tactics was to sense the officer-patient's bricks of resistance.

Resistance he proffered as a mason layering out granules of sand into palatable expression within tunes of mirth. Mirth as Mozart, who in his losses in the alluring magic flute, took a toxic dose of trauma that closed his final finale with the curtain of closure.

In the folly of mirth's last laugh, Mozart's death in tragic amusement was magical, where epiphany was reached in tragedy with comic relief.

Allan knew well that he who laughs hardest, laughs his last breath with folly where life fills irony laced in mirth in death as in birth without a clue.

Dr. Cannon knew, as he sauntered in his own free associations, that the path Freud and Brenner laid out in classic analysis was the way his modified existential blanket could warm a frozen soul.

But associations are not free in trauma and grief. No verbal associations were offered as gifts to Dr. Allan.

What could be done tactically when the party privy to the truth is silent! Silent as an oyster's lips sealed shut. Aye the rub, for in the flow of words comes concepts and inherent in each concept is the dialectic step of one door opened – as the other window closes shut.

Dr. Allan knew he only had tentative hypotheses. Allan knew, as all scientists know, that it was well worth the effort to cull out the morsel inside the oyster's shell for the meat and the pearl under the layers. Idiosyncratic, artistic and scientifically disciplined symmetry appealed to chaos along a quantum string of closed doors cajoled open by undulating waves at the portals of novel insight. His poesies underscored science at its best.

Cop Doc Diaries were an infusion of precious thoughts, where Dr. Allan Cannon laid down puzzles, queries and anomalous hypotheses as coordinates weaving his thoughts into a maze of ideas all colorful and beautiful as the mysteries gifted in him. Tenacity was a core of his essential character as was introspection.

Dr. Allan Cannon's psychiatric clinical guide's led to one path; his novels another path; his professorship and style of innovative lectures another path, his art work another path; his investigative abilities to other realms.

He mused in his mind's pining, all paths were gifts strung in deep resonating anchors in life and the joy of Living, as gifts of the Almighty. Cop Dr Allan was as complex in being personally humane, as his works of creativity and originality were becoming of his essential core.

He left a pen, paper and tissues and with an open hand gesture, articulated a gift to Antonio as he remained silent with a genuine smile. Dr. Canon folded his legs to illustrate his patience and his control of himself as a listener without an agenda save finding out the truth wherever it could lead and be pronounced. He focused on reconstructing the power of love and creativity in Tommy and Christine as facts presented: they were lovers and intense. What came to mind was unleashed as a lover sprinkles and flows his seeds inside the expanding volume of a receptive earthy responsiveness a woman embraces.

Aye, the association flows into the mystery of life, love and death – romance, and the transmigrations of the soul's immortality: other worlds, where the most erudite projections of ancient Greek Bacchus and Apollo only scratched at – try as they might have.

Antonio's core was not hubris but rather the humility of daring, why did he happen-chance on the murder scene? Why was the chief of the NY DA's Office of Homicide present for any other reason perhaps she was colluding with Antonio but how and why?

Leaping as Prometheus to glance at the light unpronounced in the darkest core of the human psyche, Dr. Cannon backed off suddenly from his free flowing consciousness and associations.

Sobering up from his own free flowing unconscious shorthand, he demanded re-routing of the flow. A dam needed to be erected in overcoming passion to infuse reason as the frame toward insight. He took succor in technique and knew he had deft ears to listen and provoke supportive responses to enable Antonio to open up in direct communication.

Frustration and anger with silence in response to Antonio had to be overcome with empathy and patience almost beyond endurances portals from purgatory to salvation. Yet, deep in the bowels of his genius, Dr. Cannon was unsure if his approach was correct. 'Unsure' left the imprint of excitement and angst strung along the shelves of an anxious mind. Anxiety embraced in the waters of healing split where uncharted waves hid undertow. Antonio took his colored pencils, gifted by Dr. Allan Cannon as a conduit of expressing himself. Gently, he placed each in his hands, which looked largely grotesque compared to his younger days of doing construction. The callous build up on the padding of his skin folded into the graphite color snapped in clean splits.

Antonio's expression was vacant at first, but in that vacancy, painful loss as grief wrapped around as a pig's blanket.

Dr. Allan felt castrated as the anxiety of his efforts lost with Antonio's bellicose splintering of pencils offered as barter fell to agitation and rage expressed in the silence hopes of an alliance slaughtered in effigy.

Potential defeated in neon and graphite hues man made and material.

A light that is spiritual is unlike the measure of color and its physical spectrum: Narrow darkness holds lights quantum leap in cubic arrangement of humane shadows. Quantum leaps of faith in pitch dark. Trial and tribulation light the infinite twists in the primal Nautilus. The spiral of the Nautilus as a living dinosaur in the depths of the driven seas where instinctual treasures hide in its cached coves that unfurl in the minds unconsciousness. Antonio took the split of the colors in his fingers and placed them in horizontal form as he used them. The hues of charcoal and cameo pastels in his fingers drew a shape of a heart in feminine form and a shield as an arrow piercing into her heart. The heart as her breast clearly had a flow of blood internally wounded. Antonio then spelled out, 'Detective Antonio too late on scene...' He then drew another shield intersecting in twain. Two shields used as piercing metal where one went in and under the heart as breast shaped the chest in shadow form. The shape of a breast – primitive as the structure of the hearts chamber was left bleeding.

Cop Doc Allan knew Antonio's offering was on one hand aggressive and on the other sexual. Muses of held hearts and lips as the craft of words swept the vision of humanity without illusion. Unrequited love emerged louder than the pits of his forced silence imposed in the chambers of his Nautilus unwound: Yin and Yang in depth and naked relief.

Cop Doc Cannon scratched out another link in the evolution of his thoughts – treatment on the wound of unrequited love left as origins in child-hood to adulthood identified in the hood, tormented in sexualized aggression.

Oh the bodings of things to come, Dr Cannon pre-intuitively closed in one his altered states of existential unconscious with light unbound. Metaphor is left better not fleshed out before its concrete mold, sets. An inverted triangle undone as redemptions lost iterations of repetition in a compulsion of solutions left for the future journal of his past record.

No verbal expression was offered and they sat in tribal acknowledgment of justice being present and unheard.

Cannon could hold his silence as he was superb in analytic technique when necessitated by the ecological and ethological niche needing identification.

Cannon drifted to his achy broken marriage of doubt and desire: He could not bridge the gap between knowledge and belief that covered over desire halted in deception she had lain in her schemes. He laid his seedling, protected from the winter of their discontent, in the garden of his ex's sexuality infused with aggressions scarlet brand of S & M provocation. Dr Cannon resisted returning to his own associations which would lead in a circuitous way to blue diamonds in Solomon's mines. His free associations suspended their erotic aggressive drive with labor intensified as it became associations which elevated the primal to the supernal dance. A dance he was wont to do with patients, and students.

Bewildered by letting go in the most dynamic metamorphosis. Cannon experimented in his method to active transference where patient became doctor, and yet as usual went one leap beyond in his existential analysis. Existential analysis and his theory that Professor Dr.

Frankl helped redeem hell into redemptions grasp – holding the fusion between the cognitive, analytic and existential worlds of therapy. The unconscious noetic dimensions could be touched in the disciplined use of classic analysis modified. In many ways, his window to the enigma and paradox of life itself melted into interpretations as fragments of science emerged in theory and technique. The need to give evidence to what is beyond normal sensory perception as intuition, insight and the Transcendental Unconscious is the challenge.

Yes, like the famous analysts of Freud's circle who supervised him, he opened his insight to the outreaches of human nature. Playful interludes in the madness that hug the fringes of society. Artists and shrinks who draw the heart of unconscious strivings into light know these trimmings fold into margins into a rough blueprint. A tapestry where punctuation of stasis is marked with ingenious leaps.

Civilization is given its legitimacy in the soliloquies of artist's communion. Without the targets, he mused – what was the center worth?

Bull's eyes, or Bull's manure; or perhaps Alexander's Gordian Knot undone! Cannon did not hang with the artists as a want to be Bohemian; he was an artist bohemian, who legitimately lived in the other world to dip his artists brush without definition – he was as allusive as his art and double in brilliance as his faith in the Almighty only grew stronger.

Dr. Cannon was a deep man of faith and culture, conserving tradition but liberal as well in independent minded tolerance for the mentally ill, no less. He belonged to no party, or schism of narcissistic society reduced to unilateral allegiance. He was an ace detective of the minds shield using his keen cop sense as the flash light into the elusive conflict of mind and soul. Dr. Cannon took the sloppy, the messy, and the hidden terror of Antonio turning out an orchestra, playing his patients anguish in his suspended state of active listening. Space now occupied by trauma with his third ear and seventh sense he allowed entry of traumas shock by the flow of reflections mirroring his defenses down and altering his state of conscious.

Conscious of his will to meaning empowered to project Antonio's trauma once identified into ports of haven from the storm. Portals of unconscious echoes reverberating ricochets of losses unspoken. Vibrating losses filling different tones picked up in his ever increasing ability to let go undefended in the wisdom unspoken as ego goes in the transient moments of genuine connection – to return in its ebb and flow to its source.

Antonio's thundering deafness rhythmically suspended articulations of the inaudible into concepts picked up in the analytic ears of Dr. Cannon. His score and epic sense of the aesthetic taste rebounded with more severely disturbed patients. Dr. Cannon facilitated sense from sensibility on the palate of taste unarticulated. Antonio lay out a primary process so primal, it was as if he was stuck in a nightmare where the womb entombed life in frozen stills. He could not say what he wanted to convey?

Dr. Allan was running out of his most ingenious methods: Eccentric modifications as his own ingenuity allowed the outer stretching, rather than shrinking of his patients will. At all costs, he avoided the Sodom evil of reductionistic Procrustian beds in places of analytic freedom of expression. Some shrinks call an intuitive attunement or interactional synchrony with his patients as he placed his classically trained third ear to pick up the inchoate as something audible.

Dr. Cannon used his natural gift, where he visualized each utterance Antonio spit out with the sensitivity of a Diamond Stylus on an old phonograph. Picking up the slightest acoustic variation felt, even the screeches.

Lt. Kevin Life, who held lineage from a genteel Masai Ethologist, without portfolio, could pick up echoes surpassing the bat using his musical radar. Echo radar as the metaphor he slipped into with boomerang skill, where spotting and devouring the poison of the recluse spider by ghosting the moth near the neon-lit flame. He wrote down this metaphor as some association Allan knew he would sort through as litter to be discarded, or gems to shine in darkness.

Dr Allen's artistic skill, in which all his caresses of his lady lovers, culminated with marriage to Sari. A place where his ability to lead her to the one place where he was the leader: Sexual prowess. Her ecstasy of small deaths and re-births in orgasm were short spent. Her extreme religiosity and jealousy – as Steckel had pointed out, was the vibrating broomstick replete with sketches of doubt and compulsion not faith. Sketches that struck chords with a healthy self-indulgence where his unapologetic politically incorrect love of the female persona left innocence unscathed in perspective.

The female chauvinism of feminist partisan politics did not diminish his male mind. He stared deeper at Antonio as he was flayed along with his analytic and abstract mind the cutting edge of silence – a coup d'état in resistance.

Antonio lifted the crimson shaded pencil once again and rubbed it as he placed 'It' on his lips as if it was lipstick and said, "Christine ... beautiful, mine too."

Cannon was unsure he heard right and repeated in the most empathic and measured articulation, unthreatening to Antonio. Silence again as catatonic inflexibility. Antonio defragmenting associations left in Cannon. He knew that the sketch, as morose as it appeared, was a type of art and quite novel in appearance. It would be evidence if reported and how could Allan not report it if asked.

Nothing is privileged in investigations: All is privileged in the therapy hour. Allan relished opening up a gallery of portraits left shelved in the last frontier of his creative renaissance. Intimate poses of his former lovers, all ladies of whom he embraced in the pith of his momentary release and sketched in Modigliani's style.

The admixture of French, Italian, Hungarian, Jew in NYC Cop Doc Style. When Dr. Cannon let go, he did it all the way with skills that disciplined the inchoate sensibility of transference in which he was so well trained. His entire self absorbed the moment in quantum pithy moments. He let go and let G-d. In so doing, Allan kept in mind the goal of healing, unadulterated by the perversions of fear and politically correct fascism. He touched the elusive boundary of the soul where the heart of life, the rhythm of carnal pleasure and pulse of the elusive eternal ultimate unfurls without words.

His skill was won in the hardest institutes of NYC and embraced the opposite camps as a way of inner-sight used in his perception of the world around by knowing thyself, his life was well worth living. Or so he thought – most of the time even in the darkest moments. Therapist meant more than a profession to Professor Dr Cannon. It meant the release of enslaved folk. Therapy as art fading in stark naked silence colored Gray became Judea's purple and Spartan Red where the universe of the patient contracts in the autistic guttural responses when a patient reaches the protective sheath of psychotic defenses.

No doubt Antonio was illustrating a split from reality that was mental slavery from unearned guilt; perhaps suicidal in the constriction of conscience.

Dr. Cannon was stuck in the hardest of worlds, as he tried to transcribe Antonio's regressed split state line on the border of a fractured cosmic line. *He transcended the splinter from inner projection scenes from childhood conflicts mirrored onto the cheap medium of illusions – modernity's delusions.*

Any means available to Dr. Cannon was acceptable material. He may have followed margins that crumbled his profession into mediocrity as the anesthetized danger zone. The age of the idiot guides, false humility, and extreme narcissism; the age of today's burgeoning consumers and producers of mental illness. Mirror reflections of death entombed in life's corridor – he was the proud Cassandra – alarm is good to wake up the soul. No apology, his work was that of his creator's path – that was his entry and exit signal. Dr. Allan tuned in and on to pick up the elusive ethereal connection with Antonio. That surrealistic sense that holds nothingness, in juxtaposition to everything around it.

The most evident solidity of that gap when all goes silent and beyond material, when it goes beyond the rational and elusive into that letting loose within the sense of G-d: Jackson Pollack throwing specks of random indulgence with the touch of G-d infusing meaning where none existed.

Prayer for a true miracle and one in which Dr. Cannon and Antonio needed to break soon as the third hour had begun and Cannon held his gut. He even held his need to piss out uric acid for the sake of his fellow officer whose life was on the line. Unless Dr. Cannon could break the impasse of psychotic splits and regression to infantile consciousness, Antonio was lost to prosecution's gateway.

Dr. Cannon put his ego on the corner of Ockham's razor and let go, while slaving at freedom's embrace to listen to his patient's despair. His thought was the world arena contracting in the space of his mission in the moment with his patient. The whole world was swept into a meaningful vacuum where Allan entered and pulled Antonio, defying exhaustion with many associations leading to endless fox holes – dug in clues that teased meaningful refuge – but too small and fragmented to launch.

His inspiration was in the most contracted space of all, where the Almighty himself stood as the master healer. He felt ever the apprentice artisan allowed the gift to taste. That was what some fools called cockiness and what he knew was the voice of the Ultimate Creator assisting him. He held on like all mortals when challenged by foes – internal or external: the Spartan King Leonitis his hero when struck with the rape of the Greeks by the Persian tyrant Xerxes held on, he would too.

It was G-d who felled the tyrant's dynasty, with little men who tried to play G-d. The famed artist and producer Emmanuel D, who took the life of a man beset with homelessness and despair through the power of freedom and faith of seeing the beauty within a vagabond named Earnest. Far from Hollywood's boulevard was a novel director who had the bloodline of Cop Doc Allan – the real passion of compassion in being humane. Emmanuel quoted, "If you have a tortured son, you will overcome the evil side, tough-love will eventually see the light on this side of paradise on earth."

G-d's love is sown in all religions and in all places at all times – illumined in the different prisms and cultures – hence the Jewish mystics do not convert but support the repair of the world within one too extend to all. Permeating the darkness his brother's energy and chutzpah inspired Dr Allan Cannon without further thought, he got up and slammed his hands together. Iterating in a hypnotic and sonorous cadence, in a loud bellow, his pronouncement as a denouement delivered in a martial tune. At the onset, rather paradoxical and measured in technique

"For G-d's sake, wake up, Dr Allan – you are a total basket case! You feel trapped, oh so trapped inside – help me, dear lord, where am I?" Allan lightly slapped his own face. "This is a nightmare, a Kafkaesque trial. Where is my conscience? What is she saying, my lover unrequited in modern bureaucracy? Help me anyone." Cannon looked directly at Antonio, and in a deep bellowing plea, said, "Can I have a 10-13 for an old Cop Doc, please, or lose my life forever? The doctor is all but lost and sick, I need help!"

Allan did this as the projection of his own despair set in ironic satire was mystically spoken. Without a word, Antonio showed alert connection to Dr. Allen moving as contextual boundaries were drawn around words. Relations pulled into articulate and rhythmic disclosure in reverse of the process laid out between patient and doctor.

This rhythmic dance moved in many different iterations for three hours. His story untold as Antonio fell with his head resting on his own chest unsure of what to do. He was trapped in his own web of loss. Dr. Allan refused giving up, such was his adaptive intuitive style as he turned on *The Ninth Configuration, Twinkle, Twinkle, 'Killer' Kane,* directed by William Peter Blatty. The author of the Exorcist, who now directed the shock treatment in place of the recommended ECT, where Ferenczi's genius of making the patient doctor was incredibly effective in role play only.

Blatty's work was a step beyond role plays in an insane asylum for officers left to madness, redeemed when they are placed in the power of the implicit power with the real psychologist and psychiatrist.

As Cannon could jumpstart the mundane science of medicine already infiltrated by the brave new world vision of a scaling of human worth based on age and intellect the new categorical imperatives. Alas, it worked!

Extreme complex trauma induced what initiates, and even tenured psychologists and psychiatrists initially dubbed ambulatory schizophrenia, or borderline states of consciousness. Helen Deutsch had presented the model in Feminine Psychology. Knowledge changed but insight was timeless, so was this epiphany. The difference here was Antonio was not in the age group, or fit any of the dynamics of the onset of this diagnosis: Dr Cannon smelled the diagnosis of Police Complex Trauma. The difference in the label was as critical as being fixed a persona non-grata as schizophrenic vs. a wounded warrior who would respond to critical intervention.

Antonio said as if he knew his Cop Doc was genuinely with him side by side and opened up, "I do remember," [he dribbled out in a slightly audible tone as saliva that congealed on his lips dripped].

Antonio looked like John Turturro in Barton Fink, until the finale surprises you and me with stunning ironic insights. Insanity posed as sanity in the inimitable work of the Joel and Ethan Coen brothers 'Hollywood Catch 22' was no match for 'NYPD Catch-22'.

Dr. Cannon reflected the fact that a long moment of association was not so different then his detective caught in the crosswinds of reality and illusion – the bell bottoms of the hip and decadent poised as social altruism. The sword in the sheath of the hero's belly. He shook off the slumber as if to awake and scream. Dr. Cannon said,

"I am listening, Antonio, I am all big ears and mine are big," Five minutes of crying waves inundated space as Dr. Cannon leaned forward, anticipating disclosure. Antonio stopped and paused,

"Doc, it is just better to not think about it, I am crazy or must be. You will never believe me – you know what I mean – believe me. Anyhow, let it pass along with me as a hero who fades, or goes crazy, something like that, okay boss! I can't believe I am here. There is nothing you can do for me. I am going to never leave here. Forget about me, will you?"

Dr. Cannon looked straight into Antonio's face and allowed him room to pause and re-directed his eyes to ensure the truth he was about to say,

"Tony, look at my eyes, I am telling you the truth. There is no guarantee you'll walk away. You'll get put away, even if you are free of guilt, or you are guilty as all hell. So, please stay with me now. What made you wake up now and decide to speak to me, unless you trusted me enough?"

Antonio nodded and remained silent, progress was surging through the stolid air, dead and now vivified!

Cannon placed his head down in mimic form of Antonio.

"Antonio, let go now. I am the Cop Doc in need of your best effort to help me figure it out with you. I am not sure, but sense there is a lot you do not know, you're more scared of being labeled crazy than being labeled a bad guy. There is even more I do not know. I do not know where it will lead us? But, for sure, I am with you. I do care. Look me in the Eye!"

Dr Allan Cannon shifted his position as he angled his whole body to a 90 degree turn of space and unity as a move forward and closer to Antonio. Without a flinching of his deep eyelashes, acting as Centurion shields with dark and heavy hewn cast as magnets for women, and wisdom for men. Cannon's ruddy complexion appeared as rue as the night shadowing day portending to accommodate a response from Antonio.

"I repeat, Detective Antonio, I know you are not crazy! I also know you are not a bad guy, no matter what! Are you hearing me, Antonio? I mean it, please let me know? Why? What happened and why? This question I will answer for you without you asking it now because you would not dare ask it. This questioning is ever present on your mind, questions we can clear in part – right here and now. You feel it will litter our communication, connection, and return for re-runs in your mind's eye again and again. You are not crazy, Antonio, for being so fearful of the label. Why? I will answer the question that plagues you. If you were bona fide crazy as a loon, you would not have said what you needed to relate as a preamble to what will follow which is the disclosure. You needed permission and absolution as a good Roman Catholic. So, although you are not religious – absolution holds a grip on your ideal and thoughts. Since you still hold life as sacrosanct – you are not a killer. In fact, I believe you may have in moments felt, or wished even, your Gumba Tommy ill, but that is normal. You have all the ability to discern right from wrong or would never have given me the layout of your rules for disclosure which was not direct in your communication to me. You re-directed me. So you are not likely insane. Insane is a legal concept but for us shrinks in part it means you'd have no ability to discern right from wrong. You do! You clearly can discern, or you would be a loose cannon with me as most crazies are: Insanely without boundaries while invading my space without care of having me or anyone believe you."

"In the second self-label, you fixed yourself as being seen as a bad guy, which is absurd. It would mean you do not care about anyone – except as means to an end to your own material desires. Being a 'bad guy', you would never be exquisitely stressed and superbly anxious as you are. You are in a bad state of mind due to having a conscience! A bad guy simply could not fake it. A bad guy is all ego and slips on the extension of his own hubris for lack of an adequate one. Hid along the stumbling stones he paves for his 'feigned' friend – takes him down – and full circle around falls hard! Take that as you may Antonio, what do you think?"

Dr. Cannon now was silent, voicing his reflection of projection transferred to the correct iterations. Like a blank screen, which absorbs the light of black and white he was no longer itinerant in a classic analytic stance. He was not plugging into a vacuum of a mirror of a mirror but one that caught a real image. The interpretation was an assessment as well as an intervention. Existence was clothed in – stark naked confrontations either taken or left as dead as dust. If Antonio understood the complex analogy, metaphor and invitation, then his heuristic test of re-directing trust and higher level thinking was a measured success. Dr. Cannon had taught his psychology graduate students the concept of active analysis with the use of '*The Ninth Configuration*,' in severe trauma cases, where Doc becomes patient and Patient Doctor. Sandor Ferenczi, the Hungarian analyst of marked genius, created active analysis defying traditional analysis and paradoxically making it more real and viable – existentially.

Ferenczi like Nietzsche and Wilhelm Reich, who fought unfolding intellectual fascism. Physical, mental and spiritual succumbed to madness, not in reality, but in illusion to escape from the doors of coercion in which geniuses must live out their lives in closed doors while open windows shine in prisms of their own lives.

Dr. Allan working in private would hold this theory till he was ready to depart from the world. The concept of the exorcising of demons was done, unsurpassed by the genius of Peter Blatty. Cannon had figured out after stopping and pausing – Father Karas was not cured by being the exorcist of his parishioner's demon, but being a doctor of the mind and priest transferring his own trial of shattered faith hidden in traumatic losses to the demon that possessed his patient he exorcised it from himself as well. This underscored his stigmata as trauma wounds – redemption came for him in death – as he cured the victim in life. Father Karas exchanged the material sale of convenience for his conscience altar in which he lay on the pyre of illusions piqued for Pyrrhic victory.

Illusions redeemed as real when his true faith sacrificed his own life for another too live. Humanity is redeemed in those whose ego is maintained in sacrifice and responsibility. It is ultimately a choice in each person's story told. Kafka's trial emerged as Cannon visualized and heard the quoted piece in the forgotten language, where the Psychoanalyst Erich Fromm pointed out in analyzing Fairy Tales, Myths, and Dreams the power of heroic and tragic irony in truths told,

"K's tragic mistake was that, although he heard the voice of his humanistic conscience and defended himself against the accusing authorities, partly by submission and partly by rebellion when he should have fought for himself in the name of his humanistic conscience. It is only in the power of dying that gave him the power to visualize the possibility of love and friendship and paradoxically at the moment of dying he had for the first time faith in life — he raised his hands and spread out his fingers."

"His fingers spread out in prayer as all living beings asking of the Almighty for nourishment even in the most unlikely places seemingly unreachable – Hell."

"Antonio, you too wanted to be a Father to lost souls. Auschwitz's martyrs as father Maximillian Kolbe where the reality of human beasts killed him, denying their stain of perfidy on humanity. Trust and leaps of faith in the humane being behind the veil of the animal being uncovers the eternal in the finite moment – where you may leap or are cut down in illusions that cross the bounds in the folds of life's margins. What do you choose, Antonio?"

Antonio, almost inaudible at first, began his oration which became a soliloquy with the razor sharp clarity re-directed as he veered to this side and that like a locomotive express.

"Doc, it is weird to say, but I loved my partner Tommy, not in a weird way, but in a way you feel about a brother. Christine was more and less than a sister. I do not know how to, begin but it is weird, real weird like a surreal dream, you know! No, Doc, forget about it."

Dr. Allan Cannon sat silently for as long as it took, perhaps 50 minutes, with focus and hovering attention. With intention to pick up each association from Antonio – the rest would come in time. As an existential analyst he knew the power of silent and active listening attunes to all senses, verbal as well as pre-verbal expression. Not just the audible sense, which reduces the metaphor in full color for the concrete path that dresses social display, not genuine connection and encounter. The intervention was a success. No time frame was set.

Labels aid the clinical psychologist and psychiatrist allowing an effective and competent treatment plan on one hand: On the other foot in glove as the lazy, too quick, too draw and the incompetent lay out easy quick fixing of living humane begins into stained artifacts, treated with chemical staining of psychotropic medications rather than existential confrontation.

The walking wounded soldiers and public safety become the walking zombies. Old school and new school – like classic and new age was transcended – ancient wisdom met novel innovation; the anomaly freed

169

in quantum release of a string of creative power overriding the force of engineering labels and coercion. Humility to the Ultimate Creator held Ultimate Meaning – all doors closed started to lower their thresholds and all seemed possible in Dr Allen's mind as his energy was returning.

He excused himself to relieve himself – a breakthrough was made as his own primal needs could be answered.

As Cop Doc Allan Cannon moved out, he saw Chief of Homicide Bureau, District Attorney Office, Ms. Lisa Wei Feng in the hallway. She approached and said,

"You're Dr Al, I recognize you from your book. I like what you wrote about complex trauma, it's very interesting. I like your method and technique, I may come in to see you, but first, I want to ask you about Det. Antonio Pacificio. Dr. Allan looked at her deeply and without glancing away with his intense green hazel eyes emerging from her stoic brown pupils said,

"I cannot say anything about Antonio. You can do your own investigation but not on my account, Ms. Feng."

"But, Doc, please, you don't understand."

"No! Ms. Feng, I do. An investigation is an investigation; however you sugar coat it. If you need anything, there is a procedure – please follow it. Have a nice day, thank you."

She looked back with the sternest and most threatening face she could muster.

"I am the Chief ADA of Homicide Investigations. Dr. Allan Cannon, you need to stop and listen to me. I have a need to know."

"Ms. Feng, I cannot confirm or disconfirm anything. You can direct your question to the Legal Bureau. Also, you can ask the CO of the Medical Division both/and Chief of Personnel. Again, thank you and have a lovely day."

Ms. Lisa Wei Feng was red with fury, she was silent and almost pouting. Dr. Allan Cannon turned and in paradoxical irony confessed,

"Nothing personal: By the way, I love your puerile taste, Ms. Lisa. Chanel hum ... Poison. It fills my olfactory canals and yours as well. Shared senses must be quintessential to you. Smell's delightful to my own mercurial dimensions. The black and white Versace bag goes so well with your Gucci dress and your .380 on your hip if I am correct. Don't answer yet. But if you'd like to meet on the QT, I am aware of your papers on Legal Issues relating to traumatized officers involved in shooting – which we can talk about. Nothing personal – I have my moral and ethical compass, as you do. Collegial relationships and aesthetic review is something else. No risk, no gain, huh?

Perplexed, she nodded assent with a genuine grin. He went on,

"Business is business. Affinity in cerebral endeavors is a whole other califlowered patch. Take my card, I have a feeling we can talk on the QT. I could say from a keen objective view – aesthetically, your cheekbones are higher than the norm, askew of an outlier becomes your facial structure as stunning and sensual, Lisa. Hum, you can call two days from now. The Red Lion has a Sporting event: The address is 151 Bleecker Street." Adjacent to Thompson Street, as in Thompson Machine gun of Bonny and Clyde Barker fame – so fire away in rapid succession of a rise and fall. Well, all in good time, Lisa, pun intended only of course."

Silently, Ms. Lisa Wei Feng blushed and looked perplexed.

Dr. Cannon glided away with a shuffle and a confident poise, slightly arched, not erect, but ever steady to the rest room. The sound of a flush was cathartic as the acid was released in the stench filled piss pot of an excuse vertically along the wall in ceramic stained yellow. Men who did not flush. That laziness annoyed Allan and he did not give a second thought to the transaction and date he made.

Dr. Cannon had a patient to think about. He knew intuitively something else happened and it was not Antonio who murdered his Pisano Tommy, or his lover Christine. He closed the bathroom door and in the meditative mind he directly ignored others and with nods went right back into see Antonio. Dr. Cannon saw Antonio with his head down and a glance that led into a stare where eyes met. Antonio had awakened, but no celebration was waiting – the door to treatment would begin with assessment as therapeutic. Antonio said,

"Doc, Jacobs's ladder was about the Hebrew father wrestling with the Angel. But what Angel? Perhaps, the Angel that destroyed Sodom. It was all an illusion or a reality in the dreams that make substance surreal, and reality illusion. The hemlock is not the bane as the witch's tit was and is the perverse desire and retraction in man's deepest desire to connect in soul with his beloved as she rejects him in his quest. I am asleep and this is a dream."

"Doc, intelligence like contrition must awake the dreamer, lest he sleep while awake and never ascent as man on the ladder. Jacob left for every dreamer following his beloved son Joseph. Please find me my Robe of many colors and help me get to light and freedoms door again. Doctor, am I a ladder in a dream or a dream in the decent of a lattice headed for perditions door."

Dr. Allan said,

"I am here and we will explore those deepest questions together. Hold on for one moment."

Dr. Allan got up and checked to ensure no one was near. Listening, he sat and crossed his legs as he leaned forward.

Dr. Allan Cannon said to Antonio,

"I am all ears, and I have big ones … please go on."

# Chapter 14

## Smell the Coffee: Awake, Cry and Weep – Brother: Frame by Frame

[Surrounding, an atmosphere of cold fog and shades grappling with light breaking and entering and then slipping away, the sun broke in with a radiating warmth that begun to oppress in its heat].

Antonio felt as if the weight of a dense fog was clearing in the head lights of a slow moving Freight train. He slowly began with a long pause and hesitation,

"Holy shit! I am up but there is no celebration here, Doc. Your big ears cannot save my torn Soul. I am so screwed – I can't believe it! This cannot be happening. I have to see Tommy, and have a coffee with Christine. No psychoanalysis can help. Why bother, Doc?"

Antonio said with agitation in his throat as he gulped in a large dose of escape. He felt the chords in his voice box click off. All articulation, once again, was narrowing. His throat felt as if his breath was closing in on its own internal vacuum where his soul was existentially sucked into the void.

Horror breathed in as if he was gasping for an offering of air to fill his lungs and inflate his brains with mindful meditation – even if only for a moment.

Cop Doc Allan sensed the horror and confusion wrestling with Antonio and holding him in its prison once again, lost in the Sea of aggression and temptations tunes to retreat into silent madness. Antonio curled out in primitive yelps,

"I can't breathe, Doc!" Antonio grappled to run for the door in sheer panic expressed in pleading gestures of fear mingled with a desire to connect humanely with Allan. He repeated, "Doc!"

Cop Doc Allan said in a calm voice that was sonorous as he placed his strong hand on his shoulder,

"I am here with you! I am going nowhere – breathe brother — brother, breathe the air …

"That's it, I hear your breathing. Keep breathing steady breaths – keep breathing. I hear the exhalations …" Antonio exclaimed,

"Doc!"

"Please, Doc … I can't – it's suffocating me. I ain't breathing boss, I ain't making it – I am dead – you're here with me… I am dead, as in dying. That's me! Can't you see me? I am a Dead Stiff – that's me! Dead stiff and shrunk!" Allan kept his equipoise with calm soothing steadiness and in a tenured calmness,

"That's it, Antonio. That's right, keep relaxing – you're doing it – keep relaxing and breathing slow and steady… Do you hear your own breath it is finding its natural balance and rhythm? Can you hear the rhythmic breathing – stop, pause and let your breath flow naturally … You are doing well, good-enough. Keep breathing …

That's it, Antonio ..." Antonio's breathing improved in measured rhythms, noticeable to him and Cop Doc Allan.

"Doc, okay, I am breathing better. It is hard, real hard! I feel as if I am not in my own skin. You hear me, man? I mean it is as if I am not me. I am lost. Lost, as in I have taken leave of my sanity and have just gone off to la-la land! Please, wake me up from this shit hole. I cannot believe it is happening. You know what I mean, Doc? It is all sur-real to me."

"Antonio's skin had the sensation as if he was a mudslinger fish: It felt stretched, like the fish that could not make up his mind whether he was a pond dweller, or a ground hunter. Antonio wanted to be rid of the pain that sketched despairs rue the day complexion with blotches of crimson hue. Escaping into madness in the cold room of the hospital was not an egress as it would presume insanity, but not justice or escape, except into even a more constricted prism of his own design.

Antonio assured himself, it was forward no matter what. He could not pull the covers over his head, or the veil of psychosis as the blanket over Cop Doc Allan Cannon's eyes. He was in Bellevue and that fact was real as dry ice. The ice that smoked visible clouds around dead bodies kept in people's homes in Irish Brooklyn Bay Ridge and Park Slope. Bodies awaiting their wake – as viewers would come by to wish them farewell in their best attire as they awaited being planted in the earth. Ancient rituals opened pages dog-eared in the Book of the Dead, revivified in Park Slopes Brooklyn NY. He sunk in as these morass thoughts descended into the dried wells that provided the parameters of the pools of his conscious awareness, slipping away into his unconsciousness. He wanted to yell, "Doc, I am drowning," and he dared not. He thought to himself as he silently struggled hard to not show desperation – not yet, no there was time if 'It' did not pass, he could then express it all. Silence again was the parley in this macabre dance of treatment having begun: Treatment was also a refuge Cop Doc Allan promoted to a degree.

"No, Antonio, you ain't dreaming, you are real as I am. This macabre place is as real as it gets – but not forever. It too will pass, and you shall pass outside the doors as long as you allow it to happen." Antonio let go and spoke out,"

"Doc, I ain't dreaming, am I? [Cop Doc Allan Cannon expressed without any smile, but with paternal equanimity and a nod]

"No."

"Doc, I am not sure you are real, except as a contradiction in my head. A dream I am having and I am unsure if you are the nightmare or the angel in disguise …" [silence for a minute passed] "Doc, you hear me? Can you understand me? I feel as if I am in a stupor, I feel as if I was half asleep and finished with a boxing match. I feel as if I am stuck in the play box in kindergarten. I am weirded out. Okay, I feel as if I am losing my mind, Doc."

With a curious grin, Antonio moved his upper lip up and expressed an ever slight tease as a query. Tease of an almost inconceivable sense of humor in the midst of all this terror. Uncanny as it was, Cop Doc Allan took it as a gift of connection and immediately responded in reinforcing this positive gesture. Allan smiled in a mimicked reflection of a mirror image, as one does when a child is anxious and full of fear. This was not a game for Cop Doc Allan. This was the struggle for healing, reparation and rapprochement as vague as those objectives were they were called for in his strategy of counter-transference.

The shrink hardly articulates the myriad interlacing of possibilities as playful advances and retreats in the dance of treatment and therapeutic gains. The lonely plight of the private practitioner is in-deed a necessity as 'love among the artists'. George Bernard Shaw, the great Irish playwright, connected to his anti-vivisection movement, which at once made him affirm the private in the social conventions thrown to the wind: At times, even with more irony, the public loneliness at the height of the artist's success leads to Alienation.

Isolation is the cost of every genius – that is, if he/she truly be so. That was the paradox of privacy of Cop Doc Allan Cannon and his inner circle. The power of gravity is the pull of centrifugal power. Yet, powerful, but not forceful as nature herself where he and his brothers dipped in her Sirens and muses of love affairs travesty and calling: The fait accompli and accomplices in his sojourn. The circular staircase of seven descending steps backward in the ascent – forward. Genius as a detective of the mind illusive as it was tempting in full swing. The mood of one door opening as the wistful winds of the other closed in triumph.

Cannon knew intuitively that Antonio needed him to waive the flag of the truce as his tools depended on verbal and non-verbal expression and reconstruction. Context, perspective and artful pixels painted and brushed with the gaps left and filled in relief comic and tragic: Feeling passion that circles the sense of – Empathy, Antipathy, and the Pathetic. The centrifugal power of One never controllable fleeing wish to conquer in all humane endeavors of being – and be-coming! The humane pathos, how laborious and complex – how delightful and exquisite!

Therapy and the healer of the mind – all emotional endeavors save being Apathetic: Apathetic the therapist's idols in quick fix like dope laced with arsenic in managed care and all types of sweeping health care: The crime of the therapist as healer is not in not succeeding, but in not giving a shit in a pile of ever returning accumulating fecal matter of fees.

As Freud understood, in place of craft and artistic medicine applied the immeasurably poverty of accumulated dollar bills – the accordion of pyres of pyrrhic victories burnt in neon lit bonfires.

Cop Doc Allan Cannon knew the shells he fired needed targets of passion and reason – the Yin and Yang of inter-coursing divine proscriptions against prescription to avoid the Healer – Un-Done.

This was the maddening dance in Dr Allan's mind as artist therapist and poet warrior, who in respectful interludes, as the art of his technique was as welcomed as Freud's Totem and Taboo, Durkheim's The Elementary forms of Religious Life and Igor Stravinsky Rites of Spring. The composers of novel theory and technique are destined to dance a stirring of forgotten language that holds the core of humanity in the starving desert where lust for blood of the hungry curs howl for genius. The masses will pervert each new window laying open the dark shadows buried with each maestro that arises to the crucible of his times. The biography of Antonio's reading room was codified and collated in the mind of Cop Doc Allan. Not all detectives or cop docs are created equal – even the best have those who are composers in the forest of chaos who imprint the borders of reason as sketches to guide new paths.

Pathfinder: The unconscious counter-existential move made visceral as the gut wrenching losses of Antonio were begging expression in Cop Doc Cannons blast. Blasts made real from the surreal splash painting in as if free associations could be freed. He was on his healthy focus with intuition. He was ready for what he knew was already a Jackson Pollack abstract. He heard in his own memory Jim Morrison send you mind to the back room – this association followed with a wet splash of a dream unanswered. He aimed to provoke Antonio to a re-direction again.

"Listen, Antonio, the only thing I ask of you now is to let any of your thoughts flow forward without any holding back. That is hard as hell and with your breath being snagged, you will breathe a lot better – trust me – even if it is painful, embarrassing, or humiliating in your mind. I care and care a lot for you and your need to let out a lot trapped in like gas, smoking mirrors and faded dreams dog-eared in fear."

"You with me, Antonio?"

Allan leaned forward again to listen.

Antonio had already modified his keen sense to mimic and learn from his healer, who gently guided him without ever letting him feel subdued as was the gift of intuitive natural leaders, professors and confessors conduits as director geniuses and the best detectives of the mind and crime, A. Kazan, Emmanuel Martin Defiliciantonio and the Cop Doc Allan Cannon. "I can reassure you Antonio, with a promise – if you offer me your paints and words, we will craft meaning and insight where non-is apparent."

"Doc, it is nothing – it is ex-nihilo in sin incarnate – you cannot understand as you are a Jew in Judea, a tribe of Judah and I am nothing but a mendicant and itinerant and you are trying to find meaning from me – but my mind and life is meaningless – you see what I mean?"

Cop Doc Allan experienced his antipathy: Anger was rising as he was ready to capitulate to the madness of confrontation. An escape from his existential attitude would be premature in the hatching of the alliance. He measured his retreat to the window of intervention instead.

"Remember nothing is not ex-nihilo, Antonio – it is something. All exists even from the brink of the abyss lay a boundary – standing as something in its nothingness. Nothingness does not exist even when nothing is apparent in total darkness." Antonio unconvinced and resistant focused with hyper-intent. Cop Doc Allan was rising with mercurial attention to what was at the core of this dance as all push and pull momentums. The force changed the dynamic in the struggle waiting to be unraveled. Especially in the caverns of the unconscious existential shadows and psychoanalytic crevices so hidden in the docks of shuttering islets at the perimeters of underwater volcanoes.

"Nothingness does not exist, Doc. If that is so and I go along with you. Then what do you call the Nautilus in the depths of the ocean, Doc? Is that not dark for you as the wetness of your lover when she runs dry and ashore in mendacity and betrayal?

Cop Doc Allan was being bated with the hyper-intuitive style of Detective Antonio, who informed him he was quite adept at applying his brush of abstraction to the dance – this, too, was a gift to be revisited at a later time. He now needed to respect his ingenuity and apparent spark of extraordinary intellect and pain expressed. Betrayal – what an incisive concept. The double edged sword, that cuts deep in the wound of trust rued.

"Antonio, is it not the occlusion of space in light inverted in pitch dark that a nautilus of illusion provides your ark of escape from the flood of passion in the suspension of embryonic reason?"

Antonio paused and stopped for a while and then jostled back in small measure and said. "Yes, Doc, but without my illusion then the light of my ark cannot shield me from Illusion. My bathysphere will breach and I will be drowned. Who will save me – you, my shrink, the father confessor? I believe in G-d. Who should I trust you or G-d?" Cop Doc Allan was not used to this parlay and allowed his creative intuition and mind to take over without hesitation he was engaging Antonio and would not let go of the rare opportunity and his own desire to play with the fringes or madness and genius – he threw the dice ...

"Antonio, the mind of G-d is not man. At times, I need let go and let G-d. I am only his creation, it is not either/or – fear and trembling as your well-crumbled Soren Kierkegaard suggests as bachelor, who could not plunge into loves confines of marriage – so lived unrequited as you have. Here, letting go, we can play as far and as fast as G-d lets us. I know you are a devout Catholic ... Let me be the doctor here and trust the process as screwed up as that sounds. I need your help and you are the only one to help me be able to help you by letting go and just let it out. Confessions of innocence are as important as guilt. I suspect, deep in the corridors of your hidden mind, we will bring to the real light what is distorted in the neon flash bites you have become accustomed too. I am going to now stop talking with my mouth and listen to you with my soul, my mind, my conscious and unconscious in what will be our work together. Please begin and let out what you need to. We can try to figure out how and why you are not losing your mind but holding on to what can clarify that. Does my offering make sense to you Antonio?"

"It does, it does – give me time and when I am ready it will emerge – you have studied me well as I do each suspect to exonerate or condemn themselves in any ongoing investigation – cold cases are not for the morgue – I keep them hot as a lioness on a hot platinum roof Doc, she can get off when the heat emerges and the other lion moves on. She, Christine, was a beauty. A seductress – that bewitched my gumba, Tommy, I did not do it! I know what you may be thinking, Doc, but it is not me – not that – other sins but not murder. I am of all places in the old asylum – nothing changes under the sun – isn't that what King Solomon said in Proverbs?"

The question was rhetorical as the emergence of new questions and links were forged with alacrity. A whip of words and rhythms crackled the dry atmosphere with explosive curiosity as quests for clarity in the silent repossession and re-direction of Cop Doc Allan.

Silence pervaded the dark and dank atmosphere of the old asylum interview room. In the dim light of all therapeutic rooms the, ambiance was as if the blues could bounce off a Mississippi bayou in a back room on a steam ship never having docked for 150 years on the River of life ending in deaths rebirth.

An asylum was the place of refuge, the safe haven of the insane who gave up on society to retreat into the abyss of life's countenance in an ever expanding thunder of silent ovations.

A steamship of the poor man blues. A man without an identity flowing along the merciful escape of the River Styx, where hell and heaven teased one another. The prize being some humane, and some inhuman beings who sauntered like ghosts in the existence of delirium and deliberation. Dreams shattered and rectified in cracked heels of Achilles tendons; awaiting faith born and re-born: Connections. It was all about connections for these two sojourners — one a cop doc and one, a cop.

Both living in the fringes of power, lust and greed: Junkies on different addictive trips that end up in the same garden of discontent and illusions. Diseased wishes, unfulfilled in psychosis, stained as the glass of the 'Bleeding Heart'.

The detective of crime and the detective of the mind evolved: Sardonic humor – it could only be as it was, and is so. The Almighty in-deed had his plan 'Truth' – beautiful and ugly, but unadulterated 'Truth'! Truth would prevail as Cop Doc Allan prayed for guidance as much as Antonio did. Antonio prayed through his unique Rabbi, Jesus, whose mystical passion and divine inspiration to the heavenly Father was his only known route.

Cop Doc Allan, as mystic Rabbi and shrink who replaced the father confessor, prayed directly to the Father: Both men, following the calling in the depths of their unique paths were sincere. Both imagined and hoped the truth would prevail.

Uninvited, Antonio looked at Dr. Cannon, and said, "Doc for what it is worth before you go on ... Man has his plan and G-d has his design. So, let's try and sort through and pray G-d will help us. He recited our father who art in heaven. You with me, Cop Doc Allan Cannon?" Silence shrouded the room and so did a quixotic sensation of light that ushered in through the blinds with a real radiance. As if a break had entered in a crack in the catacomb womb like room. "Truth be told are not the greatest romances and romantic geniuses theological and secular filled with the sparks from the Almighty – is he not the Ultimate Romantic Poet himself ..." Antonio paused and began fluently,

"It began with what Tommy and Christine knew. I mean, we were keeping it on the QT. I kind of hid it, but will let you know. Tommy and I was ghosting this case, we working on a homicide cold case. The kid, Jose Ramon Perez, was a street runner for the dealers – we found out he had a connection with the Nation of Islam. That is, he said he knew there was a lot going on in their inner circle of hood politics. Ramon wasn't a bad kid, but as usual, got mixed up with the wrong crowd. Ramon said on the QT, he would give us something if we would let him walk. Tommy did his act as if he was ready to go bananas you know what I mean, Doc? I told him Tommy had gotten a bit wild and he was losing it: I know it's unconventional and we we're building a case but Tommy would Play, or at least pretended playing Russian Roulette, he kind of got a touch of being you know a bit off the wall in his approach." Cop Doc Allan stayed silent. Antonio played the good cop and basically told Ramon, "Hey, kid – listen. I can't control him much anymore. It's like a marriage gone bad. Doc Allan, ya know what I mean? Don't you?" Cop Doc Allan just listened and did not make one sound, just a nod and a stereotypical guttural 'hum, uh hum...' "I played my role of good cop with Ramon, as I told him,"

"Listen, kid, Tommy would hammer the nail in your sleeping bag after he'd hammer you with his fist and a stray thought Ramon. That is, if my partner thought you were playing him and me for a fool." I went on with my pitch with a more serious tone,

"Ramon, if you give some good score for a real collar and we get our white shark under the radar screen in our little bay you are not a free man, you are a protected One as well. No bull, this is your chance to escape the evil eye and get into the shepherd's fold. I want to know what the fanatics from the racist branch of the Nation of Islam is forging in the hood. Let me in on 'It'?"

Antonio relayed visualizing Ramon's sweat trickling down ever slowly, from one drop emerging like dew cleansing him as all confessions promise to do – but fail in the arena of manmade ills and illusions.

Antonio went on to discuss some of the plans to sabotage himself as Allan was visualizing all this unfolding, a mystical empathic resonance reverberated in the mind of Dr Allen Cannon. A flash of brilliant light ethereal and non-material punctuated the narration between the lines as Nietzsche's warning heralding the Twilight of the Idols mocking in the foreground of perverse sardonic pleasure as anesthesia swept across streams with Mozart, Bach and Goethe: Marie Pasteur, who never dreamt their wish for fulfilling their motherland, would end in the rape of a people.

Cop Doc Allan used the material of his own ancestral guts when he silently focused on a rape of a people. His own people, the Jews. In an uncanny resonance only expressed in the bar rooms where intellectuals surround themselves in NYC as in the art galleries in Soho and other haunts – Antonio spoke,

"Doc, a rape ending on Easter Sunday in the illusory twilight of false gods in black and red neon lights of hubris and narcissistic echoes in the Streets of Marcy Projects that go down Armstrong settlements, where three story buildings end with a monster project slam dunk overshadowing the hood. The dude raped his girlfriend's sister and then threw the Chihuahua out the window. The dude who did it escaped and we did not know at the time his kid brother was thinking he was being targeted and went on the lamb. The nation of Islam attacked him, hunted him down in cold blood, and took him out by throwing him off the roof landing at Atlantic Avenue and Fulton a few blocks south of the Mall. He splattered! Can you imagine the situation – but we had to deal with it. SOP as the brass did not want to rattle the cage as much as the community; a community in allegiance with the legions of silent demons. This kid had promise he died with of all things a book with his blood in the crevices in the page. The book, I know you will ask of me was what title?" Silence pervaded Antonio's mouth and his tongue slipped the words, 'Nat Turners Confession' by William Styron the same writer who wrote Sophie's Choice."

Cop Doc Allan visualized his own nightmare as his ancestor he heard about on his father's side a French Hungarian Jew who died fighting in the Warsaw Ghetto. Echoes that erected the Obelisks like street lamps in Berlin, Kabul and Mogadishu in 1993 when Mohammad Hadid reaching Babel and even as far back as Pharaoh's slaves where blood, cement and babies place immortality of the soul in the godless machine of the brass man's machinations.

Cop Doc Allan's visualizations took him to another dimension as he was absorbing the transference of Antonio's psyche and his objectivity was gone as the contours shifted in his evolving awareness of synchrony. As all mavericks, he tolerated the ambiguity and elastic resonance of the acoustics in the relationship. Antonio resonated with the dynamic as evidenced by his next associations, Doc it was like rain of royal purple coming down hard and fast Doc. You ever hear Prince, "Purple rain." Did you ever wonder why purple? What about NYU's color? What about Victoria Secrets purple underwear as the one color women love to wear? I confess, Doc. Try as I might, my favorite stirring in the hearts mind in the vacuous 'realm of the senses' – as the bastard ingenious artist Nagisa Osima framed profane layers of the sacred in stunning numb awakenings of paradoxical intention. Existentially striking a portend of doom in the lulling moments of calm diffidence toward the human plight. A realm where lust, force, and perversion of love obsessed mocks the thrust of an empty bodkin into the sheath of purple velvet veiling silent lips wanting love in her caverns. Caverns that only an un-castrated male can deliver … You hear me, Doc, you get my message here?"

Cop Doc Allan suspended his thirst to clarify and interpret as he was absorbing every link in associations and freeing his own mind to listen with clarity as the composer he was in theory and intervention in the area of trauma and loss. The complex concrete jungle of police loss. Dr Cannon said, "Please go on." Allan would not interrupt, and after a few moments of silence, the words flowed further from Antonio.

"Doc, the score on the radio when we arrived on the crime scene was blaring a bastardized version of the real Bob Marley and the Wailers score, 'Stir it up'. It was blasting in its seductive tones encompassing confession to end doubt and uncertainty as a young man in the hood. Yes, hood: As I see it, Doc, the hood of a Cobra secretly stealing the souls of young men and women with offerings of a new brave world of illusions of forceful revolutions as iterations. I was picturing this innocent kid framed by a wanna be vigilante Justice of the Nation of Islam. We are the police and never play G-d but these thug racists, who hate a man for his skin color and religion, are the black hand as the thugs who were in Italian circles, when Lt. Petrosino was butchered in my ancestor's days.

It was no less dramatic in mass force when a young man falling under the hood from organized chaos of violence and trauma hurled into a world in which color fades to gray. Black, white, yellow or red doc are illusions in the need to measure a man's worth in nanometers as inhumane beings color his soul and nobility in reduction. Another score on a statistic sheet. That is my job to codify and to bury my own pain and loss. Is that what you mean in your books, Doc, by disenfranchised losses?" Cop Doc Allan Cannon nodded once again and said, "That is profound, Antonio."

"Please go on, Antonio." Silence was not long in the foreground and Antonio continued with zeal and vehemence in a stormy raspy voice. Eye contact was not lost this time around.

"Ramon – in fact, was caught in the web he knew this young man Darrell was innocent and it was the Nation of Islam Imam that framed him and nailed him to the door of the Mosque that was fanatical. The real

Mosque of the Sufi's was nowhere to be found – they closed communication in fear."

Hard-nosed detective, Antonio, shed tears as he now recounted the hard drops beading down Ramon's forehead. He said,

"Doc, it was a Rasta mans beaded hair of silent integrity and a Hasidic Rebbe's twirls in his sidelocks called Peyot being cut that came as an image in my Italian Catholic mind. I could not even share that image with Tommy or Christine even when I met early and we would have a tea if Tommy was out. It is not important Doc, anyhow." Cop Doc Allan interrupted Antonio for the first time,

"Everything is important, please go on with your images that intruded into your awareness Antonio." Silent Antonio finally continued,

"Okay, Doc. It was a haunting sacrifice as Aryan minded illusionists played on as pious sacrifices of dread locks from the Rasta and Hassid were clipped with sadistic pleasure – the outcast of the meek separate from the organized non mystical organized movements of a pure world of bottom lines and political correctness as the vision of fascism in America coming to ripe fruition where nomads die, as quick as a drop of a dime. The hood was under-siege by the Nation of Islam." Antonio said, "Doc!" [while clearing his throat, spitting on the floor] "I need a break!"

"Can we eat something? I am hungry." The time elapsed was three hours. Dr. Allan Cannon nodded, 'Okay, sure, what would you like, Antonio?" He was silent, as he knew the Jackson Pollack splashing of associations had more work to piece his empathic attunement without any distraction. Focus was almost worldly in the seventh dimension, and cop doc eighth sense. Antonio's glib style emerged in the silence of Dr. Allan's moments as his training analysis left its imprint as it cut with the knife of Antonio's tragedy. Ecology as moments of epiphany in the paradox of unwitting disclosure emerged unveiled in secret memoirs Cop Doc Allan and Antonio would be privy too. For Cop Doc Cannon, he was used to his identification as a Jew. A nomad, lost in a world of chaos and violence, non-spoken as all tragic losses unheard in the Organizational Man's credo, 'Arbeit macht Free.' The reality was it was emerging in the lost world in the hoods predators cached in righteous fanaticism. Was the difference really important, if it was theological fascism or it was secular – he knew the answer. Allan was hungry and ordered Antonio Pastrami with layers of mustard, pickles and coleslaw a double with Chicken Soup all from Abe's Kosher Deli. Cop Doc Allan would pick up the order and zoom back in his Unmarked Radio Motor Patrol car. Allan needed air and freedom – something he knew Antonio in the moment did not have – but he would get soon enough. At least Cop Doc Allan so conspired to prove Antonio's innocence. He knew he was guilty of sin, but not murder. He was a shrink, not G-d – unto whom judgment – is His alone.

The score on the radio from the street played the authentic Bob Marley's Exodus, and Dr. Allan moved to take a smoke although he was no smoker. He emerged from the purgatory of the Asylum as he was wont to do in his own hypo-manic reflection which felt like coitus-interruptus. He moved to do the same with the analysis with Antonio

As Cop Doc Allan walked the street, Leon Uris's work Exodus was on the curb by the sewer, thrown by a book murderer, as cast gems along an otherwise pure street. Perfidy by Ben Hecht was a few yards down. He picked them up and reflected as he reassessed Antonio describing the kid's murder and Ramon caught in the lion's lair.

Looking away and acting as if he would bolt through the door when Cop Doc Allan left the hospital Antonio looked despondent with loss, but relieved as well. More would come after eating – this was a day without stop. Antonio could take the heat of the inferno but not the flames of his disenfranchised losses and trauma – it caught up but he was not a murderer. Dr. Allan Cannon had a new window to open with Antonio as he sauntered in Abe's kosher deli. Cop Doc Cannon could not shed his Jewishness as a peripatetic philosopher knowing his own genius would guide him as all intuitions are inspired aspiration as much as ones calling. Even Beethoven heard his music in the sounds of silence, as much as Simon and Garfunkel was playing that song on 101FM. The movement of two shadow images in the darkness descending on Abe's Deli without natural light save neon and translucent gave the illusion of being bright in darkness. A sign on Abe's Deli still sought Abe's unknown murder that killed him in cold blood, a cold case in-deed.

# Chapter 15

## Liaison's: Agents Saboteur – Demons or Saints?!?

Antonio was lying in the bed and staring up at the ceiling when Dr. Cannon got back. The hot Pastrami on Club held layers of Cole Slaw and pickles with an exquisite scent. Jewish soul food permeated the ambient stale air with earthy food. Psych Doc, Dr. Anna Klover, a new police psychologist following protocol with punctilious exactitude. Dr. Klover re-asserted each holding strap – as Antonio withdrew from his presence of mind escaping with skill into madness for the moment. The sketch of his face illumined vacancy and stupor. Sketching his face to mimic what he desired presenting with expertise Antonio expressed flat affect. As a street crime cop hoping to get mugged, he could feign any mask he chose.

Getting mugged was fun for Antonio; he felt a lion's pride in wait for the gang leading Hyena ready to bite hard on an innocent cub. When the lead Hyena thinks the Lioness is alone on the flat plains of African dry winds the wistful thrills at taking easy prey – breezes through the brush until the predator swooped down on his prey. The king of the concrete jungle, a street crime under-cover cop makes the elusive predator his prey.

What does that do to a detective's mind? Even a street warrior detective of the NYPD? Dull and blank was the glaring look of Antonio to all: Like a spent .38 caliber shell his 1000-mile stare without expression enveloped his personality. The hard work Allan and Antonio forged was crushed like a sapling thrown into a tempestuous storm by Dr. Klover's crushing stamp of doing treatment by the book.

Cop Doc Allan's anger was rising as he returned to see his alliance obliterated with a few small choice moments of what could be defined as cultural incompetence. Premature constriction prompted a close down without warning.

No scheme or conspiracy, save the stupidity undergirding greed left to its own demise heralded such incompetence. Micromanaged lines of bottom feeders scavenging the remainders of heroes with tokens of nothingness given as crumbs in place of what had been potential healing and now was a closed deal. Allan knew what had happened in the vapor of greed so routine it did not even strike those who acted with such quick opportunity: The deal was sealed as his effort derailed.

Antonio stared into the vacuum of space at the linings in the stucco ceiling of a different year. Cop Doc Allan placed his hands on his shoulders and said, "Antonio, I am so sorry they acted on their own accord. This mother fuc__ shi_ is not on my orders. Please, don't let go of what we have bridged. The alliance is with us."

Clapping his hands in incredulity, he lost touch and slammed them saying, "Please!"

In a moment, Allan flashed in on an insight as he thought of Antonio being a deep cover. He realized Antonio's presentation could be an act. He whispered under a cough Antonio knew was a cue that the other shrinks and police brass would not detect.

Closing the second drapes with a bright white anesthetic look of purity, something disdained by Cop Doc Allan. At the closing of the drapes, Antonio looked up and it appeared as if he winked.

When Cop Doc Allan moved a bit to the left Antonio exposed to bureaucratic oversights turned somnambulistic as if he was under a zombie spell in some Haitian village.

Was it all appearances as Antonio acting with the genius of Lon Chaney looked doped up in concert with enchanting convention? Was he playing the mimic as he did with ethological motivation in his street crime niche? Perhaps, Antonio was really decompensating?

Cop Doc Allan politely vacated the room from the Interning new Psych Doc and the Brass. They followed soon and left him alone. The Chief with the heavy set triple chin and a still boyish charm where adipose for warmth layered his face as he chanted to Dr. Allan in a meaningful and genuine style,

"Doc, if Det. A P gives you a hard time don't hesitate to call – you've gotten a bit rough around the edges. We all do, even me. Really, Doc, I should come in to see you, ageing sucks. I lost my handsome young face, and now I am an old fart. I will not hesitate to do what I gotta do, if I gotta do it. You read me?"

Cop Doc Allan looked at him and said,

195

"Chief, I was a street cop! Remember, [pausing] Antonio is one of us. I will not abandon one of ours, not even if he's gone bad for a moment. See what I mean?"

[It was not a question, rhetorically expressed and not meant to be answered. Dr. Allan knew all too well that when one is dealing with a Chief, as his papa would say, Chiefs like Chef's serve many deserts and dishes. A Chief like a Chef has worn many uniforms from Cop to Chief. Chefs whip up greasy spoon quick fixes to Gourmet Chef Gourmet Seven Course dinners. I guess what you learn by working through sludge is when home whipped cream lies too long hidden in superficial presentation crystal hardens into layers rock hard and impenetrable.

Cop Doc Allan knew it was futile to clash with the Chief: Fighting city hall was like launching the Titanic! [The Chief looked with his head down as his chin evolved into a fourth chin. This metamorphous triggered as if by osmosis – memories in Allan's mind.

Cop Doc Allan's dad used to admonish him when he failed to study with the zeal of a Talmudic Scholar. Zeal he knew little Allan would need to make it in the world of thorns and thistles – not milk and honey. He was, after all, another Jew Boy in the concrete jungle city parks. The lowest of minorities and the greatest mendicant in prince's clothes, too tortured to take his place among the traumatized stepped on by the powers to be.]

The Chief broke into Dr. Allan's thoughts as he abruptly barked out,

"Hey, Doc, you daydreaming on me? I remember when I was your Commanding Officer in the Bed Stuyvesant Satellite Precinct in the Marcy Public Housing Projects. The reality is, Doc, you got balls! You commandeered a 1991 Jaguar bad ass and spanking new when the bad guys shot at cops from the adjoining city street crime unit. You nailed them to the wall. You are a good Cop, Dr Cannon. I mean as you are called Cop Doc Allan because we know how well you are doing. Well, you're well liked but remember [pausing] sometimes even our own good – go bad. I am right here son. Call if you need me. Okay, Doc Allan, do your magic if you can. I myself cannot believe he did it. But, what if he snapped? I have seen it happen. If he did and it looks like a duck, smells like a duck, so it must be"

[Cop Doc Allan interrupted the Chief as he said retorted without missing a bleep on his radar screen].

"As Papa Freud knew and did not say fully – sometimes a cigar is really a prick, as in a Banana. Ask any street prostie peddling her trade for a few bucks; or some gold digger who gets laid on the QT for her own pleasure while getting paid; or the wholesome woman needing her man fix. Remember, Chief, a duck can be a verb as in duck and evade. Even when an innocent officer goes into shock and is traumatized, he can appear like a duck evading justice and the justice is he is innocent as Kafka on trial for writing his work and epiphany and judgment in metaphor, for it is not what it is, but what each colludes in making 'It' for what it is and that is obsolescence as to what can be changed. Cops have a propensity to say I'm ok, you're ok, when they are dying of a broken heart and soul inside. Duck can be a tasty mandarin dish, or duck can be an analogy to take cover while regrouping. Duck is also a prey dish, not a predator that serves the dish of innocence raw. Antonio is what that hero genius, Professor Lt. Col. Grossman, calls a sheepdog guarding the sheep and ducks from mass-slaughter by hyper-vigilance. Yes, Chief, let's hope innocence is a viable option here, but first let's see if we can get Antonio back. Cover my back, Chief Julius Markowitz, you are the top Brass and the Best. By giving me my space to fill in the voids, I will show you with my assessment that there is nothing in space, which is not something. Antonio may present as if he is from out of space, but space has boundaries, boundaries form substance in all essences."

"Doc, that is why I love to hate, you even though I care for you like my own native son. You are as complicated as they come! But, rest assured that I would not trade you for all four winds as you are the Sherlock Holmes of the mind-fuckers. Help me figure out what happened here and you are set for life. I may be layered in fat like a rolled pig, but you know pigs have the best brains in the kingdom of ethology as you pointed out – Animal Farm not with-standing, Doc."

Cop Doc Allan Cannon, reflecting with spontaneity said,

"Chief, you are not a pig in a rolled blanket. That – rolled blanket is reserved for the fascists who project their shit on you and roll in their smug radical liberalism, which in reality, is as near liberalism as communism is social, and National Socialism is democratic, and the Ayatollah cares for humanity and grace served as a cold dish."

Chief Markowitz said, "You are too fuck__ smart, you are the mind behind the curtain, so go to work. Thanks, Doc. I am right here if you need me."

As soon as the Chief went out, Antonio disclosed he could not believe it but when he had changed his name, Cop Doc Allan had forgotten him. He was his childhood chum. He said I am what I am believed to be Cop Doc

Allan. They were commenting in whispers I heard well, how weird, but you did reach a shit heal like me at all. I am a sudden shit heal, or well, I became a paranoid schizo, so to speak, to give them what they want. I would rather retreat into total abject withdrawal then deal with the puritans ready to roast me in their political correctness, which is their own bloodlust in forcing their form of liberalism which is worse than communism, fascism and every ism one can think of where culture, art in classic form and diligence of responsibility is washed away in their chilling vision of what is right and wrong, based on special interests as the Judeo-Christian and Eastern World faith is drained out as archaic. Social and Psychological Engineering forced on the world of humanity is the most inhumane and subtle of all inhumanity. I am one example crucified, Dr. Cannon, as I am stereotyped as the killer and you in fighting for my treatment are caught unaware will become crucified as well, Sir."

Antonio, they could crucify, and with my sins they can as well by overstepping my own boundaries as a Cop Doc. Antonio now alone with Doc Allan Cannon moved with what was almost 'panache'. He was hatching with intensity – as when a dim flame 'ignites' into a torch unlit.

One dim, and one bright, a correspondence of numinous energy fuels the fire in war. In the shadow of innocence lies some guilt; and in the guilt of innocence lies some tragic flaw in pith. A flaw that is as beautiful and telling as a stone with a cornice chip revealed only in the future that is paved with eulogized stones. Stone cold hidden meaning that lines one's Sisyphusian task with no solace and no meaning to be grasped.

Cop Doc Allan knew he was in the presence of another mind that was great in its ability to pick up patterns in its beautiful ugliness. Cop Doc Allan Cannon was pleased as he took respectful pause. As he paused, he felt a chill in his loins as he pondered, could Antonio be a killer? He knew reasons passion as a scientist that the remote possibility needed to be laid bare and hopefully prove barren as hypothesis. Yet, as remote as any hypothesis, he would need to rule it out with the strategic power of persuasion and empathy.

Allan could not rule out Antonio as a murderer, not just yet. Antonio surprisingly broke his silence and meditation on transference and said to Allan.

"Cop Doc Allan, please let me eat some of that Jewish Soul food, I am hungry. I need to collect my strength. I like you, Doc. I know that I know you from somewhere in my past. Can you heat up the pastrami?"

"Sure, Antonio, let's eat. I think we should just gobble it down and not bring unneeded attention to you again. We have a lot to figure out together and 'you' need to educate me to assist you in gaining insight as to what may have really happened. Is that okay, with you?"

"Doc, I would eat a strip off a cow's teat if I was in the field right now and I was a bull.

Allan drew attention as his expression changed to perplexed and he realized the fact Antonio had picked it up. This was all done in nano-seconds and the analyst's self-understanding and emotional control must always be one step ahead of the next anticipated move. It was not a hostile engagement: However, a respectful parley in knights jostling for the truth by fixing the Seventh Seal unbeknownst to the other blue knight as the seventh sense.

Sleuth's parlaying and stopping by pausing with synchronized interruption after a loud and deep breath with uncanny irony, exhaling,

"Hey, Doc it was a slip – as in a slip of the tongue. Does that mean I wanted to ever do that on Christine? You may think so but not me. Sometimes, a cigar is just a cigar, did not your guru Dr. Freud say that Doc? I heard you talk with Chief Markowitz."

Although Allan knew it was not only ironic as in a style of expression, but an existential and dynamic sensibility in hidden meaning within expression was laid out here.

Det. Antonio began to un-wrap the Pastrami on heavy club and tear the mustard pack open with his teeth as he splayed it and it slowly dripped on to the sandwich.

Allan, in mimicked form, followed through in military cadence at least in Form. In his frustration with Antonio, he reverted to his structured and pro-forma analytic days.

"So, Antonio, I imagine we can talk a bit while we down the sandwich and chew the fat away from the meat. I wonder if you wonder what you meant by saying we know we know each other from somewhere before?"

"I do not know, Doc, but it was if I knew you from some past hall in the corridors of my mind with a feeling when you were out and Dr. Klover strapped me down as if I had a dream but I could not have been sleeping, Doc. Anyhow, I felt as if we knew each other in a different life. I mean as if you were a Roman General or something. Maybe a doc to the Centurions and I was a Captain seeing you. Not like in Nero times, but as in your favorite."

Interrupting Antonio, Cop Doc Allan asked,

"What favorite? What are you referring to Antonio?"

Antonio, strong in voice, bellowed out, "Marcus Aurelius the Emperor. Is it not alleged he met with the Jewish Mystic who when the later ignoble incestuous Cesar had murdered the greatest and decent Emperor of Rome. He was also secretly warred on by Bar Kochba who had tutored him privately as much as Aristotle did for Alexander the Great."

"Incredible, Antonio, where did you learn that secret?

Antonio, without any hesitation, darted out his hypothesis as to his memory.

"A friend I called a blood brother who was a Jewish kid was skinny unlike you Doc. [smile] I admired him. He was one of the toughest scrappers, we grew up with in an Irish and Italian neighborhood. He was the Jewish kid, and we had another, one black kid. But they were not our tokens in those days as we did not even know what that meant. We all actually felt they were cool and liked them otherwise it would be boring. His name was Allan, but with a last name like Horowitz. He was the smartest of all us kids, but just disappeared into the blue. I was not sure 'why?' I heard he became kind of religious in his teens. We still felt he was one of our dead end kids, but he felt awkward. I guess like that Greek/Roman Kid, he hung out with, meaning me. The Jews have their 'Rituals,' like us Catholics, Doc. He may have just felt he outgrew us, or we were not good enough. It was weird, but I never stopped thinking of him and how we were good kids and that was the best time of my life. Well, at least when I was a kid. His first name was Allan and he had a tough time as we all did as kids. But he was loyal to friends and family alike."

Silence pervaded the room again and this time it was not Antonio that had slid into a feigned look with a plastic smile of anxiety rising; it was Cop Doc Allan. He looked as if he saw Cesar's ghost as Chief Julius hawked up in a loud bellow,

"Doc Allan, you okay?"

Doc Allan Cannon pushed his phonetic ability to its best performance as he articulated in a strong voice that belied his feelings of weakness and nausea.

"Yes, all's okay. Thank you, Chief Markowitz."

Antonio's pitched anxiety with deep audible drumming in the cadence of labored breathing tented his emotions out of the blue. It was out of the blue for both Antonio and Allan like a thunder storm formation blitzkreiging with the hurling of facticity – right in the center of revelation that revealed the naked truth of ageing memories lost in time.

Cop Doc Allan had to, as always, be the Doc and return control to patients. His own unresolved conflict around faith and trauma somehow could not be resolved as of yet. He needed to move into the truth as in a Sophocles play. Like Oedipus seeking truth as ancient as the quest for truth, truth that pays with plucking one's own eyes out after the worse of sins imagined.

Antonio knew truth would be cached in the deception of Lucifer's web entranced in childhood conflicts yet to be resolved. Complicating it all was Cop Doc Allan's incredible circumstances of his childhood friend reemerging in present day as if giving room for pause as Mephistopheles laughed. Could this really be coincidence or serendipity – perhaps as a fool's volley of circumstantial evidence it is all one accident but for anyone knowing the physics of life – G-d does not throw dice, ask Einstein to Newton and one can find the answer.

He knew the metaphor was the reality as a doctor who had not ruled out the mystical artistic artery simply because it was hardest to detect. In the tradition of the mind's best detectives from Jung, May, Hillman, Frankl and Campbell, he was deft toward being humbled. Anything to distract and derail truth as the lair of Mephistopheles in all his guises would rule if allowed the valence in analysis. The devil laid his lair in the details of despair, and surrender to an illusion: Instead of the invisible but ever present – Almighty – the truth of revelations source.

The set up for both was vulnerability and then temptation and offering the most amazing setting for that tragic scene.

Tragic as the snafu – you're caught and on your own when you succumb to the illusion of greed, lust and power for its own sake as in force and domination. The aphrodisiac of man seeking pink petals to drink as woman sucks in the seminal font of masculine raw muscled power is part of the equation but not the whole. Unity and sharing what the other does not have, and in surrendering egotism to ego autonomy is inter-dependence is the only reality.

The associations coalesced as the two warrior poets needed to grab the alliance from sabotage. Dr Allan Cannon would do what was necessary and confess his sins. Salvation lies in the bosom of acceptance and forgiveness as respect and élan grown from such tuber roots in the Spring having Sprung like Stravinsky's rites of passage as the nostrils of Channels perfumes passion – even if poison – had to be drunk in rituals swooning

Bacchius too Apollonian alters. Before Allan could talk, Antonio said,

"Doc, I have to confess something I am ashamed of and always have been. I am a Pacificolini. I mean, my Dad was from the Family, and I did not want to be labeled a wise guy. They crucify Italian Catholic Americans for being part of the Costa nostra, even if Mom is partly Greek. Can you imagine for a moment what it was like to need to change your name because you were scared of being labeled and stuck to a cross because of what someone in your family did?!? I do! I stayed away and lived with my Uncle Frankie M., who my mom married. Do not ask me about her affairs – it is too painful – I love her regardless. She is a good woman but just needed my love as well as my Uncle, I do not judge her." Tears were welling in his eyes now.

"I mean I feel like I was a coward but was not, Doc. It was not fear, really, but a shame of my people if you can imagine what I mean; not about my being born Italian, but about my being born into a Mafia family. I wanted to erase my nationality affiliation. I wish I could be Jewish like you. I also wished I could be black like Kevin. But he also I know at one point went through the same shit feeling; he could not erase his blackness."

"Doc, even with you being Jewish, which I did not know until you broadcast it all over your books and lectures – I have read each one. It is a terrible goblin that I went through. Now you know. You probably think I killed Tommy and Christine."

The tears now flowed, not only from Antonio, but from Allan as he kept trying to say what he would but could not get it out at once. Cop Doc Allan taking his ego as always with patients and hanging it on the proverbial door although invisible – hung tangibly as ever as his raw genius could not be disguised.

Dr. Allan Horowitz aka Cannon began his confession to Antonio.

Antonio's breathing was labored and tears burning as they fell as he listened in empathy, confirming he was no psychopath but an empath – the opposite.

"I am that Jewish kid you were blood brothers with. I am Allan Horowitz, not in name anymore but like your past in name that is haunting you. In reality, I changed my name as well.

This is not what Allan the Cop Doc wanted, or planned on saying, but in the beauty of truth and its power waiting to be liberated by G-d's grace he confessed nonetheless.

"I realized when I became a cop two years before the academy in counter-terrorism infiltration with some undisclosed ties I could break into; I could use my new details as a way to change my name. The shocking truth reared its ugly deaths head. Like you, I too for different reasons changed my name from Horowitz to Cannon. It was at the time too much for me to carry. A decision I regret to this day. I knew since I was a kid that I was the one you felt was a real scrapper as a blood brother was me. Yes, me, the Dirty Jew to be lynched, disemboweled and burnt alive in a crematorium – never able to rid myself of the stain of being a Jew and the oppression if you can imagine that horror of anti-Semitism like being born into a Mafia Family?"

"Can you imagine that reality? Does anybody really understand how and why society can turn mad? To do that what madness and what drive pursues man to want to destroy an entire race, a religion and a whole people while screaming for individual rights and interests? Can society condone hanging a man because he is black, or fixing an Italian American for being related to Mafia members as a prison of stereotypes? I learned my family in Europe descended from Jewish Rabbis and Physicians who served Kings and Queens and the Moors in France and Italy. They had to run to hide my folks when that short, ugly monster Hitler emerged, a rogue, thief and serial killer pervert. From bohemian to madmen as Dr. Walter Langer exquisitely dissected Hitler's mind highlighted. My family kept their names although the numbers branding them was all that is left in the winds blowing Europe as ghosts that haunt. Embers of ashen oblations lit in Kibbutz's as Yarzheit candles in effigy appeal on behalf of their souls as new waves of Anti-Semitic terrorists' firebomb buses and synagogues again. Sacrifices for terrorists who herded them and recorded their identities for infamy are now doing the same all of the Middle-East. My folks in hiding fled to Hungary until Hungarians finally capitulated to the Devil's Lair and my family too were made into dust and ashes"

"I know Antonio; identity is a hard pill to swallow! As an adolescent, I felt I wanted to be just accepted as a good person, and not judged for being a Jew. I loved my people, and all peoples, but my rebellion was standing for Jewish causes without having to be fixed to the cross of Anti-Semitism. We even get blamed for crucifying one of our own Rabbis. Is that insanity, Antonio? Do you think you are a sinner without hope for fear of being crucified or will you take it from me, you are all too human and in-deed humane?!?"

Cop Doc Cannon paused and sighed deeply as he waited for Antonio to respond to him. As if in a paroxysm of guilt for being alive in a world as Mark

Twain put it — regardless of what and how well the Jew does it, and how noble he is — he is always looked at as an 'outsider'. Being a cop, he was always an 'outsider' to his civilian friends. The go to man when in deep trouble. To his patients, he was an 'Alienist', a shrink or outsider. To his own family and faith, he was a maverick at best and at times a rebel as well, since he could not sit in conformities door awaiting passively the next rise and eventual fall of the monster of anti-Semitism. It was this he reflected on in using his own disclosure to strike the heart of his patient and brother in blue such is the inside-outsider dilemma posits is here to stay. Cannon continued as Antonio stayed in silence – corridors still unreachable].

"I was nailed at the cross roads of the adolescent strum and drang of my life's epiphany. Antonio, you are in for a wake up shock, please listen to me, [in a hushed, almost mellifluous, voice that strummed a tune of confession and redemption] Cop Doc Allan had changed his name from Horowitz to the new name, Cannon. He was that little boy you played with and was your blood brother. I am your blood brother. I, too, have my shame, even though I also never negated my Faith. I like you put my life on the line for others. But now I am supposed to after our revelations do the right rule based procedures, like the patrol guide procedures. Procedures for doctors: I am supposed to let you know we are beyond assessment and refer you for another treatment."

[Deeply breathing as if at a fault line of an earthquake lever on the crust of earth bound humility clashed with virtue which lies in the inner cores sun-bound heat.]

"Antonio, I cannot abandon you to the fates at your door – for my moral compass is guiding me as my own voice of conscience. Conscience transcending the banality of the sword of man-made righteousness. There is universal truth and I must listen to my own voice and pursue justice. I now know that I must fight with and wrestle the truth as hard as it is for both of us. Truth to its final analysis – a conclusion that may blind us with the fury of unbridled insight." Pausing, and without surcease, Dr Allan Cannon in a measured austere voice,

"Can you tell me the truth, Antonio, and still trust me, even though I too cowed at one time before the illusion of fear and trembling to a false god? My own false god of fear as my own real identity as a Jew not really different then your own real identity of having a mafia Poppa: An idol which is no longer able to gain entry to my soul and I hope when we are done with assessment and treatment your own soul?

[Light that was uncanny brokered her eerie shimmer through the room. It was not known where it came from, but it did illuminate like a simple light.]

Antonio coughed up what sounded like phlegm, but it was the wafer stuck in the throat of fear as he bellowed out his lancing words unminced,

"Doc Allan Cannon, you are no longer that little boy you were. I am no longer the little boy I was. We are men, are we not? Is it not true, it is a cross I bear with that other Rabbi as you do, Kevin did, and that scrawny French kid who became a film producer genius that you are somehow still connected with. I cannot believe it – is it man made, or serendipity that brought us together or as you quote in your work, 'G-d does not throw dice.'

You are powerful and given that power by G-d for a reason! Don't throw the baby out with the bath water, Doc! We all sin, Doc, I respect you more and need your help. It is part of who we are, we were brought together again for a reason. You have awoken my faith in G-d and trust in me. I feel strangely relived and human again Doc."

[Antonio pausing with deep empowering exhalation and with passion and pain interweaving in expression sighed a sign of genuine relief perchance, even for a moment.]

"I would take a shot for you, Doc, you are family. I would for Tommy as well. I could never hurt him. Christ sake, I fucked Christine, Doc. I just remembered I loved her as he did, but sacrificed my love of her for Tommy. He deserved her more then I as a brother/partner getting a wife. She was irresistible, and I sinned major time with her! I brought her to heights and she loved me too for even more than a one-night affair. I could not lose Tommy and convinced her I was not worthy and he was. He never knew I would die for them and be crucified. I did as soul murder my own one can say. But, I do not want to be crucified now, but I will be, Doc, if you play by the books. That is, unless you help me, Doc. I know you feel you are low. But you were a fucking kid from the ghetto without a name – Ghetto and a Jewish, Irish and Italian one as well. Doc! Stop torturing yourself – you are human and so am I. Please, Doc, be real and do not throw me out with the bath water of Roman Legions gone bad. For heaven's sake, my Centurion brother, let your integrity be flexible for the sake of justice – true justice not ivory tower justice but street cop justice."

[Chief Markowitz and Maccione in choir and practiced voices ushered out a bellow of thunder in ovation to intuition of breaches in the dam of stoicism so hard it transcended all codes save the blue wall.]

210

"Doc you've been in there for two hours. You okay? Cop Doc Allan Cannon opened the door put his wedding finger to his lips in gesture to Antonio and said to the Chief to order in dinner, "Whatever you choose, boss. For Antonio as well." He went back in with Antonio and said,

"I trust you know we got to take on the crucible without any break in reality and let me do the sifting through. I want you to wash your face and stretch and take some breaths, I will get the coffee, so you could clear your head with me and then we will do an existential analysis together, Antonio. Antonio turned and said,

"Doc, only this once will I take the risk and say it as I see it in my eyes. Horowitz is a beautiful name. But think as you always say to me and others, if G-d does not throw dice, he never wanted anything for you, but for you to be named Cop Doc Allan Cannon – you are the finest and so is G-d's chosen name for you. Salute and Shalom Aleichem!" Cop Doc Allan Cannon said,

"I am with you, Antonio."

They knocked knuckles as warrior brothers and were ready to stand even on the precipice of the Abyss that the other-side is ever ready to erect with ghosts, demons and sacrifices. Both warriors unsheathed the sword and were ready to battle. But with whom? For what purpose? Who was the demon to battle and who the saint? Did either really exist or was this a folie a deux ingenious as it was invidious?

# Chapter 16

## The Red Haired Colored Recluse: Fanged Puritan Hedonist

Cop Doc Allan left Bellevue as Gargoyles that shelved their gilded edges in the corridor of his mind vanquished. Clinical notes left their mark as Allan opened up his hidden NY Cop Doc Journal and scribed his passages for prosperity.

Antonio's case resonated as did his insights into himself provoked a wish for renewed therapy. He knew as soon as he heard a message from Chief Markowitz that he was approved for promotion to Detective Sergeant for his specialized work in the department and union. This special designation meant a shift in the paradigm of the police department's bureaucracy as having a glass ceiling on mental health training and education for officers.

Allan dealing with police officers on the fringe and edge of Eden gone deep south and pulling lost officers back to sanity and investment in life itself was appreciated, after all.

A text was gnawing away at his hip like a buzzing of a mosquito when one is trying to get a moment of repose. He looked down at his buzzing ringer which could receive messages. He could not believe what he read out of the blue. He was sure he had misread the print as the shock of the cryptic letters compelled his balance to twirl as he landed on his knees. The text read in bold print,

"I love you baby cop doc, Al. I am going back to my born again Granddad I need my time and space. I will let you know when I am coming back home. I left food in the freezer for you to eat. The dog is fed and I left her, since she was your favorite not mine."

Allan Cannon rushed home, almost getting into a three car collision. Surely, her promises meant more than idle words left like spikes under the heels of a jogger ready to mount the Olympus of a star performance. Her sadistic need to flay him as her mother flayed her father was done and there was no way of undoing this. Allan was greeted by Sig-Anna, named after Sigmund Freud and Anna Freud, when as a couple, they adopted her from the shelter.

The Beatle's song, 'All alone again – naturally...' greeted him as his conscious awareness returned almost a half hour later. The Beatles he loved now grated his soul like a callous clipper on an in grown toenail as he shuddered in pain.

Numb, Dr. Allan could not trust his senses and he ran into the kitchen and found the fridge filled with some purchased food for dinner. His private car was gone. He used his department vehicle and in sheer panic he rushed to the bank and found as others had warned him his accounts were drawn. Allan had paid her debts he never incurred to care for her. Tears felt uncontrollable as did his sobbing. He rushed back home and closed the door, fed the dog and placed paper for her to urinate if she needed. He felt peed on and did not care less for a mess anymore.

Looking in the mirror, Allan stared into his own eyes, carmine red as the pain felt almost unbearable. It was agony, as if his soul was crucified alive. He wrote immediately after awakening from a sleep that knocked him out after crying and holding her pyjamas and dirty panties stained with period blood. He breathed in her smell, but it did little good, as she had abandoned him once again.

He jotted down in his diary,

"My eyes burn in the saline that emerges in a sea of bitter tears as the sweet images of dreams envelope my consciousness."

Dr. Allan Cannon lay in his bed, weeping and inconsolable. Painting with poetic license, colors of fury and passion dripped out in a melee. Dripping anguish like Goya's blood his tears fell like the Bulls of Bordeaux being readied for the slaughter.

Allan cared little for convention in his private sensibility as long as it did not harm others. Allan could be honest, even if it thrust pain deep into his own side. Such was his own overbearing moral compass which at times trickled numbness into his ankles as they bleed: That part of the ankles that holds up the legs known as Achilles tendon grew numb when he faced rigidity in his mate. His own masochistic tendencies were buoyed to the limits of tolerance with her sadistic tendencies.

Shadows of his training analysis at the most conservative enclave of Freudian analysis sketched images where great grandpa Sigmund and Grandma Anna to the present day sauntered as peripatetic and wandering philosophers trying to unravel the dynamics of conflict and compromise. He could not compromise with his betraying spouse as the NY Psychoanalytic Institute and Society intimated.

Allan learned from the best to let go in his associations that were anything but free and in doing just that paradoxically inner-sight was reached in an almost Parisian way; A paternal Parisian bon vivant nervy chutzpah lain alongside his hidden Stoic Persian Jewish ancestry. Allan was a survivor. Life as one of his close relations who survived underground sewers in Warsaw Poland was preferable to death appeased in despair.

Resistance when others were rounded up like bulls and bovines for the slaughter as Goya's shadows revealed as artist bemoaned his losses in artistic immortality for all connoisseurs' to mourn with surreptitious satisfaction. Allan's predecessor resisted and survived – defiant as Goya to the pressure of conformity as sheep being led to the slaughter a myth as cruel and invidious as conformity itself.

Allan saw Lilia's unwashed panties on the top of the shower stall, without doubt, left to comfort both/and aggrieve him in his morning. He in his forlorn sense of self debased his own sense of self-respect and sexualized his anger letting his nostrils fill his emptiness with his Cribriform Plate filling itself as her stunning odors brought relish as memories of love-making returned.

Allan allowed his libidinal energies to flow over grief, and cap his creativity with Destrudos victory in the darkest shadow of addictive escape. It was an escape from her rejecting his love and desire to love her as his wife for life.

Unlike his therapy notes, his love notes were written as if done by a scribe. His French blood dominated and his romantic heart burned,

"If poison is passion, let me drink from her chalice with eternal thirst. Awake and release me from the pit of empty dreams. Oh Lord, help me see the light, for the darkness fades and the healing must begin!"

It is hard to imagine her grace and beauty it had a mystique, hardly tangible and yet as ethereal as a fog that blinds with violence and kisses the wet dew with masculine lips. Who could understand his pain so great?

She glided across the hard steel that now encases my heart, it was warm and open prior to her invasion. It is inconceivable to have sensed her love and callous web infusing each the other as she deigned her strands downward that would bind me to her as a Swallow Butterfly on a Raptures beak.

Lilia ensnared me as her pray, culling me in a sonorous voice that begs me and haunts me in its twine. I followed as her pawn unwittingly to my wit's end with no end in sight. Yet, it is surreal and passionate, as I still love her and I fall once again. Love and hate present as poles oppositional and complex.

Yet, for Lilia all is one and linear. I am the recluse's desert. How demure is the blush of her ardor – from pink to red hot as her Puritanical withdrawal as oblation is devoured in absentia. Aye, there is the rub, the twitch of her thighs and the wink of her eyes all invitations of the femme fatale once beloved now so forlorn.

I was number three on her list of husbands down. So many more in the loops in her atypical over 200 lbs in a

5'11" frame. Her hypnotic kind veneer belied eyes, a veneer so polished she seduced her men with keen relish. I awake and cry night after night,

"I've been had?"

"Who am I?"

"I could be you!"

"A victim of circumstance," or

"A fate accompli?"

"Who is she really?"

"A wounded nightingale with tragic flaws I failed to assist?"

"A chasm, where men dare to leap head first into the abyss?"

"A Queen to launch a thousand ships into the Aegean Sea for a perish on a Hellenic whim?"

Sirens have disguised themselves as the historic femme fatales and men of honor have emblazoned the battlefield with their carcasses as so many knight benighted of honor and glory as a moth to the flame of passion – where reason is spent in a moment – where death bewitches life's erect stance.

Allan mused in a medium of madness, where passion, drenching his reason and erudition like a diluted tea percolated from desiccated rose petals freeze dried were drunk without boundaries. He spoke aloud to himself to hear the words of abandon into unrequited desire burned saline tears in his bloodshot eyes half-drunk with alcohol swallowed and with adrenalin overload as cortisol rushes impacted on his mind:

"If poison is passion, let me drink of the chalice that seduces me, let my Roman jaw lay upon her supple breasts in the pulse of her life line, even if but for a moment of ecstasy: Ek-Stasis – disruptive short breath and death. Call her Liluth, Muse, Siren, Vixen but not Courtesan, for there is honor in a woman who calls herself by her real name. There is shame and sham in one who honors herself as noble when her veins course with poison and betrayal …

To me, she was simply called Lilia and Rachel the bi-polar radiation of her iridescent sexuality to entrance me in human bondage. How that name of princess of darkness and light spells a haunting glance into the corridor of my minds secret abode.

A catacomb which drips with honey and milk spiced with nightshade in red passion. Her smell permeates my very nature and desire amidst flames of passion and fire.

Drenched in her web, she laid as a lattice of a beautiful recluse, which makes the praying mantis look trite in her pallid swallow of her mate's head as his worldly glance fades to black – she sucks my marrow relishing her bone head as I explode in the breach of equilibrium on a fault line of deaths shroud engulfed by the wet intoxication of her lips pressed tightly shut."

Realizing he was allowing himself to speak in his aloneness out loud, he reversed and slinked back into silence. The imagery swept through his mind as a real fever covered over the image of Lilia as a Lioness biting him as she grabbed the Lions mane as blood drawn felt as quivers and shakes riddled his body.

He reflected my soul slips into her canal, which with exquisite genius that is transcendent shapes amorphous clay into her elusive and creative natural sculpture pink hewn into a rough remnant of a warrior now vanquished: A real man cave. A white devil in her mind as a cast of her dark father ready to emerge when fire and ice, light and darkness, black and white chiaroscuro played like a tarantella dancing into her night. Color is obliterated on the whore and Madonna construct she has laid out as the floor of love and hate.

Call her relentless. Yes, I will survive as the haunting continues. I own it. By profession, I am the least likely victim, yet the most susceptible, a healer and doctor of the mind. That drew me in like a wave into a maelstrom.

Beauty is truly in the eye of the beholder gifted with looks and brains, she was as not a predator but seductively my superior in the carnal realm of the sensual made elusive and desirable as an addictive fix.

I found my level below the surface of her malcontent. The charm of the line of borders dim in the color I saw which was belied by the black and white lines she drew in the sand of the pit. Call me Sam-son, a judge who could have, should have, would have known better – but, alas, did not. Color her mark by the dye Lilia, a bitter sweet taste ever in my olfactory canal and taste buds.

Lilia was a master of relations that is the polis market economy no different on the West Coast of Eden as the East coast of Athens Acropolis – where gods with a small g preside in judgment.

Who she was was more defined in her pitch then the pith of moment unfurled in the wings of desire and resistance: Temptation and the temptress desiring to devour her prey without being able to relinquish her need for compulsion as much as her doctor husband. She could sell Socrates henbane and make a pitch to yield a snow storm in a desert as one dies of thirst with satiation riddled on his gnarled jaw – mirages.

It is no accident that Socrates, a healer of lost souls, drank hemlock, and Sam-son, a judge, a healer of the psyche drank the wet craving of his Lilia's seductive lips with nightshade glistening into the August night of his minds eclipse. Cop Doc Allan wrote in his diary,

"Yes, it haunts me as I write this for you to read and witness with me. It helps to give me voice without platitudes or plead for mercy to gladiators on the left and right side of the fence of life. Freud said in every marriage the father and mother stand in the corner of the betrothed room. In our society post modern it is Uncle Sam and Aunt Tabitha, think about it! Where is G-d in this G-dless society? Alas, He is still here – we chose to look away … We are all guilty of this sin. I try to embrace the Almighty, but how difficult it is in the waves of desire and passion left unmet. Awake and cast off the slumber of illusions left in the dust of abusive pasts and see the dawning of the light supernal and crisp that ushers in a new dawn. A writer no less than a poet, who is emerging from the tortured love I have lost and perhaps as paradise will never find."

Cop Doc Allan fell asleep on the hard antique roll down original Secretariat Desk he bought at the Virginia Laws Auction House. He ushered out of his sleep and heard himself say as he knocked his head upon awakening,

"Awake I say and yet the slumber of having been knocked off my center. A trial is a test to shake even the best from complacency to either despair or to meaning in the struggle for sensibility in a world at times bereft of a soul and heart. From adoration to vilification is a snug description of the Sirens call and yet as a man and a doctor I am taught to endure – where is the twain drawn? Between her lips that I as a man kiss in a deep embrace messy, wet and tumultuous as a rippled sea with a maelstrom that sucks in all she can?"

Weeping inner-sight resisted against sleep as Morpheus with Theta became visual images dancing to Stravinsky's, the Rite of Spring as a Sonata with words that emerge as elocution in his minds imagination. Dr Allan Cannon was muttering as the alcohol and sedative took effect as he accidentally swallowed both as he was trying to drown out his searing pain. The dream was neither a nightmare nor a fantasy. He was unsure if he was dreaming or awake. The cop doc lost his balance as movement and thrashing on the bed occurred in his aloneness with all but G-d.

Blinded as Oedipus in the fold of a withering and yet supple breast that heaves in the desiring chest of every man, beast, and angel as one Lilia materialized.

In light of her darkest side, this white devil was a woman who was a princess shattered by losses which he sought to heal: He scribbled again as a writer and shrink who was now shrunk to lower than any of his patients in self wallowing and pity for himself,

"Oh, never play Faust as all her majesties agents know, as the knight who lost his step from too devoted a service in an English Medieval bar ... The name of Mephistopheles echoes in a narcissus baritone as the foreground fades from crimson to blackened white hues. The image of mothers attempted suicide as my haunting image. I witnessed mom cutting her wrists open with dad's razors at eleven years old. An eleven year old child-man: I was a man prematurely hatched who never tasted the foibles of youth. My fall from innocence as I tried to stop her from squelching her beautiful life – Success: I rescued her from the succubus of her inner demons. Such is the trauma of her own past tossed on me as her son now: Pyrrhic is Victory. The healer cast back to the shores of my powerless attempts to save her life from the ignominy of each woman needing rescue. A lady in need of rescue as the trap of masochistic linchpins holding my path of salvation in the elusive plates of desire wrapped in Pyrrhic Victory. Rescue in which all else is saved except my own redemption as a man – independent from the bondage of ideals lost on the path to the Oracle of life's markings."

How history repeats itself in endless repetitions in a compulsive toss of the dice, even thrice.

Lilia's heavy body was beautiful to him and images of her nude kept reappearing in his bodily memories. The tarantella beats her erotic tunes sonorous and intoxicating. She sucks the beauty of her man as so much matter can wield to blind the heroic into the mundane catacombs of shallow conquests where love is thrust a fatal blow via greed which is always base and vengeances lust.

Awake, he kept telling himself, do not give into the force of sleep as he heard an alarm go off in his head: He managed to crack the tip of his pencil as the jarred edge shadowed words etched on a napkin of substance taken from the elegant Shanghai Restaurant,

"Intrigue presses the soul to heights one would never imagine plummeting from – heights to the nadir without a parachute I leapt from abyss: abyss … yet, as I ponder on the train without a destination empty shells of dreams splinter the rails of destiny and whose choice? Mine!"

The echoes of poverty bang at the door; still, the temptation to plunge back in with her and leap from one eternal return of promises and rent dreams mark every step of the way: Genius and madness are checked mates … both go too far! In every love relation, genius is mixed with madness and that is the comical that shadows every tragedy. It is one bewitching to another that echoes in through the hearts ability to pound its own beat. The predator finds it and the prey succumbs.

Dr Allan struggled to stay awake as he read his notes in the preface to a book called our life in love together,

"The prayer to the eternal light of G-d shields one from the fall: Fallen rise and get up as the Lord lowers, so does he raise one out of the pit. Faith infuses and emboldens every narrow strait threatened with destruction. When man and women fails, when family and friends can't share in one's own travail,

G-d reveals the way; his ways are of mercy and forgiveness and open the doors for he is not like us. Despair is when we forget who he is and his infinite power and mercy."

Dr. Allan Cannon was awakening out of what could have become an overdose of alcohol and adrenalin. Allan felt spent as fear embraced the cold in his room and exacted the price of utter exhaustion he began trembling. He spoke to himself as if G-d listened as he looked at his shelter dog as pathetic as himself in his moment of sorrow.

"I remember writing that piece, when I held my spouse, it seemed as distant as the constellations in the clear blue clouds in sight, but light years away lost in the constriction of a narrowed conscious dreaming. Dreaming, while awake in contemplation poetic and yet the culmination of my bane. Sleep has kissed my lips in place of love; grief has sealed my eyes closed. I slip into her silent lair and she is ever present again: Heaven or

223

hell I enter the tight portals allowing passage of one more embrace…"

Dr Allan's dog Sig-Anna barked aloud with ever glossy eyes from cataracts as middle life shook her puppy's innocence away. Allan shook his head at 0300 hours, indeed the headache confirmed to him, he was alive, in-deed… Allan had night terrors, in which he awoke – suddenly – shaken to his core as he felt dead while breathing. He knew the experience of terror. All cop docs, 'Do!'

Allan fell asleep as he felt the gloss cover Sig-Anna's eye lids as the film in his own descended upon the glint in his left eye resisting closure of what was and could never be in this lifetime again.

# Chapter 17

## Boomerang: Unfurled at the Altar of Peace

The fanatic pull of the Procrustean bed closed in Lilia as compulsion was too much for Cop Doc Allan to bear. He awoke! Allan plugged in his coffee drip maker: Awake from the pull of the sonorous siren of Bacchus and Apollonian poles in twain where the East meets the West and has split the Twain – the coffee mug beckoned hello as it filled dark and hot.

Cop Doc Allan had work to do. He could not help surrendering to the power of love. Perspective coursed an erring forceful path succumbing again to a love unrequited tortured and absurd. Dr. Allan held onto his faith, reflective of his belief in the Almighty: Poets, Seers, Prophets and Dreamers and Peripatetic Street Walkers penniless all held court.

How do you re-direct your attention to the power of choice and refrain to experience life? Fuck, "it is what it is."

Life is too beautiful to leave vanquished in a pool of tears of what could have been – he embraced what will be taken in life and living – now!

Herr Professor Sigmund Freud got it right. Lieber und Macht made the world spin, but Psychologist Dr. Viktor Frankl recalibrated the axis of the humane in the animal as the center of existential re-direction.

Letting go and letting love ensue cannot be pursued. The epiphany of being-humane is found in the rational left at the door frame – existential on the right post – the middle is the leap into the unknown. The love of the alliance forged in therapy was the challenge of his life work as a Cop Doc. Allan crowned each day with play as possibility.

In a way, passion kept him young and able to do the 'nigh impossible' laying on the shoulders of one Doc helped keep him from his natural tendencies of introversion. Possibilities were fragments in space that offered steps that seemingly materialized out of ether. A number of calls from the Chief of Homicide & the Manhattan District Attorney's Office came through requiring his immediate assistance.

Allan slapped his own face clean as the nubs absorbed the Passion cologne he slapped on his face. Unaware of his magnetic attractiveness, as he looked like George Clooney mixed with Tom Hanks. His green eyes looked demure and flashed sex appeal to women. Eyes for Dr. Cannon were mirrors of the mind, paradoxical as his enigmatic mind – the more insecure he felt, the bolder the hue of greenish blue coloration.

Betrayed by his red haired, blue eyed siren of a wife on a runaway platform, where her iterations spun unresolved daddy complexes. Her Cinderella wishes compelled a defense in his Nubs that pricked female passerbys with flirtatious aphrodisiac impact. Allan Cannon's shirt and tie was positioned at an angle, where slightly hidden hair on his chest provoked snuggles in its symbolic power of flirtatious hints.

Lisa Wei Feng just opened her door and almost seeming smelled him as she looked sweaty. She called herself in her irascible mood, his bitch. Beads of perspiration arouse from her porous hardened look of a bitch in heat as he saw her last. His lascivious masculine response provoked a desire for her to turn to being just a little bit bitchy in his eyes. But in Allan's eyes, she was not bitchy at all. She glistened with a flirtatious smile that made him charge as a bull, but halt with a chill in his face as his tongue held itself in abeyance.

Allan boringly licked his own lips, instead of hers. It was as if Lisa was a different woman, without makeup, and with a soft look with gentle eyes like a doe in a heath laid out with lilies as he saw her and a sparrow suddenly slammed into their glass window plummeting to her death below his window. Suddenly, becoming demure and bewitching in her trance like invitation to Allan, she presented as a lady of elegance.

Cop Doc Cannons mind drifted and he felt heat he had denied for a long while. He as much as her in a synchrony – reversed roles – she uncontrollably did the unfathomable and in compelling attraction undid his tie and licked his mouth and swallowed his chin nubs. She licked his sweat, as he felt shock and fear, but exquisite attraction.

The bounce of intensity, beyond his rational beliefs – exploded as he could not contain herself. The taboo became ecstasy for both as she made her move. He passively succumbed as if he were a Lion led to his slaughter by a doe with lilies in her eye bleached red with fiery passion and unruly lust. In an interesting, but perplexing attraction, the same strength and weirdness of introspection enflamed their passion as if each could breathe in the breath of one another, the veil of dark chambers – their ambiance. Fantasies of both were the same, except she wanted to be him and absorb his soul. She bent to his mid-waist swallowing him into herself as she tore off his shirt and biting his hairy chest and kissing his erect nipples as he began to kiss her hair and her soft and supple breast. He was squeezing her breasts together as he placed their nipples into his Roman Jaw.

Pain and losses unrequited for different reasons were released as moisture became saturated and he lifted her up kissing her thighs and then her very essence as a woman.

Lisa Wei Feng pushed him out after she moaned and swallowed him all and took him in deep and long. She moved rhythmically as his mouth was wet with her moisture and taste. Reaction formation of the opposite of desire was hatched as polemical vortices emerged in what appeared to be a compliment of perfect symmetry of man and woman merging. The fit of male and fe-male brilliance as the inevitable law of attractions and the third law of Newton physics erupted and prevailed – genius in carnal pleasure! Reflections of the supernal in liberation of man-woman in one – pregnancy as the recombinant DNA of sperm and egg – genius united.

He took in her yellow river as she flowed into his mouth and her unique taste and smell permeated his mind in the most ancient chambers of his cribriform. She muttered, "I am dirty, I didn't shower, honey, let me wash." He held her in his eyes, as he did not let go and held on for all her dew as nourishment from the gardens of her passion and heart swept asunder. She looked into his orange hue circle of pupils, surrounded by a tinge of blue portends to follow as a circle of green freshness teased an endless future in his passion filled eyes. Allan was still boyish in mid-life and she loved that aspect of him. Lisa desired serving Allen, and with passion, pulled him to her lips as she grasped the swiftness and suddenness lessening the swell of attention as she took him in. She encompassed his masculine impulse and took him to the edge of ecstasy as he tried to pull out – falling back in loves vibration – he stroked her hair and she grabbed him as she took in his power and vitality.

The Joust begun in earnest at the point of ecstasy as he thrust and she sheathed his thrust in conquest. She orgasmed as his mouth dripped and he drank her moisture till she was dry. They would be inseparable and insuperable in one cataclysm destined to happen, all objectivity lost to the power of love and desire. Chief Attorney Lisa Wei Feng licked her lips as a Spartan Queen smiling. She knew she had her man as she placed a sour dried plumb in her mouth, savoring the taste of the sour and then placed a maple sugar candy drop in her mouth. She, unlike the wife who betrayed him, had led him to the truth of what love could be.

But he resisted as she could not be who she now was. Reality was shattered as Allan felt guilt coarse his veins. Lisa Wei Feng sensed she had to have him cross the Rubicon of her fantasy and invite him into a point of no return. She bit her own lips till they bled, licked her own blood and said kiss me to him. She was biting in her taste as odd as her response to Dr Cannon's comment looking in horror, amusement and yet attraction. He in excitement said, "I imagine that is a very peculiar taste Ms. Wei Feng, it is not Sour and Vanilla."

She said, in a girlish and yet brash way, "I love new tastes of our own, you are my King and I your Empress."

Allan could not penetrate her inhibitions with enough zeal as she moaned and he laid loose the window that barred entry. She opened up her invitation and he entered: She and he merged in the genius of their bodies as a pretzel.

Messy with the tastes of souls merging into one absorbing the others missing core – centering each in balance. Her cold sore meant nothing as he swallowed her virus as he would her darker self. His genius lay in knowing her darkest fears and secrets. She knew his well and intuitively every fluid ounce she fearlessly ingested without peer. He was her lover, and she was his lover. Destined as intersecting lovers – tragic as Eagle's bound in a concrete tower. Optimism like survival grasps the last gulp of air as it soars to heaven to descend into this existence called life. Losses washed away as true genius now became united in the tragic moment and pith of human life to be whisked away as too precious to resist for either half: Each had become each other as they each lost their own masks and found power. In their united identity of anima: animus – yin and yang – force of societies bounds let loose their constriction as love yielded produce of genuine liberation.

Uninhibited flavors coalesced without boundaries of desire, which would trickle into love as polarity channels in the innermost chambers of action potentials in our nervous systems natural progress of growth. They could never be the same or look at each other in the same way.

No artificial fences and no intruders could ever break their bond.

Neither would ever admit, nor succumb, to the shallow superficial nihilism and ignorance of the high and low class fuck buddies as many a man and woman agreed on as friends with benefits which left each bankrupt in endless partners with lust and empty nights. Open marriage the lie created in the shadow of cowardice – closed. Both would agree, although never say, it is better to confess love then stay silent in the hypocrisy of surrender to the never satiable destructive impulse of anonymity and sexual fascism in the guise of liberation.

They transcended the earthly limits and were angelic in wisdom as each drank the others essence, and they both knew the elixir as energy itself in swapped spit and sweat.

They became man and woman. Ancient in modern halls of justice and medicine – applied – they defied the odds and became the image of their creator in love.

Man and woman left untrammeled: They both were romantic and intense lovers that had in a moment unplanned and un-staged crossed the Rubicon – perhaps as apart in life and living as Marc Anthony and Cleopatra.

Would their respective place of comfort and peace find solace in the Library of Fifth Avenue in NYC, or in the burnt offering of genius and madness in Alexandria posted in their bookmark titled – Liberation (Marc Anthony & Cleopatra). The Aha moment struck in the heat of her superficial feminism and his colloquial chauvinism.

Allan was all man and yet had a feminine side in her rapture he immersed in, as she, all woman, had a masculine side within by embracing his potent channel. Channels switched as East fucked West: Each had the exact fit although looking like ends and odds with each other made them inexorably compelled to compulsion of repetition. The drifting of contents was united as the East of Eden intersected and re-connected with the West fever of pacific tsunamis. Flooding all senses with sensibility of love unfurled. Lisa Wei Feng was ready to raise her voice at him as if possessed with fever biting his lips so hard without warning that an 'ouch' would have ushered out uncontrollably. Instead, in silence, a tear spilled out. He was Spartan in pain, but in emotion he was sensitive.

She looked in his eyes with dominance and licked and tasted his blood and with a tear from her eyes moved his head down to her mouth and licked and sighed as if she tasted a drop of ice-cream and maple as she swallowed.

She moved back as he began to kiss her all over and deeply. She began the same on him as they lay in his office from the couch to the floor.

Allan was erect beyond Lisa's imagination and she could smell his heat and excitement. As much as they resisted, they were overwhelmed and it was her on top from the beginning as she controlled his move which he did not resist. It was shocking and yet satiation way beyond a great fuck.

Allan and Lisa met in a dance which combined the sexual and aggressive with the center of her existence as dominant as he surrendered, she switched roles and he dominated and she succumbed. The messiness and the heated passion was beyond any experience she ever had, and to be honest beyond whatever he had tasted, and felt with any other woman. He realized after the euphoria, that like an addiction, she had tasted every part of his body, and he hers. They had obsessively shattered every boundary with the combustion of a compulsion exploding on a fault line.

"Was it love or depravity?" They smiled as Allan actually asked her. She in an almost chilling smile of love and pain, in his large ears as she mouthed his earlobes with a wince of pained pleasure whispered, "Dr Freud ala Sherlock Holmes does it matter which split in your own personality enjoyed and recoils – both of you are all mine: You'd better be!" Lisa turned red as her cheeks flushed with fire. "Doc Allan Cannon, I'll warn you, once don't let me see another woman in your lair or else!"

Allan froze as he felt a chill. "I am only fucking with you babe. Get it real babe and I will never harm you! Not as long as you are my special Freud. Fuck, Holmes, he will always get his foe and perhaps be a fawn in a lioness's jaw. Relax babe."

Allan remembered this for a moment and as quickly got distracted in his orgiastic feelings turning into emotions. Warm and nurturance emerged as they now held one another without surcease. Each licked each other's eyes and mouths as tears dropped and were vanquished in hunger appeased.

They had every body fluid commingled as his blood almost stopped bleeding and he not her bit his own lip. It spiced her own equilibrium as she oscillated in ex-stasis as he held his lip with droplets of blood for her as she licked his drop of red blood and smiled and kissed him deeply. They were both merged in their losses and trauma. She needed solace and succorance from the depths of unbridled passion with reason that transcended the mundane.

She orgasmed in multiple twitches and screamed as if in pain and pleasure as she played Gershwin's rhapsody on her portable tape-recorder beckoning him away at the same time she was pulling him in her and saying stay in me, let go!

Cop Doc Allen let go with an escalating and primal roar, as if he were a lion. He felt he was orgasming in her in a way he never existed as he held the egress from pleasure for moments in suspension as he moaned loudly to match her own gasping and singing orgasms.

They subsided for a moment. In an almost incredible manner, she went down on him, claiming him once again as she in short while excitedly kissed him and placed his head on her moisture. Both soon resurrected the small death of ex-stasis and again arouse in passion and oscillation as she mounted him on top. Lisa's mouth bent to kiss his muscles which were taut and hard with bounce and pricked skin as if goose bumps she could feel in her tongues sensation. They had impulsively delved in to the forbidden of each the other as man and woman that could not be lovers by convention and law due to status and power plays: To the law, they conveniently let go as in all the embraces without any restrictions they were literally one heart and soul.

What secrets they would have to hold in silent assent was beyond the pall of law and order. But the order of law, after all, is the convention of some conveniences and in some ways fascism when the natural order is disrupted. There is the rub of their love and passion where barriers were broken even if surrounded with the sharks that would taste blood and hone in for the effigy of two for the price of one.

A pyrrhic oblation as all tragic love relationships are lead to the dark side of light in all couplings that yield produce as Adam and Eve. If each had their own genius, together they would be light and darkness, beyond the yellow and peach hues of contrast and pixels that shine in the bowels hidden in pitch black. The parlay began and the lover forlorn boomeranged in oppositional polarity balanced in ambiguity and extreme desire. Repulsion and Attraction born in twain re-united as inter-twined as the disparate fleeing from the reality of desire and birth of mature love.

Man and woman are one and the same fit perfect in the asymmetry made symmetrical with the Almighty as Architect and the Creator. Apollonian in messy Bacchius rituals that are the primal fused with the sublime. She mused to him in his ears she loved to kiss and suck on. The ears so many tales of woe and torment passed through that she owned now. Creation enjoined in love and passion as much as the hovering of the Almighty in clouds that are dark grey and melancholic. Where wisdom hovers awesome insight, and modernity is only repetitions of splinters of the past ripping open the present again.

The genius of ancient man and woman have been swept away by the insanity of modernity – yet here lay defiantly man and woman. Epitomes of modern trappings stripped down to their primal core as beautiful and majestic. Recombinant hues of yellow and white brushed with sweat and pheromones unadulterated and uncensored natural redemption held liberation as creation. Perhaps, Wilhelm Reich was on to something. He and she were encircled by the boundary of their fusion. Allan now was musing silently as questions ragged his cortex with nagging paradox:

"But what about the soul's redemption?"

"Was this nirvana, or paradise?

"Perhaps the twain is a journey to paradise and nirvana?"; "Was love immortal?"

Could two enter in twain to ring the depth mark of one?"

Silence and sleep overcame the washing of sweat and pheromones of masculine and feminine ingested in each the other unbound. Passion unfurled the flag of sleep leaving the lovers at the altar of sleep and peace under the canopy of harmony and balance.

# Chapter 18

## Rouge, Pistols and Kisses

Allan awoke, and Lisa Wei Feng was gone in ninety days, the heat and passion left a vapid impression in the other pillow on his queen size bed. She left with a kiss as he drank her cold Scottish hot tea, shortbread, buttercream Scottish cookies with peanut butter, and a smudge of banana with a dash of chocolate truffles left behind as a clue to her disappearance.

Allan drank her tea from her lipsticked cup, and smelled her saliva mixed with his own smell from her ravaging appetite she never let lay dormant. Allan Cannon looked at his stomach, which started to bellow as he realized he had not eaten a decent meal since she suddenly departed. He remembered awakening suddenly as Lisa had turned one night in her sleep, and imagined him abandoning her. She swore she could be a Bitch if he screwed with her, but she swore she loved him and would never betray his desire.

Allan intimated that unconsciously Lisa was planning her escape, when she awoke him abruptly. Her guilt unconsciously spoke volumes. She could not be a psychopath without conscience as she awoke to confess guilt and fell deeply into sleep again. He reflected psychopaths can eviscerate without even a sneeze of pain as another wince's in agony as they are vivisected. Teases and flirtation brought their love to a crashing fold as his Alpha Style was eclipsed under her wings created like Icarus in a quest to fly to the stars. The meltdown was when both intensified the hidden Tiger of professional and personal stances of prosecutor, and the Lions roar of healer and comforter as clashes of incompatibility between a prosecuting attorney Lisa and a forensic psychologist Dr. Allan Cannon.

His seventh senses made his sixth cop doc sense seem like child's play. He was played as a child, an empath — picking up on feminine vibes like an electric rod. Lisa's thunderous temper stormed reverberations into the cold earth, when she would go off on a rant. Her rants sometimes conservative and at other times quite liberal — unsure of her leanings. Allan Cannon, Ph.D., M.D. was an enigma. He was loved, or hated because he refused to comply with party demands and politics as usual.

Lisa Wei Feng, J.D., was no different, finding the duplicity of attorneys in general – unsettling and vitriolic. It was a true mate checked with passion, reason, fire and ice all set in deep chasms of conflict and desires left unquenched. Harmony became the painful pleasure chords of sado-masochistic parlays into the night with Allan.

A night where each would cuff each other and tease the other until man ran into woman, and became one and the same. Allan and Lisa, for a moment, merged until the death of ex-stasis separated them in orgasmic release.

Allan was deeply in love with Lisa, who misunderstood his need for quelling her obsessive manic erotism, her-story. Until one night's end – day broke with the rush of a new dawn. Lisa went off like a wisp of the pussy willow in the flowing winds of malcontent.

Lisa Wei Feng would regret her departure, when he called on his old older flame to gain comfort in solace and dinner – she seduced and slept with him. He rued his own fear as he could only think of Feng. Allan quickly realized his error and cursed the seeds he dispersed to the wind of an egg, no longer fecund, rotting in sex-less without love.

Life was as messy as the forensic investigation they both were involved in. Secrets lay their wreath to the lovers whose promises fell in the moment of revelation now laid bare in the shine of disillusionments oppressive heat gone south: Deep South!

Lisa stuck to her plan of being the 'B' as Lisa in her manic moments, vetting Allan to lay himself bare and naked, reappeared. Lisa fancied herself a tigress drawing Allan's blood, as her perverse desire to reel him back in to her lair as she closed her eyes and devoured him in her imagination. She would deign to devour her Stag in her clenched jaws and elevated taut cheek bones. Her features bourn yellowing skin ran taut with freckles, and a dimple he adored the moment he met her.

Allan was no longer the confident doc or cop, but laid low in a morose bog of could have, would have been's, and should have been's, until she called three months later.

Lisa's call beckoning him out of the blues, 'as if' nothing had happened was answered as impulsively as her departure. Lisa entered Allan's life like a crouching tigress again. Transference to counter-transference Allan's compulsion to confess was unheard and unspoken to Lisa most of all as he desired to mend the error of his lewd behavior. Dr. Allan sought his training analyst who deemed him heretical for straying into other fields of existential analysis: The key competitor for psychoanalysis.

Allan let his training analyst off the hook and let go in his own un-worked through losses, reifying his old ghosts. Abandonment issues for Allan and healing his ill mother whose suffering he could never fully heal. He always sought the wounded female bird hoping to repair the wounded mother he could not save from her own demons. He had thought, when he hooked up with Lisa, that the repetition had ended with all his education and investment in working through four therapies and mastering them.

Yet, Dr. Allan Cannon was left with laces and rouge, pistols and cuffs in a melee of sex and passion unfurled as two played deep into the night of content. Allan tried to resist letting Lisa back in his lair of bachelorhood after two failed marriages.

Lisa held back the trigger of Allan's impulsive drive to plunge with Icarian wings from the edifice of concrete and steel to the depths of her own fantasies and dreams provoked again. Existential angst provokes in its steamy sultress the most sublime dreams. So her lair was woven as she raised her nemesis lover from oblivion. Lisa, after all, saved him from his ex-wife's third design as she relieved him from doom imploding as love withheld – now fully blossomed.

Blossoming into a twisted turn designed for a sumptuous feast it now became, a banquet for two 'in-love'.

He let go, and in his creative style, she had never known secret feelings he provoked of her own prowess over her man. Lisa never intended to ensue as she pursued other schemes Allan alas was her dream come true – woman interrupted by love recovered, claimed and found!

Lisa felt at times as if she could not remember why she left three months ago. Lisa had become so enraged that her lapse of memory felt like one bad dream. She let go at times and felt compelled to touch her own moisture as heat enveloped her in the mid-August cock pit of her Mercedes Benz. Lisa desired Allan from a far as she left her Mercedes Benz C350 model sports coupe running and ready for escape.

Lisa wanted Allan badly as she coyly spoke like a young 20 something year old to him over her car-phone in silly banter she hardly knew dwelled within. Lisa walked up to his Central Park Avenue Apt as the doorman let her in without adieu. She went up like a banshee to his one-bedroom flat. She rang the bell and looked like a model Catholic College coed in her 20's, not a late forty year old District Attorney with decades of experience under her garter belt. Allan was stunned as her .25 Automatic Beretta Model 21 Bobcat dropped in its sheen leather case unto his couch as she entered and took off her leather trench coat. Attached to her purple Victoria Secret lingerie were her long suede black boots and Scottish dress mid-length high exposed her piano Knee's.

Cop Doc Allan's sturdy firm .38 loaded with hollow points was touched ever lightly as she unloaded his firearm. He looked on like a naïve boy anticipating her next move. As if bewitched, she lifted the barrel of his revolver to her face and mouthed it mockingly. Her red lipstick and tongue smeared the shaft with her wet saliva as he looked on incredulously. She took her long black nail polished fingers and cusped a relationship that piqued his own hidden submission she pinched him. He seemed as altered in his conscious awareness as she was.

Allan sensed he was entranced in an addiction, yet helpless to escape from her grasp. He did not desire to run or talk but he kissed her mouth deeply. Tears ran down both his and her face sobbing in the pleasure of lovers disquieted in the night of endless repetitions on a love song of a disc never pausing. The stylus of their love was disturbingly intense and cutting — yet, neither could be without the syringe and intoxication of their hidden respite — passion with all its twists and turns engulfed the two as they merged into one.

# Chapter 19

## A Roller Coaster: Repulsion – Addiction repeats in a cup of Joe

Allan awoke and smelled Lisa Wei Feng next to him. He smelled her breath and wanted to drown himself inside her mouth. He stirred his cup of Joe. His habit was to drink coffee in a transparent mug made of tempered glass. It was stirring his soul as he pondered about their relationship.

Connecting with Lisa on many dimensions of a spectrum left Allan thinking back to his own days of being in a training analysis to become a classic psychoanalyst. Allan wondered if he had unresolved conflicts and where he had compromised in their resolution.

Like all Analysand in training analysis he knew some conflicts were mediated by more mature defenses and resolved intra-psychic conflicts by non-therapy means – some would not.

Allan even reflected on both he and Lisa being disordered per the slippery slope of the Diagnostic

Statistical Manual IV. Although he knew full well that slippery shrinks that shrunk disorders into convenient capsules of managed care were a margin over the inclusive dimension of diagnosis, most were bonafide.

Allan also knew that no Doctor of Medicine or Doctor of Psychology that ever became a clinician could ever close the door that led them into the canopy of healing. No matter how each tried to close the window, that displayed their own unique vulnerability leading to the path of healers of the soma and mind it always would be lit in their own leakage as Allan Cannon, M.D., Ph.D. knew well. Under that fragile canopy, lay the window that shadows each clinician ghosting him/her as the secret motivation that compelled him/her to heal. That is a motivation hardly conscience and almost always left as fragments of their own irrational both/and deliberate lattice that constructs their persona and their own unique defensive walls.

Allan remembered his peers, Professor Dr. Jackson Kitowitz, J.D., Ph.D., and his allergist/infectious disease specialist mentor and close friend, Dr. Stuart Yohenwitz, who in different prisms of inner sight, wrote of the fragile unity in science and biography that alas makes genius light afire. Tomes received as classics written on Forensic Psychology and in Psychobiological Illnesses palled to private communication in which they allied with Allan in preserving their traditions of excellence in Psychology/Psychiatry.

Traditions, where unique gifts bestowed on compassionate creative Doc's always surfeit the most disturbed whispers heard from students, peers and the adoring public who desire the drama and intrigue as voyeurs – hidden from fully knowing.

Voyeurs, like Screen Producers, shoot their films in the morning after their raucous trolips in the crushing vicissitudes' of their turbulent lives not realizing their art is lattices of their own biographical snippets cut from the threshold of redacting footage as much as adding in the final presentation. Allan was wont to exercise caution to the precipice of a cliff of desire, but compelled to passionate embrace. Allan could not help jumping in full throttle into Lisa as he sallied into her tempestuous soul, hidden in a persona fractionated on a split of borders lining her outer core of zeal and her inner core of desire for love and warmth that would not flee from her lair. Allan struggled with how Lisa couldn't care less about him when he was sensitive and a poet lover as well as doc and she disappeared.

To Allan's surprise, Lisa shed tears and was genuinely sweet, loving and empathic when he disclosed to her his thoughts and feelings. Allan could not believe she was not being disingenuous, but she was not. He was guided into perplexity as much as desire by her mystique and weirdness. In a cerebral way, they were piqued in intellectual affinity and dissimilitude as much as tension and friction building sexual and spiritual unity as Adam and Eve did at the portals of humanities beginning and still redo every day when man and woman – unite.

Lisa presented poetic, compassionate and balanced, as she actively listened to Allan's own collision with their situation. Calling deep within Allan was ethics and moral standards and his desire to flee from Lisa intuitively. But, Allan Cannon was drawn deeper as he tried to flee from the depth of his longing as Lisa cued into something missing in his life.

Allan was interrupted in his attention as he smelled the pungent Joe in his glass cup rise through many prisms as it hit the UV refracted light from his halogen lamp as he had turned the microwave on and had forgotten he pulled that trigger.

Allan noticed the coffee turned cold and the milk rose as a cloud in the tan hue of brown and blue in the reflection of his Goebbels Crystal vase.

A vase Allan brightened his office with as a wild lone white orchid purchased day in and out cheered him up. Allan took a sip and so did Lisa from his mouth. She imitated an acerbic taste in her mouth and smiled in a way that gave him a goose bump. Dr. Allan felt, or rather, intuited patients' feelings as he was trained to feel their loss as a clinician. Allan had hundreds of patients so traumatized, dissociated in identity, and borderline splits alike, that could not fully express their own thoughts and emotions. Allan had become an expert at reading their cues to his surrounds. Allan, in his own gut, sensed gut wrenching feelings long before patients could muster the energy to expel the words needed to color their own sense of loss, often shrouded under the unholy shroud of trauma. Allan felt traumatic loss with intensity when he was with Lisa, many times suppressing the desire to confront her.

Allan tried to ignored it. Allan worked on not letting his calling enter with a clinical tug on his inner personal voice and life. The boundary he was trained to divide between his own personal and intimate relationships from professional and vice a versa. With Lisa Wei Feng entering his life Allan could not let analysis, or anything, rue his chance to finally get it right with a lady he could rely on for life. Rue anything that attempted to disrupt his union – he would not allow her to exit his life on a damn technicality. Lisa also so appealed to him, regardless of her borderline tendencies as he believed in her variant style could be cured by marriage and love.

He imagined they could light candles in Beijing, or Jerusalem, at a Jewish convert. Lisa intimated she desired conversion with the right man. After all Jesus was a Jewish Rabbi as they would laugh at the whole fantasy before he was baptized Christ. Sticky and thorny they would enter and exit this conversation. Fantasy, shifted rapidly as Lisa bent in a momentary paroxysm after the coffee with sour cream covering the fresh Joe left the taste – bitter sweet.

Lisa motioned without voicing 'It' but miming what appeared to be a headache as she blinked rapidly and her facial expression seemingly switched.

Lisa leaned down, kissing Allan as she slowly undid his shirt buttons on the Oxford White Shirt. Licking his beads of sweat, Allan pausing and pulling slightly away said they both had better be responsible for the clients'/patients' sake. Allan watched as Lisa twitched, grimaced as if she had a headache and said she wanted to kiss his butt and pressed him against the wall. She ignored his semi-attempt to ward off her move to pin him on her wall of desire. Lisa began to do things to Allan he had never experienced before, and in a weird way, was repulsed by, but felt like he was on fire with desire as she explored him in a dominating style. It was as if he was in a trance: A dissociative hypnotic state as Lisa played all over Allan and told him to relax.

This state was a core presentation in dissociative identity disorder, borderline personality traits and complex post-traumatic stress disorders. He was unaware of how and why he was turned on by her extreme twists and turns in identity. She was one moment contrite and solemn, the next she was surly and wild, and then almost like a saint without sin. Why was he helpless to her wiles and provocations without resistance?

Allan understood his guilt and his moments of adaptative functional dissociation, when compassion fatigue and remnants of unfinished psychoanalysis failed to capture his own angst. Also called compassion fatigue, when a first responder lets all his strength sap into rescue operations emotionally. The first responder hardly remembers he/she needs to secure enough air and compassion first and foremost for himself. Allan knew himself well enough and had learned to accept his own irascible and even unseemly behavior at times. Remnants of his own trauma history compelled him, and in some ways, drove him to conquer his losses in forging a new treatment using himself first as the litmus of his crucible in treatment. Allan actively built on years of research and intervention through leafing into the tomes of hundreds and even by now thousands of trauma-laden patients. Patients who have had ordeals that would make a Spartan warrior wince in their days with shivers and trembling. NYPD centurions and other departments he vaunted into as he did his trauma therapy echoed in his own past worked through terror imprints as a street cop. Allan simply saw himself as more than one of his officers as a legionnaire Doc. But he was failing himself or was he allowing himself to leap with her and rescue her, himself and by default reach her empathic side and Antonio.

The New Centurion's by Joseph Wambaugh paperback lay as a haunting, sketched out from his own daymares and insights, no doubt experienced in seven long years from rookie LAPD cop to Sgt LAPD.

Hauntings, like the tenure of a street cop is like a soldier in the war zones of urban warfare no matter how pretty the word reducers try to paint the pain in sociological trappings as a panacea. Professor Dr. Allan Cannon, Det. Sgt promoted would fight for calling human evil no less than what it was, is and will always be first and foremost for victim, survivor, witness and warrior – human evil! He knew the first step toward human healing and being and becoming humane is to call an evil person, place or thing for what it truly is and not act as if it is other than what it truly is.

Allan Cannon never left behind in academia, department pressure or any influence, save his own conscience, his integrity as his own personal identity as a cop doc – come hell's high water or freeze. Allan realized at some level he was taken over by an addiction to a woman, who was in many ways a potential mate, and also a potential hazard.

Clearly, they both had crossed the Rubicon but she was in denial or did she really know? Could she have been in some way dissociative and hold such a critical position of law and order?

It was crucial that Allan Cannon listened to his own third ear. He knew he had to override his addiction, but in no way without help. But who could he turn to?

His realization that faith was the key to unlock the door held promise. He had to wrestle once again with the conflict within between his professional identity, his creative ingenuity, and his own faith: This triangle of all conflict born in the prisms of three dimensions was angular in its cut, but diffused in its distribution of energy and direction; Like a crystal glass, shattering and laying in a pool of its own fragments. Lisa had taken

Allan to another world as he felt her presence pull him from his need to rationalize and intellectualize, his desire expanding in the circle of her love and his for one another. Uncanny, and as if on cue, Allan holding his coffee cup of tempered glass filled with three ounces of coffee and a tablespoon of rancid milk fell from his hands grasp. The glass mug did not bounce, but cracked into slivers of shards of glass as it collided with the perfect Goebel's crystal vase. Fractionated glass refracted like lenses cast in bluish brown hues irradiated light on the table. A table where he used the corner to write his guides for others seeking to learn his wisdom distilled from a cup of Joe. That cup of Joe had seen many nights and days pass; it lay shattered. He felt shattered but knew he was ready to jump into growth or a spiral down. Allan started to take out his twelve steps, but he placed it back in his drawer. He was ascending from the descending stairs used too many times before.

The book of Psalms was in his mid-drawer next to his third firearm he never considered of any use. It was cloyed in it brownish hue cast with a blue imprint so touchable as it lay inside its original ancient Hebrew lettering. It was his Colt 45 caliber semi-automatic pistol his dad willed him in his last will and rites. The pistol lay there as if to say remember me. Allan had made a note to read the Psalms the next day as the woes of an ancient King David of Israel had written in his hypo-manic inspired genius state of unsettling conscience. David, his hero, known as much for his complexity and trouble with women as much as for being a true leader for people of all faiths and all times in distress. David fought and conquered his own depression and anxiety laden in trauma as testament to the power of his faith and surrender to the Almighty in Dr. Cannon's mind. Like his hero, King David, Dr. Allan Cannon, who fancied himself and was told by those who critiqued his work – as a modern poet-warrior – ever elusive, ever ingenious a scion of David.

Allan Cannon pushed aside his broken glass and chipped vase as he listened to Lisa get into the hot shower. He heard the loud noise of the hot water cascading hard and strong against her body he knew so well. She had taken him once again to explosive rhythms of desire and fusion. He delayed going in as she washed herself without letting a stain fall on the carpet by the rim of his bedroom door.

Allan Cannon decided instead of getting into the shower with Lisa to lay his head on his pillow and surrender to his Maker. At least for a moment of repose, he slowly opened the tome, to its ancient healing metaphors. Allan felt the crisp winds of Jerusalem on his flush ruddy face as Hebrew words stacked in two pages of the 32 Psalm transliterated sank into his minds eyes. The 32nd Psalm as a song of redemption pleading to the Almighty – answered in the silence of genuine confession, without the madness of compulsion. For a moment, he was at rest and peace. The lyrical chords of soulful repose lulled Allan's heart resonating as stokes began to undo the illusory chains of addiction. Addiction bonding his soul to the roller coaster of endless desire hardly experienced in the center of his core being and always compelling him to flee from.

Mother Theresa's small tome was near and dear to Dr. Cannon when he was down and out from therapy hours particularly trying his soul. He recalled the Saints soothing voice in the silence of determination in his darkest moment, as Saint Theresa said,

"We need to find G-d, and he cannot be found in noise and restlessness. G-d is the friend of silence. See how nature – trees, flowers, grass – grows in silence; see the stars, the moon, and the sun, how they move in silence."

Power of silence overlay the force of Allan's addiction and repulsion for raw sexuality as he turned away from lust. His power of attraction piqued as he looked at Lisa Wei Fang's nakedness: Lisa's derrière feeling infused with spiritual love as his full physical desire to be as one in her deepest darkest lit tunnel perished their darkness. The coin of transcendence reverberated in their empty chambers where the love vectored a powerful victory over lust. He was once again deeply in compassion, dripping with unparalleled genuine desire.

Allan as needful of certainty was still quite unsure.

'Why, Lisa Wei Feng?'

Never spoken in his silence as he fell as soon as he rose to challenge the compulsion, but all he knew was letting go with,

'How, Lisa Wei Feng?'

He no longer resisted the coaster that rolled under her new ceramic cup with two leafs to which he drank his new hot and moist cup of Joe as she laughed sardonically. Lisa sipped the Cora Style Peacock vase filled with Joe, she poured as she sipped the other side with him.

Lisa Wei Feng, in love in her own way, with Allan felt his conflict as a storm in her exquisite sensitivity. She experienced her bouts of bonding with Allan as madness and taunts in a thousand ways that led to orgasm as he entered her leaves blushing petulance.

Allan's own desire to flee and remain forever with Lisa almost mystically overrode her pattern of idealizing and devaluing him in explosive taunts and revelations withdrawn along the borders lining her velvet purse.

As Allan lay his un-showered passion sung in the silence suffering her love as he had turned her from playing with him to deeply and paradoxically loving him as her man. Lisa sat naked except for her flowered Chinese panties as she held his hand and in a moment of connection finally felt the trappings of contentment. She felt content she was with a man who really knew her. Allan knew her in her own fantasy as a willing master, and at the same time, a slave. She too loved the play of his words, and felt in the inane world of forceful crime, the power of her man – un-shuffled by misanthropes on the far left or far right – their unified souls Victor of all.

Lisa Wei Feng felt the power of being a woman with the power he let loose inside her as swimming poles energized her inner sheath tightening and swelling as aching pain of pleasure was filled at once. Allan's mouth opening as he took in the last sip of Joe after the climax lingered was smoking in ethereal clouds of content. Lisa swallowed his coffee, milk and his love as echoes rang and she fell to sleep. She mused a world so incorrect it needed to poison the waters of passion. Lisa wished she could drink it all as so much bittersweet poison. She placed her own urine with his drops of masculinity as an elixir to the dour taste she hungered for in everlasting union with Allan. A taste ever silent as she tasted their acerbic unity as much as she did their vanilla sweet as she looked at him, and saw herself fulfilled. The look grew in time into a stare as her eyes got glassy and far, and further away. Lisa's face changed expression as she grew more intense and his sleep ensued.

Lisa caressed Allan's curls and licked his big ear lobes. Lisa Wei Feng knew a man with big ears was destined for fame and fortune, being a great lover and never abandoning her. To these three omens, she swore.

Lisa lovingly watched Allan's eyelids move in saccadic cadence as a daze covered her vision. She was humming, thus spake Zarathustra as she took out a measuring cup and she mixed different medications and over the counter cures for a midnight cap. Lisa took Allan's L-Tryptophan at 4000 mg and diluted it in 4000 mg of Melatonin. She took ten tablespoons of Nyquil and added 3 Ambien capsules and some substance she had marked nightshade's delight. Flavoring her concoction, Allan was in a stupor from the busy night and she said, "Honey, awake," to which half asleep he supped her rum and coke as she opened his mouth with hers and deeply kissed him. Lisa used her tongue as a sieve and the interesting drink fascinatingly slid into his mouth as she relished his odorous scent as her man as it slipped out of hers.

Kissing him deeply in doses, she rocked and shook in multiple orgasms as she swallowed some for herself from his mouth. She rubbed against his muscular legs and felt him erect, imagining they were married. They would never part again, she pondered over the pint and a half Allan swallowed. Lisa the gatekeeper of Eden and their married souls. Lisa felt powerful as she lay passive in his arms. Fantasy or reality Lisa Wei Feng would never let Allan go.

Lisa never felt so alive and euphoric. Allan was deeply asleep as his beautiful eye lashes were grandly closed. Tears emerged from his eyes as they were glassy and he tried awaking almost violently after drinking her elixir of love eternal. She hushed him sweetly to sleep as she placed a pretty kerchief over his mouth and imagined he was her first love. She told him in whispers he could not hear of what she just did as a gift of love forever and ever. She licked his eyelids and as her tears fell as she placed them in a glass measuring cup and drank his saline offering saying LaChayim my love, 'Wo I knee'. Sleepy Lisa succumbed to blissful nirvana on this side of Paradise's door, hoping to never awake in earthly mundane reality, but on the side where no conflict for her and Allan would never raise its ugly face again.

# Chapter 20

## Three is a crowd: One has to be let – Go!

Lisa Wei Feng shook with pain and writhing as she remembered in terror her original trauma, which was never disclosed as she whispered the tale in Cop Doc Allan's ears. She remembered at eleven years of age getting her period and crying in the girl's bathroom. In her lulling Allan to sleep, her concoction took effect on her as she, too, let go and confessed her early marks of trauma, in-deed.

Lisa was a pubescent girl as she found herself in the twilight between wakeful alert and sleep. Unaware of why she was full of blood in her underwear, Lisa remembered being full of fear as to what was happening to her body. She was swallowed by the pit of ignorance and fear in an age when boundaries blurred without having an education about her development.

Wei's character and identity was always shifting in her own mind. She had crushes on older boys, a norm which turned into boy crazy a bit later on. Wei's character included her being attracted to the twenty something year old male teachers as being real grown up in her own mind. She was not sexual, but had feelings of warmth that were very exciting at eleven years old. Wei tried to fight her attraction to boys in Catholic School, but they emerged in her private dreams and schemes. At the time, she was moaning in fear and angst about what she imagined was her death. Wei realizing her shades of horror when she awoke to seeing her blood in her underwear. Bleeding to death as blood had dripped all over as she emerged from the toilet in abject fear – hyperventilation overwhelmed her senses.

Enter the bully, as they always do in an untimely manner. The bully came out from her own vestibule post overeating and suffering from gas that was nauseatingly loud and malodorous. The bully in her own world of farts and overindulgence heard nothing initially. Lee, a large and obese female left back student, two grades ahead of Wei and four years older than her, was of less than average intelligence. However, in sadistic skill not unusual for bullies, she was at the top of her line as the school bully.

Maria heard Wei moaning in the vestibule and in belied concern asked, "What is going on? You OK?" Maria asked of Wei behind the veil of the door.

Wei crying out said she was bleeding to death. Unaware of what menstruation was she exposed herself in underwear. Soaked in blood as the bully who fully knew sadistically and cleverly as she was coming out of the vestibule feigned not knowing anything and with no boundaries, Wei was the bullies' perfect victim.

Wei Feng tried as she did, could not stop her fearful moaning as more than pain welled in her. Lisa expecting sympathy and help in her embarrassment and fear turned into trembling, crying, and then wailing.

Fearing she would bleed to death, Wei looked in embarrassment and humiliation as other girls began to gather around her in the bathroom. She was unaware of the strum and drang of the bathroom subculture where fierce competition amongst adolescent girls reigned.

Wei suddenly was accosted by the obese bully Lee as Maria, laughing sardonically, tried to grab her by her hair. Maria couldn't, as Wei slipped away from Lee's flailing fat arms. Maria laughed so hard she farted as the other girls in fear and some like Maria in sadistic cadence giggled. Next, a punch landed in the semi-flat chested breasts of Wei, just developing. Maria did not desist as she tried to expose Wei by pulling on her dress to show the other girls her bloody mess.

Taunting Wei out-loud like a 'braying swine' as Wei would with relish mock female predators she would prosecute in her future illustrious career aimed at her. At the time, nothing but a freckled and lost girl in the swirl of development was being bullied by her competitor as Maria howled, "bleeder, loser Wei-cry baby, cry baby."

Lee heightened her pitch to a laughter of cruelty singing, "Bleeder, bleeder, little kitty Kat, what a bleeder! Cry to your mommy and daddy baby, baby. No boy likes you, ugly, skinny Wei you are a loser, loser you are."

Without time ticking along, the other large bully named Maria was enjoying herself sadistically as she made Wei her projected weak target. Suddenly, Maria sensed she was bleeding. A flash before her eye glistened and sharply stung. She looked down and saw a folk in her stomach area and her face bleeding.

Wei had swung on top of the sink and came down on Lee and then Maria with a double elbow cracking into her layered face with blood, adipose tissue and bone exposed. Lee's stomach wound was superficial. But that was the last time any bully would ever lay her hand on Wei. Wei's parents were rich and a few donations covered over the event buried in a principal's file cabinet.

A new event emerged from an ugly trauma never expressed or worked through save the spanking she received by her mother who called Wei a trouble maker. A handsome, somewhat weird boy, who was highly intelligent and gentle named Tin felt Wei's pain. In a series of some strange circumstances, he became her first boyfriend. Tin Fong approached Wei with genuine compassion as she learned the nurturance and love she could succor from a boyfriend. Wei learned what menstruation was, and how formidable she was when she struck back at her tormentors/competitors. Wei, at the same time, learnt the male body and the perfect fit she could have when sexual intercourse was achieved by a mature girl. The magical curiosity of what orgasm could be like with the perfect boy was her obsession. At thirteen, Wei broke her virginity. Her heart was broken when she learnt Tin was expelled from school, and her mother found out and beat her and reported to the principal that Tin was a bad and evil boy.

Lisa wept in bed as Allan was trying to wake and listen to her, although his aging and long work hours kept him asleep along with elixir of love and eternal bliss.

Cop Doc Allan suddenly awoke, as if he was swept away by the undercurrent of Morpheus enveloping him. He could not fully wake up, and shake off the slumber.

He felt like he had been through a marathon, but could not remember 'Why?' Overtired and fatigued, he kept hearing the alarms going off in his head. It seemed as if they were scores in his dreams – as if he was dreaming but unsure if he was hearing tower bells from a church, or he heard an alarm ringing from his boyhood Big Ben windup clock. Allan vaguely remembered awakening, somehow remembered as if he was sleeping, or awake, or was he still sleeping?

Allan, as if suddenly feeling a numbing chill – awoke. Allan tried to scream but instead looked into dark brown deep and melancholic eyes – compelled to stare into his green and orange hue pupils – he too just stared awake, but asleep. Hyper-vigilance and goosebumps jingled a tune that was like Gershwin's piano roll mesmerized with the experience – silence shelved all responses to a deafening lull.

Fighting sleep as a visceral night terror one awakens to was nothing new to Allan. In a paroxysm of fear and death sensations, while still quite alive – he would awake suddenly feeling as if he was dead. Gasping for breath, Allan pouncing on reality spoke, I am alive!

Allan's twilight state of mind and soul wrestled with one another as survival kicked reality in focus. Like Wei, Allan minimized his own maladies and illness. Relief in large gulps of air traversed Allan's struggle. Allan felt like a goldfish thrown on a marble bath-cabinet left to die, that slip-slides into the right medium to realize he is no longer in a safe round bowl, but a narrow toilet — flush goes the fulcrum of the lever of life.

The fulcrum for Allan was always a surly lady, ready to roll and rock – Sisyphus's throw of a dice – once again, naturally. Lisa Wei Feng staring at him deeply, as if in a trance, or technically as he called it a hypnotic state of mind – was looking way beyond him. She was looking from limpid pools of tears un-cried, unspoken, and hidden but opening up to view.

Surreal frames unfurled in Lisa's flowing flags colored war, misery, desire, lust, love, passion, reason, logic and rage. Lisa could experience almost in sudden shifts and at times simultaneously her contradictory borders: Borders that framed her emotional intensity and volatility born in traumatic losses. Allan knew Lisa Wei Feng's trauma colored her emotional valence in process.

Allan Cannon's photo-audiographic memory lane of encoded academic facts arrayed and combined as much as his anomalous genes: He ordered his thoughts about Lisa Wei Feng along her identity issues a serious fault line in personality. Identity dissociative disorder first discovered and called by Professor Dr. Morton Prince, when he started the first Journal of Abnormal Psychology at 52 years of age in 1906. Three years later, the psychologist-physician coined multiple personality disorder in his work, the dissociation of a personality. The work continued as Dr Freud's work on dissociation and the ego defense of identification with the aggressor. Dr. Charles Brenner, the prodigy Harvard Medical School Graduate, at 18 rediscovered the pivotal compromise formations of the unconscious as always present. Allan knew well Lisa Wei like all patients with her disorder experience compromises between the ego's super attenuated conscience that struggle with reality – never really integrating her-self as a whole person. Alters of defenses and their compromises in vast arrays leave baffling presentations.

Her primal derivatives of sex and aggression always threatened with real dangers from without and

261

unresolved ones from within are experienced as chaos. Allan knew the nature of life's portals were ever threatened with storms and deadening calm stagnation in her disorder. Dr. Allan Cannon, as an expert in grief, trauma and terrorism specialized in personality disorders, dissociative disorders and the buds of defenses that arose to shield the victim from working through the losses. But, in some cases creative flowers peppered the gardens of mind and soma.

The survivor in maladaptation had sensibility hidden from most therapists who did not have the humility to step off the pedestal of concrete knowledge as explorers in each patient anew. Learning from each patient in the analytic attitude of existential analysts, meant – one patient at a time. He used his feelings and emotions in counter-transference from patients as a window furthering insight and novel thinking about the issues that plague us all in the crosswinds of existence and conscience as choices and responsibility thrust to the wind or anchored in integrity.

Dr. Allan's strategy with Lisa emerged with a smile that was cached with fear, tears, and moodiness that was grumpy at best. He couldn't think of why's for himself as he had to get on the case and face the inevitable of Lisa Wei Feng's involvement with him while they were both working over the legal issues and psychiatric profiling of a double homicide investigation and psychological autopsy. Like the collage of a white peachy hewn Panda, the dilemma would not go away. The Panda lay with a yellowing cast sitting like a rogue Buddha in the den of their collusion in secret remonstrations of boundaries violated.

Talking of boundaries – the Panda, 'Antonio' was awaiting the renting of his stitches wide open by Bureau

ADA Chief Lisa Wei Feng's scintillating prosecutorial style: However, the stitches redone were folded on the adroit skill of ambulatory healing readied by Dr. Allan Cannon. Yin and yang or fiery brimstone vs. a comforting haven readied for redemption.

Antonio was a detective that had gathered too many ladies of opportunity he truly tried to embrace in his almost addictive rush to ward off his hound dogs. Hound dogs not of depression but trauma unfurled in being vulnerable to love interminable.

Antonio was a romantic with passion and true love to give but in his desperation for merger had come on with such force eluding the strength of his power he compelled his love ladies to flee prematurely.

Mostly and tragically, before they could truly know Antonio and love him for the good he had inside as a hero, his heroines had their ultimate poison in her dessert – 'Antonio'. Lisa was crossed instead of checked mate-d. In a moment of letting her unconscious flow, Lisa allowed her associations, which were never as free from critique and insight as she thought revealed her mind to Dr. Allan Cannon. She said, without pause, and absent the flow of context, abruptly, "Antonio is guilty"! Anger rising to the mercurial tipping point of her emotional containment blew as saliva rolled down her lips. Allan moved back instinctively as she pared the red juicy apple and she said without a grin or sarcasm,

"Adam fucked Eve and blamed her on it. The devil, my sweet, sexy, Jew Cop doc Allan is to blame. You are too naïve to know. The grisly details, honey, speak of a sick mind that is hateful of his victims especially Christine. We are going to allow Mama Lisa Wei Feng do her justice, like Athena, and you can plea for your boy Antonio and even treat him once. He is granted mitigating circumstances and allowed some treatment for the rest of his miserable fucking life."

Pausing, as Lisa's intensity switched into righteous anger she indignantly spewed out vomit inflaming her intestinal tract,

"My dear, Cop Doc Allan Cannon, unlike you, he is the worst womanizing prick dick in the world. Honey, I am talking shop off the record with you. First, as a courtesy one wrap around for you my lover boy. Isn't that the way love goes? Think, Allan, real hard – Christine was fucking Tommy, perhaps one night she had her way with both of her men: One always in fantasy; and one in reality. What if Tommy was so wasted, he allowed Antonio to deliver the coup de grace and fuck Christine twice. What if Antonio and Christine were cultivating a hot and torrid quick romance? What if Christine was playing both men in an addiction to their rise and fall – gifts to womanhood? What if it was Antonio, who in a flashing fit of rage, bashed Christine's cute little cunt head in with a razor and split her lips inside so wide that her majora labia couldn't be found except inside her own cunt. Only a man would and could do a mutilation like that. Perfect revenge for Christine, who vowed loyalty to Antonio and then fucked him over and was playing the same see-saw ride for Tommy. Christine wouldn't smile anymore, but would horrify Antonio, and his cute sweet innocent look."

Lisa, pausing in a subdued teen's voice, twitching eyes flashing signals of angst, said almost in a whisper,

"He would never cheat on me again."

Tears rolled out of Lisa's eyes and her face blushing as fluttering eye lashes shifted as her regular voice returned articulate and loud. Lisa went on in a matter of fact tone to Allan,

"Tommy realized Antonio killed Christine. He was going to kill Antonio in blind passion, so Antonio, in what was fear, did the ultimate horror by doing a double homicide. This time, he took out his 38 issued service revolver and shot Tommy dead after he cut him in his abdomen. He must have been shocked and cold as the weather was the dead of winter. He collapsed from overwhelming feelings of guilt and banged his head on the wall and was unconscious until my arrival. Your boys did the investigation. I am sure my subordinates have the particulars of the forensic evidence. I will review it tomorrow. In a state of shock, my dearest Cop Doc, it makes superb sense as you put it so well in your books as a trauma and dissociation expert he acted out but he did the cover up with cold austere maddening violence. Antonio could not remember what he did and decided unconsciously in a reaction formation to kill those he loved: one was his police partner whom, he really envied and hated; two, he killed the woman that he would not let get away for betraying him with the 'other man'. Even his own police partner, who better to kill then one's brother in a horizontal oedipal complex?"

Lisa went on with bravado as she said with an inflamed ego in a manic explosion of what could only be righteous outrage and vindication.

"Am I the legal marvel Dr. Holmes or what? Talk about cunt my Dr. Allan Cannon aka Dr. Holmes. Don't worry, as you can examine your lawyer and sleuth's sweet cunt. That is mine alone, I am only for you – that is after you process my genius and are ready for me, Professor Dr. Holmes Allan Cannon. Yes, tragic, my good dear Cop Doc Allan, but Tommy would never have his way again with Christine. Antonio ended it all in a blind fit of rage. Christine promised Antonio fidelity and broke it and so he paid her and his partner in crime Tommy with death. The ultimate vendetta like all true hot blooded Sicilians like to do. We have our crime with a motive and a means to do it with a strong enough reason. Three is a crowd, so when Antonio realized he had messed up by fucking up with the likes of Tommy he shot him with his own .38. Christine's sliced cunt was what she could be buried in as his partners shot cop cock deserved my fury."

Immediately backtracking Lisa retracted her statement:

"Allan, oh I mean, of course, Antonio's Italian fury, not my own fury."

Silence and a smile of relief passed Lisa Wei Feng's face, as if she herself had witnessed the murder laid out including the motive, the intention and the weapon and opportunity of criminal homicide – a tragic triangle – indeed. Lisa changing again in a demure and loving voice said to Allan, soothingly,

"Honey, you can, of course, do your work. I fully support you, my dearest. You know that deep down we are never in conflict. It's kind of simple, if you look it square in the center of this storm. Allan, you just take care of those I need to prosecute. You can assess, heal and fix them all to your heart's content. I love having you around, but all you need to do is fix your broken dolls after I put them in their storage cells called prisons, babe. I will first ensure they are never to see the light of day. Once they are in their dark and dank prisons, you can certainly treat them on your couch of analysis as you need to do my brilliant cop doc. Case closed and we can finally move on in happiness and love my dove ..."

[Silence followed.]

Not a momentary silence but a hard long contemplative silence. Allan excused himself to the bathroom but he disappeared into the kitchen first and then back to the bathroom adjoining their bedroom. That is, until Lisa moved in so to speak. The door did not open for forty-five minutes and then Lisa Wei Feng got frantic and began to knock hard. Allan looked upset as his complexion became ruddy with intensity. Allan had a file of papers, three vials that looked like Ambien Melatonin, and a third with L-tryptophan. Lisa Wei Feng backed away and sweat beaded down her lovely face, flushed with red. Looking down, she was silent – and looked very demure: The first time it looked like a cat got her tongue and she was at a loss for words.

Silence and eyes connected after another ten-minute wait. Not a word was said by either side: It was a draw. Allan shot the first words firmly and in a deep voice he never used before.

"Lisa, you had better start to talk now! I mean now to me, directly, and truthfully."

Lisa looked bewildered and dumbstruck. "What's wrong babe?

"You need me to reassure you, what is it that bothers you?"

Allan was silent and stood by stoically. He silently traversed Lisa's face as tears welled in intense emotion.

Allan awaiting her words held dead silent. Vexing is the quest for truth no matter where it may lead. But in Allan's heart of hearts, he was aching and in excruciating pain awaiting her words with some excuse he could buy. Allan felt Lisa's pain and his coalesce. As all man and woman connected in carnal pleasure, Allan eyed Lisa as a glint in her eye twinkled. He let go as the depths of untilled fields to the ex-stasis of supernal heights mocked heaven crashing into hell on earth. The hope the devil is in the details reverberating as Allan in his hubris dreamt of how to exorcise Lisa's extraneous details: The fucking hell too and with the devil. If he could have the woman of his love's desire, so what of the suffering?!?

Allan realized he loved Lisa, even if she was the poster chic for borderline personality disorder with histrionic petulant traits an anti-social features. She and he were as destined as fire and ice – inseparable as heaven and hell – heat and exquisite chills quivered down to the crossbow of Lisa's pelvic bone as quills marked the attraction and repulsion of their tragic synchrony.

# Chapter 21

## Love, Revelation and Grief

Lisa sat in a somnambulistic state of mind as she was stunned by Allan figuring out she poisoned his trust and safety. The intent of Lisa's special elixir tantalizing her as she could not express her thoughts and feelings. Her words dangled midstream as she became dumbstruck. Lisa's words were inaudible although she tried to utter what sounded like primary speech. Allan listened as a therapist with strong existential and psychoanalytic roots to guide his anchors as posts to understand Lisa.

As a clinical forensic psychologist, a cop-doc, and simply a man three crossroads that triangulated him in different aspects of awareness and conscious sensations he suppressed with clear intention his itching to lay it on full force as to how outrageous her behavior was and how it had sabotaged any hope of redemption for their unity as a couple and for his sanity to allow her to leave unscathed by her malevolent action.

Still, Allan, as a man, could not repress his intense and curious attraction to the femme fatale Lisa was.

Paradoxically, he was beginning to view her with the weight of gravity as the void filled with dark matter anchoring his quantum leaps of love, and desire with revulsion and distance rushing in to pique the relative pause of calm meditation. His moments of clarity became crystalline and were fleeting like fragments as she provoked haunting refrain in the turbulence of his desire to confront her madness. Madness of what he needed to confirm was more than a flirt with life and death by poisoning.

Etching the contours of his bleating heart readying for self-sacrifice for the sake of knowledge and deeply in love was his distinction of the harsh edges of his minds analytic dimension. The curve of Lisa's lips sensually beckoned sonorous appeal from her first words and their first sacred kiss. A kiss of a siren bedecked in carmine rouge covering her cheek bones, dark red lipstick smudged ever so imperfectly over her age lines she wanted to bury in puckering kisses as she blew Allan away. Lisa, in prior romps with Allan, gave kisses demure and colored with elegant words potent and poignant to discover were left parenthetically as incoherent phonemes struggling to draw monosyllabic words.

Allan's mindful meditation in clashing collision of his heart-bound resonance with Lisa was a tempest within the crushing noise of repression held for the moment. Prosaic litter from an articulate musician attorney shaped her orbicularis oculi muscles that were twitching genuine desire and fear in her rebound of conscious expression. Allan never missed the analysis of his lover's psychophysiological tempo. 'Lover', the status Lisa held, was being unhinged. Her personality as it muddied the waters of ethological imprints of his own survival began drowning resistance to his own sexual and existential needs she supplied in abundance.

Allan's rational sense could not help him as he was losing any leverage as the borders of her persona overwhelmed his own senses. In the tempestuous, fiery ice, Allan stunned again with a clear perception that Lisa was genuine, no matter how disturbed. Honesty etching in Lisa's zygomatic and frontal branches of her facial nerves hid scripts for Allan to read as her fear and laughter jumped rapidly. Transference to counter-transference of emotions were ubiquitous as he knew he read her like a script. A play unfolding hit home as psychopathic sadistic as diagnosis crept unwanted into his mind. The chills tickled its way up Allan's occipital nerves as he visualized kissing her. Lisa, looking up in uncanny attunement, sallied in with her confession. As if reading from a text, written and practiced in elocution in the mirror without shadows to haunt her, and without an echo of conscience awareness, her words left as affectless in a matter of fact style.

"Dr. Professor Cop Doc Allan, you choose me and I you. Karma means maybe this is our latest transmigration. Perhaps we were born to meet and say adieu at the end of a very long day. This existence, like many before, was a testing ground in which we almost succeed. Like Cleopatra and Marc Anthony, Bonny and Clyde, perhaps we are criminals in need of confession. I am not a real criminal, but as you see me in my zealous righteous over-kill, I fit the profile. Your silent assent in drinking my pink petals in spring having sprung confirms our love reborn."

Lisa, as if reading his mind's eye, went from sensual to sensitive and mystical.

"Allan, you are scared of me, are you not? But you as a Jew of Sephardic origin know, as I do, that as a Mandarin Chinese, we both are destined to get it right this time. Marriage and mating are never accidental. We have twelve thousand years of recorded history together in both cultures that are the longest living religions and races. I was meant to have your babies. I love you. I was meant to meet you, darling, but we both messed up till now. I messed up by almost ending us both in a very impetuous moment last night. You are right for calling me on it. It was not me but my other side, the dark mistress in me that needed you to prove your love dear."

With a changed pitch to high and almost Victorian in her gentility of oratory skill, she sang in prose clarity,

"Petulance is my name, when I am in that mood. You have no requirement to answer my gentleman lover as the breach in my cradle of locked pelvic intercourse is potent."

In heated panting and excitement of high attraction focused directly at Allan, Lisa slowly moved toward him. "I want to subdue you as my slave. I want to be your slave. You are my Master. I want you to grovel at my feet, is that a crime too, darling? I want you to lick my pink painted toes. Kiss me deeply, darling. Do it, Allan Cannon."

Allan looking at her toes moving and her beautiful skin, ever darker in yellow hues circling teasingly as the sun shading his rational mind, he bent towards her feet contemplating total submission, which scintillated his core in a paradoxical conundrum].

"You can't resist me can you, Allan!?!"

"No, I can't Lisa."

Pausing and moving upright and resisting his own urges to suck her toes, Allan held firm for the moment.

"I can resist you."

Allan pressed into the angular cove aligning the occlusion of walls separating bathroom from his study. His private practice, lined with classic tomes of yesteryear beckoned his attention and supported him for a moment of pause]

"You're disturbed, Lisa. You've lost it. What did I do to deserve your venom? How can you do this to me? I am your lover, Lisa Wei Feng! We crossed into the Elysian Fields. I thought we trammeled through and over the Rubicon together as one. Was this all a prelude to deaths unrequited crypt waiting to happen as you threw me into the carnivorous dungeon of earth when I was most vulnerable under your bewitching spell? This is the finale, and not a drama, but the end of the curtain where portends of hope close eternal. A closure of the circle of our lives where the caprice of your testing me ends like a mayfly's dance! Sudden and swift as a razors slice – we are done – as I am in love with you, but cannot trust you again!"

Lisa, looking through tears, darted clarity in acuity as she pleaded her case to her lover and best friend.

"Allan, we did cross over the Rubicon, not Elysian fields. You were not wrong in believing in us! If you want dear, I will lay my life down for you now. I have nothing else but you now. Shall I leap from your apartment window after writing my fare thee well letter dear?"

Allan moved out of his cove of tomes and dusty enclaves, meant to protect him, and moved closer to his darling.

"No, Lisa! Don't you dare even intimate suicide. We are in this deeply. We are in a world of shit! Who are you, honey? How did this happen to you and why? What did I do to cause this to you? I have been neurotic and yes, neurotic, highly neurotic – but in love and loving with you, honey? Have I let you down that badly for you to choose to do both of us in?"

Slowing and subdued to a whisper Allan began turning red as anger in his cheeks defied being subdued. His pupils dilated as if drugged with empathic vehemence and love simultaneously in colliding force.

"Why, Lisa Wei Feng, attorney, poetess, and musician lover par excellence, what do you want of me, of us, why, oh why, do you act so insanely jealous as to want to do us both in? My life, my blood, shall I blood-let my veins and let you lap it up for warm desert, after we make love? Our vampire fetish has gone overboard. We should have never pushed that boundary and even playfully swallow each other's blood. It was enough to taste each other in all our flavors. I messed up too and realize my error. Do you own your errors?"

Lisa switching to a subdued, impassioned tone of voice, coldly and methodically spoke as if in a trance state.

"Yes, I do. Allan, I wanted to test you and see if you could handle me without cheating on me. I have been cheated on by men I have loved, while slutty two bit ignorant whores have swept them away."

Silent and pausing, Lisa shifted as she rose into a stance looking down at Allan. He sat down, listened, as he cupped his own chin resembling Rodin's, the thinker. Her voice again warmed slightly. She took the tactical advantage.

"I needed to know you love me and would live with me and die with me if called on to sacrifice your precious life. If we passed last night on my love elixir, then our love would have overcome our shells of negativity and we would have become united in death. But it was not destined and now we could drink of the elixir of life together. I was following your lead my love! You wrote about the death drive in your most controversial work to date as being parallel with the instinctual drive derivatives for life."

Lisa pulled out a rumpled note, she paused and read,

"If poison is passion, as you once said, then let me drink of the elixir of our toxic flames. If I must, Lisa dear, I will burn in the fires of hells icy end for your love. If you ever need me to darling, I will drink your urine and lick your butt; nothing from you is ugly or repulsive, you are my better half." [pausing].

Allan, taken aback, defensively darted in,

"I said that to let you know we are connected and that I meant metaphorically not literally. I said we would drink an elixir of poison if that was your desire. Is that what you took literally in your mind?"

Lisa said,

"If only you promise fidelity to me as my one and only, my darling. Did you not proclaim that I was your inspiration for love and energy in your novel, my Cop Doc Allan Cannon? Is that note written for me?"

Allan remained silent. A careful stolid silence. Almost ready to give up, he pouted silently and let up a wall of resistance. Regardless of her antics, Allan was convinced that Lisa was not able to comprehend her own thoughts mitigating his anger but if correct her homicidal impulses were equal to her own suicidal impulses. It was almost beyond Allan's clinical reasoning skills as he was trying to gain a handle on her enigmatic presentation and his own irrational and intense sexual attraction for her simultaneously. Lisa's desire to end his life and hers was baffling enough for him to absorb. Lisa gave him only enough of the elixir to see him plunge into unconsciousness it seemed as he began to rationalize and intellectualize her reasons for her dip into the River Styx.

Lisa took out photos of Allan, naked, and showed him his poses asleep. She said, "You love me and here is evidence, dear, as you look so sexy and hot."

Allan, in shock, silently reflected as he pondered in contemplative questions for his own insight: Why photos of me when I was present. Was it real poison? What is Lisa's real motivation? Was she a nymphomaniac? Why did she do this? Was this a para-suicidal borderline attempt for attention and love? Was he her trophy for sexual conquests and domination? Would their addictive intensity, including his own, end tragically with an accidental death for both?

As Lisa began mumbling about his beauty as a male Adonis, he zoned out. Allan himself was drawn back in regression to his dissociation under the stress. Yet, hypotheses were narrowing down even in his state of altered identity modes. The reality of Lisa's borderline personality with histrionic traits and anti-social features emerged like crystal fractionating in prisms.

Allan's own identity as a clinical psychologist/psychiatrist and cop was pressed hard. He was reeling at the thought that re-entered his mind like a rogue storm. Maybe Lisa was psychopathic? Was she possibly a true psychopath capable of murder herself? But it did not make sense to Allan. Lisa had more than superficial remorse and grief unlike real psychopaths. Lisa's recounting of other losses in her life led to tears, turned to uncontrollable sobbing as she let out her fears. Lisa suddenly interrupted his reasoning through the reality of her incorrigible attempt at testing and possibly suicidal-homicidal behavior.

"Allan, I know I lost the very men I loved most. Yes, you are right that it was due to my *mordant* jealousy. I mean *morbid* obsession with sexual fantasies of domination and submission of my man as my own possession. Is that a crime in itself? I want my man as part of me, in me all the time, that is a woman's real fantasy of possession and sex!"

Allan Cannon in his 6'3" frame was metamorphosing as only Lisa knew. The fringe of his blue pupils started to fade to gray borders; his orange center was overcome with green envy as he heard about her other men as a deck of cards she knocked down and blew away in the wind. As his imagination caught him unaware his rational mind was blown away in the tempest of his own imaginings as images stirred a revolting collage for him.

Allan's empathy iced into a prosecutor identity mode he absorbed from Lisa. He idealized her in some ways as his heroine. Allan loved Lisa deeply and admired her for her intellect and prowess as an attorney. He also knew and sensed if she was triggered with jealousy, whether real or not his hands would be full with her anger. He empathically felt his own jealousy rise with any thought of her past where others had touched or loved her.

Allan convinced himself that Lisa's core motivation of borderline excess at testing him as a twisted test he passed was never to be done again if he could overcome his fear, anger and distrust. But, Allan lost his cool emotionally and confronted Lisa Wei Feng's audacity of arrogance in committing a crime against him and herself he could never disclose. He never could betray a lover and hurt her even an ex-lover. He let loose with his true feelings of anguish and dismay.

"I never use the following term, but are you a psycho-chick from hell. You can call me, dearest, darling, handsome lover, but, what do you mean by your terms of endearment? You almost killed me, Lisa. It was like when you showed me sites of nude male and female models in sexual positions and examined my pupils for dilation and accused me of wanting to sleep with the female models? Did I indicate any interest? Is your testing behavior weird to you? Even a trap that is sick? I did not get excited as a man for naked women I couldn't care less about, but only because we looked together at couples having sexual intercourse like us! I felt somewhat aroused, as you, dear, at my arousal. I couldn't care less for them. But just looking at naked men and women getting it on – no different than you – it made me think of us together. Are you the last Puritan? Why do that to us? Remember your law review paper when you quoted George Santayana. He warned as humane beings any of us are bound to repeat historic flaws and mistakes when anyone is incapable of learning boundaries based on history past and present as you put it so well in an individualized style." [Breaking a smile under a strong attempt to repress it] "You are brilliant as when you resurrected the Witchcraft Trial of Arthur Miller's Crucible. I am put in the role as Judge to prosecute you for presenting me with evidence as being your rescued victim. Do you realize the twisted love you show me is perverse? Do you want me to examine your perineum to anus? No, you want to do that to me dear!

Am I the Jew doc and rabbi to be laid out on your cross that crucifies me, and then accuses me of being kinky and thoughtless of your needs as a woman? I want to know why you played with our lives? I am hopelessly in love with you, darling. But what is our future?"

Allan Cannon held Lisa Wei Feng close to him. Breathing heavily, he walked over to the cabinet and pulled the prescription capsules that held the mix of over the counter and prescription meds. He then looked at her, and said,

"Is this it — all of it?"

Lisa Wei mouth was clam shut, she gestured, "No".

Allan asked, "Melatonin?"

Lisa nodding 'Yes';

He continued, "How many pills, Lisa?"

"7 cherry pills."

"What about Ambien, known as Zolpidem, my dear Lisa?"

Lisa nodded 'Yes' again. She stood with her head lowered and silent. Allan continued,

"Lisa, my lover girl, do you know Ambien is a 'sedative-hypnotic'?"

In a sardonic, almost childish grin, Lisa winced a semi-false smile plastered on her face, indicating without excuse or denial, 'Yes'.

In a perverse way, Allan was sensing his Socratic style was keying in on Lisa's need to confess to him. Allan Cannon did not want to approach Lisa as a therapist, but calling him, he felt compelled. The more Lisa confessed, the more he was intrigued. The more her intuitive senses provoked desire in him the higher his resistances compelled him to fight his own desire and primary drives. Allan ardently tried to repress his anger as his intellect piqued his need to know the truth. His analytic pursuit overcome any other need to protect himself and to exit as he knew was the only rational response to her psychopathology. Instead, Allan went on in his interrogation without due process as he queried Lisa Wei Feng,

"What else did you place in our concoction of love eternal?"

Lisa said,

"I only made our elixir from Nyquil laced with codeine from the dentist. I had some left over when I had my wisdom teeth extracted. I wanted to take pictures of you naked for my album and file. I wanted you to sleep but not forever, darling."

Allan tortured by Lisa's matter of fact disclosure and seeming lack of remorse for almost killing him stunned him. Like waves of some twisted romantic play, Lisa was acting out in her mind. Allan clearly was put to her test and he passed but to what benefit?

"Lisa, you are not mature enough to understand effect from cause," Allan said in exasperation.

Lisa said, "What does that mean, dear?"

Allan said stoically, "You quoted the great novelist William Golding in an interview on his work of good conquering evil. Did you forget your article to the Wall Street Journal, in which you explained the primal fire of aggression and beast lay in all youth unloosed? That is when law and order lay vanquished in a lassie faire society. Drives allowed without constraint in Golding's magnum opus, Lord of the Flies is the road to perdition and perfidy you said and I quote you. Further, you said

Golding presented his views on London's South Bank Show in 1980 where he put it best, when he said he knew effect was in part caused by a rational scientific cause, but intimated what about the rest?!?"

Allan rationalized Lisa's darkest nature as being part of her desire to dominate him in her lair, and her insecurity that marriage and genuine love would cure. Allan drew Lisa closer to his mouth, as if he was ready to bite her, kiss her, or perhaps both, as his emotional control was loosened. He was turned on and hot under the collar as much as he was getting angry and feeling betrayed.

Lisa's mental illness was apparent as his folie a deux with her as his parallel desire and repulsion. His working investigative hypotheses hit a momentum of insight. Her dissociation and sexual fetish for dominating her man as if he was the missing male aspect of her desire and longing for him inside her all the time was to overcome not only her inferiority fears. Her jealousy fueled her passion and itch for Allan to respond with discipline and spanking her metaphorically and literally. She, in turn, had a desire to keep his male response in her possession. She had greed, lust and envy for his masculinity to be her sole possession as he was to be her ideal slave. She would have Allan introject into her and salve her instinct in a counter-phobic way to conquer death by daring to flirt with it in the sexiest way with her man. That is her fascination with the death instinct he wrote about was compromised with her domination over it through him vicariously.

Dissociation was her best defense to avoid dealing with what may wrongly appear to be psychopathy. In her splitting into the many prisms, her altered personality presented on the podium of hysteria – reality fused with fiction. The friction of being Allan and fantasizing Allan was her and they were one whole being was orgasmic to Lisa. Allan, too, realized he found the perfect mate. As aberrant as she was in her compromise formation, he too shared in her fetish obsession and desire to merge with her.

She was sick, beautiful and yet her ingenious web was not without assent by what they both constructed as their own compromises psychosexually and in unison. Perhaps, genius needs to lay in fields where heavenly fire is dosed in chilling icy cold to awaken the light in the darkest channels unknown. He knew she could not face the reality of her unconscious desire including her need to possess him as she yearned to.

Allan retracted back like a tortoise, needing to take refuge in unconscious defenses and back off from his brilliant insights, on rationalizations that make life droll, common and ever comforting. He knew tortoises can be mistaken for red mudslingers and ready to be offered as turtle soup. Alas fantasy must remain at that level, or the flight into psychosis will conquer all gains.

Alan said nothing of this hypothesis to Lisa as it seemed confirmed in an n of 1 as the classic analysts would call a novel case example. He imagined his training analyst and supervisor admonishing him about allowing wild analysis to be taken seriously. But when it is that personal it is hard to imagine any reality exists – save the feeling of becoming one. It was discomforting for Allan as he realized his own capitulation to a great risk if he was wrong could mean his own and Lisa's death. Lisa played with boundaries. It was within their love nest of two with no interlopers – so why not leap one last time as he knew marriage could be the answer. Allan had been so hurt by his ex-wife's betrayal, he was willing to try one last time with Lisa who never betrayed him or left him cold and dry.

Allan, in resistance, held onto his hypothesis and conjecture of 'Why?' as he embraced a complimentary existential analytic perspective of how Lisa choose to be so irresponsible to him and herself?!? Allan held her in his strong and powerful hands as he looked her in his eyes that were ablaze with passion and anger,

"Lisa Wei Feng Cannon, my hope and dream. [Subduing his tempo] You are finally the one hope I have waited for as my wife. Now, look at what you did? How can I possibly ever let go and trust you? How could you possibly love me so much and then play with trying to kill me as your lover? You took pictures, I want to see them again. I can't believe you. [silence for a long pause] You actually tried to kill me – your man. I realize you drank that shit yourself! Why? I love you. Don't you know that even with your kinky desires and your incredible hunger we are already one. It is risky for me, incredibly so. Don't you know I am your mate and lover? We are unique, and for one another. Give me a reason and I will be yours as you wish!"

Lisa lit up with passion and reason.

"Fuck the others and the irrational world we live in! The mental and spiritual health is the ability to do our best for others far outside their lives as long as we have our own sphere of comfort and desire sacred and intact. I am a prosecutor and I help victims and you help victims and sometimes even those who do crime. But I love you and will never ever leave you and you will never betray me. That is all I want, and for you to put up with my mood swings and jealousy Allan."

Allan realized he had Lisa's face in his grip all along but did not hurt her. He immediately panicked as he reflected on his incessant obsessions and what if he lost it and did hurt her. His obsessive-compulsive style was piqued and he did not know what to. Almost instinctively, intuitively, he connected with the natural flow of male and female as Lisa Wei Feng continued,

"Allan, my master and king, do you want to see how sexy you are to me? Let me show you your pictures, naked. Please, Allan, I need you to fuck me now! I want you inside me! Beat me with your belt darling. I was a bad girl, but would never hurt you. I was jealous, you know, as I felt you flirt with her, I mean the Medical Division administrative assistant. I know I am wrong. I love you, just don't leave me; please don't leave me and come back home with me. Never leave me, dear. I am in love with you, Allan, and miss you very much. Please darling, forgive me for all my carnal sins and desires they are all for 'You' and you alone."

Lisa Wei felt she could lose Allan, but realized her jealousy ruined every relationship and was pathological. Allan was baited as if he was there to be a therapist and even more a psychoanalyst to understand and uncover her conflicts. But Allan realized marrying her would cure his and her ills. Allan told Lisa,

"I am thinking of reporting you. But I can't, ever, I love you. I can only say as two becoming a circle of one – I am most likely going to ask for your hand in marriage."

Lisa looked imploringly,

"Promise me secrecy Allan. I will be destroyed as a Bureau Chief of Homicide Prosecutions for the NYC District Attorney if my private life is ever exposed. Yes,

I admit I could have killed you, Allan, but I did not. I guess I could have killed me too. I cherish our love and miss you as well when you are away. I meant to play a game of Russian roulette please forgive me. It was an anomaly."

Allan returned to a place far in the distant past as he was wrestling again with a request for silence. Allan felt the tugging of dissociation as he felt warmth toward Lisa Wei Feng cooling down.

Allan slowly visualized a distant memory long forgotten and buried in repression reemerge.

A little boy standing in the basement of his parents' three-bedroom home Allan was now transformed into a nine year old. He was left by dad, his sisters and brother to take care of Mom alone.

He watched his mom in her loosely fitting dress with a turban tied around her head having another fearful migraine as he slowly hugged the old wood stairs to the laundry room. He checked on his Mom as she was suffering from a migraine headache and was moaning. He concentrated his young powers of observation not knowing how to comfort her but he tried as she suddenly looked at him and dread arouse in his gut.

"Allan, life is too hard to keep pushing on. You'll be okay without me. Your father can find a Latino whore in the factories. He loves the Puerto Rican sluts. He will gamble away the shirt off your back and you will never amount to much yourself. Yes, you're a good natured kid. Remember, like your Dad said, you and he were meant to be ditch diggers. You can dig my ditch and I will lay in there, dear Allan. My only son, as you bury me, I will cry in my grave for you and me. I wish I could give you more and we could be a happy family. I feel ill, son. I can't deal with his cheating ways and I know this will be best for you, your sisters and brother. It will make your father happy who can replace me tomorrow with one of his floozies."

Allan got busy cleaning and fixing the wooden laundry sleeves that hung the family wash next to the spiders and cobwebs. Webs by spiders spinning their own intrigue to catch a buzzing meddling fly. Allan remembered looking at his father's secret stash of playboys he also knew was hidden from mom. He remembered seeing a redhead caught in a web of elastic as a man was doing something strange with her. He knew it was nasty but he liked to look at naked woman not understanding fully what he was staring at.

Mom reminded Allan of the spider with the fly in her web. That was much scarier for Allan. He felt she was in danger but not sure of what.

Mom smiled at Allan and asked what he was thinking? Allan learnt he could deal with the different shades of mom by sensing what she needed before she asked. His intuitive skills were shaped by survival, and he knew that her life and perhaps his own depended on her being kept calm and supported especially when depressed, anxious and dissociating without much room for pause. Giving her whatever she needed was Allan's training. Mom who at times interrogated him with harsh words did not really mean for him to be hurt but cast them at him like so many poisoned barbs when she switched to her personality alter of pain and suffering. By figuring out how to get her to calm down from her excited states he somehow intuited he would always be a healer. As Allan matured other women in need of rescue prompted his adept skills exponentially increased with his innate attractiveness. He became a magnet for borderline, histrionic and depressed personality types?

Allan knew when Mom was wearing her Turban, that is her wrapped towel around her head she was having visions. Visions of which little Allan could infer her need for him to reassure her of his love. He had to read her feelings, her thoughts and what she really had in mind as a survival adaptation. It kept him from becoming mad but also gifted him with many talents. An understanding that others were struggling with in the worse of disorders was his uncanny empathic attunement learnt so well and discernible to him. Born in the harshest of needs, survival emotionally would shape his career and professional calling. Tragic as it was, the same laws of scaffolding in an unplanned experimental field trial lent the deficit of trying to rescue ladies who were way below the screen of his mind and soul leaving him bereft of love.

Allan, that very shocking day, noticed the covering over his mom wrists. As Mom began to slump, she lay on the stairs in the basement as Allan felt numbness inside. Allan remembered seeing a movie where a man saved a woman who had been ready to jump from a bridge. At nine years old, he was telling his mom,

"Mom, don't worry I will keep 'It' a secret! I am here for you and I need you, Mom. I am sorry you are feeling so bad, Mom, let me see please." Mom stayed on the stairs for what seemed an eternity. Slowly, he undid her-self applied bandage which was beginning to soak with bright red blood. He knew he had to be a man and that was that. Dad was not home and he would be very upset at Mom if she would not awake. If little Allan let her sleep, the red bandages would become redder and darker.

Allan intuitively looking up at his mom's eyes reassured her it was all going to be ok. He began to apply pressure and called on the old dial up phones to his cousin an ER doctor. He remembered hearing the number and dialed. He got his cousin, Dr. Stanley Cannon. He said,

"Mom is not well and I need to bring her to see you. We are on our way."

His cousin who was in his forties and a physician said,

"Okay, Allan, do you know what it is your Mom is so upset about this time?"

Allan said, "Yes, I do but I will tell you when we are alone and I can speak in confidence. Dr. Stanley Cannon, I am on my way. Mom had a very bad day and is sorry she had an accident. I need you to fix this and to remember Mom is good and I am sometimes very mischievous."

He and Mom kept it secret, like her many outbursts including her suicide attempt on other occasions, her anger outbursts. Many other manic moments they would share over many decades of life. Allan, remembering he was in that basement again as Lisa Wei Feng in her dress and her shroud lightly covered her face, had opened the grief hardly expressed. Allan's yearning to rescue his mom he could never fully do was now redirecting to his beloved Lisa.

Her own perfect madness, as Dr. Nassir Ghaemi called bipolar disorder type 2, plagued him in the mirror of his own overvalued conscience as his dividend paid off like his own father's trifecta. Allan hugged Lisa Wei as she moaned in tears. He felt on Lisa's first axis she suffered from bipolar disorder and dissociative disorder while on her second her borderline personality disorder with antisocial features and hysterical traits could be fascinating as much as finally cathartic for him. They became lovers once again on the stairwell of his doormen building. Lisa and Allan hugged and cuddled, moaning as he rose and fell in her silk laid strands of a Gordian knot.

A tied circle, he and she wove in the addictive hypnotic collusion of their love. Both Allan and Lisa orgasmed twice in sweat and tears as both replenished their passion with compassion and unconditional love. Born in the heat of mania and obsession as compliments in the forest of unresolved conflict.

Allan spoke in whispers heard between the membrane where salmon go upstream on a waterfall that crash and burn as the running fish is met by huge Grizzly bear jaws closing on their flesh. Oblations for promiscuity and love. Allan lulled Lisa's fear into calm as only he could do.

"I promise you silence and fidelity my lover and best friend. I will drink the poison you give me as if your lips are a chalice of sweet red wine and arsenic if you so desire. If it will save your life and prove you are lovable. I am yours and you mine."

Lisa said,

"Allan, you are as sick and twisted as me. But I understand you, darling. The mother you rescued and love so dearly and have taken care of dutifully your whole life makes me as a psycho-chick seem like a piece of cake. Eat your cake now, I am yours completely and you are mine. In exhaustion, Allan Cannon lay almost asleep alongside Lisa Wei and for that night falling into the bliss of heaven in a way only the blessed and damned could.

Allan awoke, waxing poetic as he worked off the sexual heat of the night; Lisa was swallowing his words as he sonorously lulled her as she had him,

"A reprieve from being a Demon and a Saint, a lady and a gentleman – in the epiphany of our glow – man and woman – Adam and Eve – unfurled in the naked truth. The devil is most elegant in the shadow of the angelic glow of innocence spoiled." [Gulping his breath Allan in his wet underwear from his release in loving Lisa without boundaries continuing as man uninterrupted went on without breaking.]

"Innocence yellowed in conflicts ubiquitous as the triangle of mother and father – Oedipus and Jocasta – ancient motifs reaching into the most modern of edifices. Aligning Fifth Avenues hidden dirty secrets. Secrets such as Potters field laying the bricks for Pulitzer winning poet's words aligning the Ghosts of vagabonds sauntering through memories lanes. Honey the two lions guarding the tomes of the modern Lyceum that bear witness to Bryant Park. Civil wars of a country are nothing compared to dead sworn to silence in peace as internal conflicts never rest till integration occur. A silent cadence of forgotten memories cast over a reservoir of unconscious streams."

As Allan sang to Lisa, she slipped into the cusps of sleep. Slowly, her pretty eyelids fought closure, opening a little and then again almost sealed. Under the comfort of Allan accepting her back after the almost undeniable death instinct being worshipped as a false god – she was blissful and repentant. Lisa visualized Beijing's forbidden palace guarded by the couple's symbolic animal ingenuity. Silence broke with her own poetess ingenuity,

"The King Lion in Beijing is left with all his power as balls of circular entrapment of one cycle flow into another – fads that arise and tempt are drawn in the circle of matter in centrifugal forces without surcease. Inner and outer cores of earth as hot as the inner concentric circles under the mantle protected by the fragile crust that shifts lava with water – heaven and hell – dying within life cycles many circular movements." [Gasping in excitement, Lisa went on].

"So moves the transmigrations of soul's endless quest for love and peace under the canopy of life's mortality that touches eternity in each shift as male and female pelvic eruption tips the orgasmic plates and the floods that follow. Like earth orgasms in yin and yang and creates new continents so goes the plates of pelvic inter-section where male and female collide in creative genius and explosion."

Allan got up from the bed mesmerized with her allegory and brilliance of metaphors flowing as he listened intently.

"The Lion King my dear Dr. Allan paw the concentric engraved Bronze hollow ball inside the outer shell caught in his splayed massive paws. Each outer circle returns to the origin of chaos unable to gain traction in 'It's' forceful pull: Externally restrained. Faith incarnate! Lions who are kings with power Divine retract the force with power within as the concentric outward pull of gravity is halted in resistance. Musculature refined protects and secure his Lioness. His Lioness by his side proffers his powerful large paws vigilantly guarding his beloved Queen, and their cub.

291

Queen of the jungle holding their cub under her paws grasp as he forebodes warning to interlopers to beware. The Lion mounts her stature with his shadow aplomb from behind. A formidable duo where each fulfills what the other can never do in their mirror image alone; the circle centers itself on the beginning of all creation. Reflections of the Creator, the father as Supreme Power of all force and temptation. Compare Chinese natural power with the narcissistic linear force of impotent male Lions guarding the NYC Public Library. Lions cast in concrete of asexuality as the guide to becoming perplexed. Echoes reverberating as much as the haunting civil war of pride in the courtyards where the North drilled against the South a hundred years ago. Homogenous vacuity no yin and yang is boring and uncreative as impotence."

Allan said, "I never noticed that distinction, Lisa, that is awesome." He had a boyish cast as he listened with excitement as Lisa's interpretation continued unabated,

"NYC, a palace of diversity or narcissism of the special interests acting as if they can wipe out tradition and history with their bank rolls and no soul. As if the whole world revolved around the axis of a melting pot of force without tradition and culture laid away on an impenetrable Palace of self-love. The age of Narcissism endangering the free world and social world fixed in empty tombs of reified idols. Idols embalmed far away from the origins of a social experiment called America. The America where tradition, values, religious freedom, and true diversity of respecting worship of G-d and cultural differences eclipsed under its mirage. Stretching egotism of one gender guarding the Library in the Western world, two male Lions never make a kingdom –

a King and Queen did, do and always will organically, naturally and wholesomely."

"Go on, Lisa, please," Allan intent on her ingenious view confronting the new vogue American elitism as inept held true value,

"Chauvinism of East and West fused as the polarity of differences intertwined. Creative energy enthralled the tombs of Alexandria where Marc Antony lay down his life for Cleopatra. The pride of Rome was destroyed when leaders, who were self-worshiping demagogues, took over and tried to recast culture, family, and even faith by force of exclusion in the guise of inclusion shook the world of civilization! Think, Allan, of the library of Alexandria left a pyre of the treasure cove of intellect and fertility where poetry reigned and romance fueled the genius of sexuality in their polarity. Bifurcated in compliments, where each family had their lion and lioness to guard the occupants of Potters field and aristocracy as well – left in ruins. Ruins as desolate as the volcanic eruption of Herculaneum and Pompeii where tyrants in the name of progress swept plagues over a society almost supernal in being dashed to hell in a distortion of perversity."

Allan said,

"What do you suppose can be done, dear, in such a world that can destroy itself and again rebuild. Is it not a natural consequence of the death instinct as Freud posited in all societies?"

Lisa paused and answered with depth and pith in her moment of revelation,

"Ruins today are the pyres of the affluent scourge where without a middle class they saunter over progress. This while penniless mendicants hide in the nooks and crannies of Bryant Park. Illusions as circles of force continue in posterity where the elite try to split the unity of a spiritual America. The new elitists replace the ancient while decrying the brave that fought to conserve the values against the abuses of the rich that fly in private jets as big as homes."

Allan in alliance in part with Lisa took off with his compliment to her zest for insight beyond a narrowing of life with a death drive of modernity feigning progress,

"Lisa, it is not Prometheus who stole fire for the people's wisdom. Nowadays, it is the fire of the Almighty hidden while the masses place new gods and false idols on their own illusive alter of pyrrhic victories. Failure, once again, as illusive forceful interests try as they will to change what culture and tradition hold as natural as G-d's frame is so audaciously defied in a little man proclaiming progress. Alters, where homogenous echoes narcissistically retreat in self-absorption and distance from merger. Merger in creativity and brilliance where two poles complement each other as East and West alters in civil wars. Civil wars waged in internal strife is what provokes compromise in ever brilliant unity of husband and wife. Healing is allowed ventilation via friction. Friction is killed when justice as special interests see fit legislate their distorted reality as moral truths. Legislation of Justice surfeits choice into force. Power is where the Lion and Lioness must awaken and roar my lover. Together, they will conquer inner demons and outer gargoyles that haunt the present with the past. Show and flare in Bryant Park elude being something new as the old cadence of cowardice clamoring for being a brave new world has one more turn of the screw. That screwing is buried in its own mirror image as narcissus in love with himself and herself drowns empty and alone without fecundity and profoundly alone. Brilliance, without reflection on tradition and culture as being heterogeneous as diversity only can be – is bound for the future of the Pharaohs where in-breeding breed a homogenous society into oblivion."

Lisa tried to capture the wisdom of her kaleidoscope of views and Allan's as united. She allowed herself to circle in her minds rapid flow. Dynamically teased insight with responsibility began to hatch.

Lisa was unsure who was talking in her dreams and who was the wise Sage sharing his wisdom with her. She felt as if the wind's fingers grabbed and choked her before sleep descended on her vulnerable and naked.

Unresolved conflicts condensed as reified shadows whispered through the book shelves. Lisa Wei Feng worked through eternal images in each new poem written in blood and sulfur, dripping from eyes so red from crying she could not squeeze a tear to flow forth in her nightmare. The internal ghosts of aggression and sexuality played out as yin and yang. East merging with West as man internalized in woman. Woman swallowing what is so sorely ached for inside, yet shaken by each storm on the horizon of insecurity. Orgasm condensing in the surreal elegance of her minds shadows and lights with color of red, black and gray were endless births and deaths in-deed.

Suddenly, as she was trying to restore her conscious awareness, while fighting her nightmares – daydreams experiences with trauma shattered her peace and ingenuity in shattered reflections.

Lisa's sojourn to layers unpeeled in dreams unfurled where nature allows freedom in commitment and direction of purpose. The screen protecting Lisa from memories were broken tonight as her mother's huge obesity went from hazy to in focus.

Mom's shortened hair became tangible once again in Lisa's foggy screen memory. Mother screaming at her and chasing her with a belt around the house felt like the gusts of a rogue wave as the Yangtze was lost and she was entombed in the past corridors of traumatic loss.

Lisa, at ten, was locked in the closet for hours as she was tied up to the cabinet and crying herself to sleep in a standing position. Her passive father stood mute as he sheepishly asked Mother if she could be let out for snacks. His Asperger's disorder kept him focused on teaching Lisa math and physics as language and action empathy in cerebral play which was his transitional object to protect her and by association himself.

Mom, who died of a sudden heart attack in her late fifties, while cleaning one day after she walloped Lisa with a horse tail whip of seven bonds, was immortalized. Her mom was mourned by father who could hardly fend on his own without her. Lisa was left alone as the cuts from the hits bled into her wish to disappear. She remembered thinking, before she was given up to foster parents, that the present could be retreated into the future. The books she picked up from garbage dumps and hid in her inner world of solace would deafen the rants of a cruel sadistic obese woman. An obese woman who oddly had the name Mom.

At times, she would also drift into voices in which she heard the older voice calling her a horrid little creature deserving of whippings repeatedly. If only spankings, she, at times, witnessed her classmates experiencing could be the only punishment, little Lisa would be happy. Lisa's ability to feel as if life was not real and she could disappear into the world where a prince could let her out. She could play with her far, far away boyfriend from the closet of broomsticks felt so real it became real.

Lisa saw brown wolf spiders menacing her with fangs ready to bite. She had sores under her feet and her Achilles heel was arched from leaning upward as the ropes that tied her would cut into her skin if she rested supine in the closet. At times, she dreamt of her Dad saving her and taking her away to someplace special and safe. Far away from her closet and beatings. The trauma of seeing her father screamed at and belittled as she was left alone with her mother and feeling as if no one could save her let her become the heroine of men who were thrown to the curb by femme fatales. She remembered her mother opening her father's mouth and pointing out how he was missing teeth and saying to her and any relative willing to listen how horrid he looked. She belittled him and said he was worthless, because he could not achieve anything right. She had no education, but put him down for none.

Mom would say don't choose a man like him. A no good fool and a waster your old man. Find a real man who has a real education. Yet, Lisa cried when she saw her father's soul torn down as if his persona was a rag to tatter and hang out to dry for all to see. His shame and humiliation was her mother's pleasure. Lisa remembered her humiliation, suddenly, by the bully Maria and Lee through the haze of what appeared to be dismembering her privates from her body. Atonement for their evil deeds of trying to humiliate Lisa was her borderline rage. Her hatred of female bullies or sluts was intense and caused her pulse to race with venom and headaches she still would get. No mother to identify with as a little girl who grew up without boundaries and no father to offer protection and nurturance as most fathers were wont to do with their daughters left her in search of her ideal hero and father figure who better than the little boy who suffered with her who at the same time could be the 6'3" Muscular cop doc?!?

Lisa remembered the first time she stood her ground to her mother and told her she was a cow and could not get away with breaking down her father anymore. She received the biggest beating of her life. Her scar on her hip and her welt still could be seen under her hair on her temporal side of her cranium.

Her mother, without boundaries, would argue with little Lisa about who owned what toy. Lisa was not sure of a memory of her father with mom. In the screen memory, she could visualize opening the door as Mom lay on top of him. She was hitting Dad hard and moaning like a beached whale – it was horrible and messy. She hated the image of the harsh cold hated mother who had no heart.

Yet, Lisa always wished in her ideal version of her family life as she would tell each suitor she had a perfect childhood. As she felt imprisoned and beaten Lisa remembered Allan truly loved her.

Lisa began to struggle with awakening from her nightmare. Allan did not abandon her, even though she acted badly and cruel at times to him. She tried to think well of Allan, but she began to struggle with disturbing images popping up hazily as they vanished in the ether. Lisa was trying to stay awake as her imagination flowed tacking her back to the twilight, where she visualized herself laying naked as a virgin on top of the Yangtze River.

Images of ghosts of yesteryear past one at a time. One unique man she shaved in her youth of twenty something appeared. Lisa tied his hands behind his back and dominated him till he almost cried. He did the chest-stroke as she tried to have him lay next to her: Handsome, rugged, and ruddy as his back stroke glistened across his chiseled chest and trapezoid muscles which tightened and expanded like a Lion engaging her. Lisa was licking her lips as if he was to be devoured. She could not recall his name. His name as identity remained dangling on the tip of her tongue – suddenly, the cold Yangtze laughed. He passed and she kissed him deeply. Like a deck of dominoes cascading into the haunting aura of the engulfing fog, he was dragged undertow.

Under the rapid undercurrent of the rageful Yangtze's wet and overwhelming hunger, she engulfed another man: As one emerged at a time, whether handsome, rough, refined, rugged, slight, rotund or muscular, each man she chose disappeared. Toy boy dolls she sleep with in the dark of night emerged like dead buoys. They grew as living moving beings only to go limp with the illusion of egress away from her grasping arms. Never quite holding onto any man, regardless of each one's desire to connect with Lisa. She experienced each in lust, but not with the depth of love.

That is, until Allan, love had not laid next to her dreams with reality. Each man was not good enough. Too little of a bank account, or endowed with a few inches under the acceptable pride; or shallow and without depth; or not smart enough; or too smart; or too serious, or too frivolous – none met the mettle of her content.

Hunger for restoration by swallowing each lover of her past. The Yangtze was Lisa's twin and deeply unconscious in her surly sallying with each male stallion, driven into the depths of her suffocating need for affection — rejected — drowned. She awoke as she was deeply kissing Allan's strong lips. Nubs lovely to scratch her delicate face with feeling to awaken her from repressed dreams so longed for and drunk like a hot cup of Joe: Sexual, spiritual merger, sung passion with reason in silence as the lunar coldness fell on under the shroud of darkness illuminated. Dreams and wakefulness wrestled. The sun ushered in as he caressed the moon as she bounced in his penetration. Ecstasy in Lisa's dreams where temporary parting awaited a full cycle of a day and night to join again. As if the Creator of eternity made his covenant, where man entered woman naturally and she received the chalice filled with celebrating little angels vying for entry to the doors of the palace. Lisa heard little bells ringing. Illusion placed in boundaries protected by the stability and security of love unbound. The doors were opened as the eternal rebirth of dreams and prayers – poets and vagabonds dance the song of truth.

Lisa said, as she felt Allan hard rubbing her as he slept and she wrestled once again to awake.

Two were one and once again asleep as the first band of light creased the night's fold as the sun bid his entry. Lisa, now in her hypnogogic hallucination, visualized the moon exiting in her daily small death as an eternal mourning of losing her Sun once again. Grief of the Moon. Lisa cried her comingled losses as she became the moon struggling to caress the passing sun. Her losses resonating in her civil war experiencing what felt as the pangs of birth. Her different alters of persona clashed and hid under the surface of her conscious awareness.

The sun yawned a new day, eclipsing the night in his illumination as he shone with intensity. Energy, not of celebration, but of grief as the Sun had to live each day. The world he emerged on could only be oppressed as Lions and Lionesses guarding the forbidden palace bellowing as loud as thunderous clamor in the loudness of silence.

Grief unheard where vulnerability splits under the internalization of conformity to survive another day in the inanity of the world gone grey, as Lisa's dreams slipped away. Lisa awoke and as quickly fell asleep, unsure if she told Allan, "I may be pregnant with our baby." Lisa tried to remember her vision and the horizon she embellished in her dream of the Yangtze River holding her on air. She tried to speak as her past lovers and traumatic losses slipped into unconscious. As if but a dream vaporizing as the condensation on the smog filled windows facing eastward of Allan's apartment at 20 West Street in Battery Park.

Allan, emerging with Lisa, as both mumbling about dreams they were unsure of held each other tightly. Day dawned on the lovers. Sleep resisted interruption as the lovers held time in abeyance. This night of sacred repose was revelation awaiting the dawn of a new day yet to be told. Grief was put in 'It's' place – if even for a moment.

Allan forgot about his own traumatic loss and finally felt revelation had granted insight to his own return to innocence.

Innocence or not, he felt he needed to rescue every wounded bird, and broken lady he crossed in his personal life's circle. Allan Cannon would break the cast. Determining to take a road of integrity no matter what the cost became his pathos. Remembering Lisa Wei Feng's mumbling at the crack of dawn, Allan erupted as if awakened by lightening throes,

"Lisa, my Lord, you didn't say you are pregnant, did you?"

# Chapter 22

## Triangles Undone: Det., ADA and Cop Doc

Lisa lay on her back, silently rubbing her abdomen down around her pelvis. Looking at Allan, she slowly rubbed her sensitive area, waiting for Allan to touch her there. She felt vacant without Allan. Although he was processing his question without speaking any further, she slowly grabbed Allan's hands, as she placed his hand on top of her tummy. Allan began to playfully touch her and ever so gently, explored her sensual sense of self awareness.

Allan's sense of conflict was now piqued as Lisa had claimed being on the pill. Allan's voice changed in his sensitive style. He was gentle, like a strong white rose piqued in honesty washed with pain. Silently, he believed his suffering with Lisa would make him a better man. Allan the Tragic Optimist – accepting, when even the worse happened, that there is always life and hope with the next day to take promise from. Allan's voice emerged melodious, if not sonorous to Lisa when he said simply,

"Lisa, if you are pregnant, whether boy or girl, I will be a great daddy. [Pausing, he said] Haagen-Dazs ice cream for you every morning dear or evening."

Lisa turned around as Allan checked out her smooth coccyx ending in tight cheeked elegance. She hopped out of bed. Allan loved to roll back and kiss Lisa's derriere as his silly comments always made her smile and laugh lovingly. She turned on her favorites in succession as Louis Armstrong, Glen Miller Band and the Piano Rolls of George Gershwin played in sequence as ghosts of the past spoke volumes. Allan was more into the more recent ghosts of the Beatles, Simon and Garfunkel, Jim Morrison, and Bob Marley.

Lisa, recounting the eloquence of men and women of the roaring twenties, who dressed so elegantly and with loyalty to be counted on even among knaves and outlaws. The twenties luxuriating in opulence, decadence and endless carafes emptied as carapaces' along the boulevard of deserted dreams and buried schemes. She recalled the great Depression hitting the dashboard of the farmers with a bowl overfilled with dust. Schemes where the dim lights of idealism and youth again in a manic pitch blew out its promising light. Unlit after depression, revitalization, and the ever elusive see-saw of gains from discipline, and family values now lost in a new brave world again waiting to crash as Allan agreed. A moment of pregnant thoughts filled up Lisa's empty pinched uterus as she ached to be filled with Allan's seeds, furrowed in the hearth of her center once again.

Lisa Wei Feng held Allan Stuart Cannon's hands as she readied to jump into their fate above, or below. Faith that wherever destiny would lead her and him they would be united always. Little does the flowing of Destiny disclose desire freely – she remembered her dream in fragments – as foreboding portals, opening furies unleashed on the lovers as the Yangtze River was wont to do in his power left to roam wild.

Lisa was addictively attracted to men her whole life, but Allan was equally addicted to women who were wounded as he sought the elixir of cure as a doctor of the mind, she sought to mend wounded men by the remedies of justice.

Lisa knew she had to change her violent and aggressive tendencies for vengeance was ugly. She knew her focus would change and re-direct to one man, not elusive men lined up as boy-men toys to play with anymore as she placed her dream to the scrutiny of lessons learned.

Perhaps Destiny would flow from the feminine side, she mused as the Yellow River opened her window as her excretions scoured the taste of sweet honey with devouring hunger as her tempestuous nature sought becoming one with the Yangtze in bold relief of rock and water hugging for eternity in a free fall of intercourse. Lisa would allow herself to take charge of Allan's life. She needed to guide him with her ingenious administrative skills without envy and jealousy as her husband she so waited for. Inexorably, Alan and Lisa sensed foreboding in the vanquishing outer darkness as something infernal was felt within. For Allan in a parallel process as a composer of strife and ecstasy he felt the power of Yin and Yang. It was if he could pick up in his intuitive senses what Lisa was thinking and feeling.

Allan convinced himself of the sanity that awaited in the wings of hopes promise as he whispered to Lisa,

"Yin and Yang, what a concept. My sour sweet jurist, there lay the rub. Your female soul dances in ecstatic hold with her male soul in flight. Sabbath is the day of rest in which the feminine kisses masculine. Resting in unison two splits symmetrically placed in dynamic unity fold over the obelisk face of the sun. The moons semi-arc shadows dancing on the edges of a precipice where the cliff etches song and celebration. Two imperfect halves now whole in perfect fit and purpose balances fait with destiny. Choices – align fate as destiny unfolds petals that fade in times tyrannical grasp. Genius is destiny together as only a glimpse of what is in existence – flashes of a slice in mind and sensory input unadorned – let go and surrender to the anxiety of two fusing as one."

Lisa stopped and paused, and in intense connection, she said,

"We are becoming one, my love, even in life as in death united and never ever to part."

Allan disputed within himself the feeling of destiny being dark: He placed Lisa's morbid irrational schemas as no different than overeating, indulging in gluttony, or as somatization when stress was too high. Solipsism as the Cornell Psychologist, Professor Louis Sass, postulated was the cause of Judge Daniel Schreiber who believed he was metamorphosing into an insect, and then into a female. Psychosis into madness was a retreat from the madness of a world no one who is sane could believe was not to a degree insane. It was not organic in some cases, but a retreat to a place where one could be left alone. He, again, was concerned Lisa could turn to madness even after an illustrious career. Schreiber was a Judge, after all, and had retreated into poverty of mind and soul as his psyche devolved into the lull of nirvana too.

The Holocaust framed Allan's association as he thought of other human beings putting other human beings into ovens like pizza. Humans being made into pizza, imagine that, or lampshades, what's the difference? Why? Because their faith was unique and their religion different than the majority they were burnt offerings? Sanity in a modern package – what is that really? Allan drifted for a moment in an almost hypomanic frame of thinking as he felt no clinical psychologist or psychiatrist cast aside his/her disorder of the mind in the mirror that guides their practice and style of assessment and treatment. Lisa, this time, looked at Allan and in similar synchrony of mind and soul provoked him to see a reflection she knew well enough in her borderline intuition,

"I know, Allan, your hypomania is considered the diadem of ingenuity and leadership from Churchill, Lincoln, Picasso, Beethoven, Stravinsky, and Polanski and perhaps even Pope John Paul's saintly and truly humane-being, becoming. So, become dear who you are. I can handle you in all your flavors as long as you are loyal to me alone."

Dr. Allan Cannon knew the harsh beauty of reality as those humane-beings blessed with honey were inflamed with the vinegar of disquietude in their own soul. The purging of the depression with the antidote of polarities was after all the Yin and Yang of life. The masculine and feminine free to be as meant to be and infused as compliments – not opposites. Polar dynamic play smashed from reality as a word of opposites creates a war thrust in by politics and accordion semantics rather than the artistic flow of the muses. Allan responded after reflecting,

"Muses that craft words as endless horizons and eclipses as the richness of hypo-mania. Mental anomalies in the population at large resonates with illness of the mind, soma and soul in shrinks alike as all the rest of humanity we treat. Except for training and expertise assists the healer as to where, whom, when, how and why to go for advice, assessment and treatment if their own dam is ready to overflow. Lisa, my love, you have me if you will not see any other doc for your issues. It is not the best, but better than not seeking help to let me heal you myself."

Rims of looping drapes on Lisa Wei Feng's eyelashes laced her invitation to Allan to enter her emotional darker side. Ripe with sexual tension, the dam was now inundated with messy outcomes. Their tryst was set. An impetus set in motion in perpetuity so it felt, and seemed in their – 'Oneness'. Madness irresistibly and inevitably as destiny and fate became lovers as eternal as repetitions compulsively drawn in their unique web of addictions.

Allan still was held in black and white frames, compelling him to hold on tight to illusion instead of the harsher color of reality. Allan knew Lisa was not able to gain existential and psychoanalytic insight in order to syncopate her door of perception to significant change without messing up her opening beat with him. Dark corridors and odd places would be visited, but not all at once. He mused they would bravely place their feet together in daring leaps never holding the traction of being grounded. He knew working through with Lisa would enlighten and motivate each the other in the depths of the phoenix in flight, and the roaming of the dragon in mud. Set in stone, as a pyramid triangulating shadows cast on the Obelisk's angle a 180-degree line where shadows were ominous would freeze Lisa's modes of identity as he tracked her associations to integration from its disintegration he was there and knew how hard the road to come.

Lisa was drifting in the space of time left unstoppable in momentum. Allan was anchoring his time to fill the gaps with interpretations of derivatives of base desire centered in the existence of supernal dreams and masculine schemes. A collage bridged their moments of silence as it did and would as they contemplated as each morning dawned in her lunar tears as the sun pouted his grief in multiple hues without restraint. Darkness shaded the sun as neon lights illuminate crevices of light in pitch black hues. But what darkness of heart threatened splitting the heat of the August sun of their hearts this special morning?

Allan struggled for a long time silently and internally as he wrestled with Lisa Wei Feng being the one for him – even with all her flaws – he could only abide by her now if she held their baby in her womb? Lisa Wei Feng Cannon, what a name, he mused, and the baby may be named Janet Sarah if they had a girl, as his mother, or if a boy, as his father, Jack Daniel. He soliloquized Lisa as a jurist of note and success; the right pedigree. A spirit he enjoined as being for him and with him. He soliloquized, he was turned on by their friction if it did not go too far. She would outgrow her personality disorder and it would become an adaptive style with his love.

Allan held onto his wishes in conveyance, making wisdom a vagabond he would consult and give to Lisa straight up on the rocks – only if things – got really bad.

Troubled by her darker side, Allan knew some of her sordid dark past read like a pornographic typeset in her mind's eye. Allan feared she would remember the scores of men she slept with, but rationalized, that deep inside he could tolerate her surly ways and with genuine love his love would heal her rifts within.

Allan knew his colleagues and training analyst would say while Lisa Wei Feng was entirely functional and adaptive she was torn apart inside. His training analyst the clinical director at Cornell would gently, but persuasively, attempt to convince Allan his un-worked through remnants of a training analysis still needing to be exhumed and re-analyzed. The unhealthy compromise of conflicts by his Achilles heel to save females in distress as he did his mother was extant: Dr. Allan the ever classic rescuer. His mother, who attempted to cut her wrists open and bleed her losses and pain away in pools of self-loathing undone could never fade from his own guilt of pain witnessed and his feeling he could have cured her.

Curing can only happen if the patient allows the doctor entry. She who cried in her depression and moaned in migraine pains; he suffered with her in silence as his love always pervaded his fear and worry all phantoms of his own. Allan cried helpless to his own sleep to subdue her nightmares. Nightmare sinking her into daymares that live on in his own trauma of ideals left shelved in his ego and dwelling like ghosts in his psyche and soul as in Lisa's.

He would defend himself to his training analyst. He broke from completion as a murder he had to solve after the chief of detectives asked him to analyze personally disrupted the final treatment phase. A murder in which he played cat and mouse with a psychopathic cop. Until the trial began, Allan's life was a portal on a steamship, and his own psychoanalysis cut short. But that chapter was yet unwritten in the journal anticipated in Allan's future, when time would pause as he would scribe the different chapters in his colorful life as a cop-doc. Allan's healthy narcissism had some unhealthy derivatives. All successful therapists have worked through their own unhealthy narcissistic setbacks, ideally – that is, in part. Remnants of unhealthy narcissism engulf vision until resolved.

Allan's training analysis and experiences with all therapy was to separate from over-identification with patients. Dr. Allan Cannon knew Lisa's psychopathology clearly, but he also knew his own skill as a clinician.

Dr. Allan knew, if he could tolerate Lisa's projections of what she suffered in the harm of her childhood traumas and the many losses hurled on her in her adult life she would heal completely – as Freud said, the cure for all neurotic conflicts was "marriage". He could make the leap. The time to invest in her as a lady of the time was becoming more real with each passing moment. Lisa had all he wanted in a mate, and together, they could make life larger than the sum of two halves – left dangling in the space of individual spheres they were left cleaved in twain. Dr. Allan knew catharsis lay in Lisa Wei Feng's emotional break, when she tried to poison him in a para-suicidal attempt with homicidal tendencies. He characterized her attempt as having borderline tendencies and anti-social features and historic petulance formally but with the veil of love, passion and desire, he leaped to a trauma paradigm about what Lisa Wei Feng endured as the solution he needed for his own equanimity. A solution to risk it all by marrying her.

That choice was equivocation, not clinical judgment. Dr. Allan knew all too well that any patient presenting the same scenario would be immediately advised to gain a distance and security without leaping into the borders of perditions circular spiral. A spiral to the center of what could only be a trajectory of hell.

Allan would not listen to his own rational mind. He knew well he was a maverick and that was objective in the eyes of colleagues in law enforcement and psychiatry/psychology – he could be the anomaly and so could she. Allan could cure her himself with marriage and innovation in treatment. His cure was to be effected in empathy and integrity – he knew he also was sinking into wishful fantasy, but he discounted the better side of sensibility with sensuality and desire for an ideal mate as he idealized her in his ideal. She was the perfect balance of woman and equal mate that would check desire with love and bring him happiness.

Allan overrode every argument his mind could think of regardless of insight, intellect and even his conscience. Lisa's need at times to view men subjected to sadistic poses as visual preludes to making love disturbed him. But he allowed himself to indulge her, even giving the pretense he was into being dominated by Lisa as she was wont to do in orgasming.

He, in his quiet moments, questioned Lisa's sadistic tendencies, sexually played out with him as her prototypical John. She closed her eyes and would feel his chiseled cleft chin and his barreled chest. Lisa loved dominating Allan, and while resistant at first, he began to accept and enjoy their sexuality as a couple. He even got into some of her more gentle playfulness. He cringed at times with emotional disturbance, when her grip on his groin became intense – as Allan flinched in pain as she cupped him – she moaned in pleasure unequivocally. In a paradoxical motivation that was primal her state of consciousness got so piqued in his pain with ecstasy, that he was turned on and enjoyed her delivery.

Lisa explained to Allan, after, that it was like Stravinsky's, the Rite of Spring as choreographed by Vaslav Nijinsky. Allan would not look at men in leotards, but tolerated her staring at these muscular men dancing eloquent as swan's aplomb in their element. Allan intuited Lisa's fantasy of men triangulating her as two would save her from the loss of one she invested all her heart in. She needed Allan to play out her desire with him. It was safe fantasy, as long as the play only went so far and the actors did not get so enmeshed – when fantasy ends with reality mimicking illusion as if it was real – reality becomes sur-real. Sur-real as the highway to trauma always has that flavor as does dissociative disorders.

It always led to orgasm as she imagined being totally in charge of all men as she would whisper in a hush. Lisa shook in her rite of female desire to merge with one man in the final act – the finale of small death and their unique match as prelude and prologue to the next venture on her musical and artistic journey: A journey where pain met pleasure artistically and aesthetically.

Lisa could get Allan to feel as if Lisa felt when she had yearned for the nurturance and warmth of a father protecting her from a mother who locked her in a closet and burnt her with joints she made from left over cigarettes. Her father never satiating her need for protection from a crippling mother was internalized as one central voice in Lisa Wei's head. A voice always critiquing her other alters, especially the harsh whip of seven tails with seven seals of identity modes where the innocent ones hid and never grew. When she orgasmed, an innocent naïve alter of Lisa emerged confused and disgusted witnessing her doing things with Allan that she felt a need to undo. Her finger inserted inside him and a mouth full of sticky fluid was left with no insight into what they had just done as lovers. Lisa would drift to other places where the loneliness was crushing and she felt desperate to have Allan hold her.

Memories as vague images of Polaroid shoots where she looked at herself left alone weeping, but not able to cry, as she learnt to focus on the door knob when she felt she was devoured by the places mom would leave her at. Places such as truck depots, where mom would play bop doll with men as large as her. When Mom left the cabin, she'd look at Lisa, calling her a slutty, filthy girl, trying to pry into her affairs with all the male friends she had. She was tied to the closet post in the kitchen many times to keep her under wrap. Lisa could replay in iterations the rhythms of her past trauma with her own score and color.

Colorful and red, black and grey with each chord of her choreography exhaled in a crescendo of the apex of the moment of climatic synergy. Like Stravinsky, she had spring sprung with eternal hope and energy. Her energy was not like Allan, but a dramatic flair that would leave her scared to look in the mirror. But, as she looked at others she knew, when other alters emerged as she would be laughed at, ignored, or others would look away as if fearful. Allan, as a lover first, pleadingly asked Lisa to stop with her need to touch him in ways he felt were strange and exciting. Lisa would continue in a responsive way in which she knew exactly how and where to apply pressure until mutual climax was reached but never without pain.

Lisa ruled and Allan succumbed, no matter how much he resisted. Allan's knotty drives and neurotic impulses when denuded left true love for Lisa. Professor Allan, in the context of Lisa Wei Feng's repetitive and cumulative trauma, placed her aggressive sexuality as superbly sensible from an eco-ethological perspective existentially. Dr. Allan was compelled to believe intuitively that, 'if only' he could get to her alter identity modes, he could heal the rifts better than any other clinician.

Rifts that were initially adaptive from a survival perspective or as clinically put in an eco-ethological sensibility would be the antidote to cure her existentially once analyzed, recathexted and re-directed by Dr. Allan.

If Professor Dr. Allan Cannon could help Lisa merge her altered shattered personality by cathartically exhuming and re-directing interpretation with each alter – some would grow and others would recede into the larger alter until integration could be achieved. Allan knew in the space of time unwinding that a release internalizing this new sensibility would integrate Lisa Wei Feng to a whole woman.

Lisa's dissociative identity disorder was primary and his in essence secondary and healed. Rifts in identity modes of survival where Lisa defended her adaptation to a horribly twisted reality of survival altered her cohesion as a whole person. Each split in serial identity modes emerged in the extreme vulnerability in which at times unconsciously she re-visited in the present. She was without existential awareness that her alter identities would take over and leave her with the aftermath to deal with. Paradoxically, Lisa had winced while pain racked her body and she was excited at each abuse endured by pursuing even rougher and more forceful men, who had little or no education or compassion.

Lisa's own adaptive functional dissociation requisite for survival in her ecology of trauma was frozen in the space of time as 'It' first emerged in. Lisa's legal identity mode in which her own analysis of crime, and zealous enforcement of penal law in criminal procedure and prosecution, surfeited her need for justice. The overlay of a cat of seven, not nine tails, brought such pain equal with the forceful pleasure of her sadistic release. Lisa yearned dominating Allan as a powerful brilliant man as he orgasmed simultaneously with her as she felt explosive as a volcanic eruption with the molten core of her inner turmoil erupting when she would do things to him done to her. Lisa could get orgasmic at the feeling of Allan being fiery and heated in his emotional response including jealousy as she would lay out his most sensitive issues and she would flay him in raw pleasure.

Lisa discursively flayed Allan's vulnerable and sensitive inner fears as he cringed in the armor on his outside exuded quills of pain. Lisa read Allan with razor sharp alacrity in which he would succumb to her needs. Without thinking further, Allan's addictively compelled passion for her next roust with his different sides was exciting for her alters.

He realized he conquered doubt, fear and trembling as his faith in being able to love Lisa Wei Feng became clearer. He was ready to be a sacrifice for her needs as long as he could be and it did not push his boundary of panic too far. Lisa's perverse ways with him satiated the same sore vulnerable areas in Allan needing to be penalized and be redeemed, his own masochism. Allan proved his love as requited finally after each tribulation.

Nothing was worse than death as unrequited love which would end the genius of their union with disingenuous conformity and surrender to splitting their fusion.

Allan loved Lisa deeply, while never fully resolving his own childhood traumas. Although his was not her abuse, it was his tending to his depressed mother who had suicidal tendencies that would not exit his conscience. Visualizing the old wooden stairs with discolored paint in the home that was hellish and withdrawn in all its haunted mirages he would return in nightmares. Like spirits hovering over his own vicarious trauma of Holocaust stories and the wholesale murders he experienced as a cop and doc. Allan learnt to work through his losses by confrontation and ingenuity in his calling with passion and reason. The worse image of his mother, which he felt to the core and in anguish he could not rid himself of, related to the women in his life.

Allan felt most comfortable with Lisa Wei Feng, who in his love and empathy, he could help integrate with patience and insight and not fail her as he felt he did his beloved mother, and strings of other failed love relationships. Life would become a check – mate with marriage for him as much as her: Each angle was countered with the next move of chess across the board of competition and illusion of force. No one wins as each move results in counter-moves interminably. Love lay in the corner of Lisa's coveting eyes, never satisfied as long as Allan was apart from her.

For Lisa, the very man she yearned for, she would alienate with enough time. Time for different alters to sabotage those who were innocent and lovely.

She knew deep within her psyche that her coveting eyes, where she sought so many suitors who failed her –

Allan would not. His fear and trembling of dying a fatherless man was too much to bear. She would become his wife. He would be a daddy. Surging with happiness and energy, Allan felt he grew ten feet tall and was fit to be a King.

Lisa Wei Feng said,

"Allan, I missed my period by three days according to my scheduled bleeding. I may be holding your baby, babe."

Holding a new day as Lisa Wei finally and suddenly awoke and hummed in a mood that was shifting into a feverous pitch. Lisa immediately began touching Allan as he tried hard to sleep. She would awake and sing in silence as she explored his body every morning that they were together. The past few months, she would kiss and hug him, ensuring him of her love. Lisa Wei held Allan tight and snug as she nursed him to an attention and thrust every morning. He half groaned and pouting said,

"Let's take five more minutes for sleep, come on, bunny babe, just another few winks."

Lisa's Beijing past bristled with discipline as her eyes widened as she remembered the cock crowed his morning calling. She kissed Allan deeply and remembered the tastes of their sweetly joined fluids, she said, "sour, pungent and salty, my Captain". Truly, she tolerated her own sweat and smell but only for his sake. Lisa let go of her inhibitions as a prelude for love making.

Lisa was uncannily able to envision Allan's secret turn ons from her side, and his in turn. They were very similar indeed. Like him she would tolerate his needs even when they were not hers and she got excited only because they were his fantasies. He did the same.

Allan grinned as their smiles met. Allan finally awoke to the solace of love conjoined. Lisa was cheerful and bright as she began to sing,

*"Those were the days my friend,*

*We thought they'd never end,*

*We'd sing and laugh forever and a day.*

*We'd live the life we'd choose.*

*We found we'd never lose.*

*Those were the days, oh yes those were the days!"*

A shift in conscious awareness and dissociation lapped up each undercurrent wave flowing inside as she almost aspirated on some images emerging. Pornographic photos of naked chicks she was forced at seeing at a young age as part of the male dominated milieu of the bar-room nightclub scene. Her mother left her in this trashy scene when her father was at home stupidly ignorant or blissfully in gross denial. She was turned on watching men get excited, but felt vulgar and disgusted at what excited them – women in snap shots that looked like vomit to her as photos of vaginas opened as umbrellas. Men would aim their swords into their sheaths with explosive connection without love as she was raised to see.

Lisa shifting suddenly, sounded like a bargirl more than Mary Hopkins original karaoke of, 'those were the days'. Lisa sounded like a female bartender suddenly shifting her voice, posture, and even her facial expression as a rough no-nonsense 'cat-house' purring feline.

Allan, now re-directing his attention without being swept under with excitement, viewed her for what he suspected was an altered personality.

"But who are you now dear?"

Could Allan get a name out of her identity mode alter within a disintegrated personality? Allan felt a chill, but succumbed as he felt his goose-bumps trigger lines across his thighs and along his chest. Lisa Wei Feng transformed and her voice rattled out seductive calls as he backed into a corner. Allan turned around and said,

"Who are you really, my lover girl, so sexy and hot?"

Lisa said, "I am your fascista Oh kiss me, Antonio – hard and long! Strap me down and spank me hard till I scream. Ram me deep inside. Any way you want entry you can take me as long as you are on top of me with passion. Call me Kristi, baby blue lover boy."

Allan turned to look at her as he saw twitching in her eyes and she turned pale red as her brown pupils constricted to an almost cats grey coldness. Harsh but cherubic glances pantomiming Lisa Wei's attractiveness as wincing at Allan, as if he was the last man alive.

Allan Cannon said,

"Not now, fascista. Later, when we finish with my work playmate, Kristi. We can get heavy and hot into each other. Not right now. Don't worry, I will ram you as you wish, give me a moment."

Suddenly, Allan, distracted from his tactic of eliciting what he tested as his hypothesis being partly successful, suddenly said to Lisa Wei Feng.

"Hey, what did you mean Antonio kiss me hot and long!?! Oh honey, we have to tackle this dilemma without perplexing ourselves. We need a plan to deal with the borders of malpractice either way. I actually thought you fantasized I was Antonio for a moment and you wanted him instead of me. He is your suspect, not your lover. I realize the strain must be exhaustive darling, but we need to resolve our strategy today."

Lisa went more into a trance like state when Allan delayed gratification to Lisa's alter-persona, Kristi. Allan held back without getting totally swept away. Lisa began to get very irate. Lisa's ire had gone from almost passive to vehement in a swell of ego deflated as Allan paused momentarily. Lisa Wei, turning in her angst, set a wall between Allan and herself. Suddenly petulant as classic borderline pathology fractionates into triangles as winsome pleasure, she shaped her grin and divided their love with a wedge.

A painful grin in effigy to her lover she had played one time to many in the quantum space that punctuates love. Until cured and healed of so many raw open wounds Lisa Wei Feng embarked on her repetition of petulant fancy to recapitulate once, and again. Collapsing her identity modes of furies let loose like harsh to soft tones biting in acrimony – colliding once again – sabotaging her longed for love.

"Cop Doc Allan, you can forget Kristi, it is Pallas Athena. I am one with you: Don't worry, I am going to wear your balls you've left behind when dealing with that mouse, Antonio! I will hold your balls in my grasp as a perp with a shield – is sunk to the depths of perditions grasp."

Pallas Athena, as Lisa's vengeful and cold alter, let out her damning exhalation of words cast in ironclad barbs. Her confessions unrealized, but resonating injustice unfurled in ironic twists to rupture their hope of love left undone and unfed in tragic relief – perhaps as she continued,

"I am going to rip a new piece of justice in the Annals of NY Penal Law for cops who kill other cops. Cops and their lovers left dead. I am not going to relinquish my hold on Antonio. I will bury Antonio alive in his criminal intent. His vicious desire to kill his lover Christine and her new fiancé Tommy is beyond my ability to process. Is it not beyond yours, Allan?!? I am sorry even if this comes between the love of my life – you – and me. I do love you, Allan, [pause] but this is one for the books." [Pausing, Pallas Athena emerging as Lisa Wei, quivering in the corner of where she stood as frightful even to Allan Stuart Cannon.]

"Antonio has the motive and the means to kill. He did. I ensure you he will pay for his sins, and then some, Dr. Allan Cannon. He will rot in hell for what that perp caused me in pain and anguish in my life and forever more. I mean in so many and hopes and dreams squashed by this miscreant monster in a detectives shield. I will shield the world against such monsters. If you leave me, so be it dear, dear Allan. Justice's austere tensity must test the loves tenacity bequeathed in the sheath of what is right over what is banal."

Allan, listening, was allowing his attention to penetrate past her words as he absorbed her process and its toxicity without fleeing. He grasped her unconscious hatred for Antonio which was irrational and vehement as icicles on redwood trees and as fatal. What scared him was the idea that Lisa called herself Pallas Athena. A female dowager, who was nothing but a man-eater. Freud haunted Allan's psychoanalytic ear as 'penis-envy' heard its way into motivation in part. Lisa Wei's satiation of having possession of Allan completely included having her own penis by possessing Allan. Most men would flee, where psychoanalysts would layout trenches five days a week for the next ten years of analysis.

Not Dr. Allan Cannon, for he knew and accepted he envied Lisa as well. He too wanted her completely including her coveted 'vulva' he obsessed about as much as she his penis: Tit for tat. Parallel but reverse drives complimenting the river Styx of life and death inundated his reason. It brought out the electable truth between the lovers blinding obsessive entrancement as one. But where did Antonio fit in all this? Antonio was hated but why?

Justice was one thing, but blind hatred was another. Was her need to castrate him a desire to end his male essence, and devour him in lieu in her sadistic psychopathic pleasure? She eluded to Antonio as a lover in her other identity mode.

Allan stayed silent as Pallas Athena continued,

"I want to see this bastard pay for his cruelty and frivolous life style. Public eyes and hearts can move on in their own personal lives when he burns by the stake of justice. His womanizing days are over. He will now be mine and mine only when I web him like a harsh whip. Seven lives are blown out with seven seals of fate closed as the shield of chivalry has died along with dreams like Cinderella. All chances of release into his scheming world again left in fates closing shudders on hope and love as foolish as the dreams of a young woman in love with the first young handsome man she dines her eyes on. Antonio is a dream of handsome face and harsh hearted callousness. I relish my job where I can put murderers behind bars for all time to pay for their crime and suffer in ignominy. I will crucify him with relish …"

Allan remained calm at this point, outwardly, but regrouping he was back to square one as Lisa was again dissociating to this far extreme prosecutorial side, Pallas Athena.

The alter Kristi, with her bar-room cocktail waitress catty ways purred to the wiles of men needing women in places where crumpets, eaten by strumpets, lay their crumbs, as if substantive food leaving hunger in both was the opposite.

Catering halls of empty requests never satiated in the hearts of men and women so lost they do not even know they are left bereft and wanting. Tragic in the tempo of lust one is blinded that each can fulfill for no price save the most dangerous alliance – love. What the other seeks and blindly misses in each encounter of distance in passion with no reason and direction is only a small bequest away.

Allan reflected Lisa's internalizing her mother's encounters as shells of endless returns without substance. He heard in empathy little Lisa Wei harangued about the very desires her mother played with as her own now: The endless bar room brawls with her men sucked dry for a dollar and a wishbone left uneaten. Lisa needing to excoriate her father's castration by displacing her rage on her mom's cheating ways. She could punish herself by flaying Antonio. But why Antonio? Perhaps for being a womanizer, but not a murderer – unless he was a lover – unrequited? Allan stopped and confronted Lisa,

"Lisa, darling, you are taking your hatred of Antonio too far. You said you have not even served Antonio with an accusatory instrument. It will take a lot more evidence before you prepare an accusatory instrument. Relax dear and let's work this out tonight. We will have time to reflect on the case and take a time out honey. Please! Hold off your zeal for now. We need to sort this through and do not put our love on the fierce line of pure justice. Our love is compassion which balances zeal with mercy to its counterpoise! Heracles holds Pallas Athena in his arms and she became Helen of Troy who in her feminine genius could launch a thousand ships to war. Lysistrata staving off a thousand ships bound to war back to their home ports never harmed a fly. It would take a Heracles to cull from the depth of portals needing their fill to fuse genius of masculine with feminine to turn the muck of vengeance and shedding Athena's armor stolen from Zeus for an unfulfilled wish, 'full-filled'. Yin and Yang, Mercy tempers Zeal as the wise Jewish mystic Nachmun of Breslau chants in the agony of saints never allowed voice. Triangles where male up and female down balance each the other. The fusion of friction of life and creative sparks unite as one. Two complimentary halves fused as one where trust and love sparks discontent back to the origins of creation where the content of what life is all about — love."

Lisa Wei Feng, J.D., M.P.A. emerging as the host of the identity modes heard beyond the white noise of splitting — her soulmate – Allan Cannon, M.D., Ph.D. in his sonorous love song.

In a feminine style, Lisa Wei Feng yielded to Allan's impassioned rational hope, where love and compassion conquered pure justice with tempered justice. Without defense, or oppugning back in offense, or capitulation in a pandering style — in lieu she said in judicious sagacity,

"Allan, you are my better half and succession to the union of our merger with love. This time, precludes me from challenging you. My poetic warrior, I was wrong, let's stop playing. You know those other roles are all playing with you. You are the doctor of the mind as Irving Stone called Freud. I will take pause as you love to use that expression. Please forgive me. I am just very emotional at times over my work and I am passionate as you are dear. I want to win my case and Antonio is guilty. I am exaggerating when I go overboard. I am truly a good woman and will be a great wife and mom if you give me a chance!"

Allan stayed silent and in confusion and feelings of reeling he almost fled on his first instinctive response. On reflection, Allan instead fell to his knees as he took his enchantress in his arms and made love to Lisa Wei Feng. Kissing her all over and penetrating the armor of her shattered selves he let go with all he had. In a Herculean effort, Allan tried to exorcise her demons with his love. In rhythmic synchrony, Allan fully and without creases released inside Lisa again and again – orgasm erupted simultaneously save the ensuing moment of becoming one as they erupted in perfect synchrony.

The clock stuck nine thirty-six as Allan and Lisa, after the most magnificent beneficence in their enigmatic unity, left with a deep kiss, and oddly bliss. They both parroted the words, 'I love you' to each other. Rehearsed in their minds eye for repeat performances from some time long ago as déjà vu, they hugged strongly as both tearing in their eyes left the taste of sour in the sweetness of their lightest moment. Moments alone passed and both yearned for the other in the strange space of aloneness. Tick tock, so time stole away the last minutes, without much adieu. Allan left, perplexed, and Lisa Wei felt aloneness emerging in her fear and panic as she was shifting in awareness of aloneness. Lisa Wei held her

Louis Vuitton handbag as she realized it was time for a new purchase.

Lisa went into the train station in China Town, the cross point of New York Country Supreme Courthouse at 60 Centre Street, Foley Square. She would switch to the 6 train and get off at Grand Street, today she took Broadway and Lafayette instead. Lisa's re-emerging glimpse in her mind's eye re-captured Allan's skeptic look. She couldn't hide her nailing Antonio to the crossroads of their fate, a mistake – in-erasable as she watched the subway doors coldly close the escape to call him. Suddenly, Lisa anxiously felt the giant force of the BMT line rock to and fro as brash as her own compulsive actions. Her fate inter-twined with Allan's overactive guilt over losing his ex-wife where she needed assuaging in order for him to become the husband she yearned for all her life. Lisa Wei Feng left feeling she could still straighten the crossroads of disaster laid out in deceit.

Dr. Allan Cannon was not fully aware of how deep her deceit and psychopathology dug into destroying her prospect of marrying him. Allan had ignored his adaptive intuitive seventh sense of discomfort that twisted his gut. Allan remembered, when he checked his schedule, he had penciled in an appointment to drop by his former boss and colleague from the Detective Bureau who had put in his papers to retire as he was closing down his last cases.

Allan's former Commanding Officer from the Det. Bureau was already teaching as an adjunct faculty member at the famed Police College of NYC, John Jay College of Criminal Justice, City University of New York in the Police Science, Law and Criminal Justice Department.

327

Captain Commander Det Bureau, NYPD, Professor Duffy McMurphy. Professor McMurphy, near retirement, was one of the most highly decorated Detective Commanders with a rack of commendations for extreme courage that loomed above his shield. A rack that reached its peak over his shoulder years before he retired, actually had to be custom made for his awesome success as detective commander. The best of the finest sleuths who could assist Allan on all aspects of the case including as to Antonio's likely guilt or innocence from a logistic investigative paradigm. Allan almost forgot about 'It' as he tucked away Antonio himself in the torrents of his love affair with Lisa. Dr. Allan Stuart Cannon went back a dozen plus years with Captain Duffy McMurphy. After his appointment in the Medical Division, NYPD, they worked together on the Chicken killer in Tompkins Square Park, where the son of a Chief of Police ate his girlfriend and fed her as boiled soap to the homeless of the city. Memorable, but not the most stunning in horror and malevolence successfully kept secret from the media hounds and paparazzi.

That case being left for another day and diary where the nineteenth century Jack the Ripper succeeded in slipping away into the twenty first century. Both nodded to one another as the hint came out of, "Jack ripping into this time zone unravels as times imprint left shadows portending the futures travails untouched by our sleuths of yesteryear to only be tackled today once again.

With that thought in mind, and before Allan could answer, Professor Capt Duffy McMurphy's number came up on his phone contacts as his number rang. Allan remembered Capt McMurphy's ability as uncanny. He could smell a perp like a Hungarian herring marinating in Bermuda onions sliced and layered over an inviting bed of sour cream with baco's as the cream du jour. McMurphy as usual came on straight to the point,

"Doc Allan, I knew we were going to meet. You are involved and not here five minutes late, don't fret. Hold on as I let you know what I have learnt in the Double Homicide of one of our finest and nursing's finest. I need to ask you some questions. Can you make it down to Roosevelt Hospital Lounge and schmooze about this case, Doc? You can meet me next to John Jay. Let's cross over and grab a coffee black and no sugar, correct? I will walk over in five minutes, sound good for you?"

Cop Doc Allan, feeling a rise in anxiety, softly said,

"Sure, Captain. I will be there in about fifteen minutes. What's up, serious information? I sensed you were on top of the case, any questions for me?"

Prof Captain McMurphy uttered,

"Not sure, Doc, but what I have I need to review with you and pick your brains. We have a very perplexing situation here. I called Cavanaugh and Gubiosini and they said they are unraveling the scene with interesting DNA evidence being re-analyzed at the National Crime Information Center FBI." [Cop Doc Allan's seventh sense emerged which was one notch higher intuitively than his detective days. He was now a cop doc. He felt anxiety rising as excitement and fear triggered his racing heart rate. Lisa Wei Feng came to mind. She never mentioned anything to Allan about the case until her unease when she expressed real love today. She was confronted by him on both he/she being involved romantically as crossing the boundaries. Her zeal to prosecute Antonio provoked a suspicion of 'why?' again and again in Allan's mind. Allan knew he had gone over the edge of professionalism when assessing Antonio, and doing ambulatory intervention, he was perforce ethically blocked from having a love affair with the Chief Prosecutor Lisa Wei Feng. Did McMurphy know already somehow? If so, would his former C.O. lower the blue curtain of silence, or rat him out to IAB?

Allan suddenly almost like hit by lightning awoke as he reviewed his impressions, testing, and psychiatric interview as findings that indicated Antonio was not a killer. Conversely, Lisa was sure Antonio was guilty – cock sure, guilty. Allan began to resonate on how far addiction had gone. Allan was ready to marry, or consider marrying his lover – 120 days or so after meeting her.

Hardly two seasons passed with Lisa and he had constructed the missing pieces in the puzzle of her life. One piece of her puzzling behavior was her passive-aggressive traits as extreme polar opposites. Her borderline splits cohered with a dissociative identity disorder. Perhaps he's jumping the analytic gun wildly as Lisa was his lover and fiancé within a fortnight.

What other secrets did Lisa have in her closet that he did not know? His mind began to run off like a D Train Express rolling down the tracks of his mind when he did his transit police stint years ago. Captain McMurphy knew Allan Cannon's suffix ended with the appellation Dr. Integrity. Duffy McMurphy realized like himself Dr. Allan as a NY Cop Doc had one Achilles Heel. Allan arrived promptly by Duffy's office and was welcomed in as he gushed out without further adieu,

"Aye, Dr. Allan Cannon, my cop doc," Talking to Allan, as if a third party, he continued. "The crack in Dr. Allan's cannon volley of women is to undo your multiple Gordian Knots needing unraveling. That knot is tragic circumstances of webs. Each strand with challenging elasticity sprung you into rescue fantasies, but each time you succeed assisting your lady, Dr. Allan, you are left in the buoy of surly tempests all alone. Alone on the very spear you slew the many dragons of your own mistress's nightmares – while you became their phoenix impaled."

Professor Captain McMurphy bent back and looking askance at Dr. Allan; asked him if he minded if he asked a personal question. Allan stayed silent. McMurphy anticipating Allan's stoicism took no umbrage and he just asked a rhetorical question as he drew out notes from a file titled in hand written notes, Det. and Main Squeeze homicide – black widow H1 for hypothesis one; H2 suicide homicide … too H7, Det. Antonio involved. Laying out the crime scene and the perp's factual attack on Tommy and Christine. The slim former USMC Captain and NYPD Detective Commander looked different, concerned, he asked Dr. Allan,

"Look, Doc Allan, I need to ask you a question, do you know Lisa Wei Feng the Chief of the Special Victim Prosecution District Attorney Office, I mean as a lady?"

"Of course I do, Captain. She and I have worked on this case in two different game plans. But what's new under Tammany Hall in the City of New York?"

"Doc Allan, is she your lover?" Has she seduced you into believing she is in deep love with you?" Stepping back and visceral in his reaction defensively, Allan faced Duffy McMurphy and said,

"What the hell are you talking about, Captain? You were my boss once upon a time, but you are not my boss anymore. It is not your fucking business, no disrespect to you as my former squad boss, none of your business who and when I am fucking off job time."

"Okay, Doc Allan, relax we are brothers in blue [Hooah] We go way back. Just sit down a moment – [pausing] please sit." Allan although tense and angered – relaxed enough to listen and sat. "I am asking for your sake Dr. Al, not mine, let me give you some of the particulars and you tell me what do you think?"

Pausing Allan defensively, and calmly although his heart was beating fast retorted

"Hey, Captain Professor McMurphy, you sound like me. I must be influencing you old detectives from the Mickey Spillane rooms."

Both pushed out a little grin as the dialogue opened a little.

"Ok, Captain, shoot."

"I know you don't care if you get some egg on your face, Doc. We all do. [pausing] I suppose, we all do – I certainly have. I know you are not like the lay narcissists, who imagine themselves beyond error and fallibility like headquarter icons behind rolling desks. I know your humility when you err and that is what makes you a keen investigator of crime and a healer of the troubled minds. So, here it goes. I will lay out what I know and will let you decipher the possibilities. OK?"

Allan nodded a yes back in return to the Captain.

Professor McMurphy began,

"The first telling point was the contusion on the Occipital region of Tommy's cranium. The contusion was hidden as the investigators felt Tommy was hit by Antonio with the butt of his .38. The way they reconstructed the crime scene was as follows: Tommy realized he was under lethal attack by Antonio, his police partner of a decade. In shock, but still conscious, he fought back hard. Adrenalin pumping for survival pushed Tommy to head butt Antonio in his abdomen. Tommy had his torso ripped open by the hollow point round, almost point blank."

"Tommy struggled to hold Antonio down and knock him down and out as his final defense. Antonio, oddly, received a contusion of less severity in the occipital area of his cranium and a slight area of inflammation from the head butt to his abdomen area."

"The firearm was a 38 used by Antonio. An unauthorized hornet hollow point shell in his stainless steel service revolver inflicting mortal wounds on Tommy and Christine. Oddly, very oddly, we know as of today a new bit of information that has everyone upset except the ADA Chief Prosecutor, Lisa Wei Feng, who did not even chime in with her over righteous hellfire at Antonio just came in."

Dr. Allan bent forward, listening attentively. "Well, Antonio had been knocked out by what appeared to be a hit to the back of his head. Problem is what we have is similar to what the Medical Examiner found on the back of Tommy's occipital area of the cranium. It was harder, and even as we are exploring now, may have been a fatal blow preceding the .38 round exploding his abdomen like a sliced and gutted bullfrog all over the fucking wall in a pattern that did not seem like it was fresh intestines and stomach acid, but post-mortem."

Duffy McMurphy, allowing Allan to process this newly critical information, began writhing his hands around his facial nubs, helping him absorb links in the crime.

"Dr. Allan, it appears that even though Tommy was knocked down, his abdomen was ripped open by a 38 hollow point round post impact. In other words, it appears the .38 slug is not likely to be the cause of his death. Tommy's death was a dent in the occipital area, which we have identified as a .25 caliber or .380 pistol, not from a single fired shell, but a blunt wound. Here is the kicker of all – the hit with a blunt metal object cracked the cranium with a hairline fracture. The force under that fracture was done with such intensity from above it caused a hematoma and hemorrhaging. It was directly over a prior line of duty injury that had left that part of the cranium exposed." McMurphy paused and accentuated what was to come soon,

"As you know, Doc, Tommy couldn't gain his bearing after he was hit so hard in the back of the head. This attack preceded the .38 round crushing into his abdomen from Antonio's off-duty revolver. So, the question was, how could Tommy hit Antonio with a head butt to topple him over, while he had a similar blunt instrument in almost the identical region in the back of his own head. It appears, but not confirmed yet based on clinical review by our experts, that Tommy within three minutes of his blunt injury was dying and may have been unconscious. My question in this, Doc, is one that is purely forensic psychology. But even after the 'Bear', as you know Tommy was called, was hit in the back of the head he oddly was hit right where his old hidden line of duty injury lay hidden. Even more to the pointed question, Doc, is how could a tenured DA Chief of homicide prosecutions miss a toxicology report of blood and urine?"

[Rhetorically, asking Allan], "Why?" [Duffy answered as quickly]. "It appears the ADA Chief of homicide prosecution said it was unnecessary to disrupt the dead and the family needlessly with what is a case that is clear and shut. She went on a rant about how the motives were as clear as day. Gunshot wounds and ballistics of Antonio's firearm and his being on the scene were evidence enough without any other need to dissect the dead shamelessly.

We thought Chief Assistant District Attorney, Lisa Wei Feng was right. But we found out she was not. The M.E. in charge, 'Okayed her orders'. But that Odentologist Cop Doc, like yourself, the Wyatt Earp type Doc insisted on further tests as to when rigor mortis set in and chose independently to examine the bite marks and bodies of the slain hero, Tommy, and Christine."

"Doc, between you and me only, Dr K.D. said, that Christine was stabbed and her breast mutilated. Her breast had much fat removed including the lymphatic tissues and her nipples cut off. This was no simple sexual mutilation, Doc. Sperm present in her was Tommy's, not Antonio's. But blood traces of Antonio were absent. Tommy was present and the sperm in her indicating the homicide had happened almost immediately after he came inside Christine. It appears multiple times, that two distinct moments of ecstasy passed between them right before death set in. The report highlighted that earlier Christine's vaginal secretions were in Tommy's alimentary cavity after oral sex with her. What was disturbing was unidentified vaginal secretions, as weird as it sounds, post rigor mortis were also found in his mouth, as if some unknown female as of yet unidentified placed her sexual genitalia in his mouth after he was dead. But how could Antonio have been there at the time and who is the other female?"

"Now, here comes a worse enigma, Dr. Cannon, as it appears Antonio was hit after the crime of Tommy's homicide and Christine's mutilation, which are about twenty-five minutes apart. But Antonio was unconscious for hours. Further, who ever had vaginal secretions on Tommy's penis and mouth had also entered placed her genitalia into Antonio's mouth later on."

"Perhaps as much as ten and as little as five hours post Tommy's rigor mortis set in, but not before that, Antonio was also having sex with this unknown female."

"Allan, what and to whom is the motive attributable too? Who is the team of male and female killers? Even if Antonio is one of them, what female could he have been working with, and who is that other female?

Allan motioned by a shaking of his head as he tilted and touched his ears. His mind was grasping information and analyzing what was given to him as much as his heart was pacing in attunement to his mind.

"The trick here for you is this, Dr. Allan, what motive can you present? Was this some sick sexual madness?"

"To whom are we to direct our attention, Dr, Allan?" "Hold it, Dr. Allan, more information is important for you to know first. We have re-directed the contusion on Tommy's occipital region to be approximately the same as Antonio's injury except Antonio's was less severe."

"Another fact pattern, quite odd was that the sexual mutilation on a female victim is usually done by a male rapist/serial killer, who then in power dynamics, ejaculates on the victims face. This type of crime scene has also some other dimension of hatred of women, used to dominate a man. The destruction of Christine's body is mysterious. It was exactly what we saw, but no ejaculatory fluids were present at all, and no vaginal fluid except her own was on her body. Why would Antonio have an emission when we got to him and not have any sperm inside Christine, if they all were involved including this other mysterious female?"

"The blunt wound on Tommy and the hate scene with mutilation of breasts, does not make sense, can you make sense of it for us, Doc Allan Cannon?"

"The female vaginal fluids in Antonio's mouth and Tommy's are time serial sequenced as being later than rigor mortis and strikingly, at a later time than Antonio was unconscious already."

"Christine was inundated with bleach and the male organ on top of her was unscathed but had the vaginal secretion of another woman with traces of Christine's vaginal secretions indelibly and unmistaken as being her own. What was traced to a pap smear she had done in which an active virus for Herpes two was noted and recorded but not active at the time of death. So the other females vaginal or blood secretions is absent from any traces near Christine's body."

Cop Doc Allan was piqued and buried his resentment. He was, for moments, baffled by the information. But the mystery unveiling itself was teasingly scintillating as a pivot for even his tenured investigative skills and mind. His mind had to rest with pause to give attention toward tracing the steps of the crime for outcomes. Outcomes heuristically as hypotheses tested and rejected in his mind, just as Captain Duffy McMurphy was always doing in a team approach. Dr. Allan Stuart Cannon worked alone best and only later, after visualizing a cognate review of each active hypothesis and disconfirmation, he would come

337

up with. The most feasible trajectory done as he taught his students often were uneven narrow-ways which occlude into final analysis of one path. A path the good professor knew would be piqued and would provide a missing link for Captain McMurphy. But before Allan could accommodate his mind to working in tandem with the presence of the criminologist Professor Duffy McMurphy an interruption prefaced with a cough like release exhaled from Duffy,

"Wait, Dr. Allan. Hum another bit of information for you is this. I was called by your old partner in crime in the Bureau, Det. Gubiosini, who pointed out he was suspicious about Antonio spraying unauthorized rounds to kill his police partner of many years."

"Gubiosini said it just does not fit his M.O. The whole fucking tragedy doesn't! Antonio wasting his old – QT lover, Christine, makes no sense, he said. The horrible crime scene shit is perverted and highly disturbing for me boss, I have not been in choir boy practice a long while Gubiosini said: He felt the female information was critical, although he couldn't put his finger on whom and why. He said Christine was no freak and neither was Tommy and even Antonio as weird as he could get was no freak either."

Allan let his hypotheses shape the psychological profile as he had rapidly assimilated the new information and now accommodated a motif of the crime and its motivational roots heuristically speaking; "Listen, Captain, I was debriefed by the Chief of Personnel and the Chief of the Detective Bureau when it first happened. With what you laid on me now, it is clearer to me. First, Antonio's profile and character underscore the fact he would never use unauthorized 38's, especially hornet hollow point bullets. That fact and the next one which is our Tommy was Antonio's police partner, who had rescued him in more than one traumatic event would hold back murderous rage. Even if that potential had the fulcrum of betrayal printed in bold. A cop does not forget when a partner literally takes a bullet for him. His girlfriend/fiancé, Christine, evidenced by her newly delivered engagement ring found on her finger exclude a third wheel as Antonio being in the midst of their romance would not last. Antonio had avoidant qualities and also a terrible fear in common with Tommy, which was fear of commitment as a fear of loss at its core. Repeated trauma experiences of seeing folks lose whole families suddenly when violence emerges on the scene of crimes unfurled crystallized this avoidance. Yes, they were all friends, but Antonio was likely Christine's lover in the past for one quick affair from what intelligence gathered."

However, no matter what transpired, it does not make sense that Antonio would kill either one of them. He was highly dependent in personality and from a survival point of view intra-psychically as well. In some ways, his immature personality was not fully developed as most adults emotionally needing much more inner-sight to achieve becoming a full-fledged conspiratorial murderer with a female partner in a folie a deux as femme fatale."

Pausing, Dr. Allan coughed and took a lozenge.

"Further, Captain suppose Antonio got enraged when he saw Tommy get engaged to Christine due to jealousy. Why did he never act out like this before when he was much closer to vying for Christine's love? I'll tell you why, Captain Professor Duffy McMurphy, it is because Antonio had loyalty and would never betray his partner in policing for any bribe or payment. Even after losing his son, a much more intense scene than a friend having a fling with his best buddy's girl, he still hung on to the value of life. Even if he did have one night of indiscretion with Christine, it still did not make sense. But further inquiry disconfirmed even this hypothesis too. Antonio did go into a blind murderous mutilating rage. Why?" [Allan rhetorically asked as his former boss did in this style he learned]

"Because, Antonio was a devout Catholic and even after falling from regular attendance at Church, he would not open the door to murder in cold blood. This crime scene rivals Truman Capote's account of the massacre of the Klutter family by Hickock and Smith. How do you answer that? A true female psychopathic personality being led by a dependent personality as Antonio at his core is co-dependent?" Allan asked Captain McMurphy rhetorically as he was eyeing the Commissioners Report, Medical Examiner Autopsy, and Internal Affairs Report on Antonio.

"Instead of telling you why the hell not, my friend , colleague and mentor, I will ask you, my erudite professor, Captain McMurphy, a question as the Talmudists and Jesuits like to question each other with in rhetoric and exegesis as insights shine forth from this exercise of the intellect."

Allan, as Duffy, was accustomed to this and knew an important context would be offered to him to figure out the psychological analysis he was waiting for patiently. He tolerated his shrink cop doc's professorial tone. Even though he was Allan's former boss, he knew it was Allan's style of elocution and not ego related that worked in inimitable fashion for Dr. Allan with the alacrity of lightening throes.

340

"Professor McMurphy, Captain of Homicide, as you reviewed my course for use in your department and asked me to be a guest lecturer, I have a question." [Nod of assent from McMurphy to proceed] "Do you remember Psychological Analysis of Crime at John Jay College?" [Duffy nodded] "I used Freud's most astute student, Prof., Dr. Theodore Reik's classic, Compulsion to Confess: On the Psychoanalysis of Crime and Punishment. Well, remember the compulsion to confess a crime is laid out in every crime scene. It is an offering to the investigator in the form of a confession from a psychological paradigm. Well, the unconscious motivation to commit a crime is determined by the drives hidden from the perpetrator himself, who is not able to hide his symbolic satisfaction of the homicide as he lays out the crime scene itself. The satiation received or denied from the repetition in the compulsive aspect of each crime becomes the psychological lattice leading to the footprints of the perpetrator. The imagined horror undergirding the crime scene plays out forcefully under repression. Repression needs not only expression, but witnessing it until it actually is acted out with extreme prejudice. But, who needs to witness the crime scene and tease out the motive of that crime scene. Whom Herr Professor Duffy McMurphy?

[Duffy looked askance as to where this is going in his head silently]. "I am unsure do you mean you, or me who investigate the crime and perps responsible?"

"Yes, Captain, but only when the force of the death instinct paints vengeance. Vengeance is always sought as if it comes from one perp and is directed at the victims but in this case it is not against the victims. Pause and take notice to the fact pattern which indicates that no matter how mutilation is grossly laid out – ultimately, the vengeance is against the perpetrator himself, or perhaps her-self?"

"That is the drive of destrudo for destruction's sake. Death is exacted as payment by the conscience within on others that has caused soul murder within one's heart of hearts and soul. The vengeance for a forbidden desire is exacted on the perpetrator himself and perhaps, Captain – herself."

"Think about it, Captain McMurphy. Is it not true that when Antonio was found, he was in shock and had vaginal fluids in his mouth: But what if they were forcibly placed inside him by a female who desired men even unconsciously, who could not openly see her, but experience her when she was master dominatrix over them?"

"When I saw him, Antonio, he was grief stricken. When he awoke, he was riddled with guilt and dissociation. He visualized Tommy and Christine sprawled out. The murderer had written a blood note. A note allegedly done by Antonio, scribbled, as I read I intended to read it. I lost it somehow as the detective from the PC office said they would return it to me, but I cannot remember except to say it further disconfirmed Antonio to me."

Captain Duffy had not thought of these connections and piqued asked Dr. Allan,

"What is on that note, Doc, you can remember a simple note. You have a photo-eidetic memory deep inside your mind. Funny, Doc what has been confirmed by the State Attorney General expert in polygraphs and handwriting analysis Senior Supervisor John Cayman was that it was not Antonio's but indicated a feminine style of writing discursively. We still do not know and you have figured out definitively and I am almost convinced after your analysis we are onto a female psychopathic killer. Doc, who do you know that may have unconsciously led you, maestro of the mind, to hide that note in your own unconscious mind. That is, if I may be so bold, Dr. Allan Cannon?"

"Could it be someone who is female, who you've ruled out because you are familiar with her yourself?"

Professor Captain Duffy McMurphy took out a property clerk invoice marked CONFIDENTIAL and ONLY POLICE COMMISSIONER SPECIAL SQUAD in the area for instructions typed in bold print.

"Doc, the note said as follows as I read it to you,

*The piano rolls around Eldridge, where East end meets West. The village recalls an age of poets and poetic license in art as in music. Once upon a time, only lads could win lasses until the one man and lady as two are to be cut in twain – where they ought to be merged into one: The rest of the world, where ancient meets modern and love heals not divides, will laugh in mirth's folly. Atone for my sin Antigone by marriage, not where whores and gigolos consort and are not found in this new world. A new vision of East meets West, where hero and heroine can cleanse the world of villainy and villains. A great detective will deduct the truth bleached as a whale harpooned in blood that sanctifies Moby Dick under the pussy willow. Captain Ahab in as atonement for his own compulsion to repeat an obsession he couldn't remember and so on goes the tune like burning rubber as an analyst who lost his senses in a black widow posing as a recluse as she sucks her mates head from erect to limp so goes the narrow strait and the marrow of life within to the death that now matches without in perfect symmetry."*

Allan, taken aback and feeling chilled, couldn't place something very familiar and traumatic for him in the syntax and semantic flow of a psychotic psychopathic killer with borderline features and sadistic traits. Silence blew threw his mind until he defensively postured.

"Captain, it is no one I can think of. Honestly! Perplexing as it is it sounds familiar, somehow, but I have not put my finger on the pulse of what it is yet. It is being deciphered right now, as you said. It is of key importance. I believe once my analysis with Antonio illustrates a similar script in his altered hypnotic dissociative state of mind. As when I got him to speak finally and to offer his associations ,that note confirms it is not his profile but a female. From what you wrote, it is not feigning being male but actually desires to, in a perverse way, absorb and be adored by all males with a vengeance for females who get in the way of her lust for male sex and blood."

"The crime scene speaks of a male in sexual and seductive overtones, hinting at the evisceration of the sexuality of the female as she succumbs to a man who has taken in the empty slits of a woman and filled her with his phallus."

"Antonio was straight and this letter indicates a female who is straight but with murderous hate toward females. A female, like Christine, represented her mother she hates although she identifies with in her desire to sleep with multiple men. Her mother who is that whore and Christine in sleeping with Antonio may have become if she knew what we knew. The gigolo may very well be a good fit with Antonio as she tragically misunderstands and takes him for. If a match in the crime scene surprises us Captain, we need to lean more toward Antonio as her conspirator but it 97% false I will give you 3% on your hypothesis as being Antonio involved based on Heisenberg's uncertainty principle except as the target of her rage! But I will bet a knish and canolli it is not."

Allan, still by evasion and interpretation, did not answer the Captains question about his own unconscience yearning to hide something from himself and definitively from others. He would sharply return with a snug defense as truthful. The captain was not a trained and licensed criminal psychologist and psychiatrist like him.

"Captain let's return to the crime scene: It appeared the injury that knocked out Antonio was reassessed today by the neurologist and he said it was from a small blunt metal instrument. If I got it right, and I may not have gotten it right, from your own reading of the reports that it appears the killer had a small caliber firearm like a .25 or .380. Isn't that a ghost buy and bust detectives carry? Finally, why didn't Antonio use the .25 or .380 on Tommy or Christine, since it was unauthorized for him to carry the off-duty anyhow? If he had a .25 why did he not toss out the 25 instead of waiting around for being caught by the Chief of DA prosecutions in special victim's cases? There are traces returned from the forensic lab that picked up a 25 caliber gunpowder residue on the sample of hair taken from Tommy's hair and from Antonio."

Captain McMurphy interrupted Allan and said with frank, crisp rudeness,

"Allan, it appears that belongs to a forty something year old Asian female." Dr. Cannon stayed silent for a moment and without thinking of the hints Captain McMurphy offered him. Allan blurted out, "Quite odd, is it not, boss McMurphy? Further, why wouldn't Antonio not use the .38 to do himself in, if he already crossed the line in rage?" That does not make sense, does it McMurphy?"

In a long pause and silence, Professor Captain McMurphy took in his own thoughts and awaited his colleague's analysis to spring forth as he was wont to do.

"Psychologically speaking, Antonio by doing himself in as a way out of hell into purgatory as a devout Catholic who already threw in the towel with being human – would be predictable. After all, why hold onto this last straw of decency when pressed into a double homicide Antonio knew there was no way out of?"

Well, I will tell you, Captain Duffy McMurphy, what I think happened, and why. You with me so far, boss?"

Professor McMurphy nodded a 'yes' of assent.

"Ok, then, I'll tell you, Captain Professor McMurphy. Antonio's son died a horrid death he blamed himself for. So many times, he blamed himself for this with high intensity. His catholic guilt as bad as my own Jewish guilt hovering over me all these years as you witnessed and can imagine only tortured his ability to marry and try again. Still, all these years of self enforced isolation, he did not commit suicide, and quite telling, the opposite, he never killed anyone else, but hunted down those who did. Further, it is unlikely he could find a new relationship with a woman as a new spark of hope and yet stay behind in a one or two night stand left in the dust of his experiences. It is ludicrous with his guilt

346

complex to try again in the warm comfort of Christine who was now Tommy's new finance. He had disclosed this to Antonio as a police partner being responsible so he would know he would have to change police partners or work solo during Tommy's honeymoon. Much like you and I, his private trauma took its toll. Antonio remained a bachelor. Something I intend to end with a special lady myself. But I will save that for now and spare you the details boss. Ok?"

Professor McMurphy was taking notes and looking with intense pain as he had figured, and now confirmed, Allan had slept with the DA Chief who had placed acid in her attack on Antonio and had obfuscated the investigation, which would now be sullied with an Asian suspect. In his eyes, as he saw Allan go on, he almost teared up,

"The profile of the murderer is someone carrying a .25 Semi-automatic. A .25 automatic in the hand of a woman who needed to dominate men, while flaying the other woman as excoriation for some unresolved conflict in which she victors over the other woman. Like all violent acts that are done in reality – victory is pyrrhic as the pyre guarantees the ashes of the dead will speak volumes. I tell you, Captain, that we are looking for a female detective in the Bureau, who has worked with Antonio and Tommy, and knew Christine. But I have one question for you, Captain, do we know if Christine died due to her cut breasts and removed nipples causing massive bleeding?"

Captain Professor McMurphy eyed Allan, as if dumbfounded.

"Doc Allan, you know better than to push yet another detective in the bureau as being accused.

Mutilations in certain cultures in the Arab countries as well as perversions of masochism inflicted on women by men are horrendous. But at other times, mutilations on themselves can be much worse than any man can do. That is even when they don't die automatically after such injuries. It seems Christine died of a heart attack following the severe partial cutting of her trachea, but the crime scene in the Police Commissioners Special Report indicated ... [Interrupting his sentence being completed, a ringing bell tower sound from Professor Duffy McMurphy's phone echoing a church bell alarm foreboding danger, and broke his unfinished response to Allan]. "Excuse me, Doc, just hold my sentence for a moment. It's the other cop doc, your odentologist friend, Dr. K.D., a third generation dentist and professor. You police surgeons are all eccentric as they come. Almost as brilliantly ingenious as you, hum, but not quite. Grinning, at first, to a rapid change in the expression of Captain McMurphy as his facial expression shifted to one of shock. Consternation dripped over his usual jocular expression. He told Dr. K.D to hold on as he excused himself. Putting the phone on mute, Duffy McMurphy still listening to the Odentologist with the right ear, spoke to Allan as he listened to him with his left ear.

"Dr Allan, the Odentologist Police Surgeon K.D. asked the M.E. to re-examine the toxicology reports after bite marks from Tommy's post-mortem were reanalyzed. Figuring if the bite marks were the same age and gender as the bite marks on what Antonio showed the dermatologist three nights ago on his inner thigh. He thought a red bug bit him. Our dermatologist was called to assess the bites as he had delayed telling anyone even the nurse and attending physicians. The red mole was next to his right testicle, and under his muscles that overlapped with his inner thigh. He couldn't remember ever seeing the red blotch earlier as it was hidden under his thigh. The dermatologist tested him for a mole and she realized it was not a melanoma as suspected, but an abrasion. The RN on staff in the ER was a combat medic and realized it resembled an infected possible human bite mark. It would have gone unconnected but the Odentologist had been called in for a similar mark on Tommy's inner thigh and ingeniously realized the marking was the same as the inner thigh of Antonio. The lab immediately realized it was a hematoma from an intense hard bite from a human canine in which blood was drawn."

Allan almost salivating as he was listening in intense passion to the new information said to Duffy,

"Are you saying Dr. K.D. is confirming it is the same bite radius and type as Tommy's bite and done by a human?"

"Yes, definitively Dr. Allan!"

"Tell him you'll call him back and I will speak to him after we talk."

McMurphy, hanging up politely after a brief explanation to Dr. K.D., stating as Dr. Allan requested, to return the call soon, did just that. He had Dr. Allan back and with determination knew Allan knew the inevitable as he converged on his own intuitive mind.

"Captain, what about Christine's post mortem autopsy, this is a crucial missing link for me? I am thinking hard but I need more, so please tell me all you remember of her mutilation that I have not been made privy of from the Police Commissioners private report before we were interrupted?"

"Well, Doc, Christine had no bite mark, but her vulva including her vagina and her labia majora, and labia minora mutilated beyond recognition as each fleshy mound of the majora was flapped over each the other like a bow and actually inverted with the minora stitched as a lotus leaf if you could imagine. A knife had made an incision where the prepuce of clitoris and glans of clitoris moved down to the upper portion of Christine's urethra and centering the masterpiece of horror was the penis-shaft of Tommy and his scrotum eviscerated, where two sacs hung over her urethra to perineum stitched up and erect inside her genitalia. This made the most hardened detectives' revulsion extreme and their vomit trajectories flew all over the crime scene. Resembling a gyro filled with slices of lamb in red deep blood lay her uterus, folded like a phallic symbol around her fallopian tube crossed with her ovary and sandwiched inside. Her pubic hair shaven and glued with a white substance as a mustache on her lips fixed in a plastered smile morbidly displayed – it said in some language we are figuring is Arabic, maybe Asiatic to read some weird phrase. Her Vulva looked like a hairless peach with a penis inside. It was painted with lipstick and made to look like a work of art – with lumps of feces surrounding the core of this trophy. You know what I mean? Let me show you this psychotic shit." Cop Doc Allan looked at the pictures, deeply entranced, and in a morbid way, while revolted, he could not help becoming fixated on it. A deep glance as his pupils dilated and then constricted to a pin point changing his color to an almost green hue. "Go on and do not block any other detail kindly Professor McMurphy, please?"

"OK, I do remember something weird, that is probably not significant at all. It is Det. Cavanaugh, our com stat man for the squad and the other squad Captain Patel who consulted me on this unusual case. They said the scene was laid out with 38 shells but the knife used was gone from the scene and it seemed the icy air of the apartment was a bit too cold as they found the summer Air Conditioner was running when they entered in the middle of winter-like weather."

"Captain Patel said it was not typical of Antonio, or any of their guys, to use hollow points even at the range. Cavanaugh remembered when he had spoken to Antonio a number of years back, that full metal jacket rounds, 148 grain plus was for him and that he disdained hollow points as they were too risky as effective rounds and too much trouble to clean after shooting. It appeared the ME was shocked at the ballistics report that the blunt wound had traces of female Asian hair, even though minuscule it caused so much damage to the Bear as Tommy was called, due to his size they could not ignore that hair specimen."

McMurphy paused and held up his hand with a one more moment sign to Dr. Allan to listen to as important,

"Doc, it is not only that, but one more finding now that is crucial. This is one we kept secret because we believe as you have surmised singularly Antonio is innocent. We have been trailing your DEA Delegate Det M, who is known to have been married to a voyeur and she also has some very weird habits we have ascertained in liking white men and hating white women."

"Her hatred seems more psychological than racist and she has Asian roots herself from India. We have one other unlikely, I mean highly unlikely suspect we need to address. But let me not get diverted. Doc, it appears it was not the 38 gun hollow point shots that crushed

Tommy's life out, but it was the hemorrhagic blow to an old injury only a very intimate and medically savvy perp would know where to hit him to kill him as definitive not speculative. Further, it appears the shots fired entered into Tommy after he had been dead and the same with Christine we have hid from disclosure. If female, she had to have very gifted fingers as a seamstress or musician."

"Another fact is Antonio had underwear with semen stains dried up in his Calvin Klein underwear. His own semen that means he ejaculated by the female who committed these murderers and she had to be strong enough to do this as well as drag him to that room of murder and smart enough to drug him without killing him. Or Antonio totally flipped and he wacked himself off while looking at the crime scene. But what does that all mean, Cop Doc Allan? You tell me how do we proceed on hearsay and fragments of evidence without any definitive tie in to exonerate Antonio, and to convict your friend Det. M? Hey, Doc, oh shit, I remember the weird phrase was, "Fung Shiener."

Cop Doc Allan stayed silent for five minutes and sipped his now cold black coffee. He spoke with certainty.

"Professor McMurphy, the curtain I am certain is drawn, we need to call Captain Patel and the Chief from here. It is a female perp that kills with knifes, and flayed Christine with detailed understanding of female anatomy as if she were a doll to excoriate and display for humiliation. She wanted to have us imagine it was Antonio as a pervert and to desexualize Christine while she got off her rage against her own gender displacing her anger onto Christine. She also is a nymphomaniac and intensely overly sexualized. She had fellatio with Antonio after she knocked him out, not before. She left

352

some stain in his underwear to cause the investigators to think he got off on the wholesale murder of his partner and his fiancé. The same was true after our killer immobilized Tommy, before she killed him. Leaving some spillover of semen in his underwear as well as Antonio to indicate they were bad boys being punished. But, unlike her murder of Tommy, who she took out directly, Antonio had to be severely punished by setting him up. Otherwise, Antonio's semen would have been in Christine's vagina regardless of how mutilated. It was not!" Pausing, as if visualizing the crime scene happening, Allan said after another long pause of reflection and meditation as he visibly shook with a tremble, "This female femme fatale has extreme obsessive compulsive traits and without deep insight to her own psychology. In rage of desexualizing her competitor she wore gloves and bleached out Christine's vulva as if it was a dirty mechanical hole, that needed cleaning. She did this to distance Christine from both men."

"This murderess had sex with both men after Christine had Tommy on what had to be the engagement night or weekend. Her doing her sexual act as an act of force, not love, but vengeance."

"Ultimately, she unconsciously wants to be caught doing what she did. She is unusually intelligent, artistic and creative and could be a dream lover to any man she was with as she loved to swallow all he had to offer and had not issue with excoriating a female competitor with vengeance for stepping in line with her desired male. She paid Tommy back because she forgave him and purified Christine after suffering horribly being able to leave them behind. She united Christine with Tommy in death believing by sewing them together in a stitch which is called Feng Zhen in Mandarin. They will be buried together as she envisions love in death and surrounded by death rituals, the murderess ensured that in a way she is sadistically an over the top super-ego motivated puritan and whore in one as she projects out onto the world of those she seeks punishing. A manic-depression coupled with severe trauma and identity conflict. Identity dissociation disorder rings all the bells here as a true cocktail for a messed up sadistic and obsessive compulsively manic chick. She is a puritan in her wishes of a harsh sadistic superego, which, ultimately, will masochistically leave her punished and suffering for her sins and aberrations. Her extreme libidinal and aggressive drive derivatives on an unconscious dimension is a denial mechanism in which she projects on her victims who have been mostly male that they are the effect of the cause."

"I suspect she knew both men prior to their deaths and one of which she was intimately involved with. The murder was not sexual, but profiled as extreme prejudice against Christine for stealing from her what was imagined her possession her man. What did Christine steal? She stole the love of Antonio as he was left to suffer as a cheater who once had an affair that he confessed to her or she ferreted out as an investigator close to him. She reacted in almost blind rage and forgave him – Not!"

"She never let on how anger had consumed her into the vengeance needing punctilious exactness with the certitude of a surgeon. In primitive rituals, she stole back from Christine what she stole from her. She took the purse with the goodies so to speak back from Christine by desexualizing her; rendering her sexual prowess a force to be reckoned with and to keep Antonio from

Christine forever. She is intimately involved in detective work but is also intimately involved with Antonio with passion and will return to the crime scene. This crime scene and punishment of Antonio is her zeal and motivation in crucifying him who is most likely to desire self-punishment. We know Antonio's need for his own masochistic suffering for his son's death and other sins precludes his fight for his own innocence. As long as this rings true in her mind, Antonio is safe from the murderess, but how do we manage keeping an investigation clear from detectives in the bureau when one is likely the murderess till we have in her in our crossbows. No pun intended, Captain, I know that is a bad joke. But we have a female detective murderer or a female intimate with detective procedure and familiar with police psychology as well, as art and culture. Tommy had to be sacrificed in the melee along with Christine but we now have to seek justice as well."

"Allan, you are satisfied Antonio had no part in the double homicides, definitively speaking?"

"Captain, you can rule out Antonio, from a psychological perspective. He could not have injured himself this way from a physical perspective with the exactitude in an identical way that Tommy was injured fatally. You can also note the profile is one of an ingenious femme fatale, who will take out Antonio as soon as her goose is cooked with knowing we are hot on her trail as the mandarin stitch she left on the crime scene. It is not Det M, I know her and I know that is a poor reason, but it is not her, alas. You can check all Asian female detectives, pure Asian, or not."

"Doc Allan, I believe you and your trajectory makes good sense! I will alert the nightwatch desk to get someone down to check on Antonio with you without letting onto detectives he would generally work with."

"Intel Division Threat Assessment Unit, IAB, Chief Campostosini needs to get his best investigators on this case. It is internal affairs and our first graders that must ferret out this female psychopath that did Christine and Tommy in. She may now once again try to do in Antonio as you suggest. As soon as she realizes we are onto a female suspect, I agree she will try to do him in like an asp on Cleopatra. Antonio, who is now set up on murder first degree charges, is done in already from his sustained trauma. We need to protect Antonio now, Doc. Thank you your analysis is invaluable. Anything else you need?"

Suddenly, and with alarm on his face, McMurphy, before allowing Allan a response, says,

"Fuck, I forgot, [with a long pause and face drooping] Doc Allan, we will never succeed in nailing even one of our own females who are Asian and a female if the most tight assed D.A Bureau Chief you have a crush on is the lead DA attorney. That is what I wanted to bring up besides our main suspect, you also don't agree is that Det. M. is our prime suspect and she has one hell of a crush on you, Doc. That Lisa Wei Feng is in a world of trouble with her over-zealous prosecutorial style, as we all know. She seems to get her jollies over taking down cops, especially the Antonio type whenever the opportunity arises?"

Cop Doc Allan interjects to McMurphy,

"I'll call Lisa Wei Feng myself. Let me give her some schmaltz she will understand. I will be able to convince her of reality if anyone can before we get all the physical evidence in order. She is judicious and I will get her to see it as it really is. You know we have been having been an affair putatively. Prove it, Boss?!"

"Allan, my cop doc, if it makes you happy with all you give to us in blue, I am happy for you. I hope it works out, but she is one tough number as district attorney and no one knows her well. She is one odd number to follow. If anyone can it is you, Doc. Let me know when you reach her?"

Lisa's cell phone rings and no one picks up, but her answer machine comes on and the classic inimitable Gershwin 1924 tune Rhapsody In Blue before the beep to leave a message signals an ok, as Cop Doc Allan whispers enthusiastically and a bit louder than he'd like.

"Honey, call me, I am sure it is not Antonio who is the killer. You need to take humility pie and eat it with me. We are hot on the trail of the killer. I will surprise you like a Rhapsody in Blue and then we can be like Porgy and Bess. Although we are of a different hue we have the same spirit of beauty and eloquence my lover. I am so excited, you can let go of the zeal to prosecute Antonio – we are sure it is a sick and evil femme fatale in the bureau who is Asian like you. Darling, imagine, she used the name Feng Zhou on her stitches as you probably know her crazy sexual psychosis is real tortured. But I have my finger on her pulse and don't get jealous, but I will love nailing her for the mess she has caused. As interesting a case as it could be for treatment after she is put away for a number of lifetimes she can roast in hell as a cooked goose as we are hot on her trail. Then, babe, and real soon we can move on our vacation and get married. I am finally ready to marry you. Honey, call me immediately. Don't delay. I love you always, forever and a day."

Duffy McMurphy overheard Allan and chimed in,

"Wow, I overheard you well only the part about getting married as I never knew you were like that Dr. Allan, you and the District Attorney?! Hum, well – who would figure, except me. I knew it would happen, but keep it on the QT. At least now as your work with Antonio and hers will not be prosecutorial. If you could get through to her as you can, and I believe you will best let her know, she will be reassigned by order of the P.C. himself. A cop doc, and A.D.A makes sense in this big family of law and order. You are nuts, truly, but a genius we all know and respect. I truly consider you our Cop Doc, even if your choice of women can be quite odd. I still think it is Det. M, but we will see after all is said and done."

Interrupting before Allan could respond. The phone rang with the blue tone, 'excuse me, Doc' here we go again'.

"Yes, thanks for calling back Gubiosini I am listening to you. [silence for a few minutes].

"Yeah, I'll tell Doc Allan, he is sitting right here."

"Hey Doc, Gubiosini says it is probably not much of anything, but it appears some disc, a CD was next to Antonio and he had cut his fingers on. The disc was tossed away having no value to the crime scene. It was an old time great like, hum … [putting his ears to the phone] he thinks Louis Armstrong, no not Louis Armstrong, wait it was the Arthur Miller band, no wait, he says he's got it on the tip of his tongue it is George Gershwin. Yeah, Gubiosini threw it out as meaningless, but Antonio was pointing to it and held it so tight it cut him. Plus, the Homicide Riding Attorney from the DA's office was told to not keep the tape as Lisa Wei Feng

Doc, your lady friend and prosecutor, who said throw that crap out before he cuts himself with it, and myself in a next suicide homicide attempt. He said she told him, "Det. Gubiosini you will be on official misconduct charges and I am not joking with you Det as I charge you myself. If Antonio gets that piece of crap tape just ditch it."

Chills ran through Allan's shoulder and the back of his neck hairs bristled like porcupine quills thrust inward. He was reeling as he began to remember Lisa Wei Feng's troubled world within including the piano rolls of Gershwin and the bars in Soho. Her message now and the fact he could not get her as he always did with a quick response, immediately, when he called. Aggression including biting him until he bled and licking his blood as she began dominating him. Lisa knowing how and where to touch him until he exploded and the way she so knowingly took all he had deep within herself. It couldn't be. No way could Lisa Wei Feng, his future wife, be the killer as the Chief of Homicide Prosecutions! It was sick to even think that way, a crazy coincidence, but no way is she linked to the murders not his Lisa Wei Feng. As if on cue, and in a terrible musical irony of cacophonous proportion, almost satirically the bell-tower tone rang, and Dr. K.D was again on the other line.

"Hey, Doc, it is your colleague cop doc Dr. K.D. the Odentologist. Cop Dr. K.D. is confirming your call with toxicology and confirmation of bite mark radius. Do you want to say hello, he says you need to go to military drill as you're a Captain in the Guard and he has a case to review with you besides this one?"

Allan nodded 'No' and shushed him to let go and let him know what was just said in a whisper.

"Doc Allan, you will be shocked it is as you said, a female bite clamped down hard enough to have drawn blood. The female was middle age and of strong physique to apply pressure per square inch and the radius it was at impact. It is one and the same perpetrator who bit Tommy and who bit Antonio. Dr. K.D. also said they found among all things Ricin. Are we dealing with a mimic killer, like the terrorist group in Japan in one of our Japanese or Chinese American Detectives in the bureau? We are now examining all clothes obtained from the scene to see if any airborne pathogen imprints as biomarkers with mitochondrial DNA can be identified as the perp must have poisoned all before the attack which was staged to deceive the investigators. Christine and Tommy were poisoned with Ricin traces, but nowhere enough to kill in aerosol style as a new edition to add to the complexity. It appears Antonio was struck with Ricin besides being hit with the blunt object knocking him out. Post Mortem indicates Tommy died after Christine. They both had drinks laced with some poison, which Dr. K.D. said he will be reporting on soon. Take a look at the report as the photo display read on his phone teletype of the report marked confidential Crime Scene Analysis." Allan read from the teletype and mulled over his analysis, before speaking.

"Professor Duffy McMurphy, we have hit a home run. Antonio could have not been there at the time Tommy was killed. He arrived almost a half day later. Tommy was the test for the Ricin; our Mystery murderess knew he would die even if like Rasputin under a shroud of mystery and Mayhem. He the bear would die under the guise of honey. Meaning the killer viewed their intercourse and had staged the attack on them. The knife wound to Christine was her trachea sliced in a manner that would leave her face intact. The femme fatale had access to everything and the witch was present to do what she came back to do. After Tommy was dispatched, vivisected and then had his organ stitched into Christine she must have studied Tommy and knew his style. Meaning she had an affair with Tommy earlier, and had feigned friendship with Christine as a friend. Otherwise, she would never know their love habits. She was and remains a voyeur who has stayed morbidly involved in the investigations.

Unusual for a female investigator to be manically homicidal, but this is far from the whole picture. The same identical trace of chemical aerosol was distributed in the room as Ricin with Antonio which she recalibrated in larger and near lethal doses. Explaining the extreme dizziness and confusion of Antonio in shock, but not so shocked as to not fully absorb the shock of setting up the crime scene for maximum impact on his psyche, not to mention his soma as heart, soul and gut would pay as well with her bites. His near respiratory failure and redness of the skin and eyes, vomiting and diarrhoea with blood in the stools all make sense now as heightened with pneumonia which would also be used to cleanse some of her own emissions if she had female ejaculatory responses rare but possible. She likely orgasmed again while doing the ultimate de-sexualization of Christine, while having both men fully exploited as sexual objects in her psychotic mind's eye. In her eyes, she was purifying them with sadistic cadence while masochistically gratifying her unconscious and conscious desire to be all powerful and destroy her mother figure and lord it over her. Her grandiose vision of recasting the atoned lovers Tommy and Christine for each other in effigy through death as romanticized and immortalized. She had to poison him knowing how to and when to do it with expertise, she must be a special operations, nurse practitioner, physician, or one of our own detectives which I am narrowing down to a ten to one ratio." [Pausing, Dr. Allan continued with a bit of hubris over his mastery of the case.]

"She is a nymphomaniac and had clearly had oral sex and masturbated Tommy after he was attacked with the blunt instrument in his only vulnerable spot she knew of before collapsing to deaths final crushing blow. Tommy was nude and had decided to rest after intercourse with Christine. He was poisoned with the Risin as well and taken separately before he died and she masturbated him and have swallowed part of his emission and then left him alone." Dr. Allan almost chocked for a moment and paused as he turned to Christine's vivisection and mutilation scene.

"Dealing with Christine, like a trained gynecologic surgeon, the femme fatale feeling humiliated for her failure to win every man as a devotee in her borderline narcissistic tendencies displayed with venomous hatred her opposition to Christine and desexualized her, leaving her genderless. Decapitating her vulva with an inversion and a smile plastered across her face like a clown for prosperity. Tragic comedy on a deeper level for all investigators too witness in their own trauma drama. Who, except an internalized fanatic, who felt sex was dirty and yet obsessed with it for herself?!? This is a radical type of killer, who is a high achiever and who unconsciously strives to service men and destroy her competition with a zeal and jealousy beyond anything I've seen in fusing with them. Beyond the vilest male misanthropic murderers where motivation is forceful and not sexual, her sexual crimes are. But my question now is what the hell were Tommy and Christine given to sedate them as a narcoleptic drug? It could not have been the Risin alone Captain, that is the one piece we still need to fully solve this case."

Professor McMurphy was silent and paused suddenly looking at Dr. Allan, Professor McMurphy said,

"Didn't you receive the report we got from our police Commissioners Squad not the DA's squad. It is marked internal memo, that is under the Commissioner's office for chemical analysis we got back today in the am at 0400 hours? Dr. K.D. said he reviewed the toxicology report and a lethal dose of a remarkable pharmacological concoction was ingested. It is clear it would have been the primary cause of death for Christine. But not for Tommy although if he had more time elapsed it would have been."

"Tommy's hemorrhagic hematoma and knife wounds were fatal; it was done with total surprise or he would have fought back like a Grizzly Bear, as he was called. Tommy had his old line of duty injury investigated by your girl ADA rookie at the time Lisa Wei Feng, Juris Doctor. She had a thing for his Irish ways and for whatever reason, broke it off with him. [Looking away from Allan] We had her under scrutiny. She worked at one time with Tommy as she helped prosecute the skells that attacked him, and she had them sent away for maximum sentence for attempted murder on a police officer. She was balanced with integrity at one time. [Pausing] I am sorry old boy. I know this hurts you, but you need to know the truth and it is disturbing to me as well. I would never let out your affair with her. It was not to influence the case I know that too, as I know your integrity professionally." [Pausing himself, Duffy

McMurphy goes on] "However, Dr. Allan, your notoriously poor choices of women you select as mates are as legendary as your gifts of intellect and analysis. I am sorry, but that is your Achilles heel. We all know it."

"Anyhow, the report indicated Tommy and Christine had drunk the oddest concoction of, well, I'm unsure; some very weird stuff the lab felt was done by a pharmacist. Here, hold on, let me get it for you. I'm sorry you should be privy to your Belle Lisa Wei Feng's old way as being quite a man's lady but Dr. Allan she was a man hunter earlier in her career. Taking out the yellow copy of the report he read to Allan,

"Traces of L-Tryptophan, Melatonin, Ambien and Nyquil with codeine. Fatal levels of ingested chemical contraindicated. Hey, Doc, sounds like she is one hell of a black widow. She gave all four in quantities to put a tiger to sleep. To sleep forever, Doc. What a femme fatale."

Dr. Allan turned to the waste basket and in a gurgling tone emerging somewhere deep inside his innards, his vomit projected all over. He shook and trembled as a cold chill and feverish feeling overcame him.

It dawned on Allan like a boomerang knocking him in his head as he realized Lisa's sabotage with each meeting with him. She withdrew as much as he was trying to reach out to her with love, she rejected him. Allan was stark and silent as if he suffered from lock Jaw. He could not talk and looked down his face, which became flush with extreme anguish as if all dreams of hope had exited in one sweeping slice. His mind was racing as his hypo-manic mind was triggered with tragic mirth. The fucking woman he loved Lisa Wei Feng was definitively the killer.

What a joke as the one hope he had and was ready to pursue was now in hot pursuit in reverse!

Fleeing from life and suicidal if not homicidal he had told Lisa how bad the killer had it, and was trapped like a cooked goose. Like Antonio, he too was in a Kafkaesque trial in his own mind and heart. Lisa Wei Feng was a serial dater now to his horror, her murderous side and death drive was over the top of his conscious conception and tolerance.

Lisa's dark side was not as simple as the word 'sick' – evil, perhaps, was better – even to describe the woman he loved deeply. Sickly evil, he combined as he tried to rationalize how simply spoken two words captured in verb and subject operationally defined Lisa, so well.

Lisa Wei Feng loved to work in triangles of two men and her-self. The interloper last was Christine. Lisa was a femme fatale in-deed. Too intelligent to leave a trace except in the ironic legacy of her web as the spider who died of her own gluttony when she tried to devour Antonio.

Allan would never suspect her until the final piece came through. Allan intuited but did not act on his intuition until too late. Lisa's legal acumen was as sharp as her need to dominate and yet succumb completely. She was a romantic with fatal alacrity as a razor slice. Lisa Wei Feng was a Rhode scholar on one hand and a cat house walker on the other side of her blush and rouge.

Cop Doc Allan suddenly saw the connections. Including his own succumbing to her wiles as the DA's Chief Homicide Attorney, Lisa Wei Feng sensed in her sensual mode of defense she was being scrutinized from afar and dosed Allan Cannon with the tarantella that entranced him as he fell from the grace of his ships edge like Jonah into the endless engulfing womb.

Paradoxically, he was rescued by the fact her love for Allan shielded him from his ex-wife's death wishes and now from Lisa's. The good doctor was very tortured in his unrequited love that she redeemed in her parlay and more then she could ever know left him barren as she herself.

Lisa's sexual web entranced Allan, who was on course with a permanent collision in which conscience was about to be swamped over by convention. A fait accompli accomplishing what love eclipses in one fatal move self inflicted. It was Lisa Wei Feng who was the killer. A cold blooded murderer: Tommy's lover and fiancé he wanted to marry had triggered intense jealousy in Lisa Wei Feng and she was going to exact blood to pay in a bath of fury that extended back to the womb of her soul murdering mother. Her effeminate father who created the ambiance without boundaries to guide her out of the webs she sunk into. The souls of her men she captured and sucked the life out of in perversion and ecstasy as punishment to her father who she never worked through in her own Electra complex perverse and complex in its blood lust.

Antonio had to pay the ultimate price as the targeted scapegoat, and doomed as much as the modern epic witches Arthur Miller wrote about in the Crucible. The witch hunter was the male witch in allegory and ecstasy and Lisa transferred her hate and love all into him. Allan was right his lover was ready to do him in but she did not. He remembered she spared him and her – she had a conscience but he had to reach her and confront her evil with his love, too little and too late.

Allan realized his pride and love could possibly rescue her from her homicidal tendencies. He could hardly fathom the rapid shifts in her remorse and suicidal tendencies which realizing she really loving him had given hope to overcoming her lifelong odyssey of pain and anguish which after all was coming to an end if he did not find her and alone before the job did. Allan could not fathom what to do, he was silent and numb throughout his whole body and his mind felt like shutting down for the first time. He felt as helpless as the little boy whose mother was crying desperately for help as she was cutting her wrists and saying for him to turn away from her pain. He was back to his worst nightmares and they were in the heyday of his life and career as a newly made Det Sgt. Professor and Dr Allan Cannon without hope and in the bounds of despair.

He called Lisa Wei Feng. The news came to Allan rapidly that she could not be found after he told Captain Professor McMurphy of what had transpired. She was the one they were looking for in shame and humiliation in which he hid his head in agony and Captain McMurphy equally in sadness and refrain.

NYPD Intel Division, Threat Assessment Unit, the US Attorney General Office and NY State Attorney OIG was alerted to go after her and find her. He did not hesitate to let each know through Captain McMurphy, "Lisa Wei Feng, J.D., M.P.A. is my fiancé and lover. Yes, mine, all mine, my ownership to my latest choice: Lisa, my sweetheart; Lisa, my heartless femme fatale; Lisa, my sick babe who never had a father and mother worth a shit; My Lisa, a genius who is so lost."

Professor Murphy was as dumbfounded and shocked as tears were running down Allan's eyes as he coughed hard and gasping for breath. In slurring words, but clear as day as to his intent, "I must reach her first! Give me a chance to rush and get her. I will collar Lisa Wei Feng; she is mine I am going to confront her. I have failed my entire calling if I let her get collared like a common criminal."

Captain McMurphy said, "Doc, you can't! There is protocol and she is a danger. I will cuff you if I have to for your own sake. I am an old USMC grunt I can take you if you make me."

Allan, in hyper-vigilance, stood his ground, "Listen, Captain, Fuck the protocol! I am a ranking officer with a rank of Deputy Inspector and we are colleagues and friends. I am pleading with you! I am using my calling card for saving your life right here and right now. Remember when you were scrapped off the curb after your love affair with that physician you met and had an affair with after being victimized, and going over the top with her. I love her and if anyone is going to stay by her side, it is me. I will marry her even if she is that screwed up. My choice and my stand I stand by her being healed after she is sent to the State Hospital for the insane."

McMurphy nodded to him and said,

"Go, you have a half hour and then I am letting it all out. You have one half an hour, that's all you have to get her back in custody. That's 'It', Dr. Allan Stuart Cannon."

Allan pushed himself beyond his hypo-manic energy and ingenuity as he almost collapsed at realizing the truth, in a dissociated state himself.

Allan rushed into the hospital as he opened the Room. Lisa Wei Feng sitting in a trance like hypnotic state with her pupils dilated as her blouse was shed open and her areola's red blushed. Allan tried to muster the strength to talk. He couldn't speak. His mouth shut in an agony of trauma and shock, he couldn't scream.

Lisa looked at his eyes and said to Allan as she gently held his face in her hands and her glazed eyes folded over her eye lids,

"I knew you would trace my path – you will go down in history for capturing me, darling Allan. I never loved Antonio or Tommy or the whole circus of men but you as the real true love I yearned for." Lisa's eyes were red and the pain of anguish had given her a look of pallor as she said in a voice that sounded like Kristi's alter identity mode.

"Antonio had a beautiful physique and body, Allan. I taught you about your own sexual and sensual self. I know this hurts now but, Allan, you are humane and decent I am not human, but a monster. I need to be ended as I ended others lives and spared none grief or pain which I delivered with pleasure as they reeled in pain. I spared the State the charge, of appeals and all. I have made my mark. Darling, you can hate me and curse my memory as I deserve!"

Allan in recline bent to Lisa and stroked her beautiful face and said,

"My love, you are all I need and desire. Only you! I am in love with you and forgive your evil acts as they are inhumane but you are not that ugliness. You are beautiful inside and you needed love and I have given it to you. Why, oh why, do you throw it away darling? I love you and plead with you to please tell me you will not harm your beautiful self? I know and love Lisa Wei Feng who is the artist and genius I love."

"Allan, you are like a little boy in love with me. Kiss my lips, I am pretty and you love me. Don't you want me darling as I do you? I truly wanted us to make it and be as one, truly and always my dear Allan. Life is tragic and arresting in its mirth that rocks us from cradle to crypt. Can you stop the inexorable time for me until I have atoned my sins and escape, yes escape from this horrid life now that I found you and now will lose you forever and ever Allan!" [Allan held Lisa in his muscular arms as she was breathing shallow and looking as if her breath was fading. He suddenly went to kiss her deeply. She pushed his lips away.]

"Don't swallow my saliva, Allan, my only true love. I found true love too late. Antonio had to pay for betraying me. I thought I loved him and for ending our possible life together he needed penance. He destroyed our future in his scheming rueful woes he was like me dear. Cyanide my darling is in his system was time released in the capsule in his mouth with enteric covering that dissolved when I kissed him to death. [Tears and paroxysms of deep breathing felt as if Allan was aspirating on his own gulps for air as sulfur ripped his own eyes half blind in grief and horror as he realized Antonio was slumped in his bed, and sensing Lisa had done the inconceivable to herself Lisa barely got out of her last exhalations,

"I did not kiss him, darling, in real time or anyone else since we meet. My sexual escapades had no reality just like masturbation until I did you. We made love every time. Antonio had Racin plus the concoction as you love to call what I gave you exponentially delivered IV with cyanide crushed in his mouth as he was dying.

He is dead and no way back. As he was asphyxiating, I put the uncrushed cyanide pill in his mouth and it took all my might to crack the outer-shell and send him to the hell I will join him in."

Allan fought the chocking paroxysms as tears cut the face of his lover. He felt what was coming next. He had not fear or a sense of worry for his own well being and safety. He was crushed with the prospect of losing Lisa. Not even Antonio's death could bring him to loath her as the killer she was and the twisted contradictions she presented. The betrayal itself couldn't shake his commitment to Lisa who he wanted so bad. Allan knew Lisa would be whisked away in a moment when the police rushed in.

"Darling, I am dying as I can't live with you and will not live without you in prison. Here is my last adieu. I will join the monsters you try exorcising demons from but cannot always do. Don't blame yourself − it is not you but them. Allan looked up as ESU and HNT burst in the hospital room. She looked into the depths of his soul as her departing swiftly whispered you are all I wanted and I love you forever, my dear…"

Allan held Lisa and closing in with his mouth on hers he felt the arms of Det M and the C.O. of the Intel division pull him back as saliva and froth bubbling exhaled with her last breath and convulsion of life exiting her. The violent jerkiness of her entire life emptied out of her as ashen white took away all complexion and life from her doll like stature as she slumped fragile as a raggedy doll.

Allan was held tight and pulled away as he tried to mouth his lips over hers as looked into the eyes of his fiancé and screamed a primal scream. A scream ushering in the medical staff as her life disappeared from under his clouded eyes. Lisa Wei Feng died in that moment as her soul and his eyes met for the final last waltz crushed in the power of strict of justice. It was Pallas Athena as alter who had taken the last laugh away with tears as her wreath. After she had given Antonio the cyanide crushed in her mouth, she had drunk the usual concoction at seven times the fatal dose as he drank her poison from her sweet lips Antonio lay dead – kissed by the widow maker monster.

Lisa had lived on perhaps miraculously to crush the cyanide when caught. She held on to not be held accountable for her crimes. Her humanity for Allan as he kissed her in desire and not in-deed the final breath remaining the unrequited kiss of love in effigy rather than reality. She spared his life as testament to a monster falling in love with Allan and loving him instead of indulgence which would have ended the journals undone and being left unwritten and unread.

Cop Doc Allan shook in trembles laying by Lisa's supine body after the danger of his mouthing her ended and slumped as his head nestled in her lap as Professor Duffy McMurphy arrived followed by an escort of Commissioners special squad snapping shots as Allan being led out of the Hospital room was in deep shock!

Allan capitulated to an injection of a sedative as he was brought to the police union building with a small sample of cops trickling in to see him and to offer solace.

From Officers to Chiefs, they stood vigil for him as sleep engulfed his dreams and ideals with a tantrum of discontent. The officers he helped for decades remembered their cop doc as one of their own. Allan felt as if his life eclipsing with the death of this day of infamy when it ought to have been the happiest was more than rued it was murdered.

Not another day in the life of a NY Cop Doc, this day would be one he could never live down in shame and humiliation but he could only hope to survive in its passing. In humility thanking G-d in ancient Hebrew, he fell asleep.

Allan awoke in the elegant building on 40 Fulton Street across from the South Street Seaport. He said to his delegate and the District Attorney Office Representative,

"Can we talk tomorrow, that is, if I am free to go now?

The delegate said,

"I will drive you home."

As they left, Allan said,

"Please, drive me to my office that is now my home." The delegate Det. Mo said,

"Ok, Doc, let's go. I will stay in the patient waiting room tonight. So, so fucking sorry for what you have been through. But I will not leave you alone tonight."

Allan said,

"Fine, O.K."

No words, such as thanks, came after. Allan closed the door, pulled the curtains closed, looked at his Japanese fighting fish he bought with Lisa and said, "It could be worse, I could be you. I could be with Lisa in heaven for after such hell on earth where else could she go but up in the ineffable mercy of the Almighty. A Creator whose mercy knows no bounds, perhaps at least in my wishes, Lisa."

Allan knew he was in shock but able to function adaptively to deter forced hospitalization.

Allan awoke 12 hours later. Det. Mo brought up the Daily News that read on the front page,

"Pink triangle of love-less femme fatale undone." Other tabloids scribbled in their usual tasteless mendacity, "Kinky freak ADA kills self, Det, and two others including celebrated Detective Tommy Ryan and fiancé Nurse in Roman Orgiastic murder crime scene – while Cop Doc Author Dr. Allan Cannon watches in glee."

Another read,

"Link to murder of fiancé in a bloody triangle of cop doc, District attorney and Detective: Federal Probe Expected …"

Allan looked at the beige color of the clouds of his Starbuck coffee as he poured the liquid into the glass cups he loved to sip from. He thought he saw Lisa Wei Feng extending her hands to him and her lips as he closed his eyes and kissed her back.

The incandescent light of the dark room held a shadow of the double image of two triangles in bold inter-twined relief, one down and one up, intersecting as a cross bow tie grayish with black and white motif illuminated the empty space.

Allan took out a journal and began to write the reality of the instinctual drive of death in love – a perplexing dimension of life itself. *The result of that journal will be another story in the NY Cop Doc Journals a reason to live and love perhaps again.*

# Epilogue

This Cop Doc Journal closes as Cop Doc Allan sips cappuccino and a Macanudo cigar with his Lt Buddy and President of the Historic Society of Brooklyn Daniel Jack Labonie on the roof landing of the NY Police Academy.

28 years later at 52 years of age Daniel is in tears, having read the letter un-vouchered and kept closed. Allan without ever reporting his well-kept secret breaking his heart like an old 45 record skipping a beat again and again, as, "All alone again – naturally" is playing on FM's station channel, 101.1 from another police instructor's portable Panasonic radio.

The transistor radio, carrying the tune for all to hear, was loud and strong. Cops never throw anything away including broken hearts and old transistor radios reflected Allan in a whisper. Allan reads again the missive in her own words never to hear Lisa's voice again.

"My Dearest Allan,

"It is the end, my love. I am repulsed in the mirror of who 'she' really is. That is the killer in me. I couldn't kill you, but I can kill the two sick bitches in me that bear their dual weight on my soul."

"I am on the ledge and considering direct suicide. I must free Antonio as he does not know of us. Antonio, like me, is not for this world, he is a suffering Hawk and I an Eagle with Talons."

"You are a unique man, Allan, my finance. I love you always. But I must say goodbye to you, darling. You are alive and creative in healing others and I inspired by the black widow and recluse. I am the epitome of the death drive…your hypotheses are right and I am proof regardless of the critics. Remember Joseph Goebel's and his wife who I actually feel an affinity for in my perversity of justice self-inflicted to pay for my sins as he did."

"It is not I, Lisa Wei Feng, who ever rejects you. I reject this world we live in. Life we live in, no matter how old when we die dear is lived like ghosts. Ghosts sauntering about not realizing life is so precious as the angel of death resides in all of us."

This life is transient and mortal as our flesh and blood incarnate and carnal. Our love is eternal."

"I am not a nymphomaniac, as you may believe, but a victim of the conspiracy of evil. My nemesis is not you, but me as Pallas Athena and Kristi as extremes of sexuality unfurled and sexuality repressed and aggression surfeited on the banality of the sword."

"Deep inside my deeper darker past, I could not let go of you. When you told me in your message you had the killer – I knew I had to go and take Antonio as a mercy killing. You did not send me to death. I loved to dream till then, somehow, and some way I could atone for my murderous self that committed other accidents not yet accounted for. My atonement would be loving you forever and being forgiven for my nature that nurture could never override – not even your nurturance. "I was born with a virus endogenously within my blood my Allan."

"Antonio, I loved, but he rejected me for Christine, whom he slept with. I suspect that by the time Tommy drunk that beast allowed by negligence Christine to have her way with him although he was there."

"The unforgivable tryst was with Antonio and Tommy at one point for me was atoned for by my death which is complete when you read this again and again. But with you Allan, I had it all."

"I knew in my own way Christine, that slut who ruined my little rendezvous leaving me left alone and abandoned had to suffer by atoning for her whore ways – like the bitch whore mother who bore me."

"You cured and solved my heart ache and broken heart for a moment in time, and a stitch away from that slut unworthy of men, I had to mend with her man as eternally worthy after penance."

"I will come to you when you sleep and never leave you behind Dr. Professor Cop Doc Allan Stuart Cannon. I will help you rest away from Tommy, Christine, and Antonio, and others they will uncover. But, for now my darling for giving me love and allowing me in your life I am living in you deep inside where you can't hide."

"In your conscience, I live on. So close your eyes, darling, and you will see me now and always ready to give you my sweet drink as we become one when that time comes for you to join me my last kiss. I have saved a portion for you to find of our elixir called eternal. I can give you life in death for eternal marriage as I my love am the 'Tian-Shi' angel of heaven to you my dear."

Love always,

Lisa Wei Feng

The door rang and it was the Beijing Police Bureau Det. Lt. Jim Wu, MS in physical anthropology and forensic psychology. "I just flew in from Beijing Doc," as he began to lay out a number of unsolved homicides in ten separate files.

Lt. Wu whispered,

"Dr. Allan, would you mind if I left you with the files we have gathered on Lisa Wei Feng? It appears she may have also gone under the name the White Lotus of the North, a notorious killer who seems to have been a bird of flight. She only killed three weeks between Christmas to New Year.

All in all, we have ten males who had no identifiable family who sold themselves as male gigolos to older rich females in need. These twenty year olds had their private members removed in what can only be called as grotesque oblations.

Cop Doc Allan said,

"Come in, colleague, I'd like to hear it all. I am sure you may fill me in with what I will be surprised to say I've heard it before. But in reality, perhaps I didn't. Let me get my Journal Notes Out. I will close the journal I've titled on this chapter of my life, The New York Cop Doc Journals – Mirrors of Darkness."

"Let me get the Yan Jiang Doc, it's a gift from our department to a cop doc like yourself. You've earned the gratitude of the Beijing Police from the last case you helped solve. You will be shocked at what dismemberment I have uncovered. Interesting, Doc, as you know the root of the Lotus takes in all the rot and filth in a pond of scum and refuse. White symbolizes purity and death as the last stage before bid thee fair-well. The Lotus also carries the root in which minerals are catalyzed toward energy that revitalize."

"The murderess we have nailed as a fetish Queen had taken what was potential and sent it to its rotten hell. The darkness of the mirror reflected the rot within in our diary Dr. Allan Cannon. More so I need to confess I had an affair with this vixen who visited four seasons ago. I never forgot her mark on me. She bit me, Doc, and actually tried to suck my blood and more – it was then I had the good sense to cut her off. I just was wondering if I could get a free session or two due to professional police courtesy since I have not been able to sit with the fact I allowed her in to my life for three weeks in the first place."

"Doc, the irony that twists so bad is we listened to this old odd tune by your famous George Gershwin. They were the 3 best weeks I can remember in a long time. I am unsure if you as a cop doc can relate, but I felt like one Joker down. How could I have allowed myself to descend to the roots of all evil, when I thought I was at the root of all good, Doc?"

Dr. Allan Cannon, having mourned his losses, had not heard it all. He turned to Lt. Wu and said,

"My friend and colleague Lt. Wu, let me share this with you. It is no secret to any of us that has laid our eyes or love in the storm of Lisa Wei Feng. She called herself the White Lotus attracting men in pursuit of purity of love and marriage after a life of soot and mayhem. She, in a way, fulfilled her ideal of being pure.

379

By ensuring you would never forget the lessons of infamy and murder she spun in the core of her dark roots – Lisa Wei Feng mirrored paradoxically the pureness of her evil incarnate. *That is the end of this chapter that will usher in the spring of a new one next fall...*"

"Meaning what, Doc?"

"Meaning that is if only you Lt. Jim Wu could let go of the roots that are so tasty and so poisonous. Healing takes time, and so does wisdom. Both march in silent shrouds for the fallen walking wounded heroically scared in the battles of their loves and losses. Let's meet for a session in a week. Make it Monday at ten. Good night."

Lt. Wu peered his head back in for one last quizzical look and with genuine passive approach almost whispered as an afterthought,

"By the way, Doc, when we meet again I have a question. Just something you've probably taught to hundreds of agents since 1987. But I hope you can share some wisdom with me about. Well, I never knew Lisa Wei Feng was assigned a double justifiable homicide in which you were jumped quite a while ago in 1987. You know when you had received your M.D., Ph.D. It seems you were quite a hero in taking out two international terrorists who had decided to do the dry run on you as a Det. Sgt Cop Doc with an IQ of 147 on a bad day, and 170 when you were doing well enough. They had studied you and pretended in almost perfect English and mimicking street style perps of how to feign being what you guys call muggers, we call 'Zui-fan'."

"Our White Lotus of Death, Lisa Wei Feng, had been promoted two years later in 1989 due to her handling of you and keeping everything Mum. Could you let me know your technique? Hey, Doc Allan, if you could remember that event in its important details I would truly appreciate understanding how you pulled it off? I know the case is sealed, but I figure just some tips from a legend like you would help."

"We Beijing Investigative Bureau Police were allied with Soviet Union KGB, (pausing) then. Even your CIA operatives, in more measured ways, cooperated with us on this case too. Everyone was trying to track these International Terror Cells; they were ever grateful to have you take those bad guys out. No one ever expected them doing their dry run on you and your handling of them as if you were special-forces. Incredible intuition and survival skills Doc Cop, I'd like to learn for myself."

"I know the President of the United States, NSA, your Mayor, Police Commissioner and the Provost Dean of NYU Medical School. NYU Medical and the Police Commissioner were grateful we kept it from the press. I bet they let you know personally how happy they were with your extraordinary heroism. Oh well, I wonder if you could tell me just how the hell did you move so fast? How did you know they had a room of explosives in which they had targeted the Mayor, Police Commissioner and the NYU Downtown Hospital and Washington Square Campus?"

Allan looked befuddled, bewildered, and lost.

"Sorry, I must be way too pushy. Sorry, especially after all your hospitality. Doc Cop, have a good rest. I'll see you next week Monday at 10am. Thanks for your help. Sorry to be so pushy."

Looking askance at Allan, Lt. Lu raised his eyebrows as he quipped back rhetorically.

"Hey, I am from Beijing the city that never sleeps, like the big apple we are the mammoth butterfly always metamorphosing. We cops have a job to do. Our crazies are getting almost as out of control as yours have always been Doc. Goodnight."